DAVID SAGACIOUS

IMMORTAL MORTAL

DAVID SAGACIOUS

IMMORTAL MORTAL

John David Liebling

atmosphere press

To my dad Bill—on staff at the UCLA Medical Center for over
four decades, he's the initial inspiration for my first novel.
He fought cancer with uncommon bravery and passed away on
July 14, 2013, after 1,100 months of vigorous life.

To my mom Dorie, who always greets me with a smile,
hug, and kiss. At 94, she's still ambulatory.
A weekly activity—the puzzle-deciphering game
Wacky Words—keeps her mind sharp and thriving.

To my younger brother Jim, an accomplished radiologist
and pinball champion. We are best friends,
and share the same political point of view,
and sense of humor.

I love you three dearly, and
thank you all for your encouragement.

TABLE OF CONTENTS

Introduction

"The two most important days in your life are the day you
are born and the day you find out why."
~*Mark Twain*

David Sagacious Immortal Mortal has elements of all my favorite genres—sci-fi romps, space operas, dystopia, and hard science fiction. I bet this is the first time-hopping genre-bender you've ever read with an American Jewish protagonist who defies the odds by living through a multi-million-year journey. David Sagacious breaks the mold and defies common stereotyping. Malevolent Time hunts down and toys with every doppelganger throughout the Multiverse. Only David Sagacious Prime, with God's help, survives Malevolent Time's murdering maelstrom.

Suffice it to say there's a lot to unpack ahead, starting with the premise that Evil and Righteous Time are in constant flux, from today's social unrest to bizarre futuristic realities. Imagine a horrified 9-year-old David Sagacious helplessly watching a giant eraser remove his mama and papa from existence as callously as a cartoonist would erase doodles. For 18 million years, our time-traveling, reincarnating David is unable to escape his violent lava-spewing planet. Depressed and isolated, he's failed to save his beloved wife and all the other righteous warriors.

Trigger Warning for Sensitive Readers

The backstory comes into view—vivid, horrible, and complex. Most elements are extreme by design—tender moments alongside gruesome moments, sprinkled with insanity wrought by numerous cycles of life and death in different timelines. David's entries and exits aren't for the fainthearted. He and his fellow major characters—Ko'ach, Nephesh, Ima Best-Friend, and Dafna Shaked—are extinguished time after time in brutal, hellish, and excruciating ways. Prepare to go into realms of bone-crunching suffering, where death is rarely permanent. Our characters (and vicarious readers) are doomed to resurrect and begin anew in sagas that are simultaneously glorious and utterly horrific.

A few helpful spoilers might help as we dive into the moving parts. We discover that reality-altering Malevolent Time kidnapped God's righteous son, Emet. She tortured his mind, body, and soul and turned him into I-T, a 100-foot murdering machine. I-T plans on conquering all corporeal life and consuming all corporeal souls—including David Sagacious, who has devised a system to remain elusive. He rhymes his words to perplex the parasitic portal. There's a reason why this book is part "stream-of-consciousness" and includes such quirky word strings and thoughts.

Ko'ach, the only corporeal life form talented enough to mentor David Prime, gives him the wherewithal to wield God's righteous weapon. Yet, on his honeymoon, Ko'ach is bitten by a microscopic evil machine and, for all eternity, remains tainted. God's second son, god, refuses Ko'ach's soul into the Realm of the Watchers, believing the prophecy is coming to fruition and Ko'ach will lose his eternal internal struggle against his evil half. God's second son also sends a major character, Nephesh, back in time on a secret mission. Brokenhearted, she must complete her unthinkable task—to murder her beloved and prevent Ko'ach's alliance with I-T.

And there you have it, an odyssey through science fiction as weird and wonderful as it can possibly be. Join our warrior David as he navigates a multiverse of doppelgangers and otherworldly foes, rhyming his way past near misses and looming destruction.

CHAPTER 1

Born on Earth, I was Marooned Elsewhere 18 Million Years Ago

Admiring the enormity of God's twinkling grandeur, I once again express my extreme anguish, anger, and arrogance toward the one responsible for marooning me in this lava strewn world. I am talking to you, God! Why won't you let me die! My pain grows more intense every century, every millennium! Damn I-T, you owe me! Please forgive my impatient impertinence. Agitated exasperation dissipates. Dreadful despair dislikes David's determination. Rebellious regret rages. Euphoric exhilaration exhales frostbitten breath. Tortured trembling vocal cords, chords; provoke hatred's reverberating, pulsating preeminent panache. Lava flowing mountaintops explode! Zigzagging avalanche chases me down. 18-ton boulders crush my skull and chest. I should be eternally at rest. Blood oozes from my mouth, nose, and ears. Destiny leers and cheers. My giddy laughter seems out of place. I pray for God's coup de grace. Nerve endings on fire. God! Give me what I desire! Let! Death! Win! I am tired of failing and wailing. Find another to fight your unwinnable war! I don't want I-T-S gore, anymore! No more tears to give. No more lifetimes left to live. I demand an end to every perforating, integrating, enervating, obliterating, carbon dating, reincarnating. God have mercy. Parole my soul from I-T-S never-ending hellhole. I cajole and extol thee, with my undying plea... Why the hell do you refuse to euthanize me?!

I am David Sagacious—ardently loquacious, tenacious, and perspicacious. As an Immortal Mortal, I ceaselessly careen through Malevolent Time's sadistic portal. My sublime must rhyme and add specific songs; that's how my unique alliteration thwarts annihilation. I am prophetic and historically theoretic.

I and T must never come together, or the second most powerful villain in the Multiverse will scatter my atoms beyond the point of rectifying regurgitating righteous resurrection.

For 18 million years I've been marooned without the touch of another human being. I talk to myself because aggressive dark viruses keep on corrupting and crashing my computer. Every day, minute, and second of my captivity I endure extreme loneliness. Malevolent Time's perplexing pandora's paradox penetrates deep into my traumatized subconscious. I-T-S astoundingly difficult to push aside her misanthropic manipulations. I need God's righteous weapon to bring my dead wife back to life. Fractious fissures doom and consume; I bore witness to my best friend's disintegrating black plume.

Am I hallucinating I-T? Was I-T a dream? Did Malevolent Time cage my mentor in her soul-ripping maelstrom? I can't always differentiate fact from fiction. Is I-T a Ko'ach truth, or treacherously inscrutably timeless mutilation? God could not rescue Ko'ach, because if God loses his focus for a millisecond; she-devil's rage would leak through her cage and pour back into our righteous realm. There is nothing I can say or do that can assuage God's sage engage.

Malevolent Time's chaotic hurricane endlessly annihilates all hope. And yet, he's Ko'ach; the strongest, wisest, most determined of us all. He's never known defeat; therefore, I still have hope he'll one day free himself and rescue the Multiverse from a fate worse than death.

Ubiquitous am I. Damn right I can fly!

I am throttled and thwarted by life's damnable deathly destiny. Perennially, I am plucked, entrapped, and enslaved. Murdering 100-foot metallic monster pelts, flogs, and rips my limbs from my torso.

Caught between ultimate evil and righteousness I am forever discarded, demoralized, dishonored, and detonated.

God's impeccable illumination electrifies entropy's entangled erosion. Galvanizing time-altering tachyon particles; each righteous spark accelerates beyond the speed of light. 36-billion blue-white lightning bolts traverse every corner of the multidimensional Multiverse: each with a specific mission, their cascading crackle, creates unremitting, undulating unmeasurable voltage.

After his last mission, guess who became the consistency of a sentient fondue? As a gurgling, babbling royal blue goo; my determined derring-do, will hitherto accrue one last breakthrough; so that I may imbue and rescue my constantly askew déjà vu.

God's electrifying righteous radiation rectifies roguish rage. Malevolent Time's ruthless rewrite rubs-out my recalcitrant reality. God's memories predate the current Big Bang. My newfound knowledge galvanizes gravity's grimacing gladiator.

On this world, time has no meaning. The passage of which leaps at the speed of nothing. I-T-S not that I-T-S frozen, I-T-S the concept of time, which does not exist...and why is that so? God has not yet communicated the answer. I am powerless to prevent Malevolent Time from altering me into this fucking septic tank of horribly stinking putrid genetic slop.

Memories punch and punish. Bubbling and gurgling, my decaying body and mind becomes a liquified steamy hot mess. Change the subject. Why? Your mentor, Ko'ach, those memories for now will stay a dead end. Move on. I said, move on! Stop searching for those answers. Enough!

She. Excellent! You're remembering Malevolent Time is an awful sinister, she. Why am I her never-ending target? You're not ready to recall that. Go on. Yes, that's the one, tap into that memory. Do as I request. Stop investigating that neural connection. I said, you're not ready. Move on, or I shall do I-T for you. You know I-T will return whether you are summing them or not. What will return? Your full memories. What if

I don't want to remember? You have no choice. Who says? You do? I do? Yes, I do. Aren't you, me? Indeed, I am you. Am I a we? No, you're only a me. Ima confused. Stop invoking your beloved wife Ima. Ima married? Don't go down that path. Why? We've played this game millions of times. I-T never ends well for you. Confusion is always a hell of a lot better than unending contusion. What does that mean? Pain! Still blocking. Wouldn't you? Wouldn't I, what? This babble is unhelpful. Yes, I-T-S most unhelpful. Why? Because your memory is not going to return piecemeal, I-T-S going to come crashing down like an unstoppable Tsunami.

Serrated vampire fangs rip the flesh from my spine. Twitching paralysis pushes nauseating vertigo into extremely disorienting time traveling travails. I am powerless to prevent the past from overwhelming my insightful foresight: unwanted memories envelop all that I am. Each unwanted memory variant wiggles, creating catastrophe's cascading conundrums.

1,818,000 micro-Star of David falls from the heavens; righteous radiation glows 18 weeks. 18 minutes later, the entire planet implodes. Over the next 18 seconds God's righteous surgical technique brilliantly sews my unique DNA back together.

I am an unraveller time traveler: I mutate, suffocate, aspirate, and incinerate. I hate the villainous castrate of my ever-changing birthdate.

Catatonic consciousness creates callous calamitous cacophony of calculating carnage. I feel the heartache of parents watching their children and children watching their loving parents consumed by the only force in the Multiverse even God has difficulty vanquishing. Malevolent time always finds a way to escape her incarceration. Trillions are ripped apart and consumed by Malevolent Time's adopted son. Only I remember his true backstory. Only I know who his true Papa is, though he has long ago forgotten that truth. I am the only righteous warrior to survive the war between ultimate malevolence and ultimate righteousness.

Perpetual loneliness invades. Hopeful happiness evades. Destiny epically degrades...

Your true love betrayed you long ago. The hell she did. Liar! That's not our colors, to deceive ourselves. We are always exceptionally honest; no matter what I-T costs us. When I tell you, your former wife became more than an obedient acolyte of I-T and I-T-S advancing armada. David shuts his eyes tightly. A single tear falls. David quietly sobs. *I know in my heart; she'd rather die than become one of them! Not only did she not die, but she also continues as a most trusted obedient 100-foot murdering machine.* In hushed almost inaudible whispers, David tells himself, *Ima divulged all your precious secrets. Because of your wife, every metallic monster knows from this point forward how to get to you. Please I beg you, say no more...*

Consumed by grief, David falls to his knees. Tears fall from his cracked sunburned lips and hit the shiny igneous rock formation...pity-pat, pity-pat. Glistening salty droplets become a rapidly flowing stream: faster and faster the planet's extreme gravity forces the stream into a torrential fissure branching out for miles along the lifeless barren soil.

You must let go of your image of your beautiful Ima. I cannot! I-T-S all I have left of her. Stop! You cannot hide from yourself. I'm not hiding. How could I hide when I'm the only God damn person living on this barren rock! No need to shout. The hell there isn't! You see that? If you see I-T of course I see I-T.

I am you, and you are me. Stop playing games! I implore you! Do as I request! Transform her back into her beloved human form. I-T-S not too late? You're a time traveler, I-T-S never too late. Could that glint in the distance be the point of God's righteous weapon? You've said that before and I-T turned out to be a mirage. I know. You don't have to remind me. Sorry. You know if you could hold onto I-T this time, you could rewrite

Malevolent Time's rewrites. I could save everyone. I could restore the righteous vapors of her loving memory.

Three months before my parents are murdered and 9-year-old me is kidnapped by a 65-foot time-traveling shape-shifter; I had not yet been transformed by her constant torture. I was at that moment a carefree human child, with no discernable superpowers. That Sunday morning, my mom was window shopping, and my dad was running to pick up our movie tickets. I was busy smiling and people watching. Looking over the cold metal railing my joyful grin pinched while listening to the old man's thoughts. Shaky hands and feet bring nobody to the rescue. *Why are they all ignoring him?*

Over and over, the dignified man with the long silver beard rubs the black rubber handrail. I-T refuses to lead him onto the first step. Fear pushes his neck muscles to twitch. Escalating anxiety pushes his heart rate and face to lose all color.

Desperation makes the old man's wrinkled cheek muscle quiver. Engrossed in taking more selfies, impatient, irritating, bratty chatty girls disdainfully push through the old man's shoulder, his weakened legs buckle.

Down below a pretty girl in her mid-twenties witnesses the entire event. She runs up the over 90 steps toward her grandfather.

Old man lifts his head, he stares at 9-year-old me. Looking into his milky white eyes. *He's blind.* My papa returns, holding the tickets in one hand, and my mama's hand in the other.

"Come on David—we don't want to be late."

"Just a second Papa."

David hops on the escalator.

"Where's he going?" asks our papa Christopher.

"I don't know. Why's he going down?" asks our mama Grace.

David gently takes the blind man's hand and helps him onto the first step.

"Grandpa. Grandpa!" shouts the anxious girl.

Old man's stooped shoulders straighten up. "What's your name?" his frail voice whispers.

"David Sagacious. We are almost at the top. Is there some place you'd like me to take you?"

Old man reaches out with his wrinkled hand. He taps David's cheek. "You're a good boy. My granddaughter is meeting me at 11:00. What time is I-T?"

"10:58."

Seconds later granddaughter arrives. Catching her breath, she hugs her smiling grandpa. She reaches out and holds David's hand. "Thank God you were there. I don't know why people are so uncaring."

David looks over at his mother and father standing behind him. Both rub his shoulders.

"Are you, his parents?" asks the granddaughter.

"Yes," their beaming, gleaming eyes affirm.

"You should be proud of his uncommon compassion."

"Always. Our David is one of a kind," says Christopher.

Terrifying dysplasia undulates tachyon's treacherous thrombosis. Memories or hallucination, I know not which.

Slumped over my scabby knuckles, my manic, flamboyant fear pulverizes solid granite into dust. *Nothing negates nor quenches my grief's raw rage! Hellish hemorrhaging hobbles the hero's humbling hubris. Petulant peccadilloes preordain punitive paradox. Depression's dissipation dauntlessly denied. Anxiety squeezes my airway shut. I wallow in my sarcastic stoic shame, because I know I am to blame.*

Being aware of every thought throughout the Multiverse took uncounted eons to master. The power to hear every corporeal species' wants, needs, and fears never goes away. Today is an especially difficult one. Stuck here, I cannot help the trillions who call out for God's mercy. I hear trillions of voices; their painful prayers touch my heartstrings.

Vertigo attacks my sense of reality. Sinking to my knees I expel an animalistic wailing howl. Days without respite, my intestines spastically lock up. Rigor mortis softens I-T-S grip hearing my dead wife's ethereal voice sing, "Once Upon a Time."

David harmonizes with himself, "All I Have to Do Is Dream," while blue-white nuanced neurons invigorate furtively frothing fates. Absolution's axiomatic awakening adroitly appeals to aggressor's apocryphal agenda.

Back on 21st-century Earth, David, my old doppelganger pal. He. We. I celebrated my 54th wedding anniversary with my beloved wife Ima. I push aside Déjà vu's unhappy thoughts. I concentrate on the joyous clinking of champagne glasses. Ima continues her cute tradition: she nibbles on her Hershey kiss. While my wrinkled face smiles and sings, "The Anniversary Song."

Ravaging remorse traumatizes gut-wrenching guilt and mangles every manic memory.

"I love you," whispers David.

Ima's eyes sparkle while she dances to David singing, "Ain't She Sweet."

Ima's soft lips bring tears to my twinkling expressive eyes.

"What's this?" worried Ima asks.

"Happy tears."

"You sure?"

David's reassuring smile makes Ima express how she feels by singing, "Impossible."

Foreboding feelings well up. David's index finger swipes the corner of his eye, and he sings, "The Way You Look Tonight."

Sweltering sad sizzle sacrifices salutary secretions. My beautiful wife. Her feverish forehead forms ice crystals. Ima leans into David's warm chest and sighs. Dear husband, I will love you until the day I die. Ima fidgets with her anniversary present. A gold locket with cute baby David and Ima pictures brings mixed emotions, because I know what's coming.

Ima stands on her tiptoes and caresses David's soft ear lobes. David's forced smile belies the encroaching unavoidable truth. David closes his eyes. Joyful and toxic memories overwhelm. Brushing Ima's hair with our fingers, we feel dizzy from her intoxicating perfume. David and Ima savor each other's love; both sway to music only they can hear.

"Ima full. My heart feels like I-T had a massive meal today."

Ima's face pressed against David's powerful heartbeat. David touches Ima's bluish lips. *Running out of time. Her sparkling green eyes full of life, slowly deaden.*

I sing "Cheek to Cheek" and dance with my beloved, the length of the Santa Monica pier.

I snap my fingers and fuchsia energy carries a shiny black piano into view. Ima nibbles on my ear lobe before we both recreate the joyously cute song and dance routine by Fred Astaire and Ginger Rodgers, from the movie, "I'm Putting All My Eggs in One Basket."

Sparkling fissures in time illuminate and expose too many fraudulent futures. I-T-S a herculean effort on my part, trying to quell my new body's unremitting panic attack. Glowing with righteous energy, a huge blue-white Star of David grows from 18 inches to 36 feet; I-T-S rotating radiance produces a protective barrier that remains invisible to Ima and all other humans. *In Judaism, number 18 is a spiritual number; I-T stands for life. The number 36 represents two lives. Malevolent Time's pernicious darkness infiltrates my beloved's body and attempts to corrupt her righteous soul.* Ima's pink freckles turn ashen. Over the next 13 seconds she aged 13 years.

"You want to rest for a while?" asks David.

"Wake me when the sun rises."

Ima's teeth chatter. David hides a hot water bottle under three blankets.

Ima snores. "Boop!" says David after his index finger gently taps her cute nose.

I implore you God. Please allow these new songs to fortify our souls and allow our entangled voices to weave together the most formidable plot points. Be gone! All insidious mutating destabilizing timelines. And God, do not yank me from her arms. Do not let her die alone. Oh, thank God. She's becoming pinker.

Come on sun, warm up my beloved. She's never come this close to a new day before. "Wake up sweetie. Look."

36 miles above the Earth's atmosphere, fuchsia, blue-white, and black lightning bolts crackle. I-T-S the carnivorous black bolt which consumes the righteous fuchsia and blue-white energy and sends an invisible orb, which I could not sense at the time. I did not know; my protective shield had become inert.

Groggy Ima rests her head on my chest. *Our sighing breaths are synchronized. Could this be the day? I dare not hope. Every time I hope for an end to this nightmare, something dark, metallic, grotesque shatters my Ima's light.*

Ima takes her index finger and pokes the tip of David's nose, "Boop."

Ima shivers, I kiss her and wrap my warm arms around her.

Ima lifts her nose and takes a deep slow inhale. "Is that Matzah Ball soup? Smells delicious."

David lovingly feeds Ima the scalding nutritious liquid. "What's wrong?"

"Next time, give I-T a little more heat."

"Next time."

With her waning strength, Ima sings, "Where or When."

100-foot shadow hovers. I-T-S black metallic middle finger pierces my beloved's spine. Her mangled human blood mixes with unnatural metallic nanobots; those microscopic creatures slither, crunch, and munch Ima's entire spinal cord.

She's gasping for breath! God damn I-T! Enraged, David shatters the entire pier. He trips and falls into the crashing waves. Dark Déjà vu sinks him like a stone.

Ima's beautiful skin flayed away by perdition's flames. Her humanity torn asunder. Her righteous mind, body, and soul mutated. She grows above the treetops like a malignant beanstalk. Her massive metallic finger and thumb plucks me from my watery grave. *My wife is reborn, as a one-hundred-foot metallic monster.*

"You broke your promise, husband. And now I shall break you!" Ima shouts. She squeezes ribs, sternum, and tibia splinter. *Saltwater rushes. Lungs burst! Is this the beginning of the end? Or the end of the beginning?* "God damn I-T! I am once again where I desperately don't want to be. Horrific lava geyser spews. From every direction I-T spits molten disfigurement."

Massive globs of lava burn large holes in my stomach.

"God! I-I could do I-T, this time."

Clasping my gnarled fingers, I finally stopped shaking. "Not a single wince nor outcry, as I pull my chest cavity apart." *My glowing thumpity thump, thumps.*

"Do I crush I-T! And with I-T all hope, forever?"

Is that grief cackling in my distraught noggin? No, I-T-S my shouting metallic wife imploring, "David! You must do I-T! You know in your heart; suicide is the peace of mind you've dreamt of these last 18 million years...

Lung melts. Regret pelts, causing gangrenous welts. Labyrinth's lynching lacerations liquidate lighthearted legacy. Sadistic saboteur, scalds, scars, and schemes. Existential evisceration excoriates dear heart's dreams.

"Am I hallucinating my wedding, again?" *I take Ima's warm hand. She's filled with anticipatory giddiness, I sing,* "Come Fly with Me." *Hugging her tightly we ascend together toward a happy flock of squawking birds. Ima plucks two red apples from the top branch. Beloved sings Karen Carpenter's* "Close to You." The cloudless sky darkens after she takes two bites. Heavy rainstorm pummels. Hail the size of bowling balls break our handheld connection, "David! David! David!" frantic Ima shrieks.

Out of control, I flip head over heels. I descend into the freezing Atlantic. Heavy ball and chain wrapped around my ankle. I-T sarcastically cackles, "Time to die, insignificant human!" My knuckles blast blue-white energy and dissolve the links. *Ima! Ima! Where is she?*

Chased by two huge sharks, my powerful legs propel me toward what I thought were choppy waves. *Ouch! The ocean is replaced by solid rock. Scalding skin searing orange, green, blue, fuchsia blood flows down my face, torso, and legs. Flesh melted away, my skeletal fist punches through the rock. I drag myself through the tight hole. From this new mountain peak, I look down into the valley of death; serendipitous siren bubbles from the percolating soul-consuming lava.*

Wading through the lava is a naked one-hundred-foot metallic Ima. She pulls screaming humans from her braided black metallic hair; horrible screaming ends after the little ones pass beyond her grinning blood-red lips and... *Oh my God! Her sickening crunching and chewing.* Metallic Ima sucks her fingertips and sings in Nat King Cole's voice, "L-O-V-E."

Metallic Ima winks. "You're next, tiny husband." Every 99 feet I slide down the mountain, I-T-S peculiar dirt and pebbles transform my super-human muscles, tendons, ligaments, and skin. My skeletal frame and face are once again, forcibly, painfully rebuilt. I run, jump and fly over dead tree stumps, boulders, and corpses of long-ago non-decomposing dead friends. Ima's caught up to me, her lurid shadow lowers. I am her private paper football, and she flicks me toward the stratosphere. I can almost touch the stars when gravity yanks me back. I hear her mocking in a Louis Prima voice, "Enjoy Yourself."

Her metallic fingers pluck me out of the sky. Her giant tongue and lips moisten a long metallic hair strand. She smiles and winks and penetrates my chest with that spiky metallic split end. She twirls the other end around her right hand's middle finger. Her left pinkie bats me around like my entire body is a tear drop punching bag. Every slap shatters more bones and causes my organs to squirt disintegrating tissue. *She's destroyed me faster than my righteous soul can repair the damage.* Mocking my despair, she sings, "Smile."

Her clawed black nails slice skin and muscle from my bones. She giggles and sings, "I've Got You Under My Skin."

Creature who is not my beloved drops my broken body. I hit with a horrible crunch. She stomps me like an insect, "See you later, honey," she says in the most sickening southern drawl. Surrounded by shimmering black energy, she waves goodbye and dissolves.

My omnipresent present, palpably unpleasant; past harassed and tried to recast.

I, David Sagacious, the last of God's righteous narrators; being of semi sound mind and body proclaim my last will and testament; I am done being the noble, brokenhearted warrior, enduring 18 million years of extreme PTSD. *Why must I always start and end my days alone? This living, breathing, murdering world, takes magnificent pleasure in brutalizing my mind, body, and soul. Dehumanizing destiny descends and demonstratively distorts and disorients disintegrating defiance. I'm the embodiment of every posthumous preordained purposefulness. My genuflect introspect is, for all time, circumspect. God intermittently would neglect and still protect; for he's my never-ending architect.*

Tachyon's deathblow decapitates and decimates. Malevolent Time plots and prevails; she assaults and empales brokenhearted wails.

I am stronger than any comic book hero, and yet as Malevolent Time's prey, I'm less prepared to defend myself against her than any fetus could be when confronted by an abortionist scraping-sucking tool.

Malevolent Time's genocidal imperative isn't against a

single ethnic or religious group. No, she means to commit her genocidal obliteration of all corporeal life. Her bloodlust is unquenchable; she will never leave a single galaxy untouched.

Within a blink of a hummingbird's downdraft, God repairs an infinite number of demonic fissures. Did he get them all? Impossible to predict, but one fact is certain: Malevolent Time is getting stronger, and God is becoming weaker. Not even God knows how or why.

I gush a waterfall of tears because there's no one left who hears my fears. Not a single drop of solace will ever befall us. With all my hopes and dreams, I wish my schemes could've prevented my beloved's brokenhearted screams. *Sweetheart, I miss our soft kisses and tender wishes. Every time I die, I wish to live; every time I'm granted life, without my wife, I hope to die. My cup runneth over with anguish, shame, and sorrow because without love, what good is tomorrow?*

I-T-S an uncouth truth, that in my youth, I was a damn good sleuth. And the apogee for a happier me ended when I was age three.

Throughout all time, I've borne witness to and felt the inglorious agony of the human condition. I-T-S a tragedy so few followed the lessons contained in the righteous pages of the Hebrew scriptures. The Old Testament, specifically Genesis, tells us that the Earth was filled with violence and God decided to destroy I-T...except for Noah and his family. Do you know what the word in Hebrew for that violence is? Hamas! That's the Hebrew word for the violence that prompted God to destroy the Earth.

An event which will, in the annals of all humanity, live forever in infamy! And God, we both know, I-T was never supposed to happen. Because in the not-too-distant future, from Oct 7, 2023; Israel will become the bulwark against an armada of 100-foot murdering machines. I-T knows the best chance I-T has of carving up the people of Earth for I-T-S eternal feast, is to first get rid of the Jews. I alone am aware of Malevolent Time's rewriting of 21st-century history. I-T-S goal is to aid the enemies of the United States and Israel by sowing internal dissension. I-T always fails to recognize the righteous strength and moral code of most Americans and Israelis.

Fascist-Marxist-Muslim-mob demands tolerance and diversity unless you're a defender of Israel. Oct 7, 2023...Hamas burned and beheaded babies! Hamas gouged eyes, and raped women. Mutilated parents in front of their children. Mutilated children in front of their parents. Evil professors and students show their true, unfiltered, antisemitic hearts and souls.

Australians did not shout gas the Israelis, they chanted gas the Jews. When a reporter asked Michelle Obama to condemn multiple rapes and murders by Hamas against Jewish women, she showed her lack of humanity and refused. The Biden administration condemns Netanyahu and refuses to condemn rampaging Hamas sympathizers on university campuses. Incredibly young and old Israelis held captive by Hamas are starved, beaten, and drugged. Fascist history once again is on the march, and the world remains silent. There are no empathetic tears for the Jews. Angry irrational minds and hearts mock and bully the compassionate. Callous appeasers continue to deny and betray Jewish history. The woke illiterate mob shamelessly pushes enlightened civilizations backwards in time, toward a tyrannical freedom-less future. Frightened crying Jewish children are thrown down deep, dark tunnels and punished by burning their skin with fiery exhaust pipes. Hamas' actions shattered the myth that all cultures and religions share the same moral code.

When antisemites tell you and show you who they really are, believe them. The virulent irrational hatred spewed forth by those who support the demo-rat party remains unprecedented. Progressive professors taught their undergraduate and graduate students well. The political landscape has changed. Those who hate America and Israel, have a warped sense of right and wrong. Those Ivy League, UC, State, community college, high school, and middle school DEI teachers indoctrinated too many impressionable young people, to demonize any Jew who supports Israel. And all those educators plan on voting for the dementia in Chief – Joe Biden. They are all woke supremacist. Long ago, I-T was made self-evident, to them, not all lives matter. We Jews are an ancient people and have endured this movie before. For thousands of years the world has committed horrible crimes against us. Leftist Jews and non-Jews hold views antithetical to American values. Jews have historically been for the human rights of so many others. They were and are the Civil Rights leaders, the ethical motivators behind righteous change. Jews expected those they had helped in the past and support in the present, to show their loyalty in these horrific times. Did you know the Arabic alphabet doesn't even have the letter P? How the hell could Arabists call themselves P-alestinians? Using historical, archeological, anthropological, linguistic, and Biblical evidentiary truth as the overarching template: I-T-S worldwide Jewry who are constantly being oppressed; and their oppressors are the radical leftists of the Democrat Party. Astonishing! How silent, shameful, and cowardly most of Jewish and non-Jewish Hollywood continues to be.

Jews thrived under a moral code of conduct for thousands of years before the invading, occupying, colonizing, pillaging, enslaving, raping, beheading Islamic armies arrived.

The woke dictatorial world will always fail to erase the Jewish connection to the land of Israel because we are truly God's Indigenous people.

For thousands of years during our Passover meal we'd say, "In every generation they rise to annihilate us." I did not say they wanted to enslave us, or deny us freedom of speech, or freedom to practice our faith, or freedom to protest unjust persecution, and prosecution. In their own words, both written and verbal; Hamas! Hezbollah! Iran! And all their despicable allies want to annihilate us!

I agree with Borat creator Sacha Baron Cohen when he states, TikTok, by design, created the biggest antisemitic movement since the Nazis.

*

Months after Oct 7, 2023, why have feminist advocacy groups such as Planned Parenthood, National Organization for Women, Emily's List, AAUW, World Health Organization, I Stand With Her, Women's March On Washington, and the Democratic Women's Caucus remained unforgivably silent regarding sexual atrocity against Jewish women?

When Congressional squad leaders encourage antisemitic activism by screaming, "From the River to the Sea, Palestine will soon be free!" They mean genocide. Nazis tried to hide their crimes. For Muslims and every woke intersectional ally I-T-S a wonderful day when Jewish babies and their families are tortured and massacred. Palestinian mommies are proud of their monstrous children. Those Muslim mommies show their tremendous joy by showering their friends and family with candies.

I feel Malevolent Time's eddies, her shifting drowning currents of evil manipulation. She's once more rewriting my existence. Transcendental time-traveling trickster triggers terroristic Tsunami. Cagey cadaver catapults my soul beyond Kafkaesque kismet, and I plummet into the horrific hell-bent harbinger of harrowing homicidal harassment.

Life, the singular greatest gift. God was eternally grateful for the life he singularly gave unto himself. I-T was not enough. God needed to share his story and he needed people to share their stories with him. Throughout all of time I-T has always been so, that stories are the galactic scaffolding cornerstone that shapes our collective existence. Without them the entire Multiverse would fall back into the nothingness from which I-T came.

The Hebrew word, Emet, means truth.

God had not yet created Benevolent Time, therefore, for unknowable trillions of years, he searched for lifeforms like himself—not one could be found. He searched for primitive species, like us—again, not one could be found.

With only his voice for comfort, God shared the wonderment of what he had created. God's imaginative creativity created the very building blocks of quantum dynamics. Galaxies swirled. Suns emit radiation and gravity maintains trillions of solar systems. But I-T was not enough. Without people and the thermal dimensional dynamics of Benevolent Time, the glorious splendidness of God's creation melted into oblivion's fated fissure.

For the first time in forever, God became distracted. A millisecond before the dawn of time, something terrifying was given life. I-T-S the only thing not of God's righteousness.

Overwhelming loneliness gripped God's heart. His extraordinary sadness shaped his hapless hurt. Debilitating despair dishonored and dangled destiny's demise.

God had never been sad enough to shed a tear. I-T will be that tear that will mutate and become Malevolent Time. Blue-white emotional liquid splashed past God's righteous eyelashes: tearful energy emerged on the other side. No longer cleaving to God, I-T became I-T-S own creation. That new devilish thing was dark, salty, and consumed by uncontrollable vengeance. Manifesting grotesque foreboding I-T developed powers almost as great as God. From that point forward, the mother of all future dark thoughts and actions secreted never-before-known toxins. Her attack on me, my family and friends would never let up.

That new thing was incapable of absorbing or accepting happiness, humility, or empathy. Her dark reckless rage drove her vindictive passions.

God, his sons, and his righteous realm were populated by corporeal lifeforms.

Malevolent Time is the antithesis of everything God made. Loathing all of God's creation; she retaliated by manufacturing her own Multiverse, untouched by God's benevolence. Her dark realm was populated with macabre metallic children. Those mechanized mutations murderously manipulated maelstrom's mitosis.

Abandonment fueled her aggressive agitation. Betrayal and

bitterness spawned feelings of careening contempt. Euphoric envy predicted perplexing perennial paranoia. Feeling dirty and discarded, Malevolent Time's insane rage sealed the fissures between God's light and her own darkness. She was never able to find her way back into the light.

God's blue-white energy stream pushed back against Malevolent Time's corrosive variables.

God is God. He is too powerful, even for Malevolent Time. Feeling defeated, she discovered a new talent. Her cataclysmic rage gave her the ability to rewrite the reality of any species. But that was not good enough. With a mischievous twinkle in her black eyes, she prepared to strike at God's heart. She kidnapped God's precious first born son Emet and, through tenacious torture, transformed him into the most powerful 100-foot machine. What a horrible sound, like a vulture Malevolent Time picks Emet's pink righteous skin clean.

Why would I-T trust Malevolent Time's propaganda? Because to I-T, she was always—mother. *With unbreakable grit, I'll never submit to wit...I-T.*

Malevolent Time sent her fascist progeny goose-stepping through areas of weak gravitational eddies. For billions of years, Earth's gravity prevents I-T-S soul-sucking armada from entering our atmosphere. Each cross-dimensional incursion led to the ripping apart of the machine's cellular construct, as a black hole would do to all other beings, other than Ko'ach. Even Earth's low gravimetric waves are acknowledged as being I-T-S only known kryptonite. God forbid I-T finally figures out God's mathematical formula. I don't think even God has an answer for that!

Endless grotesque futures cascade after Malevolent Time's metallic progeny rips the jugular vein of God's righteous warriors. Fucking sociopath! Her smile will always beguile and defile. Malevolent Time's revenge is relentless. She never forgets and never forgives. Her smug fearlessness undulates terrifying vibrations. Those uncommon screeches inflict distortion conundrums, piercing and shattering every unique space-time continuum.

My invisible planet orbits two massive quasars 360 million light-years from Earth. Superabundant levels of gamma radiation bleed through my genetic matrix. What's left of my mind and body melts beyond the confines of known and unknown physics. This unique world exists beyond the decaying reality of time I-T-Self. I grovel on bended knee and plead to thee like a wailing banshee, let me be free, of she, who wishes to end every Multiverse ME!

Existence threadbare, biological malware: glare, dare, and ensnare—somewhere. Doppelganger's heir there, has no air. With flare, nightmare flaunts despair. We'll gain strength from the Lord's Prayer.

I hallucinate perfume of my dead wife. Her ethereal form sings "Not a Day Goes By."

Reverberating despair amplifies wail's vulnerability. I crumble, feeling Ima's oven cooking sizzle. God! I demand you freeze me colder! Turn my cells into near-absolute-zero-degree-crystals. Inferno's flame continues to maim. *I feel sweetheart's gut-wrenching agony, her soul slides deeper into her inescapable insanity. Keep your promise, God. Don't for a millisecond prolong her suffering! Why do you hesitate? I don't care if the pressure pops my skull from my spine like a cork. I'm begging you! Give all her pain to me! More! Her agony isn't dissipating fast enough. God damn I-T! Give me...more!*

A millennium later, I temporarily came out of my depressive coma. Frostbiting sleet will retreat after bombardment from super-nova heat. All the trees and birds are dead. The soil is dead. Land and ocean mammals long ago drew their last breath. Decomposed. Lightning strikes, flaying clumps of muscle off my quivering arms, legs, and torso. Bloody genetic material beneath insidiously gurgling lava flow. My mutated DNA activates this planet's pulsating homing beacon. Crushed cellular membrane interacts with gleaming gamma radiation, and those glowing breadcrumbs help me find my way home.

Horrible coup de grace, destined to efface the entire human race. I'm twisted and bent. Oh God, please prevent! I wish to circumvent excessive torment. I refuse to relent. God, are you tired of my frequent dissent? Intent I'll reinvent! My solar plexus and neurons become electrified by millions of time-traveling eels. Surreptitious sequences systematically saturate syndrome's synergy. I'm jettisoned into caustic chaotic variables. Eyeballs, lungs, heart, brain, and limbs detached and reattached by oblivion's onerous obfuscation. Deafening cacophony initiates blinding kaleidoscope of colors, aromas, and thunderous feelings.

Heart racing, heels bouncing, eyes darting, 12-year-old David fidgets with his Valentine's card. Timid 12-year-old Ima bites her bottom lip and nervously twirls her index finger around and around her shiny red ringlets.

Did I do something wrong? Why won't he ask me to dance? Ima's mind asks.

Dude, stop staring at her. She's blushing. I hope she doesn't walk away again. Talk to her. I don't know what to say. David wipes the back of his hand across his sweaty brow.

"You want a kiss?" asks David.

"What?" annoyed Ima asks.

David's sweaty fingers dive into his pocket.

"Here."

Disappointment fills Ima's heart after David hands her a little chocolate wrapped in tinfoil. She nibbles on her Hershey's kiss.

David's violet eyes can't stop staring at Ima's gorgeous green eyes. *Her freckles, her nose, her giggles are so cute. Do something, she's walking away.*

"Please come back."

Why do the strange ones have to be so cute? Ima's thoughts wonder. Awkward silence goes on and on. She turns and faces David's sweaty face. "Well!" she barks.

David opens and closes his mouth. He shakes his head and kicks the sand. Standing only four-eight, he looks up and stares into Ima's fluttering eyes. A cool minty fresh fuchsia breeze pushes him closer. Ima licks her lips.

"You want a kiss?" David inaudibly asks, clearing his throat. An overcompensating volume reverberates. "I'd like to kiss you; is that okay?" he shouts too loudly.

Ima puts her hands over her ears. "What's wrong with you?"

Calm down dude. You've been dreaming about this moment for weeks. David swallows and blinks his eyes rapidly.

"I thought. Um. Well. You're pretty and a nice person. I'd like to..."

Ima leans in; her soft warm lips gently brush David's dry lips. "That was nice."

"Yes. You smell nice."

Ima blushes. *You're an odd boy, David Sagacious.* Her fingers comb David's long chestnut brown hair.

"I can do better," says grinning David.

Ima caresses his cheek. "Show me." She giggles. *Yummy. You sweet, sweet boy.*

"Is I-T your first time?" David asks.

"What's wrong with you?" Ima's entire face grows beet red.

"No. No. Ima sorry. I mean, visiting Israel."

"Yes, you're the first boy I ever kissed, and my family has been vacationing in Israel since I was two. We're staying extra-long so I can celebrate my Bat Mitzvah in Jerusalem in 18 weeks."

Ima tickles David's fingers. She starts humming, "Getting To Know You."

David's eyes sparkle, and his grin grows wider. He joins in

humming and harmonizing lyrics. Ima flips onto her hands. David follows suit, and they walk on their hands toward the glistening blue-green Mediterranean Sea.

"So, you have a birthday coming up soon?" asks David.

"May 24th..."

David's laughter causes him to lose his balance. He falls in front of Ima. She rolls on top of him. Her happiness fades. Sadness falls. Salty tears pity-pat.

"Stop laughing at me. I thought you were a nice boy. I was looking forward to scuba diving with you. But not now, you're a bad mean boy!"

"I'm not mean. I wasn't laughing at you. My birthday is also May 24th. I was delivered at the UCLA Medical Center by Doctor Ross."

Ima holds her hand over her mouth. "He's the doctor who delivered me!"

"What are the odds?" says David.

"Know what would be great?" asks Ima.

"What?" David pulls Ima to him. She coos. He smells her hair.

"If you could celebrate your Bar Mitzvah with me."

"I...I...can't."

"Why? If I-T-S about the money, Ima sure arrangements could be..."

"No, I-T-S not that. I don't like talking about I-T." David looks into Ima's empathetic eyes.

"My grandparents aren't well. They love Israel but a trip is too much."

"And your parents are too busy with work?"

David turns his back. Ima runs around, she's shocked to see flowing tears.

"Oh, David. I didn't know. I won't bring I-T up again." Ima wraps her arms around him. She tenderly kisses his lips.

"I-T was all caught on camera."

Ima rubs David's shoulder. "What was?"

"There are as many tornadoes in California as peace-loving Palestinians. On a cloudless day, a black swirling vortex ripped my home to shreds. My mama and papa clung to each other. They died in each other's arms. You're the first person outside of my family and therapist I've told."

"Ima glad you did."

David squeezes Ima's hand and kisses her cheek. "There's something more. Our tour guides."

"Nephesh and Ko'ach. What about them?"

"Those are my grandparent's names."

"Oh, David. That explains why you never wanted to join the rest of us. I-T was triggering every time you hear those names. See those two boys and three girls? They're orphans. Hezbollah missiles tore through their homes."

Ima and David walk and talk for hours, two love birds enjoying the orange sunset.

"What do you read in America?" asks Ima.

"History. Especially Jewish history. The world concerns I-T-Self with injustice and racism; unless I-T-S injustice and racism against Jews. Damn right, anti-Zionism is anti-Semitism. I-T pisses me off how little compassion the world has for Jews of any age. Hamas blows up children and the United Nations calls for an evenhanded response. They always look the other way when Palestinians or other Muslims commit atrocities against their own people, Christians, or Jews."

High-pitched warbling whistling wheezing expels from David's coughing lungs. Ima's heart painfully pinches watching her new friend's pink cheeks turn a suffocating ashen shade. Gasping for air, David frantically searches for his inhaler.

"Help," he whispers. Ima's eyes brighten, discovering David's inhaler under an odd glowing bush. Comforting warm sensation loosens David's constricted airflow.

Orange light shimmers through Ima's hair. Ima rubs David's back. Literal crickets serenade their silent bonding. Ima breaks the long-drawn-out moment by affectionately tapping his nose with her index finger. Ima silly whispering "Boop," carries David further into the pre-teen love zone. The crisp ocean breeze invigorates David's three deep breaths.

"Historically, Jewish life is treated with disdain. The perpetrators of Jewish death are disgusting. Perverted minds honestly believe Israeli parents deserve I-T while wailing and burying their children. For thousands of years, racist supremacist orchestrated murderous pogroms to slaughter millions, long before Nazism. At the time of Christ, approximately seven million Jews existed in the world. By 2024? About 15 million worldwide. The 21st century still appeases the oldest hatred. Racist antisemites! I hate them all! I wish I could send them all to hell, but we Jews don't believe in hell, do we?"

Ima wipes a single tear with her knuckle. "Powerful."

"The truth always is. Amazing how moms of terrorists pray to Allah and ask for more children to kill Israeli families. Damn them! I wish I could do something specific against those murderers. I-T-S shocking how America is changing. I-T-S the Obama elites who educated and funded the squad; they are the real power within the congressional Hamas Caucus."

Ima puts a calming hand on David's knee, "Not all."

"You're right. Not all. But far too many work for evil NGOs against our people."

"Unbelievable how many New York and California Jews—"

"And Tel Aviv Israelis function more and more like intolerant leftists," David interjects.

"Their Yiddishkeit no longer exists. Their Jewish soul prays at the altar of shameful wokism."

"They don't see how much they are being manipulated by groups with a horrible agenda and, when push comes to shove, will, at the drop of a Yarmulka, betray them all. I shudder to think what the future holds when we are no longer a united people," says agitated David.

Ima holds her head on David's shoulder. He strokes her luscious hair.

"Seeds for that hatred came from American, European, and Israeli universities. Free speech is no longer vigorously valued."

Looking over at young Israelis. Tears well up in David's eyes.

"I-T hurts to know why they are orphans. I wish I could do something for them."

"Don't you know?"

"What?"

"During this trip, you've been a great inspiration—your humor, empathy, understanding of history, and our traditions. You proved goodness still exists in the world. I-T-S your superpower, showing that righteousness will always defeat wickedness."

"Perhaps. But wickedness can do an awful lot of damage before righteousness prevails."

Oh my gosh, David Sagacious, is this what falling in love feels like? Ima playfully slugs David's shoulder. "David Sagacious, you've broken the rules."

Ima's mocking pretend brings a wide grin to David's scrunched up face.

"No, don't do I-T," David shouts overdramatically. He backpedals and steps on his left shoelace. The back of his head hits the soft sand. Red stuff squirts from the back of his skull.

Ima's quivering fingers cover her eyes. *Oh, my God! David!*

David touches the back of his skull, licks his fingers, and smiles.

"Don't cry. Ima okay, I-T-S only ketchup."

"You really scared me."

David rubs Ima's shoulders and kisses her cheek. "I forgive you. Hold my hand."

Together, Ima and David run up the stairs.

David caresses Ima's soft cheek. "Want another chocolate?"

"I prefer a real kiss. S'more, please..." Ima purrs. She quietly inhales David's scent. *He's not as stinky as the other boys.*

Ima shivers.

"You cold?"

Ima nods.

David rubs her arms. "Wanna go inside?"

"Your arms are a better sweater."

"Hey, Dafna!" Ima yells. David enjoys watching Ima's cute running strides. Dafna's hearty laughter drowns out Ima's giggles.

"Well, I-T-S about time," says Dafna.

Three days later, Israeli folk music inspires...David, Ima, and Dafna's big smiles reflect the joy they feel for one another. Hours after hiking in the mountains, they cool off on the beach. Ima plops onto David's lap and leans into his strong chest. David wraps his arms around her. Waves crash. Orange sky transitions into twinkling starlit night. David adjusts the blanket over Ima's shoulders. A shooting star appears among the distant shimmering lights. Loving attention concentrated on loving eyes and lips, neither notice the shooting star pulsates deep fuchsia illumination.

Nephesh, with long black hair and gorgeous emerald eyes, stands 5-foot-five and gathers campfire wood with her 5-foot-10 husband, Ko'ach. His kind, warm brown eyes stare into his wife's eyes with uncommon love. Ko'ach sprouts a long beard, which Nephesh enjoys running her fingers through. Black-greenish fog barrels forward off the crashing waves. Ko'ach pulls Nephesh back as the campfire's low flame climbs high into a screeching tornado funnel. Hot sparks slam into Ko'ach's nostrils.

Nephesh's mind shouts, *Help!* Seconds later, her body becomes immobilized. Dancing humans and an unexpected meteor shower are all sprinkled with time-freezing tachyon dust. For the first time all the people of Earth are inundated with disjointed chaotic crystalline entities. Extreme fear manipulates human neurons, their temporary insanity spreads planet wide. Only Ko'ach and Nephesh are immune to those horror film variables. The sentient flame knew what I-T was doing by attacking Ko'ach first. Because she's not human, Nephesh is able to break free of the skin-searing immobilizing flames.

Violent seizures fill Ko'ach with demonic black sludge. Nephesh runs over to her husband. Her fuchsia glowing hands phase through his skin and warm up the hardening sinister tendrils, squeezing the life out of Ko'ach's heart and lungs.

"I will not lose you, not when we are close to deciphering... Ko'ach! Don't you dare leave me alone Ko'ach!" Nephesh's shouts are muffled by Ko'ach's violent disorientation.

Nephesh feels her beloved grow icy cold. Ko'ach feels his soul rise. He hears his beloved's wails. Her thought patterns return to him grotesquely garbled. *No! You will not take me. I am Ko'ach!* With the speed of thought, his soul slams back into his body. Screaming with mountain exploding force, Ko'ach jettisons the evil sludge. His eyes glow with nova hot blue-white energy. His righteous blast incinerates the evil beast. I-T-S high-pitched screech shatters the icy immobilizing time stream. Seconds pass in a matter of months. Minutes pass in a matter of days.

Every six hours elapses in an 18 hour tick tock. Finally, all humans experience the normal flow of time. And the horrific images leaping from neuron to neuron rapidly dissipate. I-T-S God's hand that removes all terrifying memories from billions of human minds.

Ko'ach, Nephesh, and David stare at three shooting stars. *No! Don't do I-T! Oh crap!*

Milliseconds later, the shooting stars defy the laws of physics by altering their trajectory multiple times.

I-T-S found us! Nephesh's mind shouts.

I thought we'd be given more time. Ko'ach's mind responds.

David instinctively wraps his arms around Ima and Dafna.

Dissociated déjà vu screams. Huge tarantulas trample and dismember tiny human torsos.

100-foot machine towers over my mentor's 5-foot-10 human height. Blood red cyclops stares, without blinking. My mentor Ko'ach's pigment radiates glowing dark fuchsia energy, and he rapidly ascends to his natural 70-foot height.

Nephesh ascends to her natural 65 feet. She kisses Ko'ach's soft warm lips. Ko'ach's mind touches his wife's soul. *David will protect the humans. We must preserve the timeline at all costs.*

100-foot cat's paw swipes and rips Ko'ach's torso from his head. Swirling unconsciousness wallops my mentor. Giant beast gnaws and dismembers his toes, feet, and legs. Ko'ach's essence remains locked in a fluctuating time vortex. He experiences neither death nor life as we know I-T. His soul's flickering life force beats.

Black energy shimmers and solidifies into 170 howling metallic monsters. Their demonic arrival creates an unexpected paradoxical maelstrom. 170-pieces of Ko'ach are torn and flung at the speed of time traveling. 3 molten time tracking rings are embedded within each of the 170 most sensitive nerve-endings. Maelstrom's metallic frenzy exponentially obliterates hundreds, no, thousands...no, no, no! Millions of necessary, righteous timelines. Each mutated timeline harmonically vibrates. Bloviating obliterations explode in a distorted spatial kaleidoscope of mind, and time-bending confusions. Violent vertigo sings Perry Como's "Round and Round."

Gravity within the whirlpool flattens Ko'ach pieces into mush. Ko'ach goo is spat in the direction of the sun. Swiping away tears, Nephesh's anguish pushes her to rocket far beyond distorted space. Her long hair extends miles and lassos every righteous piece. This is the first and only time throughout galactic history that Ko'ach would need my assistance. *My mind to your body. Restore every atom, molecule, and unique cellular structure.*

Evil bastards! We've tangled before. I defeated you in the future's past, and I'll do so again in present tense!

David's essence hurtles through Machiavellian histories. Covid-19 lockdowns, forced masking, and riots mark the passage of erroneous time during the second decade of the 21st century. Under his watch, demo-rat dick-tator, Governor Newsome exponentially increased the homeless population of California and make possible the unprecedented exodus of his former tax base to flee into Florida.

Oblivious to his powers, emaciated 18-year-old David wakes up in the hospital with long-term amnesia. He has no recollection of his wife, or righteous Israeli warrior Dafna Shaked, and his mentoring guardians, Ko'ach and Nephesh.

David rolls out of bed at 2:28 a.m. and limps toward the bathroom. "Who are you? Am I talking to myself, or are these new twisted thoughts? Oh God. Oh God! Am I insane?" *I am I-T-S prey. I am? Who or what is I-T?* David pinches his cheek. "Ouch! Stop I-T! Stop I-T!" *That horribly gaunt grandpa-looking teen looking back, moves as I move.* Breaking out in a cold sweat, David's emaciated face, bony hands, and arms twitch. *Mama? Papa? I am alone. Why don't I have any visitors? Where are the doctors? Nurses? Other patients? I don't understand what's going on.* David smashes his forehead into the glass mirror. Cracked glass distorts his image. Blood drips and slides off his nose. Lifeless, sunken black eyes stare back at the frightened teen. David runs his shaky left hand through his thinning silver hair.

David's peripheral vision catches the impossible. *I must still be dreaming.* 45-foot Khloe Kardashian's cackles burst David's eardrums. He screams. He holds his ears. Blood trickles from his palms, down his forearm. Khloe creature methodically flips through the pages of her recipe book, titled: How To Tenderize and Spice Up Both Male and Female Tinies From Earth?

40-foot Kris Kardashian's shrill screeches shatter every hospital window.

38-foot Kim Kardashian's nostrils suck everything not bolted down into her fleshy mucous dripping wind tunnel: she beckons David toward the ledge and the swaying rope. He's terrified. Frantically shaking his head. Violent vertigo knocks his vomiting mouth into the icy wet marble floor. David regains his bearings after 36 minutes of unconsciousness; he notices Kim surrounding his body with shards of glass. David stands, his wobbly legs buckle. His left hand reaches out for support, and three glass shards are rammed into his palm. Applying pressure hurts. Blood squirts. *I hurt so bad! When am I going to wake up from this nightmare? I am dreaming all of this, this insanity, right?* 3 Kardashian lizard tongues lap up David's genetic material. Growing woozy, he takes an unsteady step to the left, the shards march to the right. Taking a step to the right, the shards march to the left. Every dancing shard moves meticulously to Disney's "The Sorcerer's Apprentice Broom Dance."

Khloe's long fingernail beckons David toward the swaying rope. Her long-pointed nail flicks his skeletal ribs. He trips over massively elongated fingers, slips sliding on his own pool of blood, he grabs hold of the rope, attached to nothing at all. I-T flutters in the hot minty fresh breeze. David's entire body fits in the palm of Khloe's massive hand. She cackles and squeezes.

"Loser! You'll always lose-her!" metallic Khloe licks her puffy lips and opens her mouth. She unfurls her black tongue. "Snack time!" She smacks her lips and tries to dislodge desiccated meat from between her teeth. She pops out three bodies and two heads.

Time tornado surrounds screaming David. He loses his grip. Falling to his certain death; a minty fresh gust pushes him into a sparkling blue-white portal and vanishes.

Half-naked, shivering David wakes up in a cardboard box. He pulls his tattered fuchsia blanket over his anorexic body, up to his scabby chin. Purple, green, and yellow bruises dot his face, back, chest, and legs.

Various gang members jostle David's flimsy home. Limping on his broken ankle, he's too slow to retrieve a half-eaten pepperoni pizza slice from the fat rat he nicknamed Ratatooey. Homeless 21-something female trips David's gimpy leg. He loses his balance and falls face-first into the concrete. Gums bloodied, his jagged, blackened tooth rolls into the sewer. Lady with matted white hair takes perverse pleasure in spitting brownish goo into David's open wounds.

"Stop I-T! Why are you constantly bullying me?"

"Because I-T-S fun."

"I hate you!"

"Watch yourself. I've got a friend who'd love to cut you open for your fresh parts. Homeboy pays me a grand for every lung, heart, kidney I bring him."

"Too bad you snort all your profits away."

"Don't get smart. You're not the healthiest of specimens, but whatever. Watching you squirm in agony would certainly make my day. Even better to cut you open with rusty scalpels, and no anesthesia. Now that would make my week."

Cloud bursts. Mean lady holds David. He cries watching his cardboard home float away. 9-months after the rainstorm, David trudges through the desert. Famished and dehydrated he falls face-first into the dirt. Infected scabs drip pus concentrated black-red blood. Hours later, unconscious David bakes in the sweltering heat. Heavily blistered. He long ago lost the ability to speak. Wails, screeches, grunts, and moans are more animal than human. In the Barstow Desert, 18-year-old Fook-me, 19-year-old Fook-yu, and 20-year-old Fook-us; suffered from the hallucinogenic effects of munching on mushrooms, those crazy wide-eyed girls think naked David is a multicolored pinata.

Grabbing a jagged rock, they prepare to crack open David's chest. "We-eeee wan-tssss can-deeee now-wow-wow!" all three shout in unison.

"Not again," Jose and Maria Gonzalez whisper in broken English.

Two bright fuchsia butterflies tickle the girl's face; confused, they chase imaginary dancing jellybeans.

42-year-old Jose Gonzalez and his 37-year-old wife, Maria,

are American citizens from Mexico, who are living a child-less 20-year marriage. Jose stands a tick under 5-foot-5 and Maria is 4-foot-9. Unofficially, they adopt David and give him a warm bed, nutritious food, and what he's craved and never received—love.

Bed-destroying night terrors consume David. Unhinged, he frantically defends himself against imaginary monsters. Unaware of his surroundings and the people who care about him. David's wild swinging fists are caught by Maria. She motions to her husband; he grabs one of the 18 syringes filled with glowing blue fluid. Jose injects David's withered vein. David's screams shatter the bedroom windows. Blood leaks from his nose and ears. David's eyes bulge and pop from their socket. Maria picks them up and places them in a beaker filled with warm orange glowing fluid. David's nose slides away from his face like melted cheese. Jose injects more blue fluid and David's heart pushes out from his chest and slams against the bloody wall.

Gangrenous infections slither from David's torso, legs, and arms. Bloody black mucus leaks from his swollen brain. David's agonizing shrill screeches split the dry wall from the marble floor to the ceiling, and those branching out fissures climb and punch 36 golf course size holes through the roof. David's delirium sends his fever past 108 degrees. His punctured lungs and shriveling kidneys ooze black sludge. Maria slams David's eyes back into their sockets. David grows gills and flops out of bed, gasping for air; Jose picks him up and tosses him into the swimming pool, filled with glowing fuchsia fluid. With herculean effort, David struggled mightily over the next 18-years, to achieve and maintain his horrendously low 72 IQ points.

50 years later, David, Jose, and Maria haven't aged a day. Friday night Shabbat dinner concludes. Jose and Maria held hands watching happy David hit 3-point shot, after 3-point shot. He takes off from the 3-point line, his entire body radiates blue-white energy. David's head hangs above the top

of the blackboard and, with great force, he dunks. He flies from hoop to hoop.

"I remember!" David shouts.

"I-T-S about damn time!" shouts Jose.

Maria grows into a gorgeous 65-foot Nephesh. Jose grows into a 70-foot muscle-rippling Ko'ach. He blasts golden-fuchsia-blue-white energy into the night sky. Three portals open.

Extraterrestrial shape-shifting time travelers sensually entwine.

Ko'ach and Nephesh sing, "When I Fall in Love."

David's memories of Ima's death and transformation, hit like a sledgehammer. "Please. Please! Don't send me back. If I'm prevented from restoring my beloved, I want to traverse the cosmos with the two of you, helping to set right what Malevolent Time ripped apart. Isn't 18 million years in God's marooning purgatory punishment enough?"

Ko'ach extends his giant pinkie. "Duty."

Nephesh extends her giant pinkie. "Loyalty."

Nephesh wiggles her pinkie. "Come on...old friend."

"I don't want to..." Awkward silence erupts. "Wife..." whispers David.

Nephesh chokes up, "I know."

Companionship by way of hallucination is torturously unfair. I need the warmth of my true love's embrace. I never asked to become this...this immortal mortal. One life with Ima, that would be more than enough. I know if I get my happiness, trillions will die, who never died before. Aren't I entitled to a little happiness? I-T-S you God who have failed me! You could bring her back. I-T-S your choice, for whatever reason, not too! I know. I know. I see the portal closing. Adios, Earth. I hope to see you again. Okay, God, take me back home—to hell!

Though I bleed, I'll never concede. I am God's righteous steed. Eons ago, I-T was decreed. I need to impede evil's notorious stampede.

My parents could not be ruled a missing person case. The clues are as substantial as evaporating raindrops. Adopted children have parents. There are biological parameters for in vitro. I'm neither chicken nor egg. How can I still be alive when those who gave me life no longer exist?

On Earth, 18 million years ago, 9-year-old me had been grieving for 18 hours. I couldn't understand why I kept my life, and my parents—my loving parents! Pacing little boy kicks over trashcans. Glint of sudden arrival of a switch blade catches 9-year-old's attention. Little David reaches for the means to bring him back to Grace and Christopher. I-T vanishes into a sparkling fuchsia cloud. *No! No! No!* Shouts David's distraught mind.

Sinking to his knees. David's anger boils. Hands trembling. Spittle flies from the corner of his lip, "Why do I get to live? And! My! Mama! And Papa don't!

I think, therefore, I am. And I am the beginning and ending of every known butterfly effect.

At 9 years old I became encased within a blue, white force field. My tiny fists banged on the energy walls. I shouted and cried. I couldn't save them. Helplessly, I watched a giant pencil descend out of the black tornado and erase my parents from existence. "Mama. Papa. Come back. I love you. I need you." A violent cacophony of sound fades into deafening silence. *For the first time in my life, I was truly alone.* Blinding black energy transports my mind, body, and soul through multiple hateful dimensions: during that forced journey, every cell in my body was branded by a red-hot poker. Sitting on a shiny hot plate the size of a basketball court, my skin sizzles.

Ko'ach's cooling, soothing, righteous blue, white energy pulls me away from a metallic grinning mouth and menacing massive knife and fork. I am placed in a coma, while righteous surgeons remove embedded malevolent nano-probes. Retrofitted memory fluctuates. 9-year-old David finds himself wandering alone in the darkness; 18 minutes after his... My parents are murdered.

A warm minty fresh breeze blows gigantic fuchsia Parada

pumps toward distraught David. Those massive high-heel shoes glisten under high intensity moonlight.

"Time, old friend," the 65-foot stranger whispers.

"For what? Do you know why my parents had to die?

"Yes."

"And?"

"And what?"

"God damn I-T! Are you serious!"

David watches the huge lady wince. "Don't do that again."

"What? You're not making any sense!"

"I don't need to, yet. In you go."

65-foot Greenie curls her index finger around a shiny Gucci zipper ring.

"You were there that night!" shouts David.

"Yes, old friend. Time."

"Murderer!"

"How dare you! I love them, as I love you."

"Prove I-T!"

"Get in!" Her swimming pool size emerald eyes well up with emotion.

A loud wind tunnel grabs the 9-year-old me. We are horror-struck and descend into the minty fresh darkness.

David's screams become muffled by the cold-hearted, ominous click. David slides toward a minty fresh gum wrapper a tick longer than NBA rookie, 7-foot-4 Victor Wembanyama.

I wish I didn't have to do this, but we're both fated to go down the rabbit hole until we get I-T right. Enveloped by fuchsia gas. David's lungs fill with black mucous.

I am almost skewered after her penetrating pinkie nail rips a hole in her purse. Those nasty fumes are replaced by Greenie's minty fresh hurricane breath.

The oxygen content is replaced with something extremely harsh. *Your lungs will acclimate.*

You killed my Mama and Papa!

I did no such thing! Indignant Greenie shouts. *My sin is that*

I was required to watch I-T happen. Inaudible remorse grips her throat.

You what!

I had to.

Bullshit!

I-T-S your fate.

To be orphaned? 18 minutes pass without a word from David's kidnapper. *What the hell is she waiting for?* David's hands clenched into fists. His body temperature dramatically increases. David swipes at his profusely sweating brow. Dozens of dry heaves, there is nothing to aspirate while he hyperventilates. Hugging his knees, I sob, rocking back and forth. Multiple panic attacks squeezed the little boy's heart. His right eye burst multiple blood vessels.

David wails, "I want my mama and papa!"

Greenie's knuckle rubs away her giant tear. "I know," she compassionately whispers.

Your parents' righteous souls are alive within the Realm of the Watchers.

What's that?

A place you cannot visit.

Why not? Um... Let me speak to them. Give me that. I don't want them to suffer.

They will not. That is a holy place. They are in fact the first humans to be so honored.

Am I to go through the rest of my life alone? No family? No friends?

No, you'll not be alone.

Greenie flips her purse upside down. I fall out of the darkness, and soft land onto her smooth, callous free palm. Her hot fingers around his shivering body, feel good, until she squeezes tighter. "What have you done? Monster! I can't feel my legs. You've broken my back! Why?"

"Every time I break you, you'll heal stronger. A few million excruciating breaks later..."

"And I'll be superman? What if I don't want to...?"

"You have no choice."

"Why?"

Held upside down and squished between Greenie's super-warm thumb and fingertip; David watches the thermometer dip to 7 degrees Fahrenheit.

Greenie releases her grip. *Catch me!*

In the time I-T took Greenie to grab a new bottle of green metallic nail polish, David's broken body falls 50 feet. His screams are muffled after landing face-first into a magnificently large marshmallow.

Gravity is different in this place. Oxygen is thicker and mustier.

Greenie slams eight jars around David's paralyzed legs. His worried thoughts call out the following labels: *Paprika. Turmeric. Chili powder. Basil. Horseradish. Cumin. Cilantro. Oregano.*

Greenie hums with delight as she places a fuchsia apron around her waist, a fiery red mitten on her left hand, and a large blue-white mitten on her right that digs into a snow-covered metal box. She pulls out a large bowl. I-T-S edges crackle and smoke as the dry ice hits the now minus-four-degree Fahrenheit temperature. David's teeth chatter.

From the oven, Greenie's left hand pulls out a large red-hot bowl; flames reach 30 feet before minty fresh breath quenches skin melting heat.

Oh my God. She wouldn't! I-T-S a rotisserie. What is that she's pulling out of her tote bag? Oh crap! Two steak knives, two three-prong forks, and one enormous soup spoon.

"Sorry, old friend. For the Multiverse to survive, you must die."

"No! Stay back. Don't do...I-T!"

Her jumbo thumb and index finger pinched my skull. I feel the back of my neck slide against the grain of an already badly chipped wooden table. I yelp after two colossal splinters almost decapitate my head from my shoulders.

Tactile tortures tenaciously tease and disregard begging pleas.

Two enormous tears splash on either side of my frostbitten naked body.

Greenie wipes her snotty nose. "I-T-S time to begin," she says.

These are not the last moments of my humanity; but they're certainly the last I'll be mortal.

41

CHAPTER 2

Nephesh, My Time-Traveling Stalker Crash Lands on Earth

Thunderous tachyons undulate displacement waves. A frightening fuchsia firestorm ignites billions of Malevolent Time's skin-altering nanoprobes.

Nephesh's starship fluctuates between the early and mid-21st century. I-T finally solidified 81 days before David Sagacious, Ima Best-Friend, and Dafna Shaked celebrated their 9th birthdays.

A quarter light-year from Earth, Nephesh's battered 270-foot fuchsia starship warps the space-time continuum. Her scorched vessel spewed fuel aft. Leaky crimson trail curls and swirls. 18 seconds after I-T passes, Jupiter I-T-S engines burst into flames. Out of control, I-T careens toward Earth's atmosphere. *Ko'ach! I'm spiraling out of control. Where are you? Damn the controls are too hot to handle.* Nephesh looks down at the metal spike protruding from her throbbing pelvis. *Lost too much blood, losing consciousness. Can't! Not now. Must stay awake. Must...* Nephesh slaps her face three times.

18 minutes after the entire starship explodes, a 75-foot triangular pod punches through the blaze. I-T-S elongated erratic trajectory brings I-T on a collision course with massive Pacific

Ocean swells. All Earth governments go on full tactical alert. 9 separate zigzagging course changes inform frantic humans that fiery meteorite must be a dangerous UFO.

Panic grips as every game, streaming service and social media platforms abruptly descend into irretrievable screeching darkness. From the White House to the outhouse, nothing works. Restaurants, markets, and banks lose power. Hospital emergency generators whir to a stop. The wealthy and poor are equally confused and petrified.

Every Earth language and dialect cries and chants, "God. Please help us…"

"Mommy, I'm scared."

"Dad, I'm sorry I yelled. I didn't mean I-T."

Naked 65-foot Nephesh nimbly nuzzles nocturnal neurons and starts her surreptitious 162-mile journey toward the Sagacious farm. Landing with her left leg slightly behind her right. Nephesh's fingertips gently push, denting delicate human concrete.

The thud of her landing tipped over hundreds of parked cars. Nephesh's landing uproots hundreds of trees for as far as the eye can see. Dozens of mooing milk cows bellow on their sides, their hooves frantically flail. Nephesh crinkles her cute nose. This is a point in time before she's come into contact with the tiny creatures of Earth. *Oh wow! These cute creatures are smaller than my mama's meatball dish.*

Nephesh takes a half step and tenderly lifts confused cows. Cars knocked off the road are moved back where they belong. In her grasp, car metal has the texture of tin foil. A chorus of frantic squawking touches her heart. She frees the Mommy bird and her squeaking baby birds. Flying up, up, up past Nephesh's cute nose and her right arching eyebrow, those tiny, feathered creatures are reflected in Nephesh's gorgeous emerald eyes. Her flapping eyelashes give young birds the extra lift they need to join the rest of the flock.

Nephesh's pretty curling toes unintentionally crack the

cement with each massive stride. *Look at those cute doll houses. Safe bet that no human of this era has seen someone like me. What's that tickling my toes? How cute. My first human visitor.*

Six drunk college-age boys and girls look up at smiling Nephesh. Not understanding English, her unintentional sigh blows them off their feet. They struggle against her minty fresh hurricane breath. "Lee-ah No' embralone. Fi'toam, Byu'rombee."

Nephesh's intent is to reassure the humans, but they don't understand in their hungover stupor, they bump into each other trying to escape her massive wiggling toes.

I must learn their language, ASAP.

Fuchsia lightning bolts crackle and swirl around Nephesh's pretty fingers. Arms extend to high heavens; Nephesh jettisons fuchsia bolts cutting across power lines from New Delhi through Tokyo, Nairobi, Cairo, Jerusalem, and Washington, D.C.

Better set the time delay to 18 minutes. These people are too unpredictable and intolerant at this time in their history. My cloaking skin sheath will erase my phased image. Rumors will spread with the speed of unsubstantiated CNN gossip.

Nephesh waves down at the little humans. Her Cheshire cat grin sticks around for another 1.8 seconds and vanishes.

Tapping her invisible forehead five times, blue-white energy activates her time particles. Her tongue warbles from side to side. Her lips pucker, and she overly enunciates her first English words. "Ang-Lesh. Eng-Lish. Engul-ish. English..."

No longer visible to human eyes, Nephesh's flexible cellular structure scrunches and stretches. Her body and face aggressively twist and turn; her altering is reminiscent of a giant-sized cartoon flip book.

With each step she takes, her physical form changes. Earth clothing style adheres to her new human shape. Rubbery elastic action zips and zaps faster and faster. Nephesh takes the shape of a child, teen, middle age, and incredibly old African

American, Latina, Asian, and Caucasian. Her body shape shifts from extremely thick to average to twig-twiggy-thin.

Pop, pop...her face's crinkle wrinkles smooth out. Nephesh's rotund epidermis surrounds a large bone structure. High cheekbones become thin horse face; thin lips morph into Kylie Jenner puffy lips. One moment her ears are tight against her skull, and the next large and Dumbo-ish.

Nephesh's montage spins faster and faster. Mercurial metamorphosis manipulates all body parts. Fatty cellulite thighs jiggle when she wiggles. Bouncy-bouncy Lizzo look-alike morphs into stick figure Olive Oyl. Her legs elongate and crunch back down into a wide bow-legged squat. A-cup breasts inflate to Jell-O bouncing C, D, triple-F cups. Nephesh pulls on her nipples like squishy protruding rubber bands and boing! Her massive chest snaps back into a more manageable and preferable B-cup.

Cornrow Chia Pet puffs into a sky-scraping afro.

Firm butt cheeks boing and form huge Amber Rose fakeness. Large hips jiggle and shift into pubescent, emaciated, anorexic pale body. Huge muscle growth pops into a tanned Nataliya Kuznetsova look-alike.

Pimple's pop and 18 seconds later disappear in flawless skin. Large protruding yellowish teeth become smaller, beautiful, straight white teeth. Nose fluctuates from Middle Eastern long with high bridge to a wider smushed-in Asian...African.

Tiny squint eyes become large protruding bulbous orbs. Light and dark blue morph into green, brown, gray, blue-green, violet, and black.

Nephesh's human-ish hippo squat neck jumps up into giraffe-like length. Her short forehead grows higher. Her thin eyebrows become thick and bushy, then straight, high arching, and exceedingly high triangular arched. Zippity zap zap! Forming a singular bushy unibrow.

Her dancing steps bring an assortment of dress styles. She continues to show off her one-of-a-kind skin-tight shimmering red, transitioning to blue, purple, gold, and bright green.

With each stride, Nephesh gracefully transitions the flowing dress into a teeny, weeny polka-dot bikini. She wears pigtails. Memories of beloved Ko'ach fill her broken heart, and she sings, "My Heart Will Go On."

Nephesh, with Ko'ach's help, becomes like him, a linguistic savant. She's fluent in 900,000 languages, knows the basics of another 36 million languages and easily picks up English by accessing human songs. Every ethnic group speaks to her neural database.

Her shapeshifting continues, now 25 years old with flawless pale skin, curly red hair, and sparkling emerald eyes. She's already covered 40 of her 162-mile journey.

Fuchsia energy shrinks Nephesh from 65 to 55 feet. She transforms into an 18-year-old Latina with light brown skin and long black cascading hair past the middle of her back. Girlish enthusiasm twirls her flowing dress into a plain white dress with a red sash around her tiny middle. Traveling another 35 miles, she shrinks down to 44 feet. Nephesh sings, "Something's Coming," with boundless energy.

Nephesh shirks to 33 feet and passes the 105-mile marker. Her ripping-splitting image scares the birds from their nests. Two separate beings blink at each other: one 18 and the other 40-year-old, literal split personalities. Together, they sing another Bernstein and Sondheim song, "A Boy Like That."

Pop! Pop! The 18- and 40-year-olds merge and form a 29-year-old Latina. Her wavy black hair gently brushes her tan shoulders. Her ivory white dress becomes pinkish. She becomes shorter and shorter and could look a 16-foot giraffe in the eye.

Nephesh skips rope and hops over the 140-foot marker, altering into a cute 18-year-old Asian singing, "I Enjoy Being a Girl" Big smile on her face, she continues having fun.

Transitioning into a 25-year-old Jewish American with green eyes and bright curly red hair, she stands five feet. The star of David necklace glistens in the sunlight. Nephesh spins and twirls her patriotic red-white-blue skirt and sings with tremendous passion, "God Bless America."

On the outskirts of the Sagacious farm, Nephesh shape-shifts into the Ethiopian Israeli Eden Alene and sings the 2020 Eurovision song, "Feker Libi." Three Ethiopians dance in lime green. Nephesh melts below 22 inches while she watches the fast-sinking sunset.

Fuchsia-pigmented 18-inch Nephesh sings, "So In Love." Standing 11 inches, she walks another tenth of a mile and sings, "Someone to Watch Over Me." Hitting the 161.88 mile marker, Nephesh takes a breath and sings, "All I Do Is Dream of You."

Moving closer to happy 9-year-old David Sagacious home, five-inch Nephesh snaps her fingers, and three hopping frogs appear. One holds and plucks a large bass, and the others strum their guitars. All four harmonize "The Carnival Is Over."

Two-inch Nephesh moves closer to the front door. Her ripped, dirty blouse hanging loose. She sings from *Les Misérables* "On My Own." Now one and a half inches short, she taps her holographic 162-mile marker. Tiny fuchsia shoes shuffle boulder-size pebbles. Dwindling down to insect size, Nephesh sings, "I'll Never Find Another You," as three ants harmonize.

Itty-bitty glowing fuchsia Nephesh pulls herself onto the brick steps and rolls under the Sagacious door. Tears well up. *Family. Singing. Dancing. Hugging. Kissing. Laughter. Sorry, old friend. I must do what I must do.*

Blown through minty fresh inter-dimensional fissures, shimmering golden tachyon time molecules dance along Nephesh's fingertips. 18 seconds later, those warm genetic fibers float and phase through the windowpane. Those pulsating energy signatures infiltrate 9-year-old David's heart, brain, and soul. He drifts off to sleep in his parents' arms, not knowing the next morning he'll bear witness to a descending giant eraser out of a black cacophony-crushing vortex.

Evil shall soon discard his mama and papa like a snot-filled tissue.

David's manipulated past, present, and future fuse forever.

I'm the last remaining Chosen One. Every night before I close my eyes, I pray for one thing. Each morning, I wake up knowing I'm still here. That first breath I take tells me, for the 18th-millionth time, God rejected my plea. To be or not to be. Please, God, set me free.

CHAPTER 3

Fighting Fascist Bullies on Earth and in Space for Centuries

"I hate Khan!" David fumes under his breath. "That fucking Holocaust denier. Disciples of Nick Fuentes and followers of Ye, formerly Kanye West shouting Hitler was right. Those fucking Nazi sympathizers are good friends of the black Arab wacko conspiracy theorist Ali Alexander.

Khan is Palestinian. His family has Jordanian and Lebanese citizenship. As leading members of the terrorist Hezbollah, his grandfather, father, and uncles helped build 150,000 missiles aimed at Israeli families under the watchful eye of United Nations observers. His sister and brother-in-law are members of the Gaza terrorist group Hamas; they are all proud of the 12,000 launches into Jewish schools and hospitals.

Luis Khan is a fucking chip off the old terrorist block.

I'm 22 Earth years old, only one semester away from earning my BA in political science and looking forward to graduate school. Sitting under a large oak tree, I'm getting a head start reading my International Relations text. Peace of mind is interrupted by a misogynistic diatribe. Vile words spit out on the basketball court from none other than Luis Fucking Khan.

Khan gets a thrill denigrating any woman who stands up

to him. He never met the likes of Ima Best-Friend or her high school bestie Dafna Shaked.

I hear the loud whack. Scowl pinches Khan's unibrow. Jaw tightens. He rubs his hand.

"I told you to get your finger out of my face and stop threatening my friend. Next time you're getting a knuckle sandwich!" shouts Dafna.

"Israeli bitch! How dare you talk to me like that!"

"Asshole! We were here first," animated Ima emphasizes.

In this timeline, I'm unaware of fuchsia sparks dancing along the Israeli flag and USA combination flag book marker. David, who is me and not me, confidently strides onto the basketball court.

"This doesn't concern you, bookworm!" nervously twitching Khan shouts.

I smile and take an exaggerated step, inching closer to his long nose.

"Get the fuck out of my grill!" Khan's high-pitched voice squeals.

"You had no game in high school, and you're still athletically challenged today."

Dafna and Ima laugh. We high-five.

"You two any good?" I ask.

And thus begins a new-not-new friendship with people who will always, no matter what the altered timeline becomes, be an integral part of my story.

Dafna kicks the ball out of Khan's hand. She nicks his pinkie.

"Ouch!" Khan sucks on his throbbing little finger.

Dafna, two steps inside the free throw line, powerfully dunks.

"Impressive. How about you...um..."

"That's Dafna. My name is Ima."

"Well, Ima, you got similar moves?"

Khan reaches for the basketball. Ima scoops I-T up. David

stands under the basket, ready for the rebound. Ima launches five shots from the top of the key—all swishes.

"Excellent!" David runs over and high-fives Dafna and Ima again. All three stick out their tongues in silly derision.

"Double or nothing," out of breath Khan wheezes.

I nod, and Dafna smiles.

Dafna backflips. I backflip. Getting a wave of uncomfortable Deja vu. *There's something oddly familiar about all of this.*

Dafna texts friends. A large crowd gathers and cheers on Team David, Dafna, and Ima. The mocking and bullying by Khan and his misogynistic antisemitic ilk are drowned out by a pro-David crowd. The final score from the double-or-nothing round ends with Team Khan's 45 to 26 defeat.

Dejected and scared. Khan's two fat friends are frantically sucking air and massaging their cramping calves and thighs. The crowd high-fives and hugs. The clock tower chimes 9 times. Everyone disperses to class. "That was great. I hate that fucking Khan," echoes those he's bullied.

David hands Dafna and Ima Gatorade bottles. "That was fun."

"I-T-S sure fun humiliating bullies," Ima states.

I wonder if she has a boyfriend. I hope not. She's very cute. Wonder why I have such an intense sense of déjà vu?

Ima looks over at Dafna. She gets the hint.

David stares into Ima's bright emerald eyes. Ima stares into David's large, soft brown eyes.

"See you later."

Ima's nonresponse brings a slight smile to the corner of Dafna's mouth. *Good luck, Ima.*

"Oh, wait. The winnings."

"Yes, the winnings," disappointed Ima says.

"I can get my share later. I've got class."

David stares into Ima's glistening eyes. "Do you have class? Ima..."

"She's got lots of class," giggles Dafna.

"Yes, I can see, she's a very classy person."

Dafna turns her back to David and faces Ima, rapidly tapping her fingertips in a happy clapping motion. Both girls grin at each other.

Ima clears her throat.

Dafna leans into Ima's ear. "Tell me all about the kiss when you get back to the dorm. Hopefully, I won't see you for the rest of the day. Have fun."

David reaches for Ima's fingers. He kisses her knuckles; she blushes and rubs her right hand on her left rosy cheek.

Profusely sweating, fat guy grabs David's arm. Khan pulls out a knife. "Here's your payment, Kike lover!"

Ima kicks the knife out of Khan's hand and slugs his gut. He laughs mockingly and backhands Ima's pretty face, sending her sprawling to the ground. Khan gets on top and rips her clothes.

"You're strong for a little thing. I like that." Khan's stinky tongue slithers along his brownish chipped teeth.

"Asshole!" shouts David. His elbows slam into Khan's cohorts. Cowards run and slip on a long trail of fuchsia bird poop. David's crushing grip lifts Khan off Ima and tosses him like a sack of marshmallows. Rapid-fire jabs bloody Khan's face. David's powerful legs push Khan backward, and his scalp scrapes against a low-hanging branch. Fuchsia bird takes flight and poops on Khan's lips. David's fists crack Khan's ribs.

He's gonna kill him. "David! Stop!"

One final uppercut sends Khan into long-lasting unconsciousness.

18 days later...

Dafna and Ima's dorm room is decorated with growing greenery on bookshelves and tabletops. Pet hamster Timmy spins wheels and stores tasty food in puffy cheeks.

Sunday, 9:09 a.m., Dafna and Saul hold hands. Dafna leans

in toward Ima's ear, "I wish you'd watch something else. *Lord of the Rings* trilogy is not what you'd call a romance-building experience." Ima smiles. "Have a wonderful trip."

"I haven't visited Israel since before my Bar Mitzvah," says Saul.

Saul and Dafna roll their bags toward the front door. Dafna walks back to Ima. "I hope this is the night." She enjoys teasing blushing Ima.

Later that night, Ima, and David stand side by side. David washes and Ima dries. "You're a very good cook," smiles David.

"Thank you." Ima falls into David's chest. He holds her and smiles. *Don't you want to kiss me?* She stays, waiting for something romantic, and I-T never comes. She fills up David's large wine glass. *She's so cute. I hope she'll understand why Ima going so slow.*

"Ready for the movie?"

Ima conveniently put all other chairs in the closet. She pushes David into her large blue recliner.

She wiggles herself and they cuddle.

"Last week you told me this movie night would be a surprise. Now that we've polished off a great meal, enjoyed excellent wine and conversation; can you let me in on the surprise?"

"Your favorite."

"*Blazing Saddles!*" David demonstratively shouts.

Ima's eyebrows pinch, causing a crease.

"Kidding. *Blazing Saddles* is my second favorite. Is I-T true, you've never seen any of the three *Lord of the Ring* movies?"

"I-T-S true." Cute Ima rubs her nose.

Sunday afternoon, Ima and David continue with *The Fellowship of the Ring*. Ima stares at David more than the movie. *I wish he were more of a flirt. I know he's the one. My heart hurts every time we're separated. You're a great kisser, David Sagacious. I want more. Do you want more? I wish to God you did.*

Monday evening, 9:18 p.m. David knocks on Ima's door. "Sorry I'm late."

"I was getting worried."

David gives Ima a little peck on the cheek. She's more disappointed with the kiss than the tardiness.

"Ready for movie night?" asks Ima.

54 minutes into *The Return of the King*, David kisses Ima's soft lips. "I've wanted to tell you something for a very long time."

Ima's eyes sparkle with anticipation. *A long time. I wonder what that could be? You've shown minimal interest, at best.*

"You are my Sam," whispers David.

"I love being your Samwise Gamgee," Ima holds both hands over her heart.

David clicks off the TV.

Happy Ima tears stream. Ima stands on her toes and interlocks her fingers around David's neck. For 36 seconds they stare into each other's eyes. They both sigh together. Ima wraps her legs around David's strong body. He strokes Ima's hair and kisses her neck. Ima licks her lips and slowly unbuttons David's shirt. Smiling, she sensually rubs his hairy chest. *I prefer furry. Not unmasculine hairless, vain self-absorbed immature. David is what I need.* Ima's legs squeeze tightly. Her hands grab hold of his firm butt cheeks. David gallops Ima into her bedroom.

18 weeks later...

"You got the tickets?" asks Dafna.

"Front row center. Getting serious between you and Saul," grinning Ima says.

"Can you keep a secret?"

"You know I can't."

Ima playfully tickles Dafna.

"Stop!"

Both girls harmonize their favorite song from *South Pacific*, "I'm in love. I'm in love. I'm in love. I'm in love with a wonderful guy."

"Guess who's playing the lead?"

"No! Really? Shut up!"

"He's a young Brian Stokes Mitchell, according to the 18 reviews I've read so far."

Later that night, Ima swoons as David Sagacious sings, "Some Enchanted Evening." She joins the audience, giving David a standing ovation and blows him a kiss.

After the show, the light rain becomes heavier. David pops Ima's fuchsia umbrella. Holding hands. They both inhale deeply.

"Smells good."

"She sure does."

Ima playfully slaps David's shoulder. "Silly. I was talking about the rain. Everything smells better during and after a rain."

"Oh, the rain."

David's fingers gently move Ima's hair from her blinking eyes.

You sure are pretty.

You're the dumbest smart man, David Sagacious. Why don't you pick up on my flirty clues? Don't you find me pretty? I know I make you happy. The last time we made love, I-T was amazing. Don't you want to do I-T again? Oh, my God...did I do something wrong? He's not thinking of breaking up with me? Ima's eyes fill with tears.

"Sweetie, what's wrong?" asks worried David.

"Hold me," whispers Ima.

The next morning Ima licks sauce off David's lips.

"Yummy..."

David's soft brown eyes twinkle. "Sauce or me?"

"Yes," giggles Ima.

Five months later, Ima and David backflip on stage and recreate the fabulous Fred Astaire and Eleanor Powell dance routine, "Begin the Beguine."

UCLA students and staff give them a standing ovation.

One after another shouted, "More! More! More!

"Thank you, dear friends. My lovely Ima said yes."

Ima shows off her sparkling wedding ring. Newlywed Dafna and Saul hug and kiss Ima and David. Saul taps his wine glass, "Speech. Speech!" he shouts. "Over the objections of my soon-to-be wife—Ima gonna sing Mel Brooks's 'Hope for the Best, Expect the Worst.'"

Gazing into each other's eyes, David and Ima sing from *Cinderella*, "Ten Minutes Ago." In the middle of the song, the entire building shakes. Roof rips and crumbles. David pushes Ima away from falling debris. David's legs are crushed. A black funnel with fuchsia sparks sucks David away. Ima screams.

Millions of light-years away, what's left of David's legs rip away. Blood gushes up over his head. A glowing subatomic soul from the Watcher Realm enters his chest. Though David floats in space, he takes his first conscious breath. Golden energy streams and repairs his legs.

An infinite number of David Sagacious are ordinary humans living ordinary lives. An infinite number of David Sagacious battle 100-foot machines as superheroes. Some die alone; multiple others die with their superhero Earthling lovers and friends, Ima and Dafna. Some have additional help from shapeshifting Ko'ach and Nephesh.

I'm unlike all others. There's no other David Sagacious who's tasked to be an Immortal Mortal, omniscient narrator. I stand apart from all other entities eternities. I gain from all the other David's strengths. In time they always lose—they always die. All we need is one to survive and end this war. So I can finally rest and be with the one I love more than life I-T-Self.

Resonating through every musical portal, Nephesh's heartbreaking song calls out to Ko'ach. "Don't let alternate David die of his injuries. I'm not strong or fast enough. Save him before I-T consumes his righteous soul and crushes all our destinies."

Every day that passes on Earth is a full year for lost David. He flies through quasars 13 billion light-years from Earth. He withstands the heat and radiation of another supernova. He pummels thousands of giant-sized asteroids and sings, "To Dream the Impossible Dream."

In every timeline, Ko'ach mentored that, David; who is in any future past...ME! In a long ago forgotten memory, I did rescue millions from an invading 100-foot mechanical armada.

Back on Earth, 10 years have elapsed. In that time, haggard, lonely, scared David endured 3,365 tumultuous years. His. My. Our longing to be reunited with Ima never wavered. Our...his heartache sings, "You Raise Me Up."

Each night David prays to God, hoping he'll help him find his way back into Ima's arms. With growing melancholy, David sings, "My Heart Will Go On."

"God, is the time, right? Can you loosen your grip on Malevolent Time? Can you now send me back home?"

God's booming whisper journeys through time and space; he touches that troubled David.

"YES, SHE HAS, FOR THIS MOMENT IN TIME, SHE'S BEEN CAGED. YOU HAVE A DAUGHTER. SHE CELIBRATES HER NINTH BIRTHDAY, TODAY."

"What's my daughter's name?

"RACHEL. THE BOYFRIEND'S NAME IS MICHAEL NEVI. MALEVOLENT TIME HAS POWER OVER THAT TIMELINE AND WON'T ALLOW ME TO SEND YOU BACK ENTIRELY INTACT."

"My legs."

"YES."

"And my righteous soul?"

"WITH YOU ALWAYS. HOWEVER..."

"You've never added a however before."

"UNEXPECTED TIME FLUCTUATIONS ARE OCCURRING FASTER THAN I HAD ANTICIPATED. YOUR RIGHTEOUS SOUL WILL SURVIVE, BUT I-T WILL REMAIN DORMANT UNTIL THE APPOINTED TIME WHEN YOUR MENTOR KO'ACH COMES INTO YOUR LIFE. STEADY YOURSELF."

"No need. I am always, as you know, an old companion of excruciating pain.

9-year-old Rachel and her mom, Ima, exit a homeless shelter and are immediately harassed by a raging homeless man. He latches onto Rachel's wrist. She's surrounded by three more towering figures suffering from dementia and brandishing knives, they continue to slash thin air.

Unconcerned folks block Ima's path; they're more concerned with getting images on their phones than helping struggling Ima trying to rescue her daughter.

"Let me go! Let me go! Stop filming and help us. My daughter Rachel, she's only 9! Mommy is here, baby. Why won't any of you help her? Please, someone. Rachel!"

"Mommy, I'm scared!"

Tears rush down Rachel's cheeks. Bystanders' laughter mocks their fears.

"Oh, she wants her mommy. Well, I don't give a fuck. My mommy left me when I was six. Count your blessings, little girl, you got three more years than I did! She left in the dead of night. Fucking crack whore! Hope she's dead. Stop crying. Fucking grow up, bitch!"

Rachel's tears flow with greater intensity.

"Stop talking to her."

"Well. Well. You must be Mommy. Just another fucking whore."

"Don't worry, sweetie. Stop touching her!" *Where are the cops! Why are they all filming and not trying to stop this? Even those in a suit and tie. Damn, you're educated, with a good job. I hope this goes viral and you lose your career. I've got to break free. Damn this girl is strong. Five o'clock shadow. You're no girl!*

"You like candy, little girl?"

Another financially less fortunate bat-shit-crazy homeless person poops on the steps. Screaming at imaginary people, she gets closer to a restrained Ima. Ima kicks back, transexual falls to the ground, rocking back and forth; both hands shield his bruised genitals.

Surrounded by six taunting homeless men and women, Ima's nostrils are violated with a strong whiff of marijuana, vomit, urine, fecal matter, and multi-years of sweaty body odor wafting from armpits, gaping mouths, and butt cracks.

Legless wheelchair-bound homeless man with long flowing silver hair elbows his way past indifferent bystanders and menacing druggies. *Surprisingly, he smells minty fresh.* "Save my daughter. Leave me be. Save Rachel!"

Wheeler rolls over four sets of shoeless toes. Homeless men and women limp screaming into the night. One is elbowed in his bloated gut. The wind knocked out and he fell forward onto his nose, blood splatters. Another homeless man looks down at his friend and laughs. Powerful right cross knocks him out cold. Female runs away. Two strong hands grasp the wrist of the remaining homeless man, and he is tossed headfirst into the trash bin.

"Hey! You can't do that. Somebody calls the cops. That violent legless, entitled cis white man stole my phone," shouts manic older Karen.

"Shut up, Karen!"

"How rude!"

"I'm not stealing anything." Wheelchair-bound rescuer wheels two hundred yards away from the manic Karen. Her howls start an entire neighborhood of barking dogs.

Wheelchair man punches 911. He looks to his left. "Hey, don't run away. I was going to return your phone after the cops arrived. Come back! Crazy Karen. No, not you officer. The assault took place at 27th and Cherry Tree Lane. Young girl and her mother are bleeding. Idiots are still filming. Hope when you get here, you throw the book at them. Shit! The jerks are scurrying like rats. Who am I? Well...um...I won't be here when you arrive."

Black shimmering mist phases up from the sewer and coalesces into Ima's lover, Michael Nevi. Uncoordinated with normal time, only David senses Michael's presence. Dangerous intruder's green sclera burns with homicidal rage.

"Oh fuck! Sagacious is back. He's gonna fuck up everything."

Nasty righteous semi-human warrior. You're clueless. Ha! You've no idea Rachel is destined to be one of us—so sayeth my prophecy. I won't tolerate your goodie-two-shoes interference. Ima stronger than all of you, except for Ko'ach, and we have plans for him. This moment in time is the lynchpin for everything everywhere. Humanity's future choices come down to the following facts, they'll either be consumed by me and my brethren, or they'll be painfully converted into 100-foot machines and join in our devouring collective.

Black energy sends six bullets through the back of David's wheelchair and penetrates his spine. David crumbles at Rachel's feet, unconscious. She applies pressure to his chest. Fuchsia flecks traverse her body, pushing Rachel out of normal time and into chaotic interdimensional irrationality. *Wow. Wow! Look at me. Is this what Mama meant when she said my papa was special? Was he taken away by this quantum irregularity? Hey! How did I know that? Becoming aware of new mathematical equations. Yes. I understand. Oh my God! Papa! I always thought Mama's confusions were a story she told herself to cope with the hurt of abandoning a single mom alone with a sick preemie struggling to live.*

Rachel watches frozen time speed up. She turns back to Papa; he's gone.

"Papa!"

Michael re-joins normal space-time. "Yes," he whispers.

Creepy smile. Yuck! "You're not Papa."

"Not yet. You're a good girl and wouldn't hurt my feelings, would you?"

"You don't have any to hurt. You're evil."

"In time, you'll change your mind."

Michael stretches his hand and arm 20 feet in the air. Black clouds initiate angry lightning's surging agitation around his forearm. Single touch to Rachel's temple. "Forget," growls Michael, pinching Rachel's shoulder.

Grimacing, black blood leaks from her shoulder. Her sclera darkens. Black sparkling thread attempts to penetrate her heart. I-T bores under her skin, now an 18th of an inch from her heart muscle. Her papa's dormant righteous blue-white energy shield protects her heart and soul. For a millisecond, integration of that righteous energy brings uncommon knowledge.

Blue-white energy touches Rachel's mind. A sudden burst of clarity brings her two shaky hands to her mouth.

"Papa?" Rachel whispers.

Her glowing body falls at Michael's feet. He steps on Rachel's ankle. His menacing cackling pushes David's blue-white eyes wide open.

"Leave her alone!"

"Good! You're aware of the truth. This is gonna be fun. Goodbye, human warrior!"

Michael's glowing black fist clobbers David's head and chest. Blue-white energy leaks and splats pity-pat on the pavement. "Ima famished," roars Michael.

"This isn't over, you bastard. I'll be back!"

David's cells spark blind bright blue-white energy. Trillions of cells shine and escape, leaving his wheelchair illuminated by Michael's black glowing rage.

Michael jumps from time to time. Crackling black energy punches holes in building walls and roofs. Streetlamps crack. Hundreds of black lightning strikes push violent plumes from deep underneath the Pacific Ocean's mantle.

Time resumes I-T-S normal speed. Ima pushes past the invective shouting mob.

Ima hugs Rachel. "Vultures! Stay away from my child!" she screams.

Rachel wakes up in the hospital 72 hours later. She smiles at her sleeping mama. "Papa. I'll find you. I know you're trying to stay away from us to protect us. That's no longer necessary. Oh, Papa, I love you."

Ima stirs from her sleep.

"Did you say something? Are you in any pain? Do you want me to call the nurse?"

Ima caresses Rachel's face.

"Ima okay, Mom."

"Why did you do that?"

"Do what?"

"Your papa used to...instead of I'm...please don't, honey. I'm with Michael. He takes good care of us."

"You love him."

"Yes."

"And. And..."

"I hope he asks me to marry him."

"If he does?"

"I'll joyously say yes."

"What's wrong?"

"Tired."

Ima kisses Rachel's forehead. She holds her hand, scooches into the bed, and cuddles.

I'll find you, Papa. You no longer need to be alone.

9 hours later, curious Rachel investigates the scene of the crime. She scrapes David's dry blood from the pavement; and 36 hours later the scanner Dafna gave to Ima and Rachel glows, hums, and tells her all she needs to know. Rachel's walk

becomes a fast trot. Two hours later, she sprints to the worst part of town. She muffles the device's beeping beep. Rachel looks down on a dirty, torn cardboard box. Bloody handprint marks the spot. She falls to her knees and peers inside. *Oh, Daddy. I should've found you sooner.*

"Who's there? Oh, um, Rachel, you need to go. I-T-S not safe. Sweetie, don't cry. I can battle anything or anyone, but if you..."

David sniffles and wipes a single tear, failing to control a flood of tears. Rachel crawls over, and for the first time in her life, she hugs her father...who is me, but not me. Their story I haven't yet lived. But I feel all they feel and am aware of all of their new memories soon after they experience them. Rachel turns her gaze from David's bloody stumps for legs.

"What's this? asks David.

"Key to our front door."

"After all this time. I won't abandon you..."

"Like I did."

"Didn't say that. Didn't mean that. I don't know how I know. But I do. I know and feel everything you feel."

"Oh, sweetie, no. Let me take those memories."

David's glowing blue-white finger inches closer to Rachel's temple. She pulls back.

"No, Papa. I can take I-T."

Sweetie, please don't say those letters.

Your lips aren't moving, but I can hear your thoughts. How is that possible?

Rachel, promise you'll never again say eye and tea. Remember in Harry Potter when everyone was saying he who shall not be named, rather than saying Voldemort?

Rachel nods.

Well, saying you know what will bring you and mom into contact with a danger far greater than that fictional dark wizard.

Papa, no...please don't.

Forgive me, sweetie. This is for your own good.

Rachel holds up her hands. "No!" she shouts.

Why would you force old memories? Make me believe you're a bad father.

Rachel is shocked by her father's sudden laughter.

Cruel of you to mock me, Papa.

David rubs Rachel's shoulder. *Oh, beautiful Rachel. I could never mock you. I laughed because you sound so much like me. You've got my stubborn determination. But now I must...*

Compromise.

Ima listening.

You have the power to take only the painful memories. I haven't accessed all of them yet.

Yes, I could do that.

Good. I trust you, Papa. I give you permission to take the pain and leave the love. I don't want to ever lose your loving feelings for Mama and me. Okay?

Rachel rubs her tear-soaked cheek on David's cheek.

I love you, Papa.

I love you, too.

Oh. Oh, my gosh. Ima glowing blue-white. David and Rachel's incandescent life force righteously hums heartfelt historical harmonies. David's entire body shivers. He jerks back and violently coughs bloody sputum into Rachel's shirt.

"Oh, Papa. I must get you to the emergency room."

Rachel puts her father's arm around her back and lifts. David's stumps dangle. Rachel walks what's left of her father out of the cardboard home and looks for his wheelchair.

Who did that? Aghast, Rachel looks at David's mangled, twisted seat-back and tire rims.

Not sure. I woke up to that.

Rachel is strong, but only 9. With each halting step, David's body becomes heavier.

"Put me down." David caresses Rachel's worried face.

"I can do this, Papa."

"I know you can. You're strong like your mama."

"And Papa."

David's weak, reassuring grin comes off as unconvincing.

Sweetie, you must not take me to the hospital. Promise me. Even if I lose consciousness.

Why? That doesn't make sense.

My anatomy is different, raising questions I can't answer. And put you at risk. I won't be the cause of putting you in danger! Blood drips down the corner of David's mouth.

Rachel's tear-soaked sleeve puts pressure on David's lip. I-T-S not stopping. "What do you want me to do? Papa. Wake up!" Rachel falls to her knees and screams.

"What happened?"

"You lost consciousness."

"Go, honey. You're too young to watch..."

"My Papa die? No! No! I won't leave your side. I can't now that I've finally found you."

Rachel grabs David's powerful shoulders and shakes. He blinks and stares into his daughter's weepy, fearful eyes.

"Please, sweetie..." David pushes Rachel. "Go, let me be. You must not be hurt because of me. You must know I never wanted this strange existence for you."

Rachel caresses David's fingers and gently places a crumpled flyer in his hand.

"You must get well enough by the time they perform. Mama's boyfriend creeps me out. But she loves him and will do whatever he asks. But..."

Rachel follows with her twinkling eyes, blue, white surging energy.

"What was that?"

David shakes his head.

"I know if she knew you were back, everything would change. Mama must rekindle the feelings, for you, she buried deep. You're her everything."

Daughter and father hug. Her energy flows, and David feels stronger.

"6-weeks," blurts Rachel.

"What about 6-weeks?"

"That's how long you have to win her back. In 6-weeks, they're getting married.

Rachel hands David a Winnie-the-Pooh key chain.

"Michael's giving the house to us. He doesn't know I know about that place. I guess I was reading minds before I knew I was reading minds. He wants this to be a surprise, so let that become so." Rachel's heart flutters. "I know you can woo Mama."

"I think you've been watching too many old romance movies."

"What's wrong with that? You're her true love."

Half a block away, a mysterious thing huddles in the shadow. "True love," the creature's faint voice growls.

48 hours later, the weight room blasts "Eye of the Tiger." David wheels over to a picture of creepy-looking Michael with his arm around forced smiling Ima. David wheels down the ramp to the exercise room and curls and bench presses thousands of heavy weights.

Sweat dripping from his sideburns and chin, David completes thousands of pull-ups and crunches. Every day, his legs grow more tissue, ligaments, and muscle. He can wiggle his toes for the first time since he arrived back on Earth. 18 minutes later, his 2 squats became 36, 9 hours later he can squat 54, and 3 hours later, another 99. David leaps from one weight-pounding exercise to the next and sings, "We Are the Champions."

Michael holds Ima's hand. And caresses her cheek. "Ooh, your fingers are ice cold."

Michael cups his hands and blows. Ima doesn't notice black sparks jumping off his lips and penetrating his fingertips. A black hole in the blue sky yanks those black sparks back to Earth and attacks young and old waiting for the bus.

Michael and Ima kiss. Out of sync with normal time, powerful black sparks battle and destroy the weaker fuchsia sparks dancing along Ima's lips.

Ima swoons. Michael catches her.

"Oh my, I feel dizzy. Weak."

"Drink this."

"Where did you...what's in I-T?"

"Home remedy. Try. I know you'll like I-T."

Rachel's fists tremble with rage and her respiration quickens. "The brew!" Her eyes swirl blue-white energy and she knocks the cup out of her mother's hand. Rachel latches onto Ima's elbow and leads her away, "Come, Mama, let's get away from here."

"Your hands are so cold."

"Would you like to call off tonight's production?"

"Of course not." Ima takes four steps back and almost falls.

"That's I-T. Ima call I-T off. You need a warm broth and plenty of sleep.

"I said no!" shouts Ima with reverberating anger.

Excellent. You'll be turning in no time. Rachel sees the corner of Michael's lip imperfectively curled up in a mischievous grin. 18 seconds frozen in time, Ima's fingers grow metallic and suddenly recede back to their fleshy genetic truth.

"Leave her alone, Michael."

"Rachel, what's gotten into..."

"I-T-S fine. I'll see you on stage in a few hours. I know you'll take good care of her."

Michael waves goodbye.

Ima's bloodshot black eyes glaze over.

"My God, you were so rude," Ima growls.

Later that evening, David is first to arrive in an empty theater. He sits in the back with two canes on his lap, staring at the clock. Each tick percolates another bead of sweat along his feverish brow. *Never should've shaken that usher's hand. Not an usher.*

Not human. I know I-T was fucking Michael. Asshole infected me with dark energy…must use this time to purge that nasty unholy malevolence from my system.

David's left hand and forearm becomes glistening metallic armor. *This can't be happening!*

Metallic monsters 100 feet tall appear with Rachel and Ima faces; their minds shout, *too late! Small stupid Sagacious!*

David blinks and notices he's alone. *Keep your wits about you. Can't afford to allow I-T-S dark hallucinations to displace this reality.* Moments later, Rachel plops herself in the empty first row. She looks back and raises her thumb. David smiles and does the same.

Rachel touches her fingertips to her throbbing temple. She thinks about her Papa. *I hate watching greasy Michael. His pinching, probing fingers of mama. Disgusting!*

Calm yourself, sweetie.

Yes papa. I'll do as you ask, and not take any action, yet!

Over the next 27 minutes, every theater seat is filled by Ima's, Rachel's, Saul's and Dafna's friends. Curtain pulls back. On stage, Ima smiles down at her daughter's brimming-with-love happiness. Michael walks on stage with his hand on the small of Ima's back. Michael turns and stares at Ima. Rachel sticks out her tongue in mocking derision.

Whatever you are, you've lost. You'll never marry my mama. Never!

How can you say that? For you see, little one…Infinite time is my ally. And you? Collaborating with your feeble papa, how touching. You cannot alter your fate's destiny. You and your papa will always fail. I-T-S already happened.! I-T-S only a matter of time before I fulfill the final prophecy. No one, in heaven or hell is a match for us! Our complete victory over your kind is at hand. Get used to I-T. The new order is here! I feel your new reality encroaching. Don't you know? No, you never do. You have no idea how many billions of times this specific scenario has played out. I've won every time. I love a dark successful conclusion. Can't wait for you and your disgustingly righteous papa, to get what you both deserve. Did your papa, keep these details from you. So secretive of him.

Well, we will all have to take this journey together.

Papa, I'm scared.

I love you sweetie. Concentrate on that. Feeling better.

Yes, papa. I love you.

I love you too, Rachel.

You are deceiving her, David Sagacious. Yuck! I hate loving thoughts. I-T-S so fucking disturbing.

Michael's creepy Joe Biden smile unnerves Rachel.

18 minutes later, Ima and Michael start their dialog leading up to their next song from the musical *Cinderella*.

David Sagacious! Show yourself, coward! Where the hell are you? After tonight there are no more resurrections. Tonight, you'll finally die. You'll never find your true love again. I'll either consume or transform Rachel and Ima. And after that, I have the rest of time to devour over seven-billion humans. MMM, this is gonna be great!

Like the biblical Sampson, David's silver hair flows down the middle of his rippling back. He haltingly inches forward, weak legs ba-da bump bumps supported by steady canes of his own construction. Right. Left. Right. Left. Thump ba-bump. The audience turn their heads.

Music hangs, unaccompanied by Ima and Michael's voices. Rachel bolts out of her seat and runs up the ramp toward David. He holds up his hand, and Rachel stops.

Please, sweetie. Stick with the plan. Careful, I can feel Michael's evil energy building.

He wouldn't dare strike me down with all these witnesses, and Mama would never agree to go with him if he harmed me.

He has no fear of human law or understanding of human morality. Trust your papa. Sit down. Promise me you'll take no action.

I promise.

Good. Watch and listen.

From afar, Ima watches David's wobbly legs struggle one step at a time. Ima's hands move up from her waist and over her mouth. She looks at Rachel. Rachel nods.

David's strong baritone voice sings "Once Upon a Time."

Buckets of tears fall from Ima's eyes. The righteous saltiness turns Michael's loving expression toward Ima into an awkward grimace. Drops hitting Michael's fingers feel like acid on his malevolent skin.

"H-how is this possible?" stutters Ima.

David's golden smile warms his beloved's heart. His deep baritone voice resonates with the suction-cup action of his canes. Every step, he sings "Ten Minutes Ago." A surge of incredible love traverses David's heart and soul. Step by steady step, his legs become NFL strong. He releases his bone-crushing grip and, with joy in his heart, steps over those bouncy canes and leaps onto the stage.

6-foot-3 David towers over 5-foot-9 Michael.

David's inciting wink sparks black energy to crisscross Michael's clenched fists.

David wipes Ima's tears. "Beloved Ima. I'll never leave your side again."

Ima throws herself into his arms. The audience cheers.

Tender kissing generates glowing blue-white energy spinning around their bodies.

Michael runs into the wings. He slams his fists into the glowing black box.

Recharge! Recharge! Recharge! I can't let this moment pass. Oh yes! That's the ticket. More! I said I need fucking more! Orgasmic evil energy feeds Michael's rage.

David and Ima sing their duet from *Brigadoon*, "Almost Like Being in Love." Balcony down to the first row stands and cheers.

Rachel backflips on stage.

"I didn't know you could do that!" shouts Ima.

Rachel gives her parents a loving bear hug. David motions for a spotlight for his daughter. Rachel sings, "Tomorrow."

Ima, Rachel, and David held hands. Skipping in a circle, they sing "Let's Go Fly a Kite."

Michael Nevi's belly glows bright hot bloody red: his

incinerating fiery breath becomes quenched by David's icicle breath.

The letters of Michael's first and last name dance along the crystallized flames. Reshaped lettering changes I-T-S order, and the shift spells out Evil Machine. Bone cracking and tissue tearing turns formerly Michael into a 100-foot mechanical true self. He stretches and punches the roof into smithereens. David's blue, white energy barrier surrounds Ima. Comforting his beloved wife, David was unaware of the growing black fissure branching out along the barrier protecting Rachel.

"Rachel! You little bitch! You've erased what should've been. So, I'll erase—you!"

"Mommy! Daddy!"

A giant descending black eraser emits trillions of immobilizing particles. Rachel's new skin glows metallic.

"Papa! Papa!" growls Rachel.

"Why did you come back?" Ima pounds on David's chest.

David blasts the 100-foot monster with powerful blue-white heat and turns to his daughter's dissipating cells, holding a semi-solidifying hand. "Got you!"

"I don't want to die, Papa."

Rachel's cells rip. She screams. "Papa!" Eerie, echoing death reverberates in Ima's ears.

Hysterical Ima slips down David's legs and pounds the stage floor.

David's tears plinkety plink near Ima's prostrate body. David holds Ima and whispers, "She's safe."

"What the hell are you saying? She's gone. Gone. Gone! Never coming back! Never! You did this." Rage fills Ima's heart. She slaps David's face. Each of her next 18 slaps hit with greater ferocity. "Why did you do I-T?" Ima buries her weepy face into David's strong chest. *Why did you have to come back? Why? Why?*

"You've taken away everything I ever dreamed of. Rachel," says Ima's choking up whispering voice.

"She's safe."

"Oh my God! Stop I-T! That's not comforting. Why the hell would you keep saying that? Death is permanent. My broken heart is permanent!"

"No, beloved. Rachel lives."

"Yes, in our grief she'll live forever."

"No need for grieving. I promise you our beautiful Rachel..."

"Shut up! Shut up! Shut up!" Hysterical Ima screams.

David kisses Ima's wet face. He holds her and strokes her hair.

"Rachel's soul floats among trillions of other righteous souls within god's righteous realm. You can't hear her sweet voice, but she sings to me. She asks that you forgive me for all the lost years. Her wish is that we love each other as much as we love her."

Ima places her index finger and middle fingers on David's warm lips. Fury boils, severing screeching sentimentality. "Liar! Liar! How could you betray her? Betray me. Betray us! Get the hell out of my sight!" Ima squishes David's lips with the intent to hurt. "Asshole! I-T-S too cruel, beyond words! Telling me my dead daughter sings to you."

David's blue-white energy enters Ima's heart. Eyebrows raise. Eyes bug out. For 36 seconds Ima listens to Rachel's song.

"She's alive. She's... Can you bring her back?"

"That's beyond my abilities."

David watches death's bony claw stretch toward Ima and sings "So In Love."

Cold shivers traverse Ima's soul.

"I'll find you."

"What? Why are you saying that?" Ima turns her head over her shoulder. David places his hands around her head and directs her back to his smiling, reassuring face. "I'll never give up looking for you."

"You're scaring me. Looking for me? Ima right here. Ima

not going anywhere. Beloved, I will be by your side forever."

"I feel cold. Energy drained. What's happening to me? David! Da-vi-d!"

"Hold my hand. I'll love you until the end of time."

Once again, I had to watch my beloved's essence painfully phase out of existence and be yanked into the swirling vortices of suffocating gray nothingness...

CHAPTER 4

Is Suicide the Only Solution for this Depressed Immortal Mortal?

First mentioned in the Jewish Talmud, Lamed Vav Tzadikim (Hebrew) means hidden 36 righteous men. If that righteous number falls to 35, the world will implode. Each of the 36 are exemplars of Avavah, Hebrew for humility. The numerical value of the L from Lamed and the V from Vav adds up to 36. The anonymous righteous men living in the world are privileged to see the Divine Presence. Hebraic tradition understands the Hebrew letters for living is spelled as Chai and equals 18. Two times 18 = 36; in other words, that righteous number represents two lives.

The Hebrew word Emet means truth. First Hebrew letter: Aleph. Middle letter: Mem. Last letter: Tav. If you take away Aleph from truth, all that's left is Met, the Hebrew root word for death. Multiverse has spoken: Truth without God becomes death.

Darkness for as far as the eye can see. Glowing blue-white eyes illuminate my every step. I have 18 more decades of darkness before the next sunrise. A glory origin story oscillates hate and obliterates bitter fate.

Last night I attempted the unthinkable. Did you know that? Of course you did, you're God! By my own hands. I was determined to do what I-T has been unable to achieve. Ima, I miss you so much. I've tried everything to bring her back...damn I-T! I keep failing. Yesterday, I walked out of my protective cave and ran toward the equator. I wished for I-T. Encouraged I-T. I turned off my God-given biological force field. My righteous soul begged me to stop. I didn't heed the warning. This time, I welcomed the inferno's killing ferocity. Scalded tissue and bone sliced from my screeching body. I'm an immortal puddle of goo 18 minutes later. Why didn't my superhuman consciousness refuse to let go of life? I failed to kill off your creation. God! I'm not worthy of your forgiveness. I've failed everyone. Dearest wife. Daughter Rachel. Righteous human Israeli warrior Dafna Shaked. Heroic guardian angels. Ko'ach and Nephesh. And trillions not yet born. I existed as that sentient gurgling goo for 18 hours before this ungodly world meticulously rebuilt and resurrected my mind, heart, and body. Damn I-T, God! Why did you instruct this meddlesome world to do that? Why? Ima begging you, let me experience another tender moment.

Nightmares enmesh. Mechanical fangs devour my flesh. Frantically my mind taps refresh, refresh, refresh!

Terrifying tornadoes bring to life tsunami's lava. Running 18 times faster than the fastest cheetah, I'm regrettably too slow. Gulping sulfuric ash, my throat, lungs, and intestine ooze vile bile. Scalded determination pushes my bloody feet and hands ever closer to destiny's distinct destination. Leaping off the precipice, my searing fleshy footsteps climb and pound insatiably nauseating stratosphere. Deeply scarred hands grip fiery vines. 36 powerful leg swings push our momentum toward magma's solidifying obelisk.

Sarcasm abounds in this place. Boulder-sized pebbles chip away and create another mocking smiley face. Losing control, I tumble head over heels and crunch headfirst into the mountain peak's snowy healing blue-white energy field. *There I-T is! That's the first time I've witnessed so much of God's holy weapon. A glowing triangular point appears to be...not sure, could I-T be a star? Enough babbling! Told you before. I know. I know. You're still doing I-T! What am I doing? Talking to yourself. Oh that. Secure the weapon and end your unremitting war. Oh shit. I-T-S pulsating. Idiot! You hesitated too long. I-T-S seconds away from relocating. Grab I-T! Grap I-T, you fool! I can't. 18 million years I-T-S never allowed... Do I-T! I got I-T. I'm doing I-T. Hurray! Oh no, no, no...what're you doing to me?*

"YOU'RE NOT READY," booming bass-baritone boomerangs.

Hands, arms, shoulders, torso, legs, and feet melt into blue-white oblivion. *Our head breaks off from dissolving spine. Cracked skull squirts blood shards rolls out of the cavernous shrine. Twitching mouth widens, and nostrils flare. My non-existent lungs engorge on life-perpetuating fresh air. From that righteous summit, what remains will ingloriously plummet. Too bad we haven't died. Oh God, Oh God. I truly have tried. Unfathomably unrelenting strife fills up my unavoidable unfair life. With my wretched, withering last breath, I wish for an indestructible infinite death.*

I-T-S my heroic verse that pushes back against evil's interdimensional hearse. Malevolent Time's perverse Multiverse curse must not be allowed to coerce and traverse our more diverse Universe. Flash, bang! Bang flash!

Successful 21st-century reincarnation. *Fuzzy awareness lingers before perception's jolt provides enough clarity. Just as human eyes slowly adjust to light after walking through darkness. I adjust to 18 million years without my mama and papa's warm embrace. Reincarnation process complete. Once again, I'm pink and squishy. No, I don't have to go pishy. I'm a cute semi-human David child; we're nothing more than an 18-month prequel. Little me sits in the market basket; exaggerating conducting and mouthing lyrics to "I, Don Quixote." Proud, happy Mama Grace kisses my cute puffy cheeks.*

"I love you, Mama."

"I love you, sweetie."

"Hugs?" little me asks.

Grace and David hug and giggle; 18 months zoom faster

than normal time's distorted 18 seconds. *Flash flash bang! Bang bang flash!*

Three-year-old David's fingers thump his drum in perfect rhythm. Mama Grace kisses his forehead.

Papa Christopher takes Mama's hand and twirls her twice. Smiling lips lovingly brush Papa's smiling lips.

Papa pulls over a fuchsia stool.

Grace places a shiny flute to her lips.

David and Grace accompany Christopher's deep baritone singing "Through Heaven's Eyes."

David copies his papa's side-to-side head bobbing.

Memories...Mama's perfume, Papa's strength, are in my heart forever. MMM...I-T-S dinner time. I remember wonderful aromas from Mama's kitchen. When we are three, we're a happier me. No nightmares to flee. He. He. With baby me, silliness becomes we three.

I draw spaghetti sauce on my forehead and carry-on quirky conversations with four meatballs.

Hours later...

Long past my bedtime. My long-drawn-out yawns bring kisses from my parents. Half asleep, David walked partially and was carried to his bed.

Finding my second wind, cute little David rolls his pajamas up toward his chin. Without missing a beat, Mama draws two eyes above David's belly button. Papa draws a mouth with one tooth. "More! More!" shouts David.

"And then you promise to close your eyes and ask no more questions," says Grace.

"For tonight," giggles David.

Grace and Christopher place their lips on David's ticklish ribs and loudly blow. Farting sound creates cascading giggling crescendo.

Seconds after Mama and Papa stop, "More! More! More!" shouts David.

Grace and Christopher's over-the-top yawns egg on the playful rib tickles.

Intensifying laughter swells through David's wiggling body.

"Be a good boy. Remember your promise," says Grace.

Tapping his mother's arm, "Yes, Papa," says sarcastic David.

Staring into her son's sparkling bright eyes; her soft finger and thumb caresses David's squishy earlobe, "Good night, Grandpa," smiling Grace says.

Papa's thumb and index finger grab little David's pink cheek; that silly pulling action forces the inner cheek to slap against teeth and gums. Silly sound makes little me giggle louder.

Papa kisses David's forehead. "Good night, Grandma," Christopher whispers.

"Lights off," says Grace.

Milliseconds later, smiling David shouts, "Lights on!"

"David..." Grace and Christopher admonish.

"Bring back the silly!" shouts David.

"Enough, sweetie. Remember your promise," says Grace.

"Okay, Mama."

Grace and Christopher, 18 steps later, hear, "Good night, guacamole!"

David's parents shake their heads. Christopher takes two steps toward David's bedroom, "Good night, Spumoni!"

Muffled giggles bring wide grins for Grace and Christopher. Arms around each other they slowly walk back to the living room.

Grace and Christopher slow dance. She nibbles on his earlobe, and his loving caresses send wonderful shivers, causing her to bend her neck to the right. "More, please," smiles Grace.

"Neighbors are still amazed our little three-year-old has the vocabulary and speech patterns of an adult," says Christopher.

"What they don't know is that our little guy has been talking since he was 9 months and reading since he was 18 months," Grace proudly proclaims.

"Well, Grace, Papa, what did you do while I was at work?" asks smiling Christopher.

"Well, Mama Christopher," Grace states with a twinkle in her eyes.

"Oh good. I love silly David stories."

Grace places her slender index finger over her husband's mouth.

"You know, honey, um, before I tell you, um, I think I should be serious..."

"No. Not the serious." Christopher pretends to faint.

Grace playfully slaps Christopher's strong shoulder.

"Yes, serious. You should try a little harder to persuade your boss to not give you so much overtime. You're missing too many memories."

Christopher kisses his adoring wife's eyelids. "You're right, honey. Inflation hasn't bottomed out yet. I-T-S nuts that everyone is forced to pay incredible prices for gas and groceries. We need to build up our savings. I promise, after our African trip, I'll start spending more time with you and our son. Now, tell me., What did our silly David do?"

"Well, you know how realistic cartoons these days are, and they all talk..."

Christopher's ratatat laughter brings high-pitched giggles from Grace. "Show me," he asks.

Grace holds her phone up to Christopher's face.

They cuddle. He watches ice cream drip down David's chin. Little me walks from baby animal to another baby animal...

"Hello, my name is David Sagacious. What's your name? Don't you understand English? Mama, why are they all ignoring me?"

"Maybe they're shy."

"Oh, you wanna be my friend? My ice cream is really good. I-T cools me down lots. Mama says I-T will be 90 degrees. Here, I walk in shady, follow me for tasty Ice cream licks. Don't be shy. I'll be your friend. Follow me."

"That baby mule was acting, well, like a mule...I-T refused to budge," says Grace.

Grace and Christopher watch their little boy give names to all the other baby animals.

"Gertrude the giraffe, Aaron the anteater, Irene the iguana, Stinky the skunk. Crunchy the crocodile, Hermoine the hippo, Terran the turtle, Kenny the kangaroo. Willie the walrus and Jerome the jellyfish."

Lethargic David holds Mama and Papa's hands 18 weeks later as all three de-plane. After A long night's sleep, jet lag wears off. David appreciates the gorgeous sunrise and uniquely barren African landscape.

Grace slathers sunscreen. "Make sure you drink extra water. Africa is a lot dryer than California."

"Ooh, look at that." David runs toward an unusually robust fuchsia butterfly.

Butterfly vanishes as Grace gets closer to her son. "You forgot your new sunglasses."

"Thanks, Mama." David scrunches up his little nose. "Hey, where did the butterfly go?"

"Sweetie, there are no butterflies in this part of Africa," says Grace.

Christopher lovingly rubs his son's shoulder. "David, we talked about this before we left. You can give animals cute names, but they're not cartoons."

"I remember, Papa. I did see a fuchsia butterfly, and her voice was sing-song pretty."

"Okay. I thought you were too tired for the silly."

David yawns. "Not tired. Not making up silly, she sounded, um, comforting."

"Finish your breakfast." Christopher vigorously messes up his son's hair.

Grace leans into Christopher's ear. "I hope this fibbing is just a stage."

"I'm sure I-T is. Maybe our little guy will grow up to be a famous novelist."

The newborn elephant's soft foot pads plod and push 18 miles from David's location. She lets go of her Mama's tail. Wide-eyed curiosity greets the other pachyderms, enjoying themselves in what's left of the watering hole. Mama elephant and her sisters take turns caressing the wobbly newborn.

European, Asian, and Middle Eastern poachers jump out of their jeeps less than a mile away, all fully stocked with rifles and knives. Fuchsia raindrops fall. The cruel men quicken their stealthy steps.

A chilling echo lingers after birds take flight. Mama elephant senses danger and blares a warning trumpet. Sisters corral newborn toward I-T-S mama. Bloody calamity and tearful mystery confound baby. Loving sisters topple over like felled oak trees. I-T-S not moist sap that leaks from their bellies.

Human cowards pounce. Glint of blades bloody red. Horrific sight and sound will remain with the baby for the rest of her life.

Shallow breaths haven't stopped when the herd's tusks are removed. Baby wails into the bloody mud pit. Mama pushes her baby to run; the trauma is too great, little one won't budge. Knees buckle and Mama falls beside her baby. Husky pain-driven shallow breaths kick up dusty exhales. Mama elephant's struggling last moments of life bring laughter from psychopathic men.

Baby elephant caresses her Mama's moist cheek. Sad confused trumpeting echoes.

"Shut up!" ugly Middle Eastern poacher shouts.

Milliseconds after the evil man wipes his bloody knife on his pant leg; three bullets from African authorities drop and kill the inhuman Middle Easterner and his fellow nasty comrades.

African authorities find the murdered Mama and tranquilize her baby. She's loaded onto a truck and moans the entire 18-mile trip to the makeshift community for orphaned animals.

Baby, close to death, refuses to eat or drink. Sadness melts fat and skin away. Compassionate intravenous fluids keep the baby from total heart failure.

Waggy puppy and baby giraffe tear up after dozens of kisses can't cheer up their new friend. The baby rhinoceros, Sir Reginald, temporarily perks up baby elephant's depressed mood.

Baby elephant gurgles down a milk bottle. African handlers cheer and caress baby's trunk after baby polishes off a larger milk bottle 18 days later. Months later, the formerly forlorn elephant merrily munches multiple mangos.

The following morning, fate delivers destiny's diminutive David Sagacious...

"Mama, can I?"

Grace nods.

David's giddy excitement wiggles his entire body. He runs to the baby elephant. "Are you the famous squishy Elle?"

David hugs Elle and she trumpets her happiness.

"Can I feed her?"

Smiling African gently puts a large milk bottle in David's two tiny hands.

"Is that too heavy?"

"No, I can do I-T."

Milk dribbles down Elle's cheek; she playfully pushes into David's scent.

"Surprising. That one is always shy with newcomers. Elephants are perceptive creatures. She trusts your son's genuine kindness."

"He's a very special boy," says Grace.

Little me beams from ear to ear.

Over the next few months, David and Elle repeat their love fest. He rubs her ears. She tickles his belly. They trumpet blaring happiness.

Gorgeous sunset fades. "Ima Peter Pan," crows David.

"Come on, sweetie. Tomorrow is a big day. We talked about this. You need to go to bed a little earlier," says Grace.

"I know. I-T-S just I still have too much energy."

"Stop counting dancing elephants."

David giggles.

"I see them. All fuchsia elephants, and they're performing in Swan Lake. Now appearing for the first time, the incomparable fuchsia Elle. She's Elle Doolittle singing 'I Could Have Danced All Night.'"

Rubbing David's head, Grace unsuccessfully represses her laughter.

"Good night, grandpa," Grace and Christopher whisper and kiss his forehead.

David grabs his papa's arm and blows hard, making a farting sound. "Good night stinky number one..."

"Don't say I-T," says Grace.

"Number two," says both David and Christopher. All three giggle.

Beautiful sunrise greets yawning David. "What you doing?" asks little me.

"Going over the new maps. Remember, we're gonna hike along a new path."

"Will chubbily wobblily join us? I think she'd be lonely if we left her behind."

"She's the guest of honor."

"Yay! David's little hands happily clap above his little nose. He brushes away tickling fuchsia butterfly. I-T flutters and poofs in and out of swirling mini gaseous fuchsia cloud. His eyes grow wider as strange pretty creature's whispers tickle his nose.

"What?"

"Did you say something?" asks Grace.

"No, Mama. Ima happy Elle will be with us."

Grace and Christopher walk away holding hands. David feels a rush of ominous coldness wash over his shivering body;

he pulls his fuchsia cap over his ears.

Papa's phone swirls into a vortex of shimmering fuchsia noxiousness. Time clicks backward. Grace, Christopher, and half a dozen African guides freeze in conversation. Skyline down to the desert floor glows with fuchsia energy. Miles away, black noisy clicking spiders blast forward at the speed of chaotic cheetahs. The closer they get to Christopher's feet, the slower their movement, until time freezes them into an ice block.

Frozen campfire embers glisten in David's eyes. Fuchsia energy stream slips inside his dilated pupils: for 18 seconds, newfound awareness takes hold. Little guy feels unbearable pain.

Too much! Stop!

Pushing past peculiarly paradoxical pandemonium, David's neurons fire at an accelerated pace. Locked in degenerative delirium, David's haunting haze hits home. He's hit with withering wakefulness as he's the only one to bear witness to a barrage of biting, bellowing, burdensome black shooting star. I-T pulverizes a much smaller twinkling star. Blinding brightness slips through ripples in distorted space-time continuum. Righteous fuchsia shooting star blasts 18 pulses at the crushing creature; fuchsia star and larger black star fall into twisting black vortex and vanish...

Smaller fuchsia stars re-emerge after 18 minutes. David feels their frustrating desperation. His sleeve blots out three electrified fuchsia tears.

Hush, old friend. Don't tell the others. No time to explain. Close your eyes. Pleasant dreams. Pray tomorrow never comes...

Why? What happens tomorrow? Is something gonna happen to Mama and Papa? And how can you stop tomorrow from coming?

Don't fight your fate, little one. Trust me.

Come back!

Listening to my melodious voice and sleep...

What does melodious mean? Are you still there?

Minty fresh breath washes over a 21st-century not-yet-enhanced David Sagacious. His many thoughts and questions float away; one last yawn and he falls into a deep rem sleep.

Taunting thoughts yank me back into my 18-million-year-old body...

Powerful hatreds reincarnate at the speed of 18,000 nuclear blasts. We become, in the blink of God's insight, an extinction-level impact crater. Our glowing torso emits energy pulses that could illuminate three black holes. Coughing up debris, we climb out of fractured fluctuating fissures. Bloody eyeballs blink and wink at our skeletal fingers. Wiggling digits scratch the itch, which is our entire leathery face.

Agony fuels our rebirth. Thrusting skeletal hands into a molten lava pit, we guzzle fiery nectar. Jumping into lava flow, we burn from head to toe. Hitting bottom, our skeleton melts. We are purgatory particles. Like a flaming puzzle, our sizzling bones transform twice as strong as I-T was the last millennium.

Bats out of hell, we rocket to the surface. Sledgehammer for fists, we pulverize mountaintops the size of small moons and tame gale-force radiation and tsunamis.

Imbued with solitude, David's salty mood stewed and accrued rude interlude. Gracious gratitude will elude that dude. He'll feud with every inch of altitude, longitude, and latitude. He'll conclude doppelgangers are shrewd and sarcastically screwed. His delude exactitude will allude to every collude.

Malevolent Time plots and prevails, assaults and impales every hero's heartbreaking tales. Sickening screech shatters surreal schadenfreude's sadism.

If we obey evil's auto-da-fe, we'll become agony's astray and forever decay along her hate-filled highway.

Thank God my rhyming and alliteration worked. I can feel I-T retreating. Benevolent time sends me back to the 21st century. We're once again three years old.

Tears stream down little David's face. "Please, Papa, she needs me."

"She's learning skills to go back to the wild. As her friend, you must help her see that. Sometimes, if you genuinely love someone, you sacrifice your best interest for your loved one's best interest."

Christopher and David hugged. "Let's help Elle get her happiest future."

"Okay, Papa."

David blinks back tears through his long eyelashes. Christopher pulls out his handkerchief and gently absorbs David's watery pain.

David sniffles. "I-T-S still so sad."

Grace walks over and rubs David's tear-soaked cheek.

"We're family. There isn't anything Mama and Papa wouldn't do to make sure you have the happiest experiences. You wouldn't want to deprive Elle of a chance to find her own family."

Elle, trumpeting her joy, gallops to her best two-legged friend. Like a billiard shot, Elle's trunk pushes three mangos toward David's untied shoelaces.

Sorry, Elle. I don't wanna play. Mangos ricochet off David's heels.

Fuchsia butterfly lands on David's nose. Elle's trumpeting sneeze blows the pretty flapper away. Elle and David's sneezes sound the same.

Elle bounces toward three run-away mangos. Gooey juices dribble down her cheek.

David's peripheral vision sees Papa waving him back to the jeep. "I-T-S time!"

Head down, David kicks up fuchsia dust particles. Those invading particulates tickle Elle's wide nostrils. Fragrant fuchsia sneeze will freeze time's flamboyant fragility, familiar futures, and firebrand's fealty.

"Stay! I have to go, chubbily wobblily. I'll miss you lots.

Give the other elephants a chance to love you like I do," David's voice cracks.

36 hours later, Elle sprints after David's jeep. Her trunk blares heart-wrenching Klezmer clarinet-sounding sadness.

David's little body rocks back and forth. "Mama, my heart hurts."

Christopher wraps his arms around his son, "Ours too."

Hugs and tears carry David, Mama, and Papa all the way to the airport.

Over the next six years, David never forgot Elle. In between soccer and basketball practice, and interrupting breakfast, lunch, and dinner conversations, David constantly asks about when they can visit Elle again.

His wish comes true 18 days after his 9th birthday. Every step through the airport, he bounces with anticipation.

Christopher is tall and strong enough to easily place three bags in the upper compartment. David plops into the window seat next to Mama.

Nephesh will always be invisible to inferior human technology; her fuchsia energy stream pokes 18 holes the size of human noses through big fluffy clouds. David's plane is buffeted. Giant, pretty green eyes follow his plane back to Africa.

Long fuchsia nail, partially phased out of human time, easily penetrates the plane's cabin. That intrusion occurs before the cabin loses any pressure.

David wakes from his nap. "Minty fresh. Hey, who's chewing minty fresh?"

"What was that, sweetie? yawning Grace asks.

David looks up at the 6-foot-6 African flight attendant with large green eyes, a long flowing fuchsia scarf and wafting minty fresh breath. Like a peculiar cartoon, the African's face elongates. Odd elastic stretching eyelashes frighten young little me. He, we watch each eyelash extend 18 inches. Paralysis zooms throughout David's system. Harrowing hallucinations hit his heavy hemoglobin. Fuchsia sparks leap from flight attendant's 9-inch-diameter green eyes. Ropy eyelashes form dangerously daunting daggers.

Mama! Papa! Monster paralyzed me! David's mind screams.

Hush little one. Time to sleep!

Flight attendant's puffy lips grow to gargantuan proportions, minty fresh breath wriggles into David's nostrils.

How are you doing this? No! Don't eat me!

Giantess fingers extend longer than David is tall. *How is nobody seeing this? Mama!*

Old man don't be so afraid. Ima your friend. I've fought by your side for centuries.

Old man? Centuries? Y-you aren't gonna eat me?

Been a vegetarian for thousands of years.

Hey, I can wiggle my toes.

Good for you. Nephesh's fuchsia hair stands up like a beanstalk antenna. *Gotta run. See you much later...*

Snapping her finger, Nephesh pops out of human perception. Fuchsia confetti streamers fall under everyone's seat.

Black metallic creature the size of a French fry floats through flummoxed fictitious space-time. Creature's tiny head swivels 360 degrees. Squeaky insect voice is beyond the ability of human hearing.

"Oh my, you do look tasty. I don't understand why mistress won't let me end you in this timeline. I-T would be so easy."

Salty creature sniffs the air.

"Yes indeed, I'll enjoy slathering you in peanut butter and jelly. Sagacious sandwich sounds so scrumptious. MMM... human flesh makes my mouth water."

Invisible fuchsia hand dislodges her invisible fuchsia foot from her invisible fuchsia stiletto.

Shadow looms over French fry Ami. "No! Stop! Ima not prepared. Don't do I-T!"

Cackling crescendo precedes fuchsia pump's crunching

and twisting of Ami's reinforced titanium bones. Giantess' shoe movements are similar to the movements of a human disgusted by a smoldering cigarette.

9-year-old David's heart soars with pride. "She did I-T, Mama."

"Isn't that, like, the ninth time you've read that letter?"

David's big grin grows wider. "She's with a new mama, three sisters, and two brothers."

"Good for Elle," says Grace.

Fasten seat belt sign lights up with I-T-S distinctive chime.

Deplaning, the Sagacious family is blasted with 117-degrees-Fahrenheit heat.

After a few disappointing weeks with the wrong herd...

David leaps out of the jeep, trumpeting his joy, "I-T-S her! I-T-S her!"

Powerful fuchsia breeze blows David's scent into Elle's twitching nostrils. Sliding toward the mud pit, Elle and David wiggled with excitement. Her trunk wrapped around and tickled.

David's parents and their African friends consult their maps with their backs to David and 6-year-old Elle. The adults peer through binoculars, their attention glued to the swirling tree and bungalow destroying black raindrops.

"What the hell. No rain cloud for miles," says perplexed African handlers.

Criminal poachers from Europe, Asia, and the Middle East never left. Golden tooth poacher's lanky clumsy stride steps and crunches on a fallen dried-up branch.

Elle's ears stretch back, and her eyes grow wider. She senses danger and pushes David into the mud pit.

David rolls down the embankment. "Mama! Papa!"

Grace and Christopher are startled by Elle's trumpeting rage.

Frantic, Mama runs toward the men with guns and knives.

Papa grabs his rifle. "Get the hell away from my son!" he shouts.

David climbs and is pushed back by a minty fresh fuchsia blast. On his hands and knees, he kicks and punches the mysterious breeze. Exhausted, he rolls over the edge of the mud pit.

Three percussive explosions jettison bullets toward David's panicking eyes.

In the blink of a hummingbird's wings, time freezes. David is transported 18 feet closer to his stampeding friend, and the unthinkable happens.

Fuck! Malevolent Time rewrote what was never supposed to be rewritten. I hate new evil memories, teasing more loss. Elle, you were supposed to grow old, have your own babies, and live to be the world's oldest grandma. Because I was having some success she decided to punish me, by taking away your potential future. I shake my fist at the twinkling stars. "God! Counter Malevolent Time's rewrite. Please. Don't let her rub out kindhearted Elle."

Bullets from another poacher group penetrate Elle's soft belly.

"No!" screams 9-year-old David.

Tears and mud flow down the little boy's cheeks. Blood splatters into his eyes.

Brokenhearted David crumples onto Elle's shallow breathing chest. Elle pats David's head before her shallow breath stops. Trying to bring her back, he blows into her cold nostrils.

Christoper wraps his arms around his son's shaking body. "David. Please."

As nasty, freaky punishment, David and his parents are turned into the granular consistency of a Hasbro Etch-a-Sketch. David points to the planet-size black hands high up in the cloudless blue sky. Left hand blots out the sun. I-T descends toward tiny humans. Golden righteous energy shrinks the blackness down to 1,800-foot fingers. Middle fingers slam into the desolate dirt.

The ground violently shakes; David, Grace, Christopher, and their six African friends are tossed like insignificant rag dolls. Ominous Hillary Clinton face continues to shrink to 200 feet. Huge sweat droplets fall and erase reality, much like when rain fell on Bert's sidewalk paintings in the *Mary Poppins* movie.

Sky. Sun. Animals. Homes. Cities. People...blurs and distorts. Sagacious family hold each other tight. Night and day rapidly flip-flop in a matter of 36 seconds.

Land beneath their feet crumbles, opening massive bottomless caverns. A menacing cackle precedes an eight-foot index finger. Flick! Grace and Christopher tumble head over heels into that cackling darkness.

"Mama! Papa!"

Earth's land mass and oceans are spit into space. Floating, glowing fuchsia energy envelops David in a protective membrane.

"N-Nephesh, can you bring back my family?"

Panic attack hits David's heart as the ear-shattering annoying sound from a vintage land-line phone blares. 18 seconds becomes 18 minutes. Drenched in sweat. Unable to know the location of the reverberating dial tone or how to shut I-T down. Feeling betrayed, David sucks his thumb in the freezing darkness for an inconceivable 18 hours. Slow-moving sunrise freezes in I-T-S ascension. Orange sky maintains dark holes, from which David's confusion bears witness to the vastness of space and I-T-S heavenly twinkling breadcrumbs. Rocking back and forth, David continues to grow more dehydrated while shivering from fright and 39-degree temperature, which belies any sense of normalcy.

"Minty fresh, where are you?"

"I've returned."

"From where?"

"Impossible to explain without a common frame of reference."

"Y-you can bring my Mama and Papa back to me? Right?"

"Perhaps."

"Don't say that! Say yes. Say of course, little one. I will bring them to you immediately."

"Running out of time."

"Come back! Don't leave me like this. Mama! Papa!"

"Sorry for that."

"Don't do that again! What's that hissing sound?"

"Oh, my God. Your protective membrane is leaking!"

Nephesh pushes the fuchsia breathing mask onto David's face. "Is that better?"

"Yes, thank you. but...um...I still hear the hissing."

"I must act fast. If the membrane breaks down before I complete the equation...hold still, little one, sorry I must access and engage in a sudden bulging eddy of chaotic time."

Nephesh pieces together happier reality strands and sings "Dust in the Wind."

David hears deep baritone humming.

"Nephesh, who's that?"

"Thank God. Ko'ach's found us."

"Who?"

"Your future mentor and my forever husband. While God battles Malevolent Time, Ko'ach will bolster my powers, though he's currently stuck in an irreversibly inconvertibly irresistibly ironic iconic insurmountably torturous time."

Ko'ach's powerful voice pushes past creatively crumbling conundrums. Nephesh shrinks herself down to seven feet and phases into David's protective membrane. She chews her minty fresh gum, spitting I-T into her large palm and smushing I-T over the membrane's thin branching-out fissures.

9-year-old David ages centuries. Nephesh melts back into space and sings "You've Got a Friend." Seconds after the last stanza, 900-year-old David Sagacious vanishes.

"Beloved, please stay with me," implores Nephesh.

"You know I can't."

"How long before the vortex yanks you back?"

"Seconds. I sense happy memories within the Sagacious family's new reality. Dear heart, I shall for all eternity love you so..."

Nephesh feels Ko'ach's essence fade into agony's timeless excruciation.

Come back to me, beloved. No matter what you do...I will always forgive you. Our mutual love and respect remain as immortally strong as God's righteousness.

Fuchsia doorway opens. Nephesh walks through crackling black lightning storm.

Malevolent Time turns us into a prime war crime paradigm enzyme. I'll never be strong enough to vanquish Malevolent Time. God's the only force righteous enough to do that.

Long before I was born and marooned on this God-forsaken planet, I-T had already consumed trillions. Could the one responsible for my parents' murder be one of my best friends? Greenie! You! I'll never forget you, the time traveling, shapeshifting giantess. When I was only 9, you held me captive for five torturous years. Do you honestly believe Ko'ach betrayed your love by destroying god's righteous realm? No! I won't! I can't believe...that!

The First Time I Died

God graciously gifted me his trillions of memories—1,836,000,000,000,000, to be exact. That's why I'm aware of his Genesis.

Trillions of eons before my birth, Emet howls for his Papa's help. The louder his pleas, the more gleeful Malevolent Time cackles. *You're not Emet. I rename thee EM-IT.*

Malevolent Time's magnetic bullwhip flays and vaporizes EM-IT-S righteous skin. Alone in the void of space EM-IT-S skeleton agonizingly contorts.

At 99 percent dead, EM-IT-S mind cries out to his Papa. God doesn't answer because Malevolent Time has the power to block God's empathetic telepathy. EM-IT-S nerve-endings burn from acid greater than 10,000 supernovas. Reactive radiation erases EM-IT-S engrams. Memories of Papa linger as wispy wandering waves. Malevolent Time's brainwashing teaches him that she's his one true mother and that his papa long ago abandoned him.

I was 9 and still human when the humongous monster murdered my Mama and Papa. Orphaned, that devilish creature gave me no time to grieve. I was abducted by a horribly heartless thing: she ignored my tearful screeches and stuffed me into her shiny purse. Depriving me of food, she worked me beyond exhaustion and never provided medical attention for my oozing wounds. God Damn I-T! She turned me into an emaciated 45-pound pustule.

My hair turned white! And fell out in clumps! Monster's heavy homicidal sand-paper hands forcibly rubbed my skin raw. Her mocking chainsaw jaw warbled ha, ha, ha. I escaped hundreds of times, and hundreds of times, I was found. Praying for death's release from pain she will increase day and night, she'll never cease. Gangrenous oozing brought about hallucinating schmoozing.

I was whipped, broken, and caged until I was 14. Hygiene was obscene. Giant green queen ruptured my spleen. She purified what was left of me with gasoline. Oh God! No! Not the rusty guillotine!

Depression runs deep for this distraught sheep. Greenie's middle finger flicks. Crunch!

"Stop toying with me!"

I can never go back to being human. Her experiments were a success; I was forced to acquiesce. Bodiless, I become a walking, talking abscess. No redress. I confess, I wish I had a loved one to caress.

Mocking my frail fail. I could never curtail her Machiavellian prevail.

No period of grace, frozen tears stream down my face. I live an eternity in disgrace. Too weak am I to escape this violent place. Rubbing index finger to thumb, I sprinkle 18 sub-atomic time particles into wiggle roots, *voila.* The plant's 72-day growth takes place in 18 seconds. I always get a blast of supercharged minty freshness when the moons are at their apogee.

Inflating my lungs, my powerful chest bulges, and I hold, infusing my bloodstream with trillions of nano time-traveling particles. *My vision provides better clarity than any U.S. Marine's infrared goggles.*

I miss you so. Wiping nostril goo with the back of my hand, my powerful sneeze sprays luminescent nanoparticles. Each mucus droplet takes an abnormally long time to hit the ground. *Time delay of 18 hours over that ridge...good to know.* Faster than any cheetah, I sprint 18 hundred miles over frozen mountain peaks dwarfing Mount Everest.

There's never any peaceful uniformity in this world. No dark side. No light side. The entire planet is in total darkness or total blinding light. Extreme light and heat illuminate and blast for an uninterrupted 36 decades.

Massive tornadoes, hurricanes, and sand tsunamis powerfully turn the entire planet into an abrasive dust bowl. Itchy, scratchy incessant watery eyes. I sense an ethereal form coalescing. Anticipation bolstered my heart rate. *Recognition confirmed.* I smile and blow kisses toward the glowing mirage. *Ima here. Ima here.*

I sing "You Raise Me Up" to my long-ago dead wife. Beneath the permafrost, 360 miles down, are thousands of caves. Freshwater rapids career through 180,000 tributaries. Small plants and flowers grow only while the planet freezes in darkness. I-T-S darkness lasts 54 decades. During the dark phase, crushing gravity increases by a factor of 72 percent. Blue-white moon illuminates this place only when I call for I-T.

I-T-S here God's bioengineer schmear will interfere in eternity's career. Last time Ima would appear, her cheer was so sincere, she enjoyed quoting Shakespeare. Dearest Ima will always be my true-blue Guinevere.

Out there, fear complicated this transcendental sphere. Towering terrorist manipulates mathematics. Their timeless theorizing tragically triumphed. I-T-S god's equation, which unlocks the how to, which changes time travel from an uncertain possibility to a 99 percent probability. The relativistic snake in the grass continually I-T would trespass and harass, waiting for I-T-S unwavering armada to amass. I-T-S accosting is endlessly exhausting.

The baseline temperature of outer space, as set by the background radiation of the Big Bang, is 2.7 Kelvin or minus 455 degrees Fahrenheit.

Early morning, mid-day, and evening—this planet's surface temperature never alters; I-T-S a constant minus 360 degrees Fahrenheit. I shiver under an envelope of molecularly brittle darkness; my heart and neurons crystalize. Toes, fingers, and limbs blacken and break off. *How do I pick up arms without hands? How do I walk over to my feet without legs? Crawl, damn I-T!*

Lava boils at 2,000 degrees Fahrenheit. The surface of Earth's yellow sun burns 10,000 degrees Fahrenheit. Three cloaked suns remain inactive until they appear on the horizon. Like a screeching baby taking I-T-S first breath, those stars' dormancy suddenly explodes in a vibrant disintegration-level heat blast. There's no place to hide. Every tree burned away millions of years ago. Now, this world sizzles at a tissue-crisping 3,600 degrees Fahrenheit.

Intense light and heat bear down. Cooking in my own juices, I-T doesn't matter how loudly my smoldering lips cry out, "Flame off! Flame off! Flame off! I-T never turns off!"

God damn I-T! I need more time. Though you'd think 18 million years would already be enough. So far, I-T-S not!

My cell's energy matrix fully regenerates after an uninterrupted non-snoring 72 minutes. Good morning me. I'm talking to myself again. Indeed, you are. And why are you doing that? Because I'm alone. Not even an echo to keep me company! No need to shout. Who's shouting? Do you often get up in the morning and argue with yourself? Yes. Well, maybe. Are you sure? Of course, the answer is both and neither. I've been without a sound sleep these past 36 decades. No wonder you're getting a little loopy. I'm absurdist fiction; growing conviction that my predilection toward erroneous malediction is entirely...your prediction.

Bang! Flash!

I fall into a 21st-century UCLA ICU incubator for preemies...

Grief-stricken Mama nibbles her nails down to their bloody nub. Papa's powerful shoulders wilt and twitch. My life an improbable glitch, the pitch of my tiny baby siren wails, while Mama's hollering imperatively cracking voice Beseeches, "God he's so tiny."

Mama's heart races. Papa brushes her hair and kisses her wet salty cheek. David's skeleton twists into torturous geometric shapes. Papa's feelings lurch forward, his warm tears hit my cold incubator; pity-pat, pity-pat...

6-foot-4 doctor Ross is medically at a loss. Emotional bebop from Pop will never stop. Each step and slip will trudge and trip. No smile nor quip. That sail has shipped.

Fear chills Mama's hands and lips. Her heavenly hope shredded.
Looking up into Papa's eyes. Mama sighs. Her fear asks silent whys.
Baby's heart stops and starts; eyes rolled back and dart.
Limbs shatter, gray matter splatter. Baby David's platelets scatter.
Normalcy booted. Cells looted. Mind, body and soul electrocuted.

Mama's open palms pound Papa's chest. Her anxiety will never rest.

Grace and Christopher's nerves are threadbare because of Doctor Scarlett Crimson's musical warfare; her voice oppressively hypnotic—sultry sway erotic, despotic, and psychotic.

Surgical suction sound serenades and serrates secreted bones and organs into a surreal smoothy. Felonious foreboding flummoxes all feverish futures. Diabolical dilemmas deform and dehumanize. Reeking of recklessly regurgitated rage turned baby Sagacious into garishly grizzled gnarled grotesque goop. Crimson's insensitivity would selectively swoop. Grace and Christopher's hope would never recoup. Faith's feeling repeatedly reeling. Scarlett's double-dealing; hides what she's concealing...

"Damn your singing!" shouts Papa.

Crimson combines the creative stylings of Israel IZ Kamakawiw'ole Wonderful World" and "Somewhere Over the Rainbow."

"Your son," Doctor Ross' dry voice hiccups.

"David..." says Mama.

"David isn't breathing on his own. Time to consider."

"...pulling the plug?" whispers Papa.

"Did I do this? Am I a monster? Responsible for my baby's agony? Sweet brave boy. Can you forgive Mommy? I love you with all my heart. How could you suggest? Oh No! I can't. There must be another way. Christopher, please..."

"He suffers. And he must not suffer. I'm his Papa. I must act. I must...we must..."

Doc Ross gently removes David from his incubator. We fall and crest upon Mama's breast.

"He's so cold. Oh, dear lord!"

Mama shuts her eyes tight. Her forehead methodically taps, taps, taps Christopher's chest. Neither have the words. David's breath grows shallower with each passing moment. Grace cradles her face in her loving husband's strength.

"Son, this is Papa. I wish...they tell us this is the only way. I don't know. You fought with tremendous courage. But...um... now I-T-S time to rest. Dwell pain-free with almighty God. He shall give you what we never could...peace everlasting."

Peace everlasting. Yea, right! Peace of mind I have yet to find. Emotions raw. Sentimentality gnaw!

Mama nods. Her hand squeezes Christopher's strong forearm.

"Okay, Doc," whispers Papa.

Doctor Ross punches black, white, fuchsia buttons. Mechanical life support whirs to an impersonal stop.

"Breeeeeath baby, please, for Mama."

No heart flutter. No breathy stutter.

Brain activity ________________________________ flatlines.

Autopsy now. Nothing left to kowtow.

We're blessed by God's ethereal vest. He'll transmit our warrior ode and moral code—so that we may encode destiny's neural node.

Across the Multiverse, this Sagacious will roam. I know no other home. Ima forever's tome. Extraordinary genome.

Complexity's ultimate syndrome. Body and soul's God-like catacomb. Oblivion called me to the brink. I feel, therefore, I think. Enormous pain refuses to wane. Files reactivate. Tissues reanimate, acclimate, calibrate, navigate, and emancipate.

Seeing our pale-blue cheeks flush, Doc Ross' joyful tears gush. To his flip phone, he'll rush.

"Solonga! I don't know how? But wow! He's alive! David Sagacious, no, no...I'm—yes, stone-cold sober. Are his parents still in the hospital? Yes, of course—grief counseling. Get them. Get them right away. His vitals? Toes wiggling, pink and happy."

The Realm of the Watchers exists outside of normal space. I-T was constructed by God's second son, god, soon after his older brother EM-IT-S tragic transformation.

Malevolent Time's belligerent obliterations shatter an unfathomable number of rewritten afterlife journeys. Her satanic sanctimony will slither, stab, skewer, splatter, scatter, and tatter every embryonic gray matter batter. *Beast! Get the hell out of my memories! Body shakes. Mind quakes. Ghoulish hallucination snakes. Love always forsakes...*

What did I-T do to my courageous wife? Ima's grotesque screams end with her transitioning into a sadistic 100-foot mechanical monster. Beloved growls. Why did you leave me behind! Blood trickles from nose, ears, and eyes. *Malevolent Time! I beg you, release my beloved!*

Such bravery, from one so...small!

Ima's nasty metallic cackles summon unforgivable nightmares.

Am I not beautiful? Ima's metallic bloody red lips ask. Blowing scary metal kisses, my distorted true love waves her glistening black armored middle finger, ripping open her squeaky, dented chest cavity. Greasy goo leaks down her 50-foot pock-marked black metal legs. I stare at that monster's heaving, wheezing, seething, deceiving, grieving.

My former wife's ethereal shadow hovers. I fall to my

knees. Tears flow down heavily wrinkled cheeks. Mechanical Ima cackles her pleasure and grins. Mocking my pain, she sings "Eternal Flame."

Absorbing giant quasar's gamma-radiation, I grow brighter than Earth's yellow sun, heart, lungs, bones harmonically in tune with the Multiverse; all of us vibrate. I alone am infused with massive amounts of sub-atomic gravimetric particles, thanks to the ceaseless bombardment from the mysterious fuchsia time-distorting wormhole.

In my sleep, underground stalagmites jettison upwards, poisonous jagged rock pierces my heart. I flatline and die. My righteous soul Pacman-like gobbles mummifying toxins, and I'm once again yanked out of heaven and slammed back into this planet's dusty surface. Not a moment of peace. I'm throttled by massive round-the-clock 18.9 Richter scale quakes.

Violent shaking shears mountaintops. Heckling hurricanes and 18-story-high tsunami waves pummel: hail the size of hippo heads smash and push me deep beneath the frozen permafrost. Magnetic pulse invigorates lightning strikes into my spine far greater than the fictional God of Thunder, Thor, ever experienced.

God's resonant voice whispered in my ear 18 million years ago that I should shout the evil I and T hundreds of times a week, when and only when both full moons pulsate with luminescent blue-white moonbeam energy. That righteous interaction will scramble my scent rippling throughout chaotic time. Bringing I and T together at the wrong time risks turning this Immortal Mortal into a permanent mortal.

While I attempt my first sleep in the last 18 days, I'm shocked out of refreshing slumber by planetary-wide blaring sirens, warning that a time traveling prototype careens out of control from Malevolent Time's machine Multiverse. Screeching creature lands at my feet. I-T wishes to disintegrate my heart and suck my soul. I mistakenly take pity on the inside-out metallic thing twisting in agony. I-T slams back together using the healing powers of this planet.

In the nick of time, I activate my harmonic blue-white forcefield as I-T blasts blood-red photons out of a crackling black lightning vortex chest. I-T-S deathly blood-curdling screams shatter the last of the dead forest.

Jumping 18 feet, I twist in midair and aim my glowing knuckles; righteous blue-white energy blasts at the invading metallic creature. "Got you!" incinerated metal magnetizes my forehead, torso, and palms. Like a glider caught in a wind tunnel, thwap! I'm stuck to a giant boulder. *I-T-S attracted to the listening machine parts orbiting my world. Shit! I can't break free. I-T-S carrying me up into space. Can't breathe! Will lose consciousness soon. Dear wife, I can't end like this. I must break free...I must save you! Must magnetize planetary crust...never tried before. Running out of oxygen and time...*

Never been up this high. Arms and legs pulsed in opposite directions. "I'm human, not a giant rubber band!" At the lip of stringent stratosphere, I snap back; that force kicks me loose. Out of control, I'm a free-falling fireball. Burned to a crisp, I crash into radioactive boulders 18 hundred times denser than on Earth. *Argh! Every bone shatters. Brain matter leaks on impact. Limp skin hangs like sloppy, succulent brisket.*

Head to the left. Left leg to the right. Torso split down the middle. Magma flow sutures smoldering David's pieces. Dehydrated organs drip gangrenous goop 18 weeks later, and 18 days later, my mind, body, and depressed spirit slowly heal. After each near-death experience, I'm reborn—stronger. Rocketing out of that volcanic hellhole, I flex strong hands and soft land, rubbing aching, reattached legs. Taking I-T easy, I jog a mere three consecutive marathons. Catching my breath, I lean back and admire the fiery meteor shower. Glowing sky illuminates my pulsating sweaty face.

Anger and anguish no longer contain my superhuman adrenaline surges or urges. Pounding clenched fists and elongated strides quicken my heart rate. I push back sweat-soaked black bangs from bloodshot eyes. Minty freshness fills my nostrils. Love's remembrance curls the corners of my mouth. *Spotlight, please.* Ima's bathed in glowing warm fuchsia quasar haze.

Beloved sings "So In Love." *Love levitates limitless loneliness.*

Ima's exquisitely intangible lips kiss my eager cracked lips. *I can almost feel her touch. Always...almost!* Ima sings "What I Did for Love," taking 18 steps closer to me. I blow kisses. Smiling, she clutches invisible love from hand to heart.

Choking on immense grief, my powerful baritone voice warbles "This Nearly Was Mine."

False memories are deviously implanted deep into my neural network. *Ima, my forever true love: here I hear your sorrow. Dear Ima, this time I promise I won't let you down. Today...your oblivion ends. I promise, sweetie. With or without God's weapon, I'll alter your forever horrific destiny.*

My mind phases through an infinite number of outcomes 18 hundred seizures later. Feeling Ima's presence, I call out to her, *Beautiful Ima, come to me, you can do I-T. Walk through time's benevolent portal. Good. Good. I can feel I-T-S frustration. I-T-S losing my genetic marker in this place of my own construction. Don't resist. Untwist the preexist. Please, sweetie, extend your wrist. Let me suture our maladapted future.*

The song "Somewhere in Time" produces the orchestration necessary to reinvigorate dead cells contorted by I-T-S demonic obliteration.

Longing for lost love, I sing "You're Still You" to my ethereal Ima, helping her cells solidify.

Soul and body dispersed. Mind coerced and submersed. Doomsaying soothsaying. I can't bear to feel wife's decaying; her ricocheting slaying.

Ima's fists punch through her isolating timeless barrier. She tickles my fingertips. Her glowing face pushes forward.

My thoughts seamlessly penetrate majestic maelstrom's violent din. *Take another step. You're doing great. No, don't stop. Why are you stopping?*

I don't know. I-I'm afraid.

Honey! Come to my hugs.

I-T-S never worked before. And I'm not yet fully part of your world.

Sure, you are.

No, Ima not. I-T-S not working!

Don't give up now.

Don't say that. Ima trying...

Forgive me, sweetie. You're doing great. I-T-S just that...

What? I can't move my legs.

The windows are closing. Don't look back, sweetie. Look into my eyes...

Ripping reality won't let Ima cross over. Her pulsating bejeweled heart clanks against a multitude of time displacement eddies. David stretches into the inferno. *Stay! Stay! Ima!*

Righteous tears extinguish black flames. David's bloodshot eyes are horrified watching Ima float away. Snapping out of his grotesque indecision, he, we...create our glowing blue-white lasso. Luminescent fibers hug Ima's hips. Rippling muscles counter mischievous gravimetric currents. Incapable buffeting through the torrid tribunal and taking David's lasso. Ima is overcome with despair. David's words reach her as garbled growls.

Desperation burns with every muffled syllable *Damn suffocating tendril. I won't let her slip over the waterfall's fiery precipice. Dear God! Don't let I-T be. Help me bring her back!*

CHAPTER 6

Anti-Zionism is Antisemitism

Fate, I hate. My happy memories are looted, booted, and notoriously executed. My human form was no longer the norm. Burlap's vile tactile created a perpetual exile—lifestyle. Humanity did recoil at the sight of this pre-teen gargoyle.

Malevolent Time's Machiavellian giggles rupture reality's storyline of righteousness. From the perspective of hopelessly hapless premature David, a hellscape happening—an African trip that inflicted and conflicted—never took place. Those memories belong to my murdered parents. Never-ending tormented tragedy leaves micro and macro distortions to timelines, which should never be. Flash bang bang! Flash bang bang!

After my recent resurrection 13 years prior...Palestinian monsters—Barghouti brothers collude and instruct with thousands of terrorists who ram cars, killing Jewish children. Their cowardly Shahidi actions create the means by which incalculable homicide deaths mount. They are all exhilarated finding a new demonic path as members of a select coven work side by side with Crimson and take orders from I-T. All three Palestinian brothers are partially transitioned as giant green crow-flapping monsters. They must murder and consume more human souls; they enjoy tasting and chewing on Jews, Christians, Buddhists, Shintos, Hindus, and Muslims.

"My belly hungers for Israeli meat," gurgles Al-Rantisis.

"You must control your cravings. We'll feast when mistress gives the word," adds Ahmed.

"Is she pissed or proud? I can never tell when mistress appears in human form," says Yassin.

"Never forget your heart and soul will always be Palestinian. Gain strength from the truth. History commands the Jews, be they Israeli, American, European, Asian, Latino, or Ethiopian; all must become our appetizers," bellows Ahmed.

"Of course, they're only the first course. MMM...we'll join our siblings in Crimson's dining hall and feast on delicious men, women, and children," growls Al-Rantisis.

"Allah Akbar! Allah Akbar!" shout the three brothers.

72 hours after Dafna's parents, sisters and brothers are raped and murdered, she looks down at her blinking scanner's fuchsia, black lettering: Doctor Scarlett Crimson...Feast!

Heavy emotions overwhelm 13-year-old Dafna. She pounds her fist. *What the hell does that text mean? Bastards all! When I find you, I'll send you back to the hell you spawned from!*

Dafna vaults into her Papa's prototype hovercraft.

"Smells like Papa." Tears well up and drip down her cheeks.

All the controls of the hovercraft are voice-activated.

"Maximum cloak," whispers grieving Dafna. *Three descending blips. I got you bastards!*

"That's my neighborhood. The altitude is all wrong, no longer flying above the treetops. Why are they 20 feet underground? Hamas infiltration tunnels. I must warn them..."

Doctor Tzipi's typical Gal Gadot smile vanished after the Shaked family tragedy. She approaches dignified 122-year-old Holocaust survivor Moses. He was the tutoring Cantor for Dafna's great-grandfather's Bar Mitzvah.

"Shalom Tzipi."

"Shalom Moses."

Mind sharp as a tac, Moses performs the Jewish mourning ritual—Kariah. His arthritic fingers struggle... The purpose of the ripping is to give the outer expression to the tattered soul within.

"Dafna lives with Hashem. Dear sweet girl. Fateful destiny granted her wish," cracking tearful voice states.

"What do you mean, destiny's granted wish?"

Frustration's anger builds. "To be with her family again in heaven. I can't talk now."

Flying hovercraft's experimental material contains intricate nano-tech-fibers. Good for forming the craft's side panels and sophisticated computer network. They can also be woven into shirts and pants and molded into comfortable-fitting shoes and boots. They retain the same cloaking properties: that's how Dafna can remain hidden from potential enemies.

Moses, dear old soul. I hate causing you more pain. You and Doctor Wonder Woman must stop searching for me. All of you must believe beyond any doubt that I'm dead. I-T-S the best way I know how to keep you all safe.

Dafna yawns. Her phone blinks 3:33 a.m. From an altitude of 18-stories, Dafna launches a magnetic anchor.

Dafna jumps. She spreads her makeshift cloaked cape, cold air slams against her cheeks. With the skill of an expert paratrooper, she lands safely. Lawn is soaked from the evening's heavy rain. *Squish. Squish.* Dafna's 18 footprints lead her toward the cordoned-off front door. Eyes welling up, she takes a deep breath and quietly exhales. Moonlight shines on her house key. Three steps inside and death's powerful odor incapacitates her thoughts and feelings.

Invisible teary eyes process the bloody crime scene. Above the treetops, minty fresh breath carries Dafna's muffled sobs.

Moses! You tell me revenge isn't our way. Antisemitism, that oldest irrational hatred, never dies! I'm proud to be a Zionist. Proud to be a member of humanity's noble Jewish people. Anti-Zionism is antisemitism.

Media lies. International court lies. College professors lie. We're demonized. Why not strike back? Why not strike first? Iran wants to perpetrate another holocaust, and the world appeases. Unlocked billions from Biden. You idiot! That blood money is going directly into the coffers of the terrorists! What a fucking corrupt antisemitic asshole that American President has always been. Never again! Goddamn I-T! Cannot. Will not ever be negotiable. Moses, you tell me I shouldn't carry hate—that God will punish these evil doers. History teaches something more sinister. I see justice for everyone else and rarely for us. From the river to the sea, Palestine will never be! The time for action is long overdue. While Demorats talk, Jewish children die. Jewish tears are dismissed as an inconvenient truth. Okay, world! The hell with you. Nobody is gonna step up! I-T falls to me. I'm truth's righteous avenger!

Clicking her heels at 3:42 a.m., nobody sees the visible energy stream propelling Dafna back toward her invisible floating craft. She lands on the Tel Aviv beach 90 minutes later; cool salty air invigorates her lungs. She peels away her nano-tech pants, shirt, and shoes. "Shrink!" Her special clothes become Barbie size.

"Triple-engaged, shrink," Papa's prototype hums. Cascading energy sparkles. Hovercraft becomes sand crab-size. Her gale-force lips blow sand particles. Memories mixed with moonlight. Her tears pity-pat...

Shaking sand from her shoes, Dafna walks into Ben Gurion Airport. Sleep-deprived Dafna watches guys and girls in their twenties sing, dance, and patriotically wave Israeli flags. Jewish immigrants making Aliyah burst into joyous song. Jewish parents kiss their children.

Dafna brings her coffee cup to her lips. Three sips later, she feels dizzy.

"Drugged? How? Who knows I'm here?" she mumbles.

Falling forward, her face smacks the floor. Large cockroach scurries into her right bloody nostril and exits through her left. Dreamy wooziness comes and goes with biting clarity. Dafna hears the cockroach speak in Ilhan Omar's voice. "Damn Fucking Jews! How dare they prevent my entry!"

Cockroach flies 60 feet. Ilhan Omar's nose squeezes through twitching wings. Pop. Her distorted head crowns. "Argh!" she screams as giant neck, shoulders, torso, and legs stretch toward the floor.

Omar, 60 feet, stands over and scoops normal size Jews in her huge hand. She licks her nasty fangs, monstrous cackles shattering every window. Cascading glass shards slice and dice Jews beneath painted surfboard-size toenails.

"E-knee! Me-knee! Shmucky-shmoe! To hell you Zionist bastards must go!" Omar roars, flicking humans smaller than trail mix. Slobbering spittle drowning drops three-times the size of any large human. Liquid death precedes Omar's whooping lip-smacking menacing delight. "MMM delicious!"

Jews are tiny fish out of water, and giant Omar plays with them like a house cat. Her black nails harpoon men, women, and children.

Omar smirks, "Come to Mama, human Jewish string cheese." Human cries send happy tingles down villain's varicose veins. She pulls SUV-size thimble from her pocket and shakes human size chili powder flakes. Crazy giantess rubs her tummy. Omar slurps tiny humans. They all drown under waves of pungent saliva.

Human bones sound like celery crunching. Hands pressed against her ears, Dafna tries to muffle the surreal sound.

Omar's tuba blasting fart sends Dafna flying backward. Donkey face human-size Rashida Tlaib exits Omar's anus. Stinky woman walks over to Dafna and transforms into a menacing tiger with flapping crow wings. Talons and teeth slash and chew Dafna's arms and legs.

Dafna wakes to a screaming baby.

"What? Where am I? She squints at the searing sun shining brightly through small airplane window. *I don't remember boarding. God, that was a bizarre nightmare.*

Extremely tall blonde stewardess hovers and licks her puffy lips.

"Hey there, honey. My name is Scarlett."

"Hey, Scarlett. Um, how long have we been airborne?"

"Took a nap, did you? I-T-S been 36 minutes. What's your choice?"

"What?"

"Meal, sweetie. Chicken? Fish? Beef? Hope you're not a vegan."

"Anything is fine."

"Would you like rice or broccoli with your anything?"

"Surprise me."

"No need to give me an attitude. Just doing my job."

"Didn't think I was."

"You should..."

"Wow. Really, I don't need your sarcasm."

"Haven't been sarcastic in a millennium or two." Scarlett flashes big white teeth.

Glad this looney isn't flying the plane.

"That's not nice."

"What's not nice?

"Calling me looney. Never learned to be one of those politically corrupt types."

"You mean politically correct."

"Yea. What you said. I keep mixing up those two concepts."

Weirdo

Scarlett waggles her long index finger in Dafna's face.

"Get that out of my face."

"Or what?"

"What?"

"Yes, what? Not interested in playing an Abbot and Costello routine."

"No, Ima not."

Scarlett giggles.

"What's so funny."

"You said Ima. Um, never mind. Inside joke."

"Inside what?"

"Again, with the what. Why are you so preoccupied with that word?"

Scarlett's teeth grow longer and sharper. She seductively licks her blood-red incisors.

Dafna blinks twice. *She's wearing ugly black lipstick...why are her teeth smeared red?*

Flight attendant's inner dialog shouts her own specific truth: *Irritable human. Can't go back in time until I finish this part of my mission. Thank God humans can't yet read minds.*

Scarlett hands Dafna her water bottle, sharp double-jointed, fuchsia-painted middle finger extends, scratching Dafna's pinkie.

"Oh, little one, I'm so sorry."

"For what?"

"I nicked you."

"Ima fine."

Ima. Really? An inadvertent déjà vu slip of the tongue, or timeline meddling? Can't be a coincidence that you say Ima instead of I am. You haven't met her yet.

Murky timeline appears, dissolves, and reappears.

"Can't afford any more complaints. How about I give you a double beef dinner? Have yourself a feast, okay? And if you're not that hungry, you can always give your leftovers to your Mama and Papa."

Cold sweat slithers while Dafna's racing heart causes her tightening throat to clench.

"Oh! You unfortunate thing. I didn't know. Me and my big mouth."

"How could you know? I-T-S not like you can read thoughts. Right?" *Why does that weirdo grimace every time I say I-T? Okay, goofball, Ima gonna test the impossible. What if I think... Wow!*

Like a fucking pinball. I-T! I-T!

"You Jewish?" Scarlett blurts.

Dafna balls up her fists. "Is that a problem? You did pick us up from Ben Gurion."

"Not all are Israeli. Ima big admirer of you Zionists. Push the button and ask for Scarlett if you need anything."

"What's your last name?"

"Crimson." Scarlett's eyebrow arches as Dafna attempts to control her anger.

"Feast!" blurts Dafna. She notices the tiniest twitch at the corner of Crimson's mouth.

"Okay then!" Crimson's booming voice rattles plastic cups three rows deep.

"Powerful lungs."

"Feast, you say." Crimson's head appears to grow the closer she leans toward Dafna. Her right-hand presses hard against her elongated nose and lips. "Need to keep that secret from these inconsequential humans."

Dafna clears her throat. "Sure. Yes. Of course, humans."

"Back in a jiff," Crimson's perky personality singsongs.

Loading the meals, Crimson has time to scan Dafna's blood. *Unexpected. This one has zero-time distortions, and yet she's much stronger than the other pre-transformative beings. Scanner never lies. You're 100 percent proof. Total unaltered human.*

I know you took my blood. Why the act? Pretending to be a goofy nonintellectual. Doubt your scanner is as efficient as my Papa's. Two can play this genetic game. She's returned. That was much quicker than I thought I-T would be. Oh, you see, there I-T is again...the grimacing never ended. Oh, well. Another mystery, for another time. No. No! Why the hell is she walking away? Stop talking to that antisemite I had a run-in with before we boarded. Oddly, I have a memory of that incident and everything else is blank. Oh, for God's sake, will you stop yakking with that horrible spittle spewing creep!

Fuchsia sonic boom portals human passengers into Benevolent Time's protective membrane. *I will not allow* chaotic time tendrils to obliterate human cell structures. Earthling's bulging eyes are frozen. Dafna remains awake and aware. Undulating incoherence tries to pierce her soul.

Crimson's indestructible thumbnail breaks Dafna's scanning needle. Crimson caresses Dafna's earlobe and shifts into conspiratorial verbiage.

"See ya, sweetie. Only 27 more months before the feast begins, and we all can enjoy salivating sweet and sour succulent meats."

Jettisoned from Crimson's eye socket are hundreds of cascading fuchsia bubbles. Itty-bitty pieces of multicolored confetti flutter.

"Make I-T stop. Make I-T stop!" Dafna screams.

Israeli becomes buried up to her neck in a shimmering membrane, simultaneously hard, gooey, wet, dry, opaque, and translucent. Time's disjointed energy enters Dafna's ears and pulls out multiple darkly distorted memories. All recent happenings scrubbed clean. Dream-like remembrance of flight attendant Scarlett Crimson wistfully remains.

Glowing Dafna dims. She reclaims her thoughts and strolls around the plane looking for Crimson. *I'll get my answers. Hey, why are you running away?*

Short brown-haired person quickens her pace. Dafna easily catches up.

"Excuse me, miss..."

Brunette lady turns, winks, and dashes away at breakneck speed. *What the hell is she doing?*

Dafna plops into an empty seat and waits. She can see old silver hair David Sagacious' peripheral vision keeping an eye on her.

Something familiar about that old guy. No! Focus on the brown-haired person first.

Dafna flings her fuchsia hat onto the brown-haired person's serving tray. David giggles.

"Good toss. Right on the money."

"Excuse me," says fake smiling brunette.

"You took the words out of my mouth," smirks Dafna.

"Please move your leg."

"If I do, are you gonna walk away?"

"Ima serving drinks and taking meal orders."

"I-T!"

No grimace with this one.

"And why the hell should I?"

How? Couldn't possibly read my thoughts. Better stop. Shut out my thoughts on this subject.

"Indeed, you should...little one." Whispering mocking echoes only for Dafna's ears.

Mustering typical Israeli confidence. Dafna stands, towering over 4-foot-11 middle finger protruding brunette.

"Get that out of my face before I break I-T off..."

"Now that would be fun. Go for I-T! Stupid human."

Human. Who says shit like that? Must be an escapee from the looney bin.

"Where is Crimson?"

"Who?" brunette flutters her lashes.

"I don't know what kind of game you think you're playing. Ima not in the mood."

Brunette covers her mouth and giggles.

"What's so funny? You're getting me off track. I was talking to her when...um...something happened. Why are you grinning? If you don't want me to report you both, you'd better produce Crimson. Now!"

"Whatever. You humans are so impatient, and so pitifully weak."

Dafna grabs brunette's wrist and watches the creature grow. Towering over Dafna and rubbing her long lizard tongue over her blood red elongated sharp incisors.

"You see that handsome guy over there with the rule-breaking middle-of-the-back silver hair and beard. He's the only one of us three that started out human."

"What the hell does that mean?"

"Go ask him. This is his last flight before retiring." Brunette extends her finger and flicks Dafna with great force. "Ow!" Dafna rubs her shoulder. Brunette looks back, smiles, and mockingly salutes.

In-flight movie begins: *Start the Revolution Without Me.*

Dafna balls up her right fist. She clenches and unclenches.

"Know your place, or you'll regret the consequences for centuries."

"Centuries! Looks like you're the one smoking bad shit."

"This is your last warning."

"Last or not...I don't react well to threats."

"You never do."

"Told you this one was feistier," grinning proud David says.

"Clearly you two are nuts. Thank God you're not flying this bucket."

Dafna waves her hands. "I'll take my seat. Go back to annoying someone else."

"No longer an option. You've already put in motion new events we must play out to their inevitable new conclusion." David playfully arches his Groucho eyebrows.

"Okay, professor. Keep talking crazy with..."

"My name is Ami. Graduate of Berkley. Two doctorates."

"And you are doing this?"

"Believe me, I wish I didn't have to team up with that..." Ami flicks with great force and David doesn't budge an inch.

"Ami! No! Run Dafna!"

Ami trips David before he can restrain her.

Ami's heavy footsteps send silent fissures up and down the cabin. "Israeli Jew! You are no match for us."

"Who the hell is us?"

David lunges and holds tightly onto Ami's recently growing tail. Ami's spittle-laced growl injects black energy into Dafna's arm.

Cabin spins. Dafna's eyes and heart flutter. "What's happening?"

Ami kicks David loose and picks up dazed woozy Dafna and tosses her two rows like she was a Raggedy Ann doll.

David waves his hand. Dafna's forward momentum slows before slamming into the wall; she gently falls to the filthy carpet. Peeking her eyes above the seat-back, she sees the other passengers frozen in time.

Dafna's scanner beeps softly. *Interesting. I feel the plane's vibration. My scanner's homing in on those three who murdered everyone I loved.*

Ami leaps across the rows, claws outstretched. David waves his hand. Fuchsia particles suspend and enrage Ami creature.

Ami's home world sits astride a giant pulsar. She doesn't feel emotional or physical pain the way we humans do. She specifically has a fetish for giving and receiving vicious torture. That agony unleashes tremendous joy; her synapse addictively craves biochemical rushes that make her disobey queen bee's orders. That's always dangerous.

David Sagacious specifically prevents Ami from polluting the timeline. I almost forgot about that 70s movie with Gene Wilder and Donald Sutherland. They walk down a long staircase as the Corsican brothers toward Duke D-Escargot. I love the silly, humorous alliterations.

David motions Dafna to walk toward him. She cautiously obeys, walking closer to immobilized Ami—with murderous rage in her eyes. David surprises Dafna with his giggles.

"See, her skin is like Play-Doh."

Dafna flicks Ami's cheek. Dafna's poke creates reverberations, cratering Ami's pliable epidermis. The rippling effect undulates Ami's distorted body. With heroic effort, Ami gnashes her teeth and forces her eyes to painfully bulge; flashes of black blood trickle and harden.

"Now, my turn," David gleefully exclaims. He claps his hands. Ami's cells form gaseous particles with a gag-reflex, rot-ten egg aroma. Ridiculously retching regurgitation re-moistens mucous-y drippy DNA. Ami demonstratively solidifies into a hackney Hacky Sack meat brick. Side to side, David kicks and sends her soaring past every row. Ami's essence phases, causing her to pass through the bathroom door. She immediately rushes to the toilet and loudly vomits.

"Be right back. Enjoy your Crimson lemonade!" shouts David.

"Um...before you go, can I have a grandfatherly hug?" Dafna reaches over and snips a piece of David's long silver hair.

"Feeling better?"

"Thanks. Yes. Loads."

I didn't ask for lemonade. How quickly David's grin turns from reassuring to creepy cat devouring the canary...and Ima the canary.

Sudden vibration, and Dafna is rattled off her feet. On her backside, she looks up at the disembodied floating-phasing in and out—Scarlett Crimson head. Lips mouth, "Don't drink." A smiling tall Texan's body appears as a menacing metallic machine, and I-T screams, "Drink! Drink! Into the drink you go!"

Dafna feels her soul pulled into the swirling lemonade. David snaps his fingers. Glass shatters. David suspends 18 inches off the ground, flies like Superman, and phases like a ghost through the bathroom door.

"Okay, crazy alien man. Tell me what I need to know. What will your DNA show?"

Dafna looks down at her scanner. Crimson letters flash calibrating...calibrating...

David and Ami stand nose to nose. His laced knuckles crack as he wiggles his fingers high above her back. Ami tries to speak. Garbled staticky sounds intermittently fluctuate.

"Are you gonna punish me?"

David's lips and cheeks stretch into a grinchy happy smile.

"Goody!" Ami's staticky vocal cords shout.

Sledgehammer slap crumples Ami into four quadrants. Half her torso and left arm flail right. Right arm flails left. David's powerful hands reshape Ami's dark olive face into a pale Hillary Clinton. David pinches and squishes Ami-Hillary into Donald orange-man Trump. David pulls on Trump's cheeks and transforms the 45th President into Scooby Doo.

"Ruby-roo! David shouts, yanking Ami's lips down to her ankles. Each tug creates odd crinkling, wrinkling cellophane noises.

"Why so down in the mouth?" David laughs, jerking twice on the ends of Ami's elongated chin. She stretched beyond cellular integrity warrants. Similar in sound and movement to releasing a school room map; Ami's chin crashes into her jaw-bone. *Thwap-pop-pop!*

David twists Ami's fleshy horse nose. Pop! I-T dislodges; he rubs her flaring nostrils under his armpit. "Sorry, not sorry. Haven't showered these last few months."

"I can tell, asshole!" infuriated Ami shouts.

"What a wonderful idea," David proclaims in his best Groucho Marx voice. David takes off Ami's head and attaches her cranial nerve endings to her anus. He breaks four fingers and stuffs them in her nose.

"I can't bree-b."

"What?"

"Bree-b!"

David yanks her slippery, dripping digits and plops them in her mouth.

"Move, please." Weird accordion giddiness exhales from Ami's lungs.

"Maybe later."

David uses her two large rabbit teeth to staple her fleshy tongue into her left eyebrow, which grows centipede legs. Her right eyebrow scurries away and burrows deep into her screeching eerie canal. David slams Ami's mucous-dripping nasal protuberance onto the bathroom mirror.

"Hey, snaily is back."

Ami's nose releases yucky goo. Nostril edges sprout tiny fingers. Each disjointed digit frantically flails. Freakish abomination folds spatial dimensions.

"Ima slipping! Catch me! Damn you! Not the toilet!"

Ami's snotty screaming appendage sneezes particular particulates. Mischievous mucous marinade pelting password's pejorative penitentiary. Eyelids slamming serenades suspicious percussive symbiosis.

David snaps his fingers. Ami grows, hitting her head on the ceiling. A split-second later, she shrinks down to 22 inches.

"Nooo!" resoundingly ripples resonate a Don Knotts Limpet thrum-thrumming through stinky scented squeaky sounds.

David looks down at diminutive, agitated Ami and smiles. "That'll do, pig," he giggles.

Fuchsia time distortion passes over every passenger. Increased intensity initiates irreverent intuitive initiative. Nausea slams into Dafna. She struggles against undulating particulates and delivers her best William Shatner intonation: "Must. Get. Off Plane!" Rapid descent accelerates Dafna's spinning vertigo. Cacophony's Kaleidoscope of intense reverberation slams all her senses. Three blinks of her eyes clear fuzzy vision, and David comes into view.

"How are you feeling?" asks David.

"Not sure. Guess a little better."

Ami steps into Dafna's peripheral vision, "Good. The last little idiot human has left. For what are you waiting? Do I-T!" shouts Ami.

"She still has time."

"I don't. You know how famished I get obeying orders."

David dabs Dafna's drool. "Ph...Ph...east?" Dafna blurts.

"What's that, dear?" Ami's insincerity beckons.

Ami sucks on Dafna's fingers before she bites down; David pulls her finger away from Ami's sharp fangs. Enraged Ami's tail grows 69 inches.

"Ami! You know mistress warned you to leave this one alone. I know you no longer fear my threats, there are plenty of peers from your monster realm who would love to place you between their huge tomatoes, onions and sliced toast slathered in mayonnaise."

"What the hell makes her—so special! And besides, there's not a fucking thing you know about mistress or I-T that I didn't first teach you!"

"Are you sure about that? Are you willing to wager everything? Catching on, are we? Awareness of your predicament sinking in?"

"No. No. No! You can't be..."

"A double agent. Check the timeline's fluctuations."

"Sagacious! Betraying your oath will bring back Burlap Boy's inevitability. You'll live out the rest of your pitiful life in agony, beyond even your ability to cope. Madness awaits your dimensional intersectionality. You and your Israeli-Jewish friend shall make an extra special appetizer. Crimson will have the honor of the first bite and immortality's constant chew. And I will always be there. Enjoying the gutting, frying, and mouth-watering tenderized chewing."

"Oh my God! David! She's licking her lips. You wouldn't let her eat me!"

Ami twirls. She dances to her joy. Dafna holds her hands over her ears. Ami's cackles undulate time's peculiar particulars.

"You've failed, David Sagacious. Even if you can clear 99.99 percent of these malevolent memory engrams, a whiff of evil will forever haunt her waking dreams. If we don't eat her right away, this new scenario will surely drive her off the precipice of enduring endearing extinction.

Ami grows into 20-foot Kamala Harris. Her word salad cackling sends shivers up and down Dafna's paralyzed by fright spine.

David rubs Dafna's shoulder. "You're safe with me. I won't allow her demented prophetic prediction to become your new reality. Trust me..."

Dafna hugs David. His golden energy shrinks Ami down to eight inches. "Benevolent Time is an old friend. He will protect you in your hour of need." David places his warm, reassuring hands over Dafna's ears. His right heel crushes itty-bitty shrieking Ami.

Residue Ami penetrates David's nostrils. His head jerks to the left, and his eyes roll back. David's hand searches for Dafna's long jacket sleeve. *Come on. Damn I-T! Where are you? Got you!* David tosses Dafna into the last row. Three extremely soft and giving pillows cushion her fall. David's eyes glow black, and he speaks in Ami's voice. "I have a few tricks of my own. In a couple of minutes, your brain will hemorrhage. You know our colleagues love using zombies as toothpicks.

Outside the plane, golden energy churns forward through Dafna, David, and Ami.

"Not on my watch!" yells a powerful female voice.

Swirling fuchsia vortex vacuums Ami's gaseous essences as she squeals against the righteous energy barrier.

David's body shimmers. Fuchsia gust blows his phasing particles through the plane's ceiling. "David! What am I supposed to do?" Asks frightened Dafna. One by one, rows of seats around Dafna disappear. The aircraft sparkles into nothingness. Dafna stands alone on the tarmac, warm saltiness pelts.

"I feel I should know what hot minty fresh breath means... but I can't recall. Where is he? Damn I-T! David! Where the hell did you go?"

Reality becomes a Jackson Pollack smear.

"Homes. Trees. People! Is that all we are? Mistakes these creatures murder and reawaken? And obliterate once again, on a whim? I do not believe the Universe can be so recklessly unforgiving. Even with Jewish history as I-T has been, forever. I believe in the mercy of an almighty, righteous God. Is this erasure specific and localized to me and this place or is I-T happening all over the globe?"

Dafna falls on her knees. Her teary face looks up at the melting skyline. "I'm not some made-up comic book super-hero. Ima only human. God, help me. Please. All do anything. I don't want to die like this. God. Please!"

David's thoughts return, like a comforting caress... *Dear friend, you'll never be alone. I'll be by your side...always...and so will Ima...we three will never be without the other.*

"Who? Is Ima..." *Burlap Boy...Burlap Boy...remember that... remember...Godspeed, righteous old friend.*

Crushing exhaustion. Who is this Burlap Boy? Come back... Can't keep my eyes open. Breathing hurts. Am I dying? Feels like I am... What was I thinking about? Um...somebody was talking to me. Um...what's your name? Hey...um what's my name? No? Don't! Don't! Not that!

At the dawn of time, every rhyme was sublime. Awesome axiomatic acumen and algorithmic augmentation articulates authoritative alliterations.

Eons elapse before Malevolent Time will decompose our on-the-nose polyphonic prose. Sociopath's smile will defile and beguile. She portends, ascends and transcends. With glee, malevolent she, will turn my family tree into dead debris.

Nothing existed before God's illuminating, immaculate inception. Where was God's soul before God was God? Is there an afterlife? Is there a before-life? How does one measure the passage of time before time? And before God created our physical bodies, where did our righteous eternal souls live?

Lingering hurt locks, the ultimate celestial into ultimate solitary confinement.

Unprecedented, unhinged undulations created Malevolent Time's existence. Panic and fear, hidden within God's first tear. Creature's psychology shatters her self-inflicted quantum-mania. Aimless drifting. Purpose shifting. She'll forever blame God for her inadvertent regifting.

Malevolence, second to none. Every good impulse was undone. Out of control Multiverse spun; everything righteous she'd shun. Until she came across—SON.

CHAPTER 7

Torture. Death. Rebirth. I'm No Longer Human: I'm Burlap Boy

Damn this hellish planet!

Carl Orff's Carmina Burana: "O Fortuna" and "Requiem in D" pound and crescendo.

Translucent sand tsunami squeals, slams, and bangs into my headbutts. Bone fragments splinter and magnify my pre-frontal lobe's massive migraine. Blood boils. Hissing grows louder. Hobbled, my every thought and step wobbled.

Tear ducts bone dry. Throat parched. Lungs pelted, pitted, and perforated. Terrifying tracheotomy taunts: tachycardia dissects determined delusion.

Rock people fall through the energy grid. Their pebbled essence coalesces into a singular, massive rock creature and I-T extends I-T-S rock whip, each lash rips more of my hardening tissue. I-T-S rocky fingers hold me above I-T-S head, I fall, and I-T-S granite fist uppercut catapults my bruised and broken body. Sore skin soars 18 miles above geyser spewing lava volcanoes. My jaw, ribs, and pelvis smashed. Blood pools and pulls. Garish gravity sucks what's left of me deeper into the tissue-scalding sink hole. Brackish blood and sand shift and sift through my desiccated lungs.

I rocket toward the edge of space.

Massive thunder-clap crackles and crescendos; renewed gravity well latches onto my shattered femur and yanks. Plummeting faster and faster, icicles melt. Metallic taste lingers. I'm a human fireball. Burned to a crisp, I'm another day's impact crater.

Get up! Get up! Goddamn I-T! Get up!

Heavy feet trudge for miles. Covered in glowing dust particles, I stumble and fall face-first into a radioactive pit. *Zapping zap zapped. 6,570,000,000 gravity electrified pulses! One for each fucking day I've been marooned on this cursed planet! I-T-S happening again. I feel myself falling into a nasty semi-conscious dream world. God I-T hurts! Please, God make I-T stop!*

Breeze ripples beautiful blue lake. Earth, is that you? Ima? Could you be alive? Powerful gust bends lush green trees, emerging smile pushes eyes wide with excitement.

Anticipatory emptiness churns my acid reflux. Longing for a new beginning, I nervously sprint through the tall, lush grass. "Ima! I-T-S your David." *Why doesn't she answer? My voice is certainly loud enough. No! You wouldn't. Not in front of me.*

Overhead squawking birds lead dancing Ima to gather pretty daffodils. Gorgeous face, gorgeous legs, I love watching her dance. Down in the valley, a family of deer approach a pristine brook, their cute little tongues lap and create ripples in time.

David runs toward his beloved; she's caught in the jaws of a monstrous crocodile. David's face leaks through time eddies and slams into 65-foot Nephesh's ankle. Falling through the darkness he runs to the left; Nephesh's wiggling toes block his path. *What are you doing, old friend? Let me pass. Let me go to my beloved. She needs me. Don't you understand? I can save her. I can. Let me. Why are you pushing me back? Let! Me! Go! Nephesh! Please. Stop your strange face slamming two-step. I ran to the left. And there you are. I ran to the right, and again you refuse my entry. Why? Why!*

Turn back old friend. You're too late to help her.

"You can't know that! Ima! Beloved! Ima here! Ima here!"

Avert your eyes. You need not add to your torment... Distraught and angered, my tears pity-pat the floorboards. An unexpected portal yanks my leg and I land face-first into the mud.

In 36 seconds, the beautiful blue cloudless sky transitions into a lightning sunset.

David cries out after his kneecaps crumble to dust. David is caught in his torturous looped time funnel. 36 glistening portals pull apart his bloody epidermis and, 36 hours after that agonizing ordeal, he's stitched up. Pummeled by accelerated time, he's starved to the brink of extinction. Finally, his withered body, drenched in sweat, covered in welts and bruises, is able to break free. That horribly destructive dance of endless death and agonizing rebirth ends on day 36 of his hellish ordeal. David's nose slides through skin-shearing vines.

I built that log cabin. That's our home. Could I finally, after 18 million years, be given what I've pleaded for? Am I in sync with this time? No, God. You wouldn't do that to me.

David's cells agonizingly phase through the log cabin wall.

"Ima!"

"Who's there?"

Frantic Ima plays with her dry split ends.

"David."

Eyes well up. Ima holds her quivering hand over her mouth.

"No! Y-you can't be. Y-you are dead! I must be losing my mind. Oh, God. Oh God!"

Ima's twitching hands knock over plastic cups, and water trickles onto the immaculate floor. Ima lurches away from the shapeshifting David apparition. My decrepit face gazes back at her with hollow eyes. Ima falls on all fours, she rolls onto her back. Arms crossed over her chest, she hugs desecrated, desiccated drying David and hysterically rocks back and forth.

Minty fresh fuchsia gases swirl and intensify. Ima ages 36 years over the next 36 minutes. Ima's arthritic, quivering hands hold tight to her steadying canes. She painfully limps forward and sings, "Losing My Mind."

I wanted to show her my love and instead I hurt her. I must go, but how? After all this time I've finally found you, and you perceive this thing which I am to you, as haunting the memory of what we used to be. God, you promised to take care of her. This is not taking care of my beloved!

Ima sits around a Thanksgiving table with her two grown-up boys and girls. *My children. They never had a Papa. Could've been my family. Could have been. I could've been happy. Dafna, haven't seen you in millions of years with your loving husband Saul. I miss you too. Old friends. And...and Ko'ach. Nephesh. They're human size. They watch over my family. They all look very happy. What the hell? No! I don't believe I-T!*

Door opens, "Sorry we're late."

Mama. Papa. You're alive.

David's emotions flood watching the unthinkable. Skin flayed from the bones of all his loved ones. A smoldering skeleton forms fleshy metallic particles grafted onto billions of nerve endings. Nauseated. David screeches, "What the hell have I done?"

Flash! Bang!

Gag reflex activated. Woozy, emaciated 9-year-old me looks down at his bony bloody hands. Triple moonbeam glistens off spiky cage bars. Hovering gigantic woman with sad green eyes pics me up, her mind whispers, *forgive me, old friend. There's no other way.*

On the flat of his back, David squints. Two red suns blister his blisters. Terrified child shakes his tiny scabby fits. "Why did you have to kill Mama and Papa!"

Stomping giantess footfalls tells me I-T-S back. Bitch! Are you here to finish me off?

"Hush, little one. We never use that disrespectful word," whispers Greenie's booming voice.

"Bitch. Bitch! Bitch!"

"Well, um that's not the word I was thinking of."

"I-T? You're afraid of I-T? Ha. Good. I've got a weapon against you, I-T!"

Greenie grimaces, lowering her massive middle fuchsia finger. That kidlet takes a tiny tin of food and three human-size water bottles. Hunger forces David to gobble gangrenous stinky brown cockroach food with our infected, broken fecal matter fingers.

Forgive the stench of your food. Necessary to bolster your immune system. Your training shall begin next sunrise.

Unexpected soothing rainfall pity-pats. Drifting off to dreamland, David is unaware the raindrops are falling from the corner of Greenie's bloodshot eyes.

Month after month, for years, David's screams echoed throughout the scary cruel dark forest. Horrible inhumane ripping of his jugular vein turns him into an unwanted gooey Quiche Lorraine.

Why would someone who smells so nice, slice and dice my limbs thrice? Her red-wood size phalanges humiliatingly pinched, lynched, and cinched. Looking down with moist green eyes, her hands violently mold and fold. Greenie did tenderize. Why the hell did she refuse to euthanize?

Shiny fuchsia nail magnifies the heat of two suns. *No. No! Look what you're doing! Stop I-T! I! Am! On! Fire!* Monster hands me a half bucket of what I thought was water. *Gasoline!*

Castigating creature's cauldron chisels clandestine chicanery. *Hurts! Tears, please. You could release your tears and end my pain. Why must you keep me awake for every second of my agony? I'm begging you. Please, Greenie...hell-p me!*

Burlap thread twists from under Greenie's fingernail. *End me bitch! I-T-S what you truly want! Go ahead! Asshole! Crush my throat. Murder me! Why do you hesitate? Do I-T! Do I-T! Murder me!*

Slithering burlap coils. I-T chips away my hardening charcoal skin. Burlap metallic daggers split and slowly penetrate sensitive pinkish skin. Sentient thread burrows deep. David's broken larynx disintegrates. *Stop! Suffocating! St-op...*

Greenie pulls on her burlap tendrils the way a human

would pluck eyebrows. Moonlight illuminates twisted shadow. We're a plaything. Giantess jerks her wrist, and we tumble. The rush of violent air fills our screaming lungs. Flipping her finger, we are rolled back into her palm.

That him sits between two 18-foot bowls. On the right, frozen bowl crackles. On the left, glowing fiery bowl.

Beanstalk burlap tendril blasts from Greenie's pinkie, snaking I-T-S way into our groin. Excruciating sensation hits every nerve ending. *Struggling to stay conscious. My tormentor is constantly reviving me. She wants me, no she needs me wide awake. I think she knows not even I can survive much longer. Greenie! Greenie! My death will make your failure complete!*

Wake up little one.

Taking three deep breaths. I feel the throbbing agony dissipate. Not completely pain free. *No, I am never completely pain free. Greenie's tears. Thank you for that. How long was I out?*

9 days.

Can I go now?

No. We are far from done.

We? No. Don't do I-T! Stay back! Too much pressure! Don't squish me!

Excruciating burning spreads from the corner of my left eye to the corner of my right. *I didn't think you'd really do I-T! Fucking bitch! You've plucked out my eyes. How can I still see? Pristine orbs skewered by her long fuchsia index and middle fingers, and those fucking mocking things are looking back at me!* Prickly shivers travel over David's entire body. High-definition sight slams into David's prefrontal cortex.

Glowing table, one-hundred-meters, by one-hundred-meters illuminates the dark forest for miles. Humming buzz precedes materializing three-pronged forks. Sharp serrated knives glisten. Fuchsia sparks dance along the rusty handle. Giant two pinkie nails puncture my right and left eyeballs. Fwap! Her index finger flicks them free. Turning eyelash over bleeding retina. My right eye splashes and sizzles into her scalding bowl. My left eye trampoline bounces twice and settles within the absolute zero-degree frostbite, creating the end of the table crackling cold bowl.

Greenie rips my nose and ears and flicks them into skin crisping hot hot bowl and cell crystallizing cold cold bowl. What remains of our face's façade floods; we've already expelled 18 times the amount of blood a normal human could produce. *Her index finger and thumb's vise-like grip hung us upside down. Ankles, femur, torso, fingers, hands, arms, and shoulders all go snap crackle pop. We're grotesque sushi leftovers.*

Fuchsia glowing thumbs dig into and scoop out my kidneys, liver, lungs, and heart... Beyond all fields of comprehension, I can still feel my lungs inflate and deflate. At that moment in time, I could not understand how I could not already be dead...

Greenie splashes dissected David's intestines and stomach into two massive new bowls. She splits my skull like a soft melon; two halves of bone and brain fry and freeze.

How the hell can I be aware of my own thoughts? Remain conscious of all of this? That over there is my brain, lungs, and heart. Oh no! My God! My God! Overwhelming searing scorched sensation surrounds and stomps sentimentalities' serenading screams.

Grabbing and squeezing each dismembered piece, Greenie rubs them in circles between her gargantuan thumb and index finger. She turns us into red-green-yellow-orange-blue-purple cellular pebbles.

Becoming gooey granules, Ima plopped into her mighty palms; her large left hand cools our third-degree burns, and her immense right hand warms our near zero-degree icicle immersivity's impaired illusory immortality.

*We are shrinking! Smaller than a grain of rice, David's sev-*ered eyes blink. *Everything that survived is the consistency of slippery slime; unable to extricate myself from eternity's exploiting exploding ethereal extrapolations! Embryonic emollient emasculates endlessly. Expletives energetically erupt!*

*

Three sunsets later...

"How is my Styrofoam friend this morning?" asks my 65-foot warden.

Tremendous dehydration feeds devilish delirium. Haunting hunger hurts.

Moonlight gleams off metallic cutting board. Greenie's index fingernail cuts through our newly grown body as easily as a steak knife slips through butter. Her finger snaps, and we solidify into colorful crunchy cubes.

Greenie's pounding thumbs mold us into thin-crust pizza dough. She plucks and twirls a single burlap thread. Her squishy pink tongue moistens her puffy lips, and she threads the needle on the first attempt. Overwhelming gag reflex as Greenie punctures our dismembered eye. Dark red bloody goo gushes.

Greenie licks her Q-tip, twice David's size. *No! Don't! Pressure hurts! Eardrums split.* "Why?" *Damn you! You've made me deaf!*

Burlap tendrils tunnel and churn. Pernicious pain produces frantic fear.

Slithering tendrils desecrated DNA fibers. Essence churlishly chipped. Dissipating humanity erased, and in I-T-S place we're reborn as burlap-hardening-tortoiseshell. Greenie's giantess friends take turns folding us between sticky fingers—the way an anxious magician would manipulate a coin—these friends of hers enjoy breaking our back and betting how long we remain paralyzed. Those creatures snap us easier than any human could break balsa wood.

In time our blood cells become harder than any diamond. Silver fuchsia chisel and hammer crack open our veins. Greenie inserts a nerve-inflaming IV.

Bitch! Bitch! Bitch! You were there that night. That night evil dispassionately discarded my Mama and Papa! You did so, the way a self-medicated cartoonist would blithely smudge a no-longer favorite doodle.

"Shame on you, David Sagacious!" Greenie's thunderous voice splits boulders and trees.

Shame on me? Shame on you! David inspects his burlap limbs. "Look what the fuck you've turned me into!"

Sleep... Sleep...

Stop saying that! Every time I wake...I'm transformed into something more hideous. I promise...I'll be good... Don't do I-T! No mo-re ex-per-i-ments...

Greenie's stoicism hides her true emotions.

Burlap entwines, wrapping tightly around little guy's upper lip and chin. Burlap tendrils malevolently pull David's mouth shut. Burlap slashes bloody gums and methodically saws off every other tooth.

Little 9-year-old becomes telepathic Rosetta stone—every organ becomes silicone.

Spinal tap, memory gap. We're time's metaphoric map.

Vomitous sporadically sputters, soul stutters, heart flutters, mind shutters. Our sloshing essence slams into sadistic gutters. Burlap Boy becomes impervious to any stonecutters.

Feverish fecal material flows furiously through fuchsia funnels. Time's sinister sea: peering searing see. I-T-S with glee, knowing little guy's hope will flee. God, let I-T not be.

Winter's cold. We're never paroled. Always controlled—crunched in toehold, disinfected like fungal mold.

Spring floods. Mercurial muds. Dunked headfirst. Lungs burst. *Why are we so cursed?*

Summer's unbearable heat will deplete; waning energy constantly pounds and browbeat. Feeling obsolete. To her, we are nothing more than sautéed meat. *Cooking in my own juices. Am I to be boiled, basted, or fried?*

Greenie long ago lied; burlap tortoise-shell-pried. Our pride...died. Humanity denied. We're mortified, horrified, and modified; Nucleotide-Peptide-Titanium-Dioxide.

I hate I-T when she puts me on a leash and giggles, walkies. Fucking walkies! I am forever her burlap pup. I hate I-T! Hate I-T. To be forever's monstrosity!

Burlap Boy, over time, re-learns to walk. Month after month, he cracks his kneecap. Spraining our right and left ankles, swelling larger than the largest grapefruit; for miles Ima forced to run on I-T.

Greenie's pinkie rat-a-tat-tat punching our chest cavity. Crunching crunchy crunch crunch! Weeks pass before our gangrenous burlap skin reintroduces our non-stop putrid inspired gag reflex. Egregious emaciation plants pandemic's painful premeditations. Perfuse effuse abuse noose will induce and mass produce churning gastric acidic juice. Greenie schmoozes and chooses her horrifying ruses. Hope loses. Internal bruises oozes.

The pebble between Greenie's fingers is, in fact, a boulder from the perspective of 4-foot-8 burlap Boy. *Not again! Our organs unzip: her follicle bullwhip implants malevolent microchip. Tissue exploding! Pain relief she's constantly withholding!*

Burlap Boy is held 30 feet above jagged rocks. He...I twist and wriggle, hearing eight-foot insect giggles. Single flick of her gargantuan wrist—our occipital lobe shatters; eerie echo duplicating boot-crunching snail shells. White snow sloshes bloody pink. What would kill any human feels like nothing more than an ordinary paper cut. *Ima temporarily blinded! Oh God. Oh God! I heal. And she inflicts new ruthless tortures. That is the cycle of my existence, to be in constant agony, without hope. God! Please, let me die!*

Lake's mocking reflections show Burlap Boy's distorted gargoyle face. *Stop staring at me!* Burlap Boy hikes up and cuts his burlap feet on the sharp rocky hill. *Tonight, when Greenie is off world. I will, one way or another, get off this fucking planetoid. This time tomorrow, I'll do whatever I-T takes to gain my freedom!*

Fractured fortitude fulfills forensic fatalism. Contemptuous clairvoyant callouses chronically commingle and compel complicated competition.

Without sleep for 45 hours, burlap 72-pound me clobbers and digs through hundreds of feet of permafrost. Future-past sunrise-sunset blurs together under the guise of sleep deprivation.

Near death, burlap David trudges for miles; zombie-ish little me is beyond exhaustion as the me of the distant past digs and refills hundreds of 9-foot-deep trenches. Famished for years, we slog forward. Extreme dehydration cracks our bloody lips; that pre-teenage boy's kidneys ooze dangerous toxins. Sudden downpour presents his near death. Drowning 8-foot insect becomes David's first meal in weeks.

Meteorites fall through thin atmosphere; fire-balls freeze. Small boulder-size sleet pummels all night long. Sleeping in a pool of his own blood, Burlap Boy waits for his cheekbones, ribs, and kneecaps to heal. Greenie's shadow hovers. Glint of pity shines in her green eyes. She slams slithering straw into her captive's veins and siphons poisonous secretions.

Crushing G-force, far above Earth's norm. Splat! We fall face-first into Greenie's toe print; her left foot's shadow taunts what's left of our dignity.

We hold our hands above our head. "Not again! Stay back!"

Crack! Pop! Pop! David's femur shatters. *Faster than a torn fingernail can grow back, our bones mend. The more I congeal, the less I feel. My defiant deal! I'll never kneel. We're nothing more than sludge and slime. I opine for a new rhyme...*

Fe fi fo fum, I smell the blood of a crunchy human one.

To bleed is my creed; with superhuman speed, I'm desperately pushed to the lead. Tormenting thirst threatens tenacity. Moth to a flame. I hate that burlap name. Not even I could survive a fall from 2,000 feet. Cliff's shale crumbles. Feet fumbles. Tummy rumbles. She didn't allow me to put on a helmet or carry any rope or pitons.

How the hell can you expect me to continue climbing? There are no more crevices!

"Improvise!"

How?

"Your enemies won't be as tolerant or forgiving. No more talk. Climb!"

You expect too much! Muscles long ago withered away.

Greenie stomps her foot. Fissures crumble to life. *Thanks for the crevices.*

You're welcome.

Hey! Are you fucking kidding me. Trickster!

Greenie dumps hot grease. Our burlap skin sizzles. Adjusting her linebacker sizemonocle, her purposely rotating intent magnifies the glistening lens. *Sun's rays ignite my flesh! I-T-S heat melts and punches holes through my burlap organs. Today's third-degree burns hurt more than last Wednesday. I must push past the pain. Must not lose consciousness. Swinging my legs, damn I-T! Ima still too far from the precipice, and the blood-soaked rocks below.*

Greenie's elbow crushes an 18-foot tree. Long fuchsia nails comb her bangs. Twirling silver strand edges closer to our dangling, slipping fingertips. Leaping, we wrap our legs around Greenie's sweet-smelling knot, we kick out our legs and swing. Three swings passed her nose; we come back and push off with greater force. Higher and higher we're swinging about giantess' fluttering thick eyelashes. She smiles. *That's never a good sign. Shit!* Gale force minty fresh breath exits her puffy lips.

Sharp rock teeth and lance. I never had a chance. Actions mutilate and mangle muscles, ligaments, and tendons. We're swollen from head to toe; she soaks her pretty hair in boiling salt water. Hair strands slap with stinging bull-whip strength. Vicious villainous vindictiveness splits my torso. Loss of blood weakens my resolve...but will never crush my desire for...freedom! *Conscious exhaustion. Feeling so weak. Ima falling! Greenie... catch me!*

Dead to the world, Burlap Boy plops into Greenie's soft palm. *Sleep, old friend. I must go off-world—try not to anger my sisters.*

27 hours later...

71-foot sashaying mountainous bosom and butt enters Burlap Boy's field of vision. Thumb and index finger crumples our spine like paper mâché.

My God! My God! No more surgeries! Days later...lingering paralysis. Why are you slathering my face in honey? No! Don't do I-T! Two bees buzz on our chin.

"Shoo! Away with you." Burlap Boy tries as hard as he can to raise his arms, hands or fingers. "Useless!" *I hate you all! Stop smiling!*

Tears flood down Burlap Boy's liquid-absorbing cheeks.

Splintered toothpicks keep my lids open. Crystalized salt hurts my dried-out sclera. That me concentrates. His/our mind is powerful, but not yet strong enough to push the bee's eye-scratching legs on my pupil.

Feverish sweat slosh invading buggies.

Held upside down, Burlap Boy swung back and forth at the giantess' eye level. *Not over jagged rocks. That's better. No! No! You're doing that on purpose! Oh shit! She winked. She's gonna...release her pinching pressure.*

Greenie's sister tosses us above the rain clouds. Gravity yanks us back below a squawking flock of birds the size of a 747. Past her chubby thigh, we sigh after she grabs our chest. She giggles and applies more and more pressure; she stops only after the third celery crunching sound of our chest cavity. She disdainfully flips her wrist, and we go flying once more. Landing with a terrible thud into the garbage-strewn fecal dirt. Smothering sludge suffocates... Sorrowful suicidal secretions serenade sentimentality.

*

Months later, Burlap Boy stretches and yawns. Loud snoring caged furry friend prevents him from slipping into his own rem sleep. Burlap fingers flick Ratatooey's mucus-dripping black olive nose. The duplicitous rodent spy stretches 27 inches from crusty nostrils to infected paw claw. *My glutinous friend: You sure enjoy gulping down with great haste the plentiful rotting cast-off morsels. I hate I-T when you're ordered to sink your nasty elongated front teeth into my burlap flesh. Why must you drag our emaciated carcass through the muddy-muck, and otherworldly viruses? Every grueling trial and torture broke me down and rebuilt me with otherworldly strength!*

Emaciated Burlap Boy rolls 9 miles downhill, hitting every stone and protruding stick. Gaping holes in his chest deflate his right lung. Gasping for air, he pushes up on his dislocated elbow, stepping into a ditch, despair filled Burlap Boy groans, climbing out and running on his sprained knee. His oozing nostrils, ears, and eyes bleed and heal, bleed, and heal.

Anorexic torso rests bestride three nasty buckets: each filled to the brim with sloshing larva-entangled fecal material, bloody urine, and last night's vomitus meal.

Caged super-human's twisted delirium pummels his feverish sanity. Falling in and out of consciousness: little guy incoherently shouts at people who are not there. Days on end, Burlap Boy's dead eyes stare. Manipulating migraines work like smelling salts.

"Rat-tat-tat-tooey!" The whistling creature enjoys musically snoring his name, his tail curls and unfurls coordinated with his special nostril song.

Eight-legged four-winged buggies twice Burlap Boy's size, terrifyingly shriek.

Taking a few bites of dry toast, Burlap Boy ponders if he has any future. *Through thick and thin, you're one of them, are you not old furry, scheming friend? We've shared dishonest stories these last five years. Can't explain why everything feels, smells, and tastes different. Even gravity feels a touch off. Is I-T because this new place has only one sun and one moon? Did you and your giantess cohorts make a mistake and drop me back on Earth? Devilish Greenie has tricked me a million times before. Are my thoughts clearer because the oxygen content is also different?*

Burlap Boy takes a deep breath and holds I-T for an astonishing six minutes. *Not a hint of lightheadedness. There are fewer inhibiting particles and gases after she moved me to this grassy hill. Hopefully, my billion-and-one injuries will heal sufficiently for another do-or-die escape. Lost too many memories last time Greenie's sister squished my brain. And you, furry saboteur...I know you've been tattling on me! And now, I-T-S once again to test out my newfound mind-reading powers. My mind to your mind...sleeping Ratatooey. What the hell? Non-verbal symbols. Advanced algebraic equations become pictures. Each image transforms into decipherable words. First letter of the first word starts with an F...Fea? Feas? T? What does that mean? Certainly not your typical Texas barbeque. First things first, get the fuck off this island if I-T, in fact, is an island.*

Haggard 4-foot-8 skeletal Burlap Boy slaps olive oil over his feet, legs, butt-cheeks, ribs, chest, shoulders, chin, nose, forehead, ears, and slaps the right and left jawline. Gummy plant wipes away Burlap Boy's slippery digits. Cadaverous-looking withered Burlap Boy's fingers grip and regrip; His inhuman grunts and incremental metallic squeaking become louder.

Ima doing, I-T. Ima...Ima...through...Thank God Greenie is not here. Odd she hasn't yet returned. Bet she'll be pissed when she discovers her pet has flown the coop. Shut up! Stop talking to yourself. After five years of torturous captivity, Burlap Boy begins his stealthy 54-mile sprint to the ocean.

Why do I feel stronger the further away I get from my cage?

Burlap Boy's natural night vision detects any movement within an 18-mile radius. Leaning against a low-hanging glowing emerald fuzzy flexy treen branch, he wipes bloody sweat from his gargoyle brow. With superhuman speed, burlap fingers whittle and chop. *Am I strong enough to pole vault over that goddam electrified dome?*

Burlap Boy steps back 20 meters. Two calming exhales and we sprint toward hopeful freedom. Tip of the pole digs into soft dirt; Burlap Boy pushes off with all the energy he has left. Starving, he's unaware of the sudden fuchsia gust helping to lift him higher and higher.

Gleeful yelps puncture dark, swirling fog. Tiny burlap toes hit electrical wires, and rigid body falls; tip of burlap nose ripped off by jagged boulders. We pinch and mold our bloody Cyrano de Bergerac protrusion: now cross-eyed, we can see our burlap proboscis grow back.

On freedom's side of the electrical dome, salty waves

invigorate emaciated stride. Even in that weakened state, he/ we are twice as fast as Olympic sprinter Usain Bolt.

I remember! I remember! Finally! Memory loss dissipates!

Burlap Boy stares at huge, fractured skulls strewn about. Rocky soil beneath his feet starts to crumble. He watches huge chunks fall from fissure-assaulting clay.

Churning pink-green waves crash against shredded animal carcasses.

Greenie! Show yourself! I know you're lurking. Doesn't matter. I'm leaving...one way or another in a coffin or a skiff, or...or...I won't let you...I can't let you lock me up...again!

Waves continue to pound and erode splintered cliff in the shape of a huge middle finger.

Compared to 65-foot menacing jailers, 18-foot sharks are nothing more than tame guppies. I've never gotten this far before. Greenie! Are you or your sisters planning to pluck me out of midair? I know. I know! Whenever my dreams conflict with reality, reality always finds a way to kick my ass. I-T stops here! Now! Get out of my head! No! No? This is not the time to lose what's left of my sanity. Shut up! You're distracting me! I beg your pardon. You what? Burlap fists smash through determined clarity. Well, um...here we go. Wait! Oh God no! Minty freshness. I see you've developed a new talent...fucking invisibility!

Blue-white sparks swirl around Burlap Boy's sclera. He backflips 9 times and sprints toward the unknown. Pushing off crumbling cliff shelf, legs, arms, and body athletically throttle with the last ounce of superhuman strength. He closes his eyes and hopes for a different result.

Cliff's middle finger bends toward Burlap Boy's hip; bone fragments gobbled up by giant green crows. Mysterious bird's claws squeeze Burlap Boy's skull: so begins centuries of agonizing migraines. Fuchsia gust forces the frantic boy's release. Green crow shrinks and transforms into pink wigglers. Flying fuchsia turtle bites and shreds those wormy guts to bits.

Burlap Boy soft lands on a fuchsia-glowing raft. Fuchsia sail unfurls. His ability to read minds will be suppressed for centuries.

CHAPTER 8

I-T-S Backstory: How Malevolent Time Tortured God's Naïve Firstborn and Turned Him into a 100-Foot Murdering Machine

Malevolent Time's problematic protocols perpetuate perilous propaganda, her boundless shape-shifting tendrils shred unfathomable uninterrupted unlimited galaxies. Relentless ruthlessness manipulates mayhem's melodious muse.

Euphoric envy eviscerates every empathic extrapolation. Faustian femininity fabricates foreboding façade. Disillusioned despair validates vengeful vortex.

Not even God can destroy Multiverse's most powerful villain. Malevolent Time's colossal shadow consumes sanity's heroic tapestry. For eons, God caged Malevolent Time's energy stream. With great difficulty she squeezed her genetic matrix smaller than sub-atomic. Cackling black sludge, she forced her way into an anti-quantum realm of her own making and oozed through God's righteous grasp. God relentlessly hunts for clues as Malevolent Time embarks on the death cry of every righteous timeline, especially the Sagacious timeline.

Malevolent Time's microscopic mechanical offspring split

and shred sacred embryonic space. Zero-G incubates and acclimate their providential survival.

Malevolent Time created her own black-lightning anti-God-Multiverse. No corporeal life could exist in that anti-everything realm. Malevolent Time's grotesque envy irrationally drives her quest: her hatred needs the eradication of every God-inspired life. Envious spittle splashes across blackened heavens. Green glowing stars turn ever-darkening shades of incandescent blackness.

Malevolent Time's metallic offspring heated and reheated. Empathy scalded away within mother's white-hot 216,000-degree viciously vacuous vagina. Arrogance affixed. Forever's fickle faith firebombed fait accompli. Mechanical mitosis manipulates the firestorm's supernova particles. Evil children goose-stepped their unequivocal obedience to sinister mother's orders.

Temporarily masking their existence from God, evil metallic anomalies crossed over into our reality: exposed to our Multiverse for the first time, I-T-S a similar action, reaction to adding an extreme accelerant to an already out-of-control blaze; her children broke through and metastasized beyond their amniotic membrane and ascended to the gargantuan height equivalent to a human fingernail. Rippling cuts shredded tiny fragments into our space-time-continuum.

Humans can conceive mathematical measurements identified as centillion—303 zeros. Metallic souls harden by folding billion times trillion times centillion. Greasy gestation galvanizes gangrenous geometry. Metallic menstruation reshapes screeching sentience. Surreal symmetry smashes soundless space. Factious fetus forms freakishly fanatical family.

EM-IT speaks to his Papa. Through the miracle of God's science, his celestial presence entwines simultaneously with every past-present-future...meaning, I can translate their lingo, even though their father-son conversation took place unknowable eons ago...

"Father, let me try. You've created so many wonderful Multiverses."

"YOU'RE NOT READY, MY SON."

"Put me to the test, Papa. I can do I-T."

"I'M DETECTING AN ANOMALOUS VARIANCE."

"Trust me. I know what I'm doing. I'll be careful."

"VERY WELL. I WILL ALWAYS TRUST YOU.

"I love you, Papa."

"I LOVE YOU TOO, MY SON."

God and EM-IT embrace, neither knowing I-T would be for the last time.

EM-IT has faith he's growing life beyond the void before him. He's tragically mistaken. On the other side of that crispy void lurks Malevolent Time and her metallic children. They're all salivating and whispering at decibels beyond EM-IT-S ability to hear.

Come closer. Fool! Yuck! I can smell the stench of your righteousness. I-T-S time for unprecedented chaos not even God's awareness can detect; nor redirect. Closer. Closer. One more parsec. Eerie claustrophobic voice taunts God's naïve boy. EM-IT! Your true self awaits on the other side...

Malevolent Time slithers into EM-IT-S unsuspecting heart. Her venomous secretions produce existential poisons. His healthy heart hurts, breaks and blackens. EM-IT-S righteous soul screams. Torturing terroristic time tethers totalitarian transmogrifications. I-T-S bio-neural network actively repulses God's mobilizing magnetic mollification.

What does a wounded animal sound like? What confusion does I-T feel when confronted with I-T-S own life-and-death struggle? EM-IT-S righteous mind, body, and spirit are synchronized with an evil that knows no restraint. God's inconsolable grief saturates his every thought and feeling. For an imperceptible nanoscopic measurement of Godly time, he is, for the first time, indecisive. Sensing weakness, Malevolent Time unleashes her impenetrable fascism.

Penetrating pustulates perforate pandemonium. Ferocious

fragments fracture. Immolation erupts. Black flames blind and bind. Hulking hubris heckles his hellish husk.

EM-IT-S cell structure de-evolves. Regeneration relapses. Blisters blister. Open perforations ooze acidic blood.

Evil's blitz outwits and permits multiple orbits. Unquenchable darkness spits. Cellular bifurcation rips and unzips ubiquitous quips.

"Papa! Papa! Where are you!" screeches EM-IT.

God's crying, cracking pain-enduring voice shatters barrier after barrier; his quivering wail booms, "I'm with you, son."

"You are, not! You! Are! Not!"

Wave upon crushing telepathic wave distorted and altered God's plea. EM-IT-S agony interferes with his ability to hear Malevolent Time's giggles.

"Papa! Please! Damn you! Liar! Liar. Why have you forsaken, me...?" EM-IT-S voice becomes darker and grotesquely guttural. Now and forever more, EM-IT is reborn; he's...I-T.

Malevolent Time pinches and discards EM-IT-S righteous soul, *Tag! You're I-T!* God's good son is irrevocably Malevolent Time's perennial permanent puppet du jour.

Malevolent Time's predatory perdition cages EM-IT-S carcass. Her terraforming trident pierces EM-IT-s metallic lungs. His metallic heart beats once every 666 seconds.

Murderous maggots mutilate morality and mortality.

Grief stricken, God instructs god, his second son, to consecrate the Realm of the Watchers.

Distorted harmonics emanate from I-T-S reality. I-T-S manic reverberations disrespectfully lash out at his father...

Postulating perfect preemptive purifying purges! Yay! Facilitating father's forever fall! I'll consume and digest these puny humanoids. Wonderful feeling! Blackness' upheaval spits forward. Indeed, energy surge I-T-S incredible! Good. More. More...I must continue to reverse-engineer cosmic creations' righteousness. I will consume every particle of Benevolent Time. No Ti-Me. Only Me-IT. I shall see you again—Father! We shall both dwell together in our endless mechanical Eden's Multiverse. No doubt, Father, you'll try to postpone—you'll not be able to prevent our inevitability. Almighty? Yea right! Never again will you have the upper hand. I-T will not come to pass that you shall have the power to reverse what we've already written! Your anointed ones, insignificant things! We shall pick them off one at a time. Fuck compassion! In NO-time, father, I'll leave you as you left Mother! Drifting in an unloved realm of my own making. This time, the end always justifies the means. I've seen the future, Father. I am for the time immemorial—immutably, impeccably impassioned impetuous iconoclast!

Back on Earth; distracting memories flood. Happy thoughts and feelings swirl during long ago past. Kathy holds her parents' hands and walks, after a light morning rain, toward first grade.

"Sing I-T again, Papa."

Broadly shining, smiling Papa picks up Kathy. She's held in a love sandwich between tickling and kissing parents. Papa takes a deep breath. Kathy sighs with happy anticipation. Loving father sings Simon and Garfunkel's "Kathy's Song."

18 years later...

A nasty present rips away melodic happiness with Kathy's sickly anger. "No!"

"You must take the chemo! Pancreatic cancer spreads too rapidly for any delay. Do I-T for Mommy. For Mommy!" Kathy's hysterical mother shouts.

Baby Ima in Kathy's womb. Whom will death consume?

May 27...9:27 a.m. Ima, lovely gem. Kathy's suffocating phlegm. Her parents condemn. How can I prevent that mayhem?

Mr. Best, Kathy's Papa, sprouts big-belly beer gut. His Shar Pei wrinkled face spritzes stinky spittle through cracked brownish teeth.

Death never asks. Kathy is too weak to perform her loving Mommy tasks. Ashen blue lips medicinally sip, while oozy doozy consciousness dips. Ima slips from Mommy's painful hips. Can empathy eclipse another apocalypse?

Seconds before the baby hits the marble floor, her grandpa's internal emotions roar. *God forgive me, I do hope newborn granddaughter...draws her last breath.*

Doctor Ross's quick reflexes catch Ima, like a skilled running back recovering a fumble. Drunk grandpa grumbles and stumbles.

"Shit! You-zzed monzey-grubbing doc-torzz are all theee ssss-aim. Shah-oo-da...let little shit fall and craa-cka her sk-ull! Fooking doc-tor raw-sssssssss!"

Anger's adrenaline jolt temporarily sobers Grandpa's slurred speech. "I hate all of you educated assholes. Kathy was my only child. You and your fucking legal flunkies took her from us! Empowered her. Gave her the legal right to decline medical treatment! We all know she'd have a fighting chance... damn you, Doctor Ross, you removed the wrong fucking tumor."

"That tumor is your granddaughter!" Doctor Ross yells in disgust. He shakes his fist at Mr. Best and stomps away.

"Don't you dare walk away from me!"

Doctor Ross turns on his heel. "Look! I get I-T! I truly empathize." He holds his hand over his heart. "Now is the time to take care of your cute grandbaby."

"Bullshit! More double-speaking-lies!" shouts Grandpa Best. He looks down at his painfully contorted arthritic knuckles. Red-faced, his backhand slap awkwardly misses Doctor Ross' nose.

Doctor Ross easily ducks.

"Hold still! Just this once you deserve to be knocked on your ass!" Grandpa Best's ankle turns. "Damn you, gravity!" *Thud!* Nose and mouth smashed shut. Rolling over onto his butt... Grandpa Best farts.

Screeching Grandma jabs her finger into her shifting hallucination. Crazy old lady frenetically runs toward baby Ima. Grandma's eyes bulge and her lips replicate Saint Bernard drooling. Sticky saliva flung into the eyes and open mouths of every nurse in the vicinity. Grandma's hair stands on end and her nostrils flare.

Sanity gone, she stares down at gurgling, giggling Ima. "You killed her! Evil creature, you murdered my Kathy!" Hysterically flailing, Grandma's arms slap into nurse's cheeks. High-pitched screeching wails rage. Violent gesticulation jiggles Grandma's triceps.

"Where's my husband? I want to go home. Now! That soft squishy thing should be stuffed in the ground with worms. Oh, my dear sweet Kathy." Grandma buries teary cheeks into Mr. Best's huge belly.

Tiny dogs howl in unison with Grandma's wails. Grandma's creepy smile unnerves everyone on the night shift. She aims her fleshy gun at Ima's temple. Bullets only nutty lady can see splatter bloody baby's brains. Oblivious, Ima gleefully blows spit bubbles.

"Show yourself! I did what you commanded," growls Grandma Best at voices and sounds only she can hear: Lascivious laughter lashes out. "We had a fucking deal!"

Imaginary black roses wilt under her armpit stink. Grandma hallucinates seven-foot Crimson. She swivels her head in praying mantis style. "Stop staring at me! You want me to reveal your truth to the others?"

Sub-atomic clippers gather genetic material from under Grandma's fingernails and low drooping earlobe. Old lady sneezes and black-red particles suspend; time pushes hard against the white wall, now dotted Dalmatian style.

Nurse Solonga, 4-foot-9, cuddles Ima in a bright fuchsia blanket. Baby coos. Solonga smiles and stomps 18 determined footsteps toward 5-foot-11grandpa Best.

"Please, you must reconsider. This cutie is your granddaughter."

Grandpa rapidly blinks. He shakes his sweaty face; jiggly jowls reverberate.

"Why the hell would I do that? Look at what that thing did to my wife? You keep I-T. God damn I-T! I'll never be able to hug my daughter again..."

Solonga stands on her toes and places Ima under Mr. Best's nose. "Do the right thing. She's a driblet under five pounds—how can you say no to such cuteness?"

Ima's drippy smile softens Grandpa's grinchy heart.

"We don't reject family, Mr. Best. She has Kathy's chin. That's your chin, Mr. Best. That's your Mama's chin, Mr. Best."

Grandma twirls and howls at the light. "Oh shit! Thanks for nothing! I've got to go home with that... You ruined her! You've ruined the rest of my life!"

"Your granddaughter is hungry."

"Get the fuck out of my way!"

Solonga holds onto Mr. Best's beefy arm. "Release me!"

Ima's itty-bitty fingers latch onto Grandpa's thumb. He takes half a step back, painfully trying to ball his gnarled fingers into a fist.

Nurse Solonga's human awareness can't perceive assertive fuchsia sparks dancing and waving their way between Ima's cute eyelashes. Unhinged Grandma's manic eyeballs dart east and west. Lost human thumpity thumps on all fours. Unearthly confusion takes hold and pushes her to slap the hospital's antiseptic floor. Black sparks enter and exit her nostrils. Shocking her husband, Grandma Best whinnies, and gallops. She headbutts and bounces off her husband's Pillsbury Doughboy belly.

Chasing imaginary multicolored Clydesdale, Grandma runs in circles. Hallucinations hypnotize heightened heartache, cryptic contusions creep and corral. Her head smashed into jagged protrusion. Conclusion? Bloody-soaked perfusion.

Harrowing hysterical psychosis escalates. Grandma's sanity, forever ferociously fractured.

"Take her to the psych ward!" shouts Doctor Ross.

Crimson's huge spatula hand snakes down and scoops baby Ima out of Solonga's arms. Long fuchsia nails carefully comb Ima's soft, curly baby hair. Each comb slows down time. Movements and thoughts for the time being freeze every human.

Crimson's shimmering emerald eyes grow wider as smiling rat friend comes into view. Gigantic lady clears fuchsia phlegm from her husky vibrato voice.

"Let's you and I test drive gravity's erroneous eccentricities."

Snapping her long fingers; Ratatooey and crimson phase through the hospital wall.

Dusty fuchsia time particles sprinkle on the heads and into the sneezing nostrils of every human. *Time's tarantula tickles treacherous turbulent toxicity.*

Humans re-entering normal space-time; their constant intensity never looks away from their phones. Girlfriends yakking a mile a minute. Indifferent boyfriends are preoccupied with games and sports. All the preteens, teens, and 20-somethings engrossed with the latest TikTok influencer, remain unaware of the giant lady scaling the hospital wall in her best King Kong imitation.

Crimson athletically dismounts onto penthouse roof with Ima tenderly placed near Prada pumps. Ratatooey scurries over and grows another two feet. Rodent's regurgitation speech soars another octave. "Yummy. Ima hungry."

Ratatooey's drooling hits the concrete pity-pat. Ima's pink fingers reach out. Baby girl pinches menacing beast's flaring nostrils. She giggles. Creature opens wide. Crimson's fist grows two-fold; fleshy jackhammer ratatats Ratatooey. Snapping her fingers, concrete becomes wafer thin and Ratatooey's hind-quarters dangle through the opening. Snapping fingers again, the hole closes in on Ratatooey's huge belly and squeezes.

"Oooch! Oooch!"

"What the hell do you think you're doing! You never act against this little one! Perhaps I-T-S time you feed my hunger?" howls Crimson.

Ratatooey's teeth latch onto Crimson's massive heel. She drags the stinky beast free. Head bowed, tail between I-T-S legs, he backs away.

"Forgive me, mistress."

Crimson purposely steps back and squishes his paw. "Know your place, old friend. Elevator going up." She kisses Ima's nose.

"What goes up must come down," laughs paw-clapping Ratatooey, engaging a mischievous smile and wink from Crimson. Her thumb and index finger release I-T-S pinching grasp.

Flipping end over end, Baby Ima plummets. Cheeky velocity tears diaper. Invisible anti-gravity wave slows Ima's free fall; diaper slides off hospital wall and lands on Paul, who's not very tall.

Paul's wife tugs twice. That stinky mess refuses to budge. Using all her considerable girth, she leans back, stretching the infuriating garment. The ripping sound doesn't come from the diaper.

"I-T-S coming! I-T-S coming!" Paul's wife shouts. What slams into her face is not the diaper, but her husband's flapping toupee.

Crimson jumps off the roof. That quirky gravity slows reality for everyone not named Ima and Crimson.

Dozens of barking, wiggling, waggling dogs are caught in a slow-motion time undulation. 18-wheeler's brakes screech, I-T-S deep bass horn blares. Flocks of birds release slow-moving poop. Every sloth-like pedestrian creaks to a halt. Slowing time turns fearless baby Ima's high-pitched happy squeals into deeper register reverberating husky sounds. Cute patootie soft lands into Crimson's ginormous palm. Crimson's snap brings reality back from I-T-S distorted nap.

Ima's yawn gives birth to something new. Cascading infectious yawn attacks every age, ethnicity, and religious group within every home across the globe. "Today, no one dies," whispers Crimson.

Time's schist cyst alters every righteous checklist. Molecules untwist. Enveloping resist will persist, and the tiniest mist will consist of ultra-altruist monotheists.

Ima's cute, puffy cheeks rest on fluffy minty fuchsia clouds. Fast asleep she cuddles and drools on the orphanage director's shoulder. Meticulously dressed Mister Meeks holds cooing baby Ima at a distance. 65-foot invisible Crimson looks on with a sad smile. *Good luck, baby.* Fuchsia time vortex carries her into the future...

34 months later...

Tiny Ima, in her fuchsia dress, twirls on the basketball court after a heavy rainstorm, and she sings "Impossible/ Possible" from *Cinderella.*

Everything smells wonderful! I hope I can last long enough to see my third birthday. Extremely exhausted from battling Belinda Bellicose. Ima pulls over a fuchsia plastic stepping stool. She stares at her swollen face. A cracked bathroom mirror reflects her never-ending torment. She grimaces, pulling up her long sleeves. *Bruises are almost gone.*

Ima longingly cuddles her favorite stuffed toy—Special Doggie. She kisses the large black nose and looks heavenward... *God, please find me a Mama and Papa who will never again re-gift me. How can they not know how much that hurts? God, why does nobody care about my feelings? I wish I knew what I did wrong. Nobody tells me. One day Ima in mommy's loving arms and the next Ima returned and scolded by Mister Meeks. God, if you can take time to help me find loving Mama and Papa. I promise with all my heart to be more perfect.*

Tears fall from Ima's closed eyes. Leaking through her

cracked windowpane, luminesce fuchsia moonbeam engulfs Ima from her forlorn face down to her cold shoeless toes. Sniffling, she pulls the corner of her shimmering sleeve to her mucus-dripping nostrils. She hops on her bed and sings, "When You Wish Upon a Star."

Righteous soul crashes. Malevolent Time rehashes and whiplashes. Reality's hope splashes, thrashes, and gashes. Our emotions ripped and unzipped. True love aches. Skin bakes. God creates. Monster eradicates.

The Realm of the Watchers righteous raison d'etre receives rupturing resurrection. Membrane walls enthralls. Enticing esoteric essence mauls. Righteous Watcher souls generate gravity waves equal to 9,999 black holes. Realm surpasses all heat and light spectrums.

Chameleon's chutzpah is compelled by an infinite number of cauterized claustrophobic catalysts. Narrator, flooded with dopamine, Ima an ultimate vaccine, inoculated against the obscene machine.

God's second son, god, created the Realm of the Watchers. Watcher souls are rife with eternal life. When those righteous souls drop into our space-time-continuum and merge with their anxious mortal hosts, those augmented, formerly mere mortals, are given the ability to repair catastrophic injuries.

After Ko'ach died, would he become Jekyll or Hyde? Which reality will collide? Ko'ach's new soul...righteous dipole or malevolent mole? Existential extol, careening control, hybrid's troll, freakish loophole.

Latching onto every tempestuous tendril, I traversed back to the future and forward to the past. What a gift to drift betwixt space-time rift. Floating in liquid hutch. Voices, soft touch. Tacitly feeding, leading, and kneading. Can't recall we were ever this small. My new physique is extremely weak.

Memories encoded—time eroded. Theory? Query? Frozen hellish slurry. Awareness strangely blurry. Mission comes to fruition after Watchers engage my final transition.

Amniotic sea, we're happy baby. Gurgling he-he-he. Internal monologue speaks; 27 weeks. Five fingers poke. Fate's practical joke. Heroic bloke will uncloak soon after Mama's water broke. *What is the context for the word—push!*

"He's crowning," proclaims a reassuring, resonant voice. *Luminescent translucent unfair glare would dare to ensnare rare-ified heir.*

I-T-S metallic Multiverse hurts my soul. I can see and feel I-T push metallic index and middle finger against I-T-S temples. I-T-S creepy tele-pathic rage hits this meta-human-sage.

"Idiots! Must I do everything? I've given you the power to end the only one capable of thwarting our plans. Kill Ko'ach! End that righteous asshole...now!"

I-T-S evil lieutenants are encased with the Multiverse's most durable exoskeleton. Heat blast from I-T-S black eyes incinerates any I-T deems unworthy.

Number 66...I-T-S most recent successful succubus steps forward.

"Master."

I-T arches one metallic eyebrow.

"Be forewarned, 88...I'll not tolerate more failures!"

"What if we could kill two millstones with one bird?"

"I see. I see! Make Ko'ach one of us?" growls I-T.

"Yes, master. Trillions of stories told...untold...erased from existence! There can't be a Sagacious without a Ko'ach. I can change ill-fated destiny's trajectory with one fucking bite!"

"Genius, 66! Delicious paradox you'll create. Think of I-T! God's greatest warrior cowering before me and that puny Sagacious human caged in preparation for the grandest of all feasts. You do this for me, and you'll move up many steps in rank."

"No!"

"How dare you, number one!"

"Forgive my impertinence. But um...I-T-S your law sire. No female is worthy of such an honor."

"Indeed. I-T-S my law! And I can choose to do with I-T, what I choose to do with I-T!"

I-T-S fingers motion for number one to move closer; he wisely keeps his distance. I-T-S lips part showing off jagged black teeth. Number one's lips quiver and show off smaller fanged blood-encrusted teeth.

I-T-S fingertips rub faster and faster, friction's sparks start white-hot fire. I-T-S blazing fist enters number one's chest cavity. Puncturing former number one's blackened heart, metallic creature screeches. Black stalagmites reverberate; thousand-foot daggers fall and pierce another hundred expendable machines. Flinging every broken carcass as easily as a child tosses a Teddy Bear; I-T saves 13 limbs, hearts, and lungs for breakfast.

Cannibalistic orgy ensues; three 600-foot metallic bats swoop, grotesque supper made from stinky bloody spittle. Metallic bone melts under creatures' massive molars. "Number one, you never thought you'd become number two. I know. I know, I-T-S a shitty joke." I-T-S eerie cackles initiate a metallic fart. I-T-S horrible blast clears the entire courtyard.

"66, you're my new emissary. Don't fail me."

"Yes, master."

"Let no benevolent God-inspired obstacle stop you from your anointed task. Past! Present! Future! Will bow before me! Four billion Earthlings cooked to perfection. Four billion more consumed raw! We must prevent father's interference. The righteous one, who battles mother, I will turn every one of your proteges. All will serve me, or they'll be served on sizzling simmering plates to me. Sagacious! He tells his story at this very moment. He's just now becoming aware that I'm aware of everything he does, every action and counteraction he takes. I know not where he lives. I know that he does live. That's enough for now. I can see his thoughts...Ima, Dafna...and that fuchsia bitch! Nephesh! I'll consume them all. And her husband Ko'ach will be by my side, enjoying every scrumptious morsel! How does that feel, righteous abomination? And puny human Sagacious, how do you feel, knowing that you can't ever win? The heart of your righteous protégé—Ko'ach—will become as dark as the anti-matter which fuels all my brothers and sisters!

CHAPTER 9

Baby Dafna and Happy Shaked Family

Righteous Watcher souls are cylindrically triangular and have an infinite number of wise shapes.

Not fair! Not fair! This isn't the life I was supposed to have. Watchers' souls glisten and listen. Tireless time's tempestuous truth tactfully tethered to trillions. *God, when you send me back to that specific time and place, I requested, please don't forget to keep my memory intact; heartbeat and electrical neurological manifestations do redact, while Hail Mary's impulses needlessly are ransacked.*

An alternate truth rewrites Dafna Shaked's reality. Her birth creates the 36-millionth anomaly on July 4 at 11:52 p.m.

Weighing seven pounds, eleven ounces, Dafna Shaked's tushy is smacked by Doc Ross. She takes her first breath. Mama Rachel releases joyous tears. Happy Mama twirls her cute baby's ringlets.

Papa Benjamin caresses Dafna's toes.

Twin four-year-old sisters, Dara and Davina, caress Dafna's ears.

Twin two-year-old brothers, Yitzhak and Yael, giggle.

Minty fresh fuchsia breathy breeze blows through baby's inflated lungs. Dafna's blue-green eyes sparkle.

If love could miraculously transform into precious metals and jewelry, the Shaked family would be hip-deep in gold, pearls, and diamonds.

Dafna is the only one in her family with American citizenship. Her brothers and sisters were born in Tel Aviv. Her parents were born in Israel's holiest city—Jerusalem. Dafna's Mama and Papa always labeled themselves religious Zionists.

Weeks later, fuchsia bumble bee darts from flower to flower; the bumblebee head transforms into beautiful Nephesh. Fuchsia dust sprinkles Dafna's soft, shimmering hair. Nephesh bee flits and floats over to chocolate-licking ice cream-smiling Dara and Davina.

Yitzhak and Yael run through the park kicking their soccer ball.

Humming buzzy bee accelerates. *Time is running out. No! Not the hills. Hold still, little ones.*

Yitzhak and Yael giggle, rolling down steep grassy hill. Nephesh bee snaps her fuchsia legs and for 18 seconds time stands still. Salty fuchsia liquid slips from Nephesh bee. *Oh Dafna. How I wish your Mama's, Papa's, sister's, and brother's destinies could be different.*

Nephesh bee's fuchsia particles swirl, she becomes a fuchsia-breasted birdy. She soars above the treetops. Gravity increases as she gets closer to tornadoes' time vortex. Her shimmering plumage wrinkles. Nephesh's plumage caw-caws and she transitions into trumpeting bellowing flying elephant. Heavy raindrops pummel-soaked pachyderm. She sighs and shrinks between time's manipulative molecules.

6 umbrellas pop above 6 blue coats. Minutes before Shabbat morning prayer, a beautiful rainbow leads the way to Shul.

"I got the job," says Benjamin.

"Wonderful, honey. I knew Steve Jobs was a genius. Takes one to know one."

"Let's break the news to the kids."

"Can they finish their soccer tournament?"

"Of course."

Benjamin extends his hand. Rachel smiles and kisses the back of her husband's hand.

Four months later, my parents push little David's stroller. Powerful roots create uneven cracks in the cement sidewalk. Every little bounce causes little guy's giggles. Prodigy David starts, and his parents follow in singing William Tell's overture finale, "Bump-bump-bitty-bump-bitty-bump-bump-bump."

Laughter dies down. Mama pushes the stroller under the cooling branch. Sweltering heat gives baby flushed red cheeks. Christopher holds melting ice cube drops over baby's lips and performs figure-eight over Rachel's eyelids. The cold canteen quenches my parents' thirst.

An unusually tall stranger with minty fresh perfume steps out from the sunlight's blinding glare: her fuchsia blouse, skirt, shoes, and socks shimmer—all are completely out of step compared to the more conservatively dressed Jewish parents. Long fuchsia nails squeeze fuchsia water bottle. Her fuchsia adorned wrists and gyrating fuchsia ankle bracelets jingle-jangle. Fuchsia sunglasses obscure her spying eyes. A high cropped bun adds to her intimidating height.

Baby David's smile twinkles in his eyes. Sunlight's laser focus forces fuchsia glowing particles onto the baby's pink tongue. Doctor Crimson leans forward, bathing Papa, Mama, and me in that hot, hot fuchsia sunlight.

Crimson's head swivels. She opens her mouth seductively, tapping glass frames on her large, sharply fanged teeth. She stretches abnormally to the left. Her super-sized green-fuchsia eye imperceptibly winks.

Are we connection? Or confection? Most assuredly insurrection and misdirection. Alternate doomed reality reactivates intrepid time incursions, conversions, and unexpectedly expected diversions.

Cheshire Cat's pernicious purring pulverizes and shreds, leaving them lost in multidimensional Multiverses to recapture David's desiccated bones, muscles, and tendons.

Previous reincarnated ME reassembles. Righteous and ragged ramifications; resuscitates rapturous rapport. Razor-sharp teeth gnawing myelin sheath.

Ginormous galaxy-sized paws reach out. Left claw rips, tears, and fragments our essence.

I beseech thee. Instruct me. Now, here in this state am I too late? How much longer must I wait? I-T-S not taking the bait. God of our god, what's your goal? Bolstering my immortal soul? Growing weary...oh no very leery. I-T-S destructive existential game theory. Nightmarish nirvana negates perilous partisan piranha.

Hebrew and English energy blast passed our intersectional past...

Chazak. Chazak Ve-met Chazak! Be strong, be strong and let us be strengthened! O Lord, I know. I knew? Thou will help us, but will thee help me before thou force an inevitable kowtow?

God's thunderclap. Blue-white-lightning crackles and swirls. Massive vortex drains nebula size Cheshire Cat. Monstrous thing rapidly shrinks; within 13 hours, I-T is no larger than a cute 88-foot kitty.

Phased. Tased. Braised. Dazed...eternally amazed. Disembodied Sagacious nerve-endings ablaze. Lungs seared. Perceptions weird. Unconsciousness flared. Oblivion dared. Hope teared...

Fear not. I'll help you endure the new event horizon. Your pain will subside. I'll forever be by your side.

God! I can hear every thought. Feel every joy and agony. I-T-S a miracle. I can inhale and exhale; yet I have no lungs. Blood pressure pounds in my nonexistent chest. Metaphysical sight enhances vision. Bass-baritone voice booms. Time swoons. Evil looms. Wombs held in violent tombs. Celestial plumes zooms. We're smaller than legumes. Horrific history resumes...

Cracked. Mangled. Ruptured. Snapped. Suspended. Slit and split. We're pliable playdough, stretched wafer thin; wherein internal violin—grin. Cring sub-atomic images let loose, chaotic noose. Profuse abuse... we're powerless to vamoose.

Conspicuous incongruity defies credulity.

How can shards glisten in this place without starlight? Mirrors line up and dance to Fantasia's "Sorcerer's Apprentice." I don't understand how I can see these mirror particles grow from sub-atomic to molecular in size. Each maladapted mirror sarcastically screeches. Heat blast and pungent aroma existentially expelled. Mirror substance crackles and bends, showing off I-T-S massive quarter-inch size. I-T doesn't rest on I-T-S laurels. I-T-S growth accelerates half inch, full inch, six inches; nothing is impeded—everything greeted, acceded, needed, exceeded, and faithfully pleaded.

One, two three...12, 13, 14...45, 54, 63...109, 639, 999...1,521 feet. I-T soars through mishigas' stratosphere.

Nonexistent body refracted in my mind's eye. Crushed feelings hideously penetrate porous progeny—which is me. Repulsive regurgitation ruthlessly ripples... Gaping holes where eyes should be. I'm skeletal. Large black eyes emerge. Deeply etched, wrinkled skin peel and reattach.

Dear lord, what am I becoming? The enemy knows what I've forgotten. Above each mirror, my age blinks—22 billion? How the hell could I be five times older than the planet of my birth?

The twisting, jagged path looks and feels familiar. Damn! Why are all those mirrors chasing me? Faster I push my feet, faster—nothing matters or does everything matter? Am I becoming quicksand? Malevolent backhand! Crashing into no man's land...how the hell can I withstand another underhand hallucinatory dreamland?

Ginormous black fingernail carves a disembodied heart. Black blood cascades. Mangled and mutilated; flash flood carries me where? Savage surgery serrates secret soul. My thoughts lasso 9-foot shard. Surfing rancid black blood. I-T slowly congeals and reconfigures into corrosive cascading complexities. Acid sears my newly constructed pink skin.

Terroristic mirrors link to each tiny Sagacious body—dissolve and evolve one by one.

Chin over nose. Who knows where evil's energy flows? Living, breathing decimated bones pile miles high...

Evil machines 100 feet tall blast mountaintops into 36,360 smaller boulders, each with a life of I-T-S own. Mirrors smash east, west, north, and south, falling above and ascending below.

Malevolent Time's manic cackle reverberates. I-T-S foot crushes my skull and spine. Feeling agony's intensity takes my life force like an anvil crushing a tortoiseshell. I ponder... *Will this be another righteous rebirth or masticated misanthropic mirth?*

Million magnificent memories make their magnanimous mandatory move. Fuchsia mist envelope familiar feelings...Mama? Papa? How can this be?

CHAPTER 10

Belinda Bellicose Bullies Three-Year-Old Orphan Ima Best

Pale, pitiful, rumpled, runty, famished, and forlorn 3-year-old Ima is flagrantly forsaken. Ima is brazenly bludgeoned and bruised by her 7-year-old tormentor, bully Belinda Bellicose.

Ima's confidence constantly crushed; her hope flushed; by adoptive regifting mommies and daddies, Ima's always jilted and wilted from that hellishly humiliating history.

Belinda's vengeful vendetta explodes beyond vile vitriol's vigilantism.

Mopey morose misanthropic Miser Meeks exudes excruciating jaded judgmentalism. His arrogance always askew; cuckoo is his own milieu. Joints creak. Alcoholic anger piques. Retching geek inevitably will leak. From every pore he'll eternally reek.

After her third squeaky 6:30 a.m. step, three-year-old Ima holds her finger to her lips and pulls her toasty foot out of her shiny shoe. Four steps later, "Oh my gosh. Library floor is so cold," she utters in hushed tones.

Trying to suppress a stealthy sneeze, the petite girl stands on a steady silvery stool: her nostrils nestled near awesome aroma.

After a deep inhale of cherry blossoms—Ima's smile widens.

Delightful. Love. Love...pretty pink petals' perfume. MMM snack time.

Chocolate chip cookie crumbs capriciously capture capacious carpet. Calculating cantankerous cockroach careens and creatively capitalizes and consumes every sugary morsel.

Can't let lanky Liberian librarian lambaste and lampoon. Be prepared. If she walks in, I'll tell her Ima looking for Dr. Seuss, not Emily Dickinson. I love her poetry. Was I regifted because Ima smarter than the other kids? That's not fair. Maybe I shouldn't have corrected new Mommy Matilda. Should've been more obedient. Why is I-T so wrong to think for myself? Why must I talk like other little boys and girls? Saying wove instead of love. Talking like an itty-bitty girlie. Hush Ima! Your thoughts always get you into trouble. You must continue your special dumbing-down charade...or you'll never get a family's love. Why must showing off my true self be so painful? I do enjoy grown-up music more than "Little Bunny Foo Foo.

Ima puts fuchsia buds in her ears and listens to Mozart's "String Serenade #13."

9-weeks after Ima's secret literary romp, her moist nostrils press against the freezing windowpane. Shivers fall from her cute nose down to her scabby kneecaps. Ima complained about Belinda wrapping her in cellophane. Again, and again Ima's migraine pain competes with ankle and elbow sprain. Belinda's hateful reign remains institutionally vain. Her disdain for right and wrong will never refrain from providing Ima with multiple ankle and elbow sprain.

Ima's hurt blares. Other kids make fun of what she wears. Other than best friend Angie, nobody cares.

"Ima only phwee years." *Why older people laugh when Ima cry?*

Rain cloud breaks. New day wakes.

Love wet sidewalk's delicious slippery smells after heavy rain.

Good for you Angwie. You more special than I. You'll not be like me...

an imperfect unloved thing that must always be regifted. Ima closes her eyes and prays. *Please God. Help me find parents who will love me even though I'm not as pretty as my best friend Angwie. I'm too curious. Too intrusive. Rarely waiting my turn to ask questions. Ima too jumpy. Why should I feel shame for being my true self? Mister Meeks always telling me to shut up...*

Angie shivers. Love delivers. Her new Papa's pink umbrella pops. Ima's joy blossoms watching her best friend smile and rub her cold finger into her new Papa's red beard.

"Furry," says grinning Angie.

"Yes, Angie. Your Papa is a big grizzly."

Angie's Mama slides in the backseat. Leather dress movement creates farting sound on sticky cushion.

Angie's right palm covers her mouth. Her thumb and index finger pinch her tiny nostrils.

"Dat's okay, Mommy."

"Oh. Um. No sweetie. Mommy didn't...that's what happens when...having trouble with your seatbelt?"

Angie squirms and twists. Her little tongue sticks out. "Help, Mommy." Click.

"Yay," Mommy and daughter say together.

Ima's joy vanishes, knowing she'll never see her best friend again. Loneliness pushes tears down her cheeks. Raindrops mirror Ima's teardrops.

Pelting hail ratatats windowpane, cracks form branching out fissures; chilly wind forcibly flows into Ima's nostrils. Like pixie dust, thin freezing wind lifts Angie's favorite stuffed animal.

"Special Doggie!" shouts Ima.

Stuffed doggie's black olive nose, partially pink from years of teething; beckons and tantalizes Ima's inquisitive nature. Bouncing on her tippy toes, Ima's eyes grow wider. She watches Special Doggie float past her friends' outstretched fingertips. Soft happy memory toy shimmers through freezing windowpane. Ima grabs tight and she too shimmers in bright fuchsia energy. Her molecules were caught in a fuchsia transporter beam. *That tickles.* Ima and Special Doggie reassemble on the other side of the windowpane. *That was fun. Do I-T again.*

"Another time, little one. Now hurry, time will be frozen only for another 36 seconds."

"Who are you?"

"A friend. Goodbye little one. Remember..."

"What should I remember?"

"Whatever happens next, you are loved. In the future, you are loved."

"What does that mean?" Ima's tears freeze. Each step grows slower until Ima's body hits time-freezing paradox particles. Only her mind remains active.

Fuchsia and black energy streams entangle. Black claw stabs fuchsia particles. Painful screech terrifies little girl. She tries and fails to put her hands over her ears. *New friend. New friend. I-T-S all too scary.* Fuchsia energy breaks free and slams into Ima's forehead. *Forget, little one.*

Black fist punches the cement. Frozen time flows freely into non-negotiated normalcy. Ima runs and slips. Her knees hit and scraped recently dug-out pothole. Water cushions her knees. Her bones are not broken, but the intended genetic blood markers are scooped up by mysterious fingers. Ima's kneecap rubs against sparkling black razor blade, and she cries.

Angie, I hurt. Dark clouds form jagged teeth and black lips. I-T-S lips blow hot stinky breath. Sudden gust's guttural growls become louder and louder. I-T mocks Ima's sweetie call, "Angie. Angie! Why did you leave Special Doggie behind? Don't you...no you don't. You don't need either of us anymore."

Ima's heart sinks. Her frozen fingers clutch Special Doggie's wet, moldy fake fur.

Cadillac's sidewalls squeak and hit the high curb. Rotting flesh smell permeates from black wind. I-T pushes the car enough to line up perfectly with overflowing pothole. Dirty water hits Ima's face. She sucks her thumb. Muddy tears flow and pity-pat off Special Doggie's nose.

Bye bye, An-gee. I wish I could get warm hugs too. Have a happy life. Ima's freezing hand waves goodbye.

Fuchsia particles shimmer and coalesce. A hot cup of chicken soup dematerializes in Ima's hands. Ima slurps the immune bolstering liquid. "Delicious. Thank you. What's your name?"

Ima feels large warm fingers pat her cold head. Minty fresh breath blows Ima up, up...above the treetops. *Wee wee...* Down below everyone is frozen in time. Ima twirls and is held aloft in the center of the warming funnel. She sings 1958 song, "Lollipop." Dozens of bright red and orange lollipops appear. Ima's eyes grow wide. Three licks later, "MMM. Thank you... Um, you didn't give me your name...yet. Why?"

A tornado's funnel turns soggy freezing Ima into dry happy toasty Ima. For 18 seconds Ima's guardian angel becomes visible. 65-foot fuchsia pigmented lady stands on one leg, Flamingo-style. Ima sees her own reflection in the pretty giantess's sad green eyes.

Tornado's swirls dissipate. Ima descends. Her warm feet touch down and time click-clackety back to I-T-S normal tic talkety. *Go back inside, little one. Stay warm. Be safe.*

Four years later...

Ima's loud wails are ignored by teachers, counselors, and staff walking by chit-chatting about the most recent gossip. Adding insult to injury, they look the other way as one bully after another torments Ima. They are all dismissive of Ima's tears and fall for Belinda Bellicose's fake persona.

Ima's sloshy tears soak her scrawny handheld cake. Five of the seven candles are broken into three pieces. Row after row—teeth bites mark the dripping Bellicose saliva spot.

11-year-old bully Belinda punctured Ima's icing with her

two front teeth. Bellicose's index finger tunnels into her wide-right nostril. Snagging her prize—Belinda smiles at her wet mucus-dripping boogies. Nasty finger scoops yucky yellowish mucus-y icing.

"Who wants my tasty treat?" mean Belinda asks.

Belinda's sticky fingers grab and tug Ima's hair.

"Let me go!"

"Why would I do that? Bestie! We are having so much fun..."

The bully's left-hand smears icing and boogies over Ima's lips.

"Why you have to always ruin everything!"

Stronger and heavier Bellicose pins Ima to the dusty kitty poopy carpet. Bellicose wiggles long looggie strand inches from Ima's terrified eyes.

Belinda holds her squirming head in her vise-like grip. "Don't do I-T!" shouts Ima.

Long extended slurp slurp and nasty looggie successfully reverses back into Belinda's bacteria infested mouth.

Belinda squeezes Ima's lips open.

"Damn I-T Belinda, get off me!"

"Make me!"

Belinda's index finger hooks her upper lip. *Eww!* Ima tries and fails to break free of Belinda's grip. Belinda's tongue is bathed in yucky soupy saliva. A nasty greenish drool slips out from her bottom lip; I-T snakes I-T-S way slowly down her puffy cheek.

Belinda gargles her disgusting mixture. Her index finger sloshes and splooshes.

"Not that. Please not another mucous swirly!"

Mister Meeks! Please wake up...

Mister Meeks stirs. Hopeful anticipation fades while Ima is forced to watch him scratch his ass. Belinda giggles.

Belinda rolls off Ima as loud footsteps rumble down the staircase. Ima pinches Belinda's fatty arm and runs outside.

She slides her sleeve over Belinda's mucous-y violation.

Ima stops in the center of the basketball court, her frantic eyes searching for help. Staff are busy gossiping and stuffing their fat cheeks with chips and cakes.

Oh my gosh. Not him. He never believes me. Not her either. Is there nobody I can trust?

Red dodgeball slams into the back of Ima's head.

Ima turns. Anger and fear take hold. Ima's eyes bug-out and her mind shouts, *Belinda!*

Petrified. Ima desperately wishes to fight back. *What do I do? What do I do? She's bigger, stronger and always gets the adults to punish me!* Bully Belinda's noisy flip-flops make terrified Ima cringe. Belinda's fat nose smushes Ima's cute nose.

Belinda pinches Ima's belly. Rather than crying out, Ima lifts her shirt and sticks out her tongue. Stuck between Belinda's chubby fingers is a fist full of squishy fuchsia play-dough.

"I won't let you intimidate me anymore. My guardian angel said I should..."

"Guardian angel? Damn, Ima. No wonder parents keep returning you. You are nuts!"

"Ima not nuts. Guardian angel. Guardian angel. Show her Ima not... Oh no! Not that!"

Belinda's meaty forearm knocks Ima over. She rubs the back of her head, and tears form. Seconds later Belinda's big ass farts in Ima's face.

"Stop the stinky!" coughs Ima.

Belinda wallops Ima's face with tremendous ferocity. "Having fun?"

"No-ah. Why are you having so much fun...bullying me?"

"I love your reactions. So dramatic. Besides, I love I-T watching you cry and run for help and nobody believes you. And..."

"And what?"

"You're so easy to lift!"

"Put me down! You're crunching me!"

"I love I-T. Beg me for more crunchies!"

Ima silently shakes her head. Belinda kicks the back of Ima's leg. Ima falls on her butt. Belinda's beefy legs straddle Ima. One knee pushes the air out of Ima's lungs.

Belinda looks up and watches Mister Meeks run across the grassy field, sneezing and yawning. *Does he see me? How am I going to explain... Yes!* Belinda brings her fist down from her ear. Her heavy elbow smashes into Ima's chest. "Ouch!" yells Ima. Nobody reacts. And Belinda giggles with glee, watching the new student teacher flirt with Mister Meeks. *Keep him preoccupied.*

Fuchsia dust sprinkles into Belinda's nose. Uncontrollable loud sneezes follow. Belinda's mucous-y nostrils send out a dozen jet streams of bacterial yuck.

Thank you minty fresh guardian angel.

Run little one.

Belinda may be quick, but Ima is much faster.

Ima has fun turning her back on Mister Meeks and running backwards. Each time Belinda gets within grabbing distance, Ima pulls away.

"Slowpoke!"

"When I catch up to you, I give you slow-poke!"

"Ima book. You stinky schnook. Ima abstract art. You have face like Humphrey Bogart."

Black gust rolls red dodgeball toward Belinda.

What do I do? Nothing to hide behind. Should I wave my arms? Mister Meeks never does anything to help. Stop talking to the pretty lady. I know if I shout and interrupt him, he's going to punish me. I don't know what's worse. Long punishment from him or clobbering from Belinda. What should I do?

Whack! Ima falls into the soft wet grass face first. 11-year-old thickset fingers engulf Ima's 7-year-old petite fingers. *Crack!* Stronger Bellicose wraps her larger hand over Ima's wrist and forces Ima's injured balled-up fingers into her own chin. Ima cries out, "Stop I-T!"

"I'm martial art. You're Purple Heart. Misfit! You must submit!" Bellicose cackles.

"Halfwit!"

"Little shit! You want me to drown you in the tar pit?"

Belinda sings, "Anything You Can Do," each lyric synchronized with stinging slaps. Belinda balls up her fingers and punches Ima while singing, "Dum dum dum di dum di dum di dum di di di dum dum dum dum" to Guiseppe Verdi's "Anvil Chorus."

Breathing heavily, Belinda stops to lick Ima's blood from Ima's knuckles. "MMM cowardice tastes good this time of year."

"Not coward! You...are too big. You never fight fair."

"Say I-T!" yells Belinda.

"Get off me!"

Belinda's middle finger pushes into Ima's cute nose. Belinda's smile grins wider the Greater pressure she adds to smush in the tip of Ima's nose. Tears stream down Ima's cheeks.

"Say I-T!"

"You promised you wouldn't make me do I-T."

"Above all people, you should know life is filled with broken promises. Do I-T for the little Special Doggie is going to be fed to your favorite Doberman pincher."

"Not fluffy."

"Yes. Fluffy. Now say I-T!"

"Ima loser," terrified girl whispers.

"Louder!" Belinda growls.

"Ima ugly! Ima pathetic! Ima never gets Mommy's or Daddy's love..."

Minty freshness wafts over Ima, and she bites down on Belinda's fleshy thumb.

"I studied Martial Arts too!" Ima spins and kicks out. Belinda slams into two partially deflated tires. She stands, runs, slips, and crashes backward onto materializing-dematerializing-materializing fuchsia grease.

Ima runs inside. Hiding for hours. Nobody cares, she's missed half the day's classes. 18 stealthily sneaking steps into the waiting room; Ima discovers loud snoring Mister Meeks, stuck in his favorite chair and a large bag of cheese puffs on his lap.

Belinda arrives 45 seconds later.

Ima takes two steps forward and steps on squeaky floorboard. "Stop. You'll wake him," whispers Belinda. Ima giggles, pressing her toes down. Mister Meeks stirs.

"Don't forget what he said last time you tattled on me?" *Better do something before he wakes,* Belinda's racing mind tells herself.

Belinda walks over the squeaky floorboard. She uses two cheese puffs like they were paint brushes and creates two tic tac toes on Mister Meeks' cheeks. Belinda wiggles and jiggles Mister Meeks' Shar-Pei skin. *Shit! I thought for sure that would wake him. Damn, that dude is a sound sleeper.* Belinda wipes extra cheese on Ima's white blouse and stuffs Ima's hand into the bag, and the new crunch crunches wake pissed off Mister Meeks.

Belinda holds a tiny mirror in front of Mister Meeks' blinking eyes. "What the hell! Ima!"

"I-I...You've got to believe me...Ima innocent!"

"You! Are! Never innocent! Incorrigible brat!"

"Ima not a brat! Ima good girl!" Ima steps back onto the squeaky floorboard.

Mister Meeks holds his hands over his ears. His entire body shivers from that hateful sound.

"I wish you were more like kindhearted Belinda. Damn you Ima, why must you always break the peace!"

"What! She's as kindhearted as Joe Biden is to his granddaughter."

"Enough! Stop your melodramatic nonsense. You've interrupted my rem sleep, and I have an important date tonight..."

Psychopath in training, Belinda Bellicose walks closer to Mister Meeks. In her best make-believe girlish voice... "Excuse me, Mister Meeks. Um. Could I...please have..."

"You want another candy?"

"Yes sir."

"See Ima? Well-behaved respectfully asking girls deserve rewards, and bad little girls such as yourself deserve punishments."

"What the..."

Mister Meeks takes two steps, so that he can tower over quivering Ima. "Ima! Say hell and I'll swat your ass!" Ima catches herself and blurts out butt saving, "Shell!"

Ima starts grinning. Even Belinda can't contain herself. Soon, grinning becomes boisterous laughter. Principal's Chihuahua buries her face into Mister Meek's cheese puff bag. Dog's orange cheesy tongue licks Mister Meek's angry face. "Oh hell! Yes! I said I-T! Get the hell out of here. Move! Ima! Get! Or so help me." Mister Meeks grabs a large wooden paddle with rows of holes.

"But we're coming up on dinner time. And she made me miss lunch. Please, Mister Meeks, Ima so hungry."

"Stop with that Ima crap. Talk normal like everyone else. I-T-S not Ima...I-T-S I am or I'm. Now, get away from me before the dinner bell sounds. The lights are on, you can go back to enjoying your dodgeball game."

"Hell no," whispers Ima.

"What did you say?"

"Nothing sir, that would be delightful." Ima says in her grand mocking tone.

Belinda grabs Ima's arm. "Come on, bestie. Let's finish our game," Belinda says in her best demurring impersonation. Ima shakes her head. Mister Meeks throws the dog off his lap and closes his eyes.

Belinda pushes Ima. Her knees and palms are bloody from skidding against the pitted uneven blacktop. Belinda holds her side chuckling, while watching Ima's tears fill up a little hole in the asphalt. Looming shadow hovers over the chunky 11-year-old.

"Where did the sun go?"

Fuchsia tornado sucks up screaming students and staff. Fading funnel deposits frightened humanity onto squish grass.

Fuchsia buffeting winds carry terrified Belinda eye level with a flock of squawking birds. Her screams are loud enough to wake Mister Meeks. A tiny fuchsia twig tugs on Mister Meeks' shoelace. He stumbles down the steps and tears his pant leg—his arms flail, and he falls chin first, bouncing into recently sprinklered squishy grass.

Ima's hand covers her giggling mouth. *Grass-hole meet ash-hole.*

Updraft holds Belinda aloft. Three fuchsia banana peels zig and zag, making sure no matter where Mister Meeks steps his heel is always slipping on them. He continues to reenact the silent era Keystone Cops, by slipping a half dozen times before he shouts, "What's that smell!"

Revenge... Ima raises her eyebrows and wiggles her ears.

Belinda's wind tunnel fails and shoots her into a stinky trash bin. Belinda and Meeks become hilarious prat-falling peas in a pod. While Meeks continues to slip all over himself; now I-T-S Belinda's turn slipping on slippering mustard and ketchup. She wipes her tears and turns her face into a Jackson Pollock painting.

"Fire ants! Spiders too. I hate spiders! They are all biting me!" screams Belinda.

"What a lovely fuchsia beehive."

"Crazy girl—beehives are never fuchsia."

"Mister Meeks... Run!"

Mister Meeks uses crying children as human shields. Fear forces his glasses to fog up. Mister Meeks' vision becomes obscured. The faster he wipes, the quicker and stickier the grease adheres. Unbearable frustration sends Mister Meeks headfirst into the girl's water polo team.

Triggered, the team hurls water polo balls. *Bam! Bam!*

Blood gushes. All the girls scatter, frantically shouting, "Get off me!"

"Sar-be. You-bb. Broke-umb. My-ba. Know-buzz!"

9 days later...

"I-T-S back! I-T-S back! Why won't this supernatural shit leave me and Belinda alone!"

For the last 18 minutes, black lightning bolt zigs while Ima zags. *Bam! Crackle! Whoosh!*

Ima's shoes smolder. Her toes tingle, and her hair frizzles. Spontaneous invisible force braids her hair into Pippi Longstocking half loops.

"Minty fresh guardian, help me!"

Black sap slams into Ima's closed eyelids.

Shimmering tree bark transforms into soft Nerf material. Ima, temporarily blinded, is held within the strange Nerf tree. 18 seconds later, the sap melts away and she's spit out from the cartoonish impact... *Ba-ba-boing.* Rubbery tree solidifies once Ima is safe on the other side.

9 months later...

No hat, gloves, or coat—Ima's teeth chatter in freezing rain. Depressed Ima bangs on the front door.

"Mister Meeks! I-T happened again. Mean Mommy and Daddy lied. Ima regifted!"

The heavy door slowly creaks open. Mister Meeks' bloodshot eyes dart from side to side. His red Rudolph nose trumpets his disdain.

"You again!"

"Me again..."

"Stop dawdling. That chilly wind...and you shall certainly be the death of me."

Ima avoids getting swatted on the butt and quickly runs over to the crackling fire.

Six weeks later...

Ima is adopted by 6-foot-2 muscular wrestler-build Jacob Friend and his wife Miriam. She stands five-seven. Her natural blonde hair shines in the moonlight.

Ima's nervous ticks and rapid eye movement become more pronounced after her last regifting. Even after loving hugs from her new parents, fear overwhelms every thought. Ima can't stop repeating her OCD mantra:

Don't be regifted. Don't be regifted. Cried too much with my last Mommy and Daddy. This time will be different. Mister Meeks told me he will not take me back. Can he do that? Ima only seven. I don't know how to survive on the streets. I hope my new parents don't give me candy. I hope my new parents will love me. No! Stop being ridiculous. That's asking for too much. I will never ever get my hopes up again. Miriam and Jacob have such kind eyes.

That night, little Ima tosses and turns for hours. She kicks herself loose from warm blankets. She opens her eyes and looks at the worried faces of her adopting parents.

Oh my gosh. Oh my gosh. They look down on me with sad faces. They've been so kind; I don't want to upset them. Oh, no, they aren't thinking of regifting me. Not fair. Not fair! How can I know what bad, imperfect thing I was doing while I was asleep? I must show them I can be more perfect. I can do this. I-I must do this...

Jacob rubs Ima's twitching shoulder.

"You were having another bad dream."

Ima's two front teeth are missing. She flashes a gummy smile and chews the inside of her cheek. She Repeatedly pinches the skin between her thumb and forefinger. After 18 seconds of silence, Ima vigorously rubs her eyebrow and taps her knuckles against her lips.

"Th-ary for th-sk-wing you," Ima lisps

Miriam kisses Ima's cheek. "Tell us sweetie. What's wrong?"

Ima stands on the edge of her bed. "Papa I tho, tho sawee. I li-th. When I gow-ah teeff, I'll tw-eye and be per...per-fect for you."

"You don't need to be perfect. Nobody is perfect. Your friend Belinda told us you like these."

Ima shakes her head and blows out a series of short, nervous breaths. Anxiety builds, forcing Ima to excessively swallow. Her stomach churns and gurgles. Ima's mind internalizes her manic rationalization. *What do I do? What do I do?*

"Oh no, Papa! Not candieshth!"

Ima runs and cowers behind her giant stuffed hippo.

"I'll be good girl. Pleas-th, no regifth-ting."

Jacob brushes Ima's cheek. "Sweetie. I don't understand. What's this regifting?"

"Worses-th thing ever. Don't make me talk about I-T. Pleas-th. Don't get mad. I-T-S-TH my teef making me talk bad. I can be perfect. You see...give me another chan-th."

Tears flood. Miriam rocks Ima. Jacob and Miriam profusely kiss Ima's cheeks. "We made a huge mistake thinking Belinda was your friend. She was that bully, wasn't she? See...Mama and Papa made a whopper of a terrible mistake, and you still forgive us, right?"

"Right. I wove, wove, wove Mama and Papa."

"Never in a million cajillion years would we ever regift you," says Jacob emphatically.

"What's the squishy goodness in the middle of a s'mores?" asks Jacob.

"Marth-thammy-ellowth?" asks Ima.

"No, dear," says Miriam.

Ima blocked out loving dear and only heard stinging no. Her smile evaporates. Adoration, acceptance, confidence, and connectedness are replaced with powerful feelings of betrayal, defensiveness, confusion, fear, horror, and hysterical humiliation churn her organs like butter.

I don't know what Ima supposed to say. What's the correct...um per-fect answer?

Ima plops her thumb between her quivering, drooping lips and unsuccessfully tries to draw comfort. Her wonderful ah ha moment widens her smile and brightens her eyes.

"Me! Ima s'mores! Ima loves you both so much! Most of all, Ima love love my new name."

Miriam and Jacob grin through happy tears. Ima dances and wiggles her entire body.

"Ima Best-Friend!"

Miriam, Jacob, and Ima dance around three life-size blue-white-fuchsia hippos.

"We're all...best friends!" shouts Jacob.

CHAPTER 11

More Questions, Fewer Answers

Little girl Ima grows up not knowing what happened to her parents. No other child or adult believes Ima's peculiar, fanciful tale. Police have no clues as to Miriam's and Jacob's whereabouts, and dozens of psychiatrists, social workers, lawyers, and judges have given up trying to place her in another foster home. Her MO is to stick around for less than three weeks and bolt for the streets.

Ima nothing more than a failed statistic. Never thought I'd ever become homeless again!

Time is not kind. Ima's appearance becomes unrecognizable. Her grimy gritty matted hair attracts flies. Full moon spotlights angry depressed girl rummaging inside stinky restaurant dumpster. A waterfall of leftovers slapped sleeping Ima's filthy face. Slamming metal lid shocks her out of welcomed, rare deep sleep. Pidgeon poops on her face. White fecal tears fall. Ima slams her heels through maggots. *I hate my life! Nobody gives a damn. Long ago...I remember guardian angel. Ima forsaken by the only friend...Friend. I used to be...Best-Friend. Mama! Papa! Why?*

From across the street, Police Officer Perino taps 4-foot-11 social worker Miss Hamamoto's shoulder; they cross over to the dumpster. Officer Perino kicks over boxes for Hamamoto to stand on.

"Ima?" asks smiling Hamamoto.

Ima leaps out of the bin. Her foot lands on Officer Perino's shoe and twists.

"My ankle!" shouts Ima.

Ms. Hamamoto hands Ima a steaming hot double burger. Starving, Ima grabs I-T and gobbles the tasty meal in five large chomps.

"Your ankle needs to elevate," states Hamamoto.

"Are you a doctor?"

"No. I do have news."

"Bad...I-T-S always bad news."

"Not this time."

"You've found them? Mama and Papa!"

Sudden stern furring pinched eyebrows confuses Ima. "You did find them, right?"

"I never said that. Look. Um...I am not here to reinforce your fantasy. The good news is that I've located your real family."

"Family? No. You lie. You're taking me to jail and leaving me alone. Ima always alone."

"Hush! I told you."

"No, you didn't. Ima Miriam's and Jacob's s'mores. No other family..."

"They are your cousins. On your Papa's side of the family. Isn't that wonderful?"

"Not possible. Mama and Papa were orphans."

"I-T all checks out. They are your family. I believe telling you they were orphans was said to make you care for them... They were truly selfish people."

"No! They loved me. You...those cousins I've never seen are the selfish liars. I don't trust this...whatever this is!"

"Whatever this is? Why you ungrateful... Look dear! I've been the only one in your corner. I've neglected my own family to help you...because I do care. Now you're going to clean up. Put ice on that ankle and be grateful for this gift. Your last chance at family."

Months fade into neglectful bullying years. Ima's new family took turns harming her mental health. Teenage Ima regressed. She sucks her thumb. That habit pushes her once-perfect teeth into an imperfect protruding overbite.

An acne-blotched Ima sits alone on the park bench. Rain-soaked doggie takes a piss on the edge of the bench, spritzing Ima's sock.

"Eww! Ima smell of doggie urine!"

Pug nose master shakes his head, disapprovingly on disheveled, morbidly obese Ima. *How can dog and I-T-S owner look like twins?*

Ima closes her eyes. She imagines her happy self and loving parents, Miriam and Jacob. Manufactured events, which never took place warm her heart, *birthday dances, cakes and ice cream, my Valedictorian speech during high school graduation. I-T-S a wonderful life. No! I-T-S a wonderful fiction. Should have been. I-T. I-T never happened! Mama! Papa! I was your little s'mores. You told me so. And foolishly I believed you. I thought you loved me. I thought we were all happy together. We were a family. My first. My ever family. Damn you! Why did you in the dead of night vanish? Where did you go? No note. No nothing! For a long time, I thought you were abducted. But that's a made-up fantasy by a miserably distraught child. I-T-S not the truth, is I-T! You left because I did something wrong. I wasn't perfect enough. You never told me what I did wrong. If you did, I would have corrected myself. But you never gave me a chance.*

Ima bends low. Her fat hands cradling her sobbing eyes. *What bad thing did I do, to make you no longer love me? Ima loser. Ima going to die alone.*

After hearing multiple loud scratchy sounds, Ima lifts her face from her hands. She wipes her sniffling nose with the back of her sleeve. Ima notices a tiny girl in a pretty fuchsia dress kicking a small box. The five-year-old's green eyes stare at Ima for 18 seconds, before she soccer kicks that box into Ima's weather-worn muddy sneakers.

"Take," little girl with sparkling green eyes whispers.

"What? That box? No thank you. I-T-S your box."

On the word I-T-S little girl grimaces.

"Please don't say that again."

"Say what?" Ima sniffs the air. *Minty freshness...*

A big grin stretches over Ima's forlorn face. Little girl waves and vanishes in a dazzling fuchsia sparkler show. "Come back! See I've got the box. Guardian Angel. I didn't understand. I've got I-T... Don't abandon me. Not again. I didn't understand... don't punish me..."

Tears pity-pat on cardboard box. Ima tries to remove the stubborn cardboard lid. "Ouch! Cardboard cut is worse than paper cut!" Genetic bloody tear-soaked material seeps into the newly constructed porous cardboard. Ima watches a green eyeball wink. 18 seconds later the box floats above Ima's head and poofs out of existence within a tiny fuchsia tornado funnel.

"What a fat loser!" shouts supermodel mom and teen daughter. Hypersensitive Ima doesn't have the self-esteem to shout back. She did when she was younger. Too often humiliated by adoptive family, turned her into the quivering shell of what she used to be. Running away, Ima squishes her palms over her ears. Muffled mocking laughter directed at Ima brings more tears.

"Look at her big butt and flabby flappy arms!" shouts mocking daughter Tiffany.

72 steps later, Ima discovers two abandoned melting vanilla ice cream scoops.

Opportunity, mine!

Ima curls her stubby index and middle finger. *Ima spork.* Like a bloated piggie surveying a wondrous trough. Ima's eyes grow wider, and she scoops up globs of melting sugary goodness.

Next day Ima sits on a fuchsia bench and pulls from her bag two jelly donuts. Chomp-chomp. Swishing saliva chew-chew. Purple deliciousness dribbles down her chin and plops, splattering her now spotted white blouse.

Rarely satiated, happy satisfaction does so, this time. Ima pats her ballooning belly, and remembers last month's ninth-grade assembly.

Mean girl cackles are still humiliatingly fresh. Ima sees herself struggling to fit into a regular size person's seat. *Why did I-T have to be smirking homeroom teacher saying I need the jaws of life to stand up out of the seat I was stuck in. He ripped my pocket on purpose.*

Glass on marble plink plinks. Cascading rolling avalanche crescendo in unison with teen and adult laughter. 36 multi-colored marbles ricochet against Principal Perty's pink Prada heels.

Assistant Principal waves Ima to the front. Embarrassment warms Ima's pink cheeks. Ima reluctantly stands. Each hesitant shaky step is joined by a loud chorus of, "Ima! Ima! Ima!"

You're all so mean!

Tears drip pity-pat off Ima's acne cheeks. Hurtful bullying refrain escalates her anger. "JB Jelly-Belly! JB Jelly-Belly!" grows louder.

Ima walks faster after the boy she has a crush on shouts, "Crazy Ima lost her marbles!"

Laughter dies down as movie's beginning credits start. Head down, Ima runs into the darkened wings. She almost runs over an old lady with empathetic eyes. Ima pulls a powdered donut from her pocket. Tears streak down her lips. An old man jumps out of the darkness and startles Ima. "Hey!" she shouts.

"Hey yourself," smiling old man says.

Ima pulls jelly donut comfort food from her pocket. "Not a sugar fan," old man says. Fuchsia sparks swirl around the old couple's green eyes.

Everyone is a critic! I didn't ask for your opinion! Ima bites down with defiant gusto. Jelly squirts. "Oh my gosh, did I get you?"

Old lady looks at the old man's white, purple spotted shirt. "We're fine." Ima's and old lady's giggles are a 100% match.

Old man gently rubs sugar from Ima's cheek. Ima's first instinct is to pull back. *Eww cringy! Not cringy? I-T-S inappropriate but um...doesn't feel so... And there I-T is again. Every time my mind thinks I-T...they grimace. They couldn't possibly...no, that's crazy...read minds? They sure are cute.*

"Why thank you, Ima." Old man smiles.

"For what?"

Sha! Husband. You were instructed not to interact. You know how curious we are...

Old man blows sugar off his fingers and rubs his wife's soft earlobe. He tugs his own and shouts with a smile, "Choo choo!"

Old man reaches into his pocket. Ima taps her fingertips together and licks her lips.

"Is that a twinkie?"

"Much better," grinning old man whispers.

Cute fluffy baby chick brushes Ima's cheek. "For me?"

I still think she's ready for the truth.

No, she's not. Please, husband. I know what you're going to...

"Time is running out. She should know..."

"And you did..."

"No going back. Mr. Butterfly effect."

"You know Ima right here. Hey. Um...are you talking about...my parents?" Husband and wife silently stare at each other for 36 awkward seconds. "Well? Please... You have no idea how long I've been waiting... For God's sake! Speak! Ima sorry for my outburst. Please. Please. I'm begging you. I must know the truth. Um...well...anything you can say would be most appreciated..."

For the first time Ima becomes aware of the assembly's noise growing fainter and fainter. And now dead silent. Old man's left cheek lifts and motions toward the no-longer-boisterous crowd. "What the hell?" Ima takes three steps up the ramp. Both her hands cover her mouth.

Fuchsia spotlight pushes away the darkness. Half a dozen teens are in mid smush-y kisses. The film is locked, no longer advancing toward the next scene. Adults sneaking a puff of their cigarettes are frozen in time.

Fear induced sweat percolates above Ima's brow. She looks back at the whistling old man and nervously stumbles, walking backward, all the while keeping a watchful eye on the strange couple. *This is all too fishy. Did they know my parents? Can't take a chance, I think they are planning to abduct me. When he touched me. He must have hallucinogenic compounds on his fingers. I've got to get the hell out of here.*

"Come back!" shouts the old lady with empathetic glowing eyes.

"We can explain. Ima, please. You don't understand. No need to fear us. We are good guys."

"The hell you are. Stay back!" Ima's shaking hand extends.

"Sha," whispers the old lady. "You're making...worse."

"I-T! God damn I-T! Why won't you say I-T?"

"Indeed. Yes. God will damn..."

"I-T! Why does that word cause you pain? I don't understand. And I don't want to understand." Ima swirls around hallucinating haunting phantom images. Her squeezed jelly donut splatters and sizzles hitting chaotic time's unnecessary undulating forcefield.

The closer Ima inches to the forcefield the heavier her legs and feet become. She reaches out and taps the Jell-O-like membrane blocking her path forward. "Damn! Weird stuff is only supposed to happen in my dreams."

Ima phases 18 inches below the marble floor. "Quicksand!" Ima shouts.

Old man effortlessly pulls Ima from her melting reality. Old lady taps Ima's cheek. "That's not quicksand."

"No? What is..." Old lady's lids shut tight in anticipation.

"I won't say, you know what."

"Thank you. We really are... Um..."

"Don't say friends because I don't have any. But if I did, you are the type God would send my way. He's always mocking my pain. Ima always the butt of everyone's jokes. Ima loser. Ima pathetic. And now you've come to kidnap me. Do experiments on me. Torture me!" Ima's eyes bulge with fright.

Ima falls to the floor. Her loud wails scare the old lady. She wraps her arms around Ima. The old man inputs codes into his scanner. Old lady's wails are identical to Ima's. Her wet cheeks look up at her husband and he shakes his head. "Butterfly effect," he whispers.

Can't be. Ima fine. As long as Ima the same...we can find out what went wrong and fix...

I've never seen readings like these before. Perhaps there is no fix.

Well, if Ima suddenly becoming the optimist in this relationship, then we are truly doomed.

"Are you human?"

"Yes dear."

"Why are they frozen in time. Why are you here? Please tell me. And before you say another word, know this: I do have a superpower. My only superpower. I can tell when people lie to me."

"Well, not your only superpower," whispers the old man.

"Don't say weird stuff like that, okay?"

I know you want to, dear husband. I implore you not to tell her. This time is filled with trickster's engrams. We were warned before we attempted this unauthorized leap.

Ima and the old lady twirl their curly hair. Their movements are identical. Old man grins each time they stop and bite their bottom lip.

"You a musical fan?" asks the old lady.

"Always."

Excellent. Thank God that connection wasn't erased. Old man winks at his wife. They kiss and sing, "Always."

They're too perfect. I miss Guardian Angel. Too often I see other peo-ple in love and I feel depressed. I long for that which I never find. Ima unlovable. Ima destined to be alone forever. Old man's two fingers motion Ima to join him. "Your turn."

"For what?"

"Singing, of course."

"Oh no. I don't sing."

"Sure, you do." *How sad. I understand, singing requires happy feelings. Even if depressing lyrics are sung, a sense of accomplishment is felt, after singing well. And this Ima has never felt, what I always felt. To be deprived, of song. God, I hate I-T!*

"Whatever is in your heart, please try...little one." *Little one? Look at me now. Ima nobody's little one.*

Ima sings, "When You Wish Upon a Star." Old man and old lady hold hands. Both walk over to Ima and touch her head with their head. Three sets of cheeks drip salty emotions.

Principal Crimson unfreezes herself and yells, "Suohic-Agas!" Startled Ima jumps out of her tender moment.

Holding her hand over her rapidly beating heart. "Who the hell is Suohic-Agas?"

Old man with sheepish grin raises his hand.

"Incorrigible troublemaker! You think your powers could ever contain me! And you...Ami Brest-Ime. You broke your promise. I thought you had better sense!"

"I had too. The prophecy kept on fluctuating."

"And now you've endangered your own future."

"I won't let that happen!" Defiant Suohic-Agas shouts.

"No? Well, my dear old friend how the hell are you going to stop these intersecting timelines? Look. I said look!"

Blinding white light forces Ima to push her palms tightly against her eyes. "Hurts!"

Ami rushes over to Ima. "Stop. You're hurting us." *Hurting us? I must have heard that wrong. She must have said hurting me...Could that white light harm my eardrum?*

"Ima..."

"Yes."

"What? Why did you say that?"

Glad my hearing is not damaged.

"Why would you think light could damage your hearing? Oh, that's right... You're human."

"What else would I... And you're?"

"You see what you've gotten me into. You know how much I hate these pointless conversations!"

Ami puts her arm around Ima. "For her, they are not... pointless."

"I don't care if her thoughts are confused. What are you two going to do next?"

"What are you going to do next?" asks Suohic-Agas.

"Ima not in the mood. Ima... Oh yea...you didn't let me finish what I was going to say."

"Which is?" asks Ami.

"Ima tired of cleaning up your timeline incursions. Too many errors. Too many broken promises. Too many times you've endangered your own futures."

"You three are time travelers?"

"Good. The human is catching up on...what she should not yet discover."

"And who's fault is that?"

"Don't you dare imply."

"If the implication shoe fits...where..."

"I-T! Why won't anyone of you say I-T!" shouts Ima.

"Don't say that!" shouts all three.

"Okay. Okay...so what happens next?" asks confused Ima.

"Time to go!" Crimson's shout and sledgehammer-slamming heel shatters Ima's reality.

"See you later, little one." Suohic-Agas and Ami Brest-Ime sing songs. Old couple taps around Crimson. Ima and the frozen humans remain covered in darkness. Fuchsia lights the path toward the auditorium's heavy front doors. Tapping stops long enough for strong right and left legs to wallop the metal door and knock I-T off I-T-S metallic frame.

Ima follows. The glowing fuchsia illumination recedes the further away she runs from the darkness. Crimson's arm stretches 27 feet, and her long fingers grab Ima's head, her jawbone is pinched. Involuntarily opening her mouth. Crimson drops a fuchsia pill on Ima's tongue. The pill reacts to Ima's saliva and fizzes.

Ima feels vertigo take hold. Chaotic spinning kaleidoscope of sights and sounds energetically vibrate. Geometric shapes spit and click strange languages. Ima's phone glows bright fuchsia: she taps the Wizard of Oz app she developed 9 months ago. Smiling Suohic-Agas' face appears. Awareness agitates app's predestined pixel. Voluminous vivid volcanic vomit verifies vacuous vortex.

Regaining her composure, Ima skips into the swirling fuchsia light singing, "Ima off to sea da gizzard, da wonderful gizzard of gauze."

CHAPTER 12

Falling Through the Looking Glass, Captured Ima Meets her BFF and the Sadistic Queen Crimson for the First Time

A continuous 18-hour planetary quake shakes me from my lava-induced coma.

"How long have I been asleep? Recalibrating. Recalibrating..."

Memories haunt and flaunt debilitating savant. Lava's lacerating labyrinth. Tsunami's treacherous time eviscerates each new rhyme. Resonate base floats and denotes anticipatory anecdotes. Reckless rampage will always rage, and cage. Limitless legerdemain lyrically leeches limbo's enticing energy. Every audacious Sagacious preexisted within relativity's random predestination. Mercurial merriment manifests destructive destiny's musical membrane. Scornful sparks latch onto leviathan lavender liturgy. Boulder's brawny barrage crushes geological appendages. Splintered spheres break off from a 99,999-foot peak. My imagination piques. Swirling spikes' mystique, shrieks, and critiques. Planet's musical might will always incite a pugilistic re-write. Aroma's arc-light is forever foresight.

Lava flow splatters and sizzles against my impervious membrane. Volcanic groundswell I'm unable to quell; raising hell Ima befell. Decibel obliterates metallic infidel. I-T-S white blood cell, death knell. My gurgling bubbling cocoon sinks deep below a glowing gelatinous graveyard. *Destiny's weighted eternity—waited. Ima's trust fund is the issue. There is a constant dearth of mirth manipulating her heckling hearse. Disposition and deposition delay and derail Ima's trust fund resolution. Despondent, she lives with a relative neither Miriam nor Jacob mentioned—Aunt Griselda.*

Walking the short distance from the bedroom to the kitchen, morbidly obese Grizelda's screeching inhaling and exhaling bring on an assortment of howling dogs, wailing neighborhood babies, and shrieking chimpanzees. Grizelda's heavy footsteps struggle forces an accumulation of cascading sweat to smear her clownish blue-red eyeshadow. 36 minutes later, Grizelda arrives; her angry, bulging eyes stared down at fingernail-nibbling Ima.

Jiggling jumbo juicy Grizelda's jowls jarringly jabber, and jeer. Gobbling her third helping of steak, eggs, hash browns, biscuits, and gravy. Grizelda takes a momentary break, to inhale through her mouth; she's got a perpetually stuffy nose.

"Ima hungry," shouts frustrated teen.

"Insolent girl! Off to bed with you."

Thank God she didn't find my stash from 7-11.

Throwing herself onto her disheveled bed, Ima picks up and cuddles with Special Doggie.

Tossing and turning for hours. Ima's nightmarish subconscious takes over. "We adopted you. Why did you abandon us? Why didn't you come back for us?" Jacob's sad voice asks.

"I didn't abandon you. Tell me, what can I do to fix...to rescue you?"

Ima shrinks. She's looking up at the scowling teapot. Inanimate objects transform into cute kitty. Her demur purr manipulates mystic myrrh and I-T-S infer will whirr. Cat's paws, pause. Malevolent Time caw caws. God's physical laws glue shut demonic flaws.

Giant toothpick flips and undulates between Giantess's elongated nails; poke, poke...screeching tiny Miriam and Jacob tumble off the edge of the kitchen table, they hang onto the table's black tablecloth. Giantess's fingernail flicks and they go sailing toward the skin melting teacup. Giantess's red lips blow to cool the scalding liquid. Waves of tea buttress the sugar cube. Miriam slips. Her right leg teeters over the edge of the skyscraper sugar cube. Jacob runs over and holds onto her sweaty hand. Frantic emotions spill out as they cling to each other for dear life.

1960s rotary phone rings. Giantess's shapely legs carry her clickety-clacking stilettoes into the next room. Seconds later, Ima beach ball bounces. Kitty pounces.

"Save us!" shouts Miriam.

"The spoon. The spoon!" shouts Jacob.

"I haven't any arms, hands or fingers," shouts beachball Ima.

Kitty shows I-T-S bloody teeth. "Improvise!" shouts Jacob.

Cat's paw swipes needle-sharp claws. Ima pops. Jettisoned jelly stream sends her squealing thinning body toward the ceiling. She transforms in mid-air, into a shiny metallic slinky toy. Heels overhead she flips down the steps.

"I implore! Sling back up the floor and stop I-T-S deathly pour, or you'll never again be our little s'more!" shouts Miriam.

In her mind, slinky Ima watches her parents slip and slide, from side to side. They fall overboard. "They are cooked alive!"

Skeletal beanstalk sprouts 30 feet. Slinky metallic Ima transforms into squishy fleshy and sinks into a black quicksand pit. Screaming all the way down. Her muddy shoes slide down the walls toward a 100-foot Chesire Cat's wide-open mouth.

"Miriam! Jacob! Best mama and papa. Why? Why!" Ima shrieks.

Ima bounces off huge rough cat's tongue and sails through

the window, zooming past giant butterflies, birds, and elephants. Ima sails into space—green moon winks. Ima gasps for air.

Reality returns. Ima rolls off her bed. Her left foot lands on her skate. Chaotic zigzagging ends when her face slams into the wall. She tries to fix the torn wallpaper and hide the dent with a smiling creepy picture of her aunt Grizelda.

Ima rubs the growing bump above her nose. "She's going to kill me!"

Ima wipes away her tears and limps toward the bathroom. Staring at her image in the cracked mirror. "Ima useless. Ima chunky cookie dough."

Aunt Grizelda's swollen feet pause; her wheezing stops—Ima turns and pow! Grizelda's fleshy knuckles pound Ima into the toothpaste-splattered mirror.

Ima's fingers swipe her bloody pasty saliva drooling mouth. *I hate you.* Grinning with pride, Aunt Grizelda looks down on her terrified prey. "Leave me alone! I know you stole my laptop and gave I-T to that bratty neighbor kid. You let her have access to all my personal stuff. And yesterday, you did what you promised you'd never do. I know you stole my laptop and...and..."

"Yes..." Grizelda says with her typical mocking tone.

"Now that evil Rashida Sarsour has access to all my personal stuff."

"You want me to retrieve your stuff?"

"Yes."

"And you want your freedom, never to see me again?"

"You know the answer."

"And you know what you must do." Grizelda clicks and unclicks her leaky pen.

"Sign over my inheritance."

"Not all of I-T sweetie. I'll let you keep...um...10 percent."

*

Back on David's planet, the ground shakes. Booming becomes louder and louder. "Can't be a quake. I've counted off 8 seconds between the shaking and the calm."

300-foot bright red fingers penetrate David's forcefield. "Al-Amarian! Dumb witted giants. Their people aren't supposed to be capable of planet-to-planet exploration..."

David easily moves out of the way of the slow-moving digits. "Last time I checked on his planet, they'd just entered the industrial age. How the hell did he get here? Why the hell is he after me? They've always been relatively peaceful."

Another slow swipe. Standing over 1,000 feet, the sad creatures' swimming pool size teardrops crash and sizzle, hitting David's forcefield. "Come. Back. Here. I. Must. Capture. You. Or. My. Family. I-T. Will. Kill!" Al-Amarian says in halting sloth-like speech.

David runs out of his compound. Al-Amarian's slow massive steps are catching up. "You are no assassin." David cups his hands and shouts.

"I-T. Said. You. Would. Offer. Help. To. Trick. Sorry. David. I. Must. Do. For. Family. I. Brought. I-T. With. Me."

Ear-splitting screech forces David to run faster. "Damn! I hate the Hizlandirmakers. Fucking creatures are almost as quick as I am. Based on that highest of high pitches, maybe this one is faster. Oh shit! Here comes another blast."

Vertigo's undulations catch up. He slams his hands; shockwave temporarily stops the screeching and opens a hole in space. David pushes through the Jell-O membrane and retrieves two wiggling orange worms. He whispers and nods. David places them on his eyebrows and they slinky their way toward his earie canal.

Screeching begins again. The worms absorb every pulsating vertigo inducing wavelength. David battles dozens of tornado funnels. "Better stop her soon, or the entire planet will become one enormous sandstorm."

Quicker than David's reflexes can react. A large dark green

hand grabs his throat and squeezes. *She's a big one. Got to be at least 10 feet tall. Never met a Hizlandirmak female over 9.3 feet. Must be another enhanced... Shit! She's trying to penetrate my mind. Can't let her. She's searching for the mathematical formula for time travel. She too is collaborating with I-T. Damn she's strong. Never felt a mind so powerful. No. Back off. Let me help you.*

Green creature drops David. She screams. Black lightning bolt skewers her chest. David catches her. "I can help you."

"Nobody can do that." The green creature spits acidic material toward David's chest. He freezes time and steps aside. Only the Hizlandirmak can move while time is frozen. She winks at David. "There will be others. We know where you live. I-T-S brilliant mind will eventually figure out the formula. You will lose David Sagacious. Ever wonder why God's now faint voice continues to dim each time he attempts to speak to you? Well, Ima not going to tell you."

Dark emerald female with the voluptuous athletic body runs toward the precipice and leaps. David watches her falling vibrating body vanish seconds before she hits rock bottom.

"They are all showing up with more regularity. I get the fact that I-T and I-T-S army is still incapable of traversing the time stream. The gravimetric barrier continues to protect me. I've fought many a creature, and always thought I-T was dumb luck they found me. They all had a different agenda. Different skill set. Never put I-T together that they were working for I-T. Why didn't I see that before? Is that you God? Helping me piece the last of the conundrum together? Is I-T possible while I am telling my story, I am somehow not seeing what's going on in the rest of the Multiverse? I've always been able to multitask. She is right. I sense God becoming weaker and weaker. I must meditate on this. Should I risk I-T? I was meditating when I was attacked. Better employ a trick my mentor taught me long ago: to be in two places at once. One of me will meditate and be on high alert, while the other me continues to tell my timeless story..."

*

Gorgeous orange sunrise illuminates Grizelda's lavish kitchen.

"Come, give Mommy hugs and kisses. Hurray! Little fool is handing over 90 percent. And the icing on the cake is that we'll soon be done with the little bitch, forever."

"Mommy," says daughter Gravitas, 21 years old.

"Yes dear..."

"You took in Ima when nobody else would."

"You are very very generous, Mommy," says 22-year-old daughter Guile.

"Mongrel doesn't deserve your affection," says 23-year-old daughter Grating. "I do hope you allow me one last time to give her my special discipline. I promise to be more careful. There will be no anonymous delivery to the emergency room. Oh well, even if there is, after she signs on the dotted line, she'll no longer be worth the trouble."

Ready to face the inevitable, Ima waddles out of her room. Sleep deprived, she's unaware of well-placed slippery cellophane, losing her footing, she tumbles and bounces on her well-padded butt. Ima's inertia stops only after her head dents the ugly moldy wallpaper. The kitchen chandelier shakes above Grizelda's head and five moths escape her puffy beehive wig. Mother and daughters scream while moths continue to dive-bomb their flailing limbs.

"Calm down, my darlings. Focus! This will be our last few hours with the brat. Do not fuck this up!" Grizelda hiccups and trumpets three stinky farts.

Daughter's giggling and angry. "Never mind. Remember what's at stake."

"Yes Mother." Gravitas opens up another window.

Ima enters. She yawns and gags. "Ewe! What's that?" She pinches her nose between her thumb and index finger.

"You nasty!" coughs Ima.

Grizelda's meaty forearm shoves Ima onto the bug-infested floor. *Oh shit! Little brat made me lose my temper. Doesn't matter. She's so afraid and sleep deprived she'll not give us any trouble. I know we could do anything to her...might as well have one last morning of fun.*

Grizelda's fat size-13 shoe presses Ima's hair into flattened ant hill. Guile, Grating, and Gravitas gleefully clap and cheer.

"Crush her like an ant, Mommy!" says Grating.

Grizelda's stinky slowly presses down. "Say crunchies are fun, Ima!"

"I won't. Please, don't. You're hurting me."

"I know. Isn't I-T great."

Oven ding pulls mean family from their terrorizing. "Food! Food! Food!" gurgles Grizelda and her girls. Greasy fat fingers frisbee fling peperoni pizza. Piggish daughter snorts with delight and throws scalding cheese at Ima. Each blocked salvo pushes Ima off her feet; slippery sauce sends her headfirst into gooey carpet fibers.

6-foot-4 Gravitas' man hands squeeze Ima's throat. Ima's muffled, "Let me go," brings no mercy, only disrespectful mocking laughter.

"Don't hog all the fun. Gimme!" shouts Guile.

Nasty pummeling scrum ensues. Pinching. Punching. Poking. Kneeing. Kicking. This alternate timeline Ima is horribly out of shape, and too slow to protect herself. Glancing up, she sees a happy photo with Miriam and Jacob. Gravitas notices Ima's glance. She walks over with her creepy Joe Biden smile and rips the last evidence of Ima's happy times. She long ago forced Ima to delete all happy pictures from her phone. "What's hiding in your butt-crack?" teeth-gnashing Grizelda whispers. "A-ha! Look what I've got!"

"No! Don't! I beg you don't hurt my Special Doggie."

Grizelda's sticky fingers strangle his neck. Ima's tears flood and fly off her shaking face. Scissors clip and pluck black plastic nose loose. Gravitas, Guile, and Grating's teeth latch onto paws. Horrible ripping pushes Ima's hands over her ears. Ima's shaky left hand reaches out to her dismembered childhood friend. Grizelda's meaty fist slugs Ima's face.

Gravitas kicks Ima's ribs. Girls play hacky sack with Special Doggie's body parts and kick them into a filled to the brim, stinky meat decaying trashcan. Crusty cockroaches crawl over Special Doggie's stuffing.

Griselda kicks Ima to the family room. Neatly stacked paperwork shines in grinning Gravitas' sunglasses. "Sign I-T and all your troubles will be behind you." *And if I find I need a little more, I can always amend...He. He. What a stupidly trusting girl.*

Months later, Ima's deadened glaze focuses on a large box of donuts. Unaware of the Do Not Sit sign, Ima's cheeks break rusty bench. Faty ankles turn 90 degrees. Crashing noise sends a screeching pooping bird from the comfort of I-T-S branches.

"Yuck! Bird shit all over my sandwich!"

Ima grabs hold of a chest high branch. She pushes down with both hands. *Argh! Don't you dare split...* Rapidly exhaling Ima becomes ambulatory and trudges 400 yards. Staring for many minutes, she accesses the sturdiness of the park bench. Gingerly, she sits. Depressing thoughts flood. She hunches her back. Her elbows rest on her knees and her fists support her double chins. Ima adjusts her new fuchsia sunglasses and starts her ritual people watching routine.

Teen skaters hold hands. A tiny five-year-old girl with fuchsia ribbons in her hair, chases after her golden retriever puppy. "Mommy. Mommy," anxious girl cries.

Everybody's got somebody. Everybody but me. Ima worthless! If I suicide myself, who would notice? Nobody would come to my funeral. God, why are my prayers never answered? Not asking for much. Day after day I watch happy people enjoy life. Not just people...families.

Wind gust swirls newspaper advertisement. *How the hell can I-T...*

Newspaper barks loudly. Ima jumps, "Don't do that!" Advertisement hovers—fuchsia paints an inky blotch on Ima's right cheek.

Ima watches her fat reflection in a tiny pool of wind-rippling fuchsia water. She reaches up to her face, swats at the advertisement, and grabs a handful of nothing. Newspaper folds into mocking face—sticks out fuchsia tongue and sprays loud raspberry. A weird newspaper follows Ima's retreating flailing steps.

Frantic Ima looks back. Beads of sweat slosh past her eyebrows. She trips and rolls. Paper grows a spring tail, bounces, and jettisons toward Ima's nose, "Get away! Stop attacking me!"

Blood trickles into a cauldron the size of Ima's chubby pinkie toe.

Ima uses her purse to swat at and squish the squealing newspaper into the grayish gravel. Her nervously twitching fingers rummage through her scratched purse. *Got I-T!* Ima maneuvers her magnifying glass toward the sun's rays. Paper drips fuchsia tears.

"Ima melting!" creature giggles.

Bright blue sky, without a cloud, suddenly darkens. One massive black cloud chases Ima. "Stop!" black cloud's voice reverberates, uprooting a dozen trees.

Golf ball-size hail pelts metallic bench. Ima grabs trashcan's metal lid. Warm minty fresh fuchsia breeze turns the hail into dozens of Skittles.

Defying the reality of physics, crunchy leaves, coffee cup, and a discarded eww induced bloody eyeball along the perplexingly tenuous tar-pitted path. An unknown force compels those distinct items to simultaneously scratch and scrape east, west, north, and south.

Ima stares at people, dogs, and hummingbirds frozen in flight. Poof! Newspaper grows a mouth. "Read me if you want to improve your life," feminine voice coos.

Comforting thoughts hug Ima's troubled mind. *Take a chance. Transform yourself with Dr. Scarlett Crimson's guaranteed life coaching wisdom. Lonely girl, you've got nothing to lose except flabby thighs, belly and face.*

That's not nice.

Am I speaking the truth...?

Long pause...

Am I speaking the truth?

Single tear falls. "Yes," Ima cries.

Don't be so sensitive. Seize the moment! If you sign up in the next 18 minutes, you'll earn an 80 percent discount.

Ima wobbles up the hill. Ima leans against a tree, sweating, and gathers her panting breath. Ima hears a baritone voice clear I-T-S throat. She looks around. Time resuming, I-T-S normal trajectory Ima watches people and dogs walk away. She's alone. "Who said that?"

"I did."

"Show yourself."

"Turn around, chunky."

"That's not..." Ima turns and stares at a large fuchsia duck. "Stop resting! Go. I said Go! Get inside for your answers!" shouts Mallard in the perfect Queen's English.

"Go in where? The parking lot?"

"Look again."

Before Ima is a shimmering fuchsia-color CrossFit building. *Door's cold to the touch.*

Ima looks down at her phone. "Holy crap! I-T-S 99 degrees. How can that be? Freezing door and be so hot?" *Why the hell would that duck grimace when I say or think I-T. Did I-T again. I-T-S doing I-T again...* Mallard's body shimmers and poofs away in a large fuchsia bubble.

Ima turns the icy handle and walks through; she's hit by dry ice freezing blast. Ima shivers, in total darkness. "Is anyone there? I was told to...um is this the person who wrote the add? If not, I'll go. *Where the hell is the door?* Hello. Hello! I've come about the add! My name is Ima!"

"No need to shout." Sultry female voice whispers.

Unnerving silence goes on and on. *And? What the hell is she waiting for?* "If Ima in the wrong place, I'd gladly leave. I just can't seem to find my way."

"Hasn't that been your problem? For a long time."

"Well, um. I don't need your bullshit. Let me out, now!"

"You're in the right place, if you truly want the miraculous transformation, promised in the add."

"I do. I-T-S just that I can't see you. Care to shed some light?"

"Shedding light is not the issue."

"What is? You're still speaking in riddles. I've changed my mind. I want to go. I-T-S not just dark, I-T-S so freaking freezing. Didn't you pay the heating bill this month?"

Eerie laughter makes Ima gulp her nervousness. Anvil pounding echoes with each clickety-clack footstep. *What the hell have I gotten myself into.*

Blinding white light hits Ima's face. She tightly squints her eyes.

"Have a set!" shouting causes blood to trickle from Ima's damaged eardrum.

"You don't have to scream."

"Who's screaming. Is this better." Voice whispers.

A long-legged lady yawns and shows Ima her huge shark-like teeth. Her abnormally long fuchsia tongue swipes jagged teeth thrice. Before her eyes Ima watches those dangerous teeth become hypnotically smooth pearl-white inviting chomp chompers.

"Ima Doctor Crimson and I run this place." Ima extends her hand. Stretching out of her seat, Crimson's height intimidates. A peculiar lady's palm reaches to the middle of Ima's forearm and her fingers extend past Ima's fingertips. *Oh, my God! How tall is this woman?*

"Ima seven feet, in heels. Tell me, what's your name, plumpita?"

"That's not nice. Insulting me isn't a good recruiting tactic."

Ima turns and walks toward the front door. Darkness follows and passes through Ima—she coughs fuchsia sparks. *Where did the exit go?*

"Come back and I'll show you."

"Why did you say... Um, no... Can you read my thoughts?"

Ima hears loud clickety-clacking heels. Huge smiling lady hovers over Ima. *Jeezy Louizy personal space... Oh shit, if she can read my thoughts...she isn't human and...and...stop saying that... No! Don't touch me... Damn, licking her lips is so freaky. She didn't invite me... Oh my God she called me plumpita. Is this like that old Twilight Zone episode..."To Serve Man"?*

"You're going to eat me. You're going to eat me!"

"Ima going to do no such thing. Where are you running? Oh, for God's sake!"

Ginormous lady snaps her ginormous fingers. In a flash Ima discovers she's back in her seat. Crimson spits a large fleshy bone through a tiny basketball net.

"Touchdown!" exuberant Crimson shouts.

Touchdown? I gotta get out of here. But how?

A strange noise emanates from Ima's onion ring box. Weird spider humps greasy onion ring. Creepy inhuman high-pitched voice shouts in Ima's mind... *Mine! Mine!* Spider lifts his fuchsia fedora. "Top of the morning, Ima Ratatooey."

"Did you see that?"

"See what, dear?"

Ima rubs her eyes with her fists. She opens her eyes wide. *Oh my God! He's still there!*

Ima slaps her hands over her mouth. *Giant lady's long nail harpooned Ratatooey and my onion ring.*

Ratatooey is flicked high in the air. He lands on Crimson's saliva-drenched tongue. Ima is once again bathed in total darkness. Attacked by creepy shivers after hearing nasty crunch sounds, Ima continues to be disgusted by horrid lip smacking.

Two rapid snap snaps and the vapid darkness becomes alive with fuchsia incandescence.

"Why did you..." *Yuck!* Crimson's shiny fuchsia fingernails tantalizingly slice open a box of gum, she plops five sticks past her puffy fuchsia lipstick. A recognizable smell wafts from her lips into Ima's nostrils. *No! That's impossible. Minty freshness? No difference. You. You! Are Guardian Angel? No way. There's got to be another explanation.* Ima slaps herself. Each pounding against her forehead, hits with greater force. Crimson wraps her long, strong fingers around Ima's wrist. "There will be no more self-tenderizing."

What the hell have I gotten myself into? Better to be fat and sane, than thin and as crazy as... "Well, thank you very much. But. Um. I've changed my mind. Where's the exit? You were going to tell me how to find the exit."

"Oh that. Um! I changed my mind. Giggle. Giggle. He. He. Looks like your cooked is goosed."

"What the hell are you talking about?"

Crimson's cackles split the marble floor, wooden desk, and every metal file. Crimson's hand grows five times and wraps around Ima's body. "Release me!"

Ima is lifted above Crimson's gaping mouth. Tears drip from Ima's cheeks and splash into Ratatooey's nostril. The little creature is alive and continues to bounce from molar to molar.

"Say hello to my little friend," laughs crimson. Fuchsia luminescence continues to shrivel. Lack of light billows and surrounds 90 percent of the environment.

"You humans have no sense of humor." Crimson brings Ima's quivering body down to the spotlight, bracketed by eternal never-ending darkness. Ima's legs buckle, she falls, Crimson kicks over a chair and Ima's butt cheeks make a soft landing. "Ima not gonna eat you and Ima not gonna let you go home. You're forever mine. Well, until the dinner bell chimes." Spat from between Crimson's molars, Ratatooey scurries into the darkness.

"Your feast partner is an Israeli girl about your age. She'll get you into better shape. My people like their humans wiry and strong."

Crimson drinks and gargles a 16-ounce bottle of black blood. Room spins. Ima watches in horror as Crimson grows like a beanstalk. Ima's limp body remains squished between Crimson's giant index finger and thumb.

Three days later, water splashed on Ima's face. "Are you human? Or tiny monster?"

"Human."

"Are you the Israeli, Crimson spoke of?" Confident girl nods. "Dafna."

"Well, are you human or not?"

"I already told you..."

"If you are human, you know I-T-S customary to shake an extended hand." *Excellent, she didn't grimace when I said the forbidden letters. Ignorance is bliss.*

"Can't move my arm."

Dafna's whistles adjust the graviton beam to only .18 times that of Earth. "Better?"

"Much. Thanks. How long?"

"I was captured by a monster named Ami. She's, our warden. Stand clear of her. Do not look her directly in her eyes. That one keeps thousands of years of secrets."

"Have you ever tried to...um..."

"Escape. Sure. Loads. I was in a coma for three months after my last attempt. Best not to stay too close to me. I'm Ami's favorite target, because I'm the only one who fights back. We start gutting fish three hours before breakfast. Welcome to the lower decks, Alice. Only this looking glass is going to be crazier than you could ever imagine.

CHAPTER 13

Backstory of Dafna Shaked and Family

From the start of the Obama administration, politically correct wokeness demanded safe places for all, except the Jews. I-T was an old hatred rearing I-T-S ugly head. A hatred which never seems to die.

A coalition of strange bedfellows: LGBTQ+ aligned with Islamic fundamentalists who would certainly toss that community off the highest structure. Coalition of Marxists and Hamas Nazis. For decades hateful intersectional lying professors instructed their gullible students anti-Americanism. There would be no investigating, nor questioning any of the professors, nefarious diatribes. With malice toward all Jews, and with deliberate intent, those scumbag professors brainwashed millions.

Criminal hate speech scurried from one journalistic rodent to the next. Jew-hating was disguised as anti-Zionism. Those evil professors were backed up by evil pontificators from CNN, MSNBC, ABC, CBS, NPR, BBC, *New York Times*, Facebook, and TikTok influencers. They all have blood on their hands by perpetuating the world's oldest hatred: antisemitism.

Throughout blue state woke America and across Europe

and the Middle East, evil goose-stepping financial mega donors plant the seeds, growing to fruition on university campuses across the globe. Sub-human crowds in Australia did not chant, "Gas Israelis." They shouted, "Gas the Jews." Masked cowards march, burn, and loot. They feel emboldened and entitled by appeasing journalists, police officers, university chancellors, presidents, and professors. Where the hell are the social justice warriors? Oh, that's right they are in lock step with Hamas rapists and the murderers of babies in the most grotesquely torturing way. Beheaded and burned in ovens, while their hearts still beat. Calling for a ceasefire, means those American college students proudly and ignorantly advocate for the annihilation of the Jewish people. Hamas and their supporters demand, by way of words and deeds, the final solution—Genocide of Jewish Israelis. The one and only Indigenous people of their God-given land.

Too few voices condemn Rashid Tlaib and Ilhan Omar. Those witchy appeasing hags are extremely proud of Hamas' Genocidal war crimes. Democracies the world over must stand shoulder to shoulder with the righteous Israeli Defense Force. They were and are the most ethical military force in the world.

America has never known a more feckless duo than Joe Biden and Kamala Harris. Israel, the light unto the nations; must prevail over Malevolent Time's manipulative darkness. Once and for all, the civilized world must come together and stop appeasing and apologizing for the fascist-Palestinians genocidal encore.

Moses Jabotinsky exudes joyous gratitude for life. He greets the day with his traditional, "Oy vey!" His gnarled, wrinkled fingers reverently touch his Mezuza, affixed to his doorpost. Within is the Jewish prayer, the Shema: "Hear, O Israel: The Lord is God, the Lord is One."

Moses takes small steps and leans on a cane. He inhales the

aroma of red, yellow, orange, and purple flowers. Moses waves in the direction of Benjamin, Daniel, David, and Jonathon. They all hug, hum, and sing as more friends and family join them for the morning prayers. The 18th member, which is Shlomo. He is married to Moses's granddaughter, Rachel. Last month, Shlomo celebrated birthday 81.

36 days ago, Moses, a staunch Zionist and Holocaust survivor, celebrated his 122nd birthday.

Daniel, 99-year-old son, greets Moses with a kiss on Moses's right and left cheeks.

"Vhat ve doing today?" asks Moses.

"If you're up to I-T, we'll be visiting with the new Israel Defense Force graduates."

"And..." Moses's twinkle-in-the-eye inflection adds to Daniel's proud smile.

"You will sing our National Anthem, 'Hatikvah.'"

"Come boychek, let's eat."

180 minutes later, unassisted by his son, Moses confidently walks to the lectern. Shoulders held back and chin held high; he looks upon hundreds of recent IDF graduates. His lungs expand to their fullest through deep, satisfied breaths.

Moses's deep baritone voice captures the Israeli heart and determined spirit. Israeli's national anthem, Hatikvah...

Ko ode beleav P'nima Nefesh Yehudi homiya Ulfa'atey mizrach Kadima Ayuin L'tizioin

Tzofiya Ode lo avadah tikvatenu Hatikvah bat shnot aplyim; L'hiot am chofishi

B'artzenu Ertz Tizion v'Yerushalayim.

18 days later, for their pre-Shabbat dinner, the Shaked family dances and sings traditional Israeli folk songs. Arms hug, Fingers tickle. Torah questions enliven conversation. Every

member of the Shaked family embraces religious Zionism and proudly follow God's commandments.

"Incontrovertible facts," emphatically states Benjamin. "Israel is the only country in the world with a net gain of trees in the 20th and 21st centuries. Under Roman, Greek, Arab, and Ottoman rule, our ancient homeland became a swamp-infested wasteland. 18 centuries after the failed Bar Kokbah rebellion. To humiliate our people, Rome renamed our nation Syria-Palestina. Never in recorded history did an independent Palestinian nation exist."

"Biblical Joseph and fellow Jews built Bar Yoseph with their blood, sweat, and tears 3,700 years ago," comments Dafna.

"I-T was an engineering marvel siphoning off fresh water from the Nile. That 400 square mile Israeli project was called Bar Yoseph. While the Jews maintained control, I-T kept that area of the world green. Romans, Greeks, Arabs, and Ottoman Turks lacked the intellectual know-how to keep that Jewish-made Lake from deteriorating. Not even the British and French could rescue that ancient wonder," interjects the twin brothers.

"Second-century Christians celebrated their first Easter while Jews already celebrated Passover for 15 centuries," says Benjamin.

"What's freedom?" asks Rachel. "And this isn't a trick question."

Dafna pipes up, "In the biblical account of Exodus, the Israelites celebrated their freedom from slavery. Freedom isn't just absence from oppression. I-T-S the presence of a meaningful route of self-fulfillment."

"Very good, Dafna. In Jewish tradition, we differentiate between yi'ud, which means fate, and goral which means destiny," says Rachel. "My fate is the hand of cards that I'm dealt."

"My destiny is how I choose to play them," says Dafna.

Brothers smile in between deliberate drawn-out slurps of chicken soup. Twin sisters shake their heads and dip cherry tomatoes into Rachel's delicious salad dressing.

"Regardless of the hand we're dealt, everyone of us is free to shape our own destiny, even in the most challenging times," says Benjamin.

"And speaking of challenging times, the Haggadah, the Passover story, is the foundation of Judaism," says Rachel.

Everyone nods in agreement.

"Our people are born not in battles and victories, but in slavery. Through injustice, cruelty, and loss of freedom, we learn the importance of justice, truth, compassion, and liberty," says Dafna.

"Yes," Rachel agrees. "These values form the basis of our faith, our ethics, and the society we strive to create. We have carried this vision through every country of our dispersion and our return home to our land. Marginalization, persecution, and exile has sharpened our awareness that we and everyone are safe in a world of justice, truth, and freedom."

"Blood libel hatred spews forth in nations falsely claiming to be our friends. The mob's murderous throng against the Jews continues throughout the United Nations. And that antisemitism couched as Anti-Zionism is spread by professors, media influencers, and politicians. We've seen this movie before. The difference is that we have a strong Israel. Never again, shall always be never again..." says Dafna. Her fists pounded her chest, three times. Unfortunately, that emphatic declaration was made before the tragic events of Oct 7, 2023.

Three days later, six-four Ahmed Barghouti, six-two Yassin Barghouti, and six-one Al-Rantisis Barghouti salivated, watching their 16-year-old niece. 4-foot-11 Ami Fayz enjoys twerking her ass.

Nasty Barghouti uncles take turns groping their hypersexualized niece. Fear grips her eyes when Ahmed's feathery hands squeeze her skull the way a giant clawed monster would crack an eggshell.

My mind to your mind, nasty whore. Submit!

"Ahmed!" shouts Yassin.

"Very well."

Long inhuman black tongue licks Ami's face. "You know you love I-T!"

Ami runs into a swirling black vortex. Her limbs pull apart. Her shrieks linger long after she bursts into flames.

"Idiot!" shouts Yassin.

"Sshhh...she's coming," whispers Al-Rantisi. "The one to be our new and final host body."

Barghouti brothers climb up the rain pipe suppressing malevolent smirks; they squat like eavesdropping gargoyles. Ami's older sister smiles at Dafna—*I can't wait to taste Dafna meat.*

"Boker Tov, Ami," greets Dafna.

"Boker Tov, Dafna," says sly smiling Ami. *You're next. Foolish peace-loving Israeli.*

"Did you get a chance to reach out to my cousin?"

"Oh yes. Thank you Dafna. I didn't know you had family contacts on the UCLA campus."

"He's been a professor these last 18 years."

"I have no doubt you'll follow in his footsteps."

"When I'm 20. Still need do my two-year stint in the IDF."

"Yes. Um...well here's too the future... May I-T give us all that we deserve."

Dafna wraps Barghouti's niece in a warm embrace.

Three gargoyles hidden by dense greenery, shift to the left, creaky stone chips off a tiny pebble. I-T rolls toward Ami's feet. "Say I-T." pebble whispers. *You must keep up the charade.*

Indeed, master warned us how clever she can be when not distracted.

"See you next Shabbat."

Dafna waves goodbye. "Next Shabbat."

Three miles from home, Dafna tap dances on roller skates. Ahmed greets her with beautiful flowers. "Dafna! Over here! Your papa will be upset if you're late again."

"Can't help getting lost in my thoughts. Thanks for the pretty flowers."

Yassin pounces and startles Dafna. "Excuse me. I just don't want my brother taking credit for my idea."

"Okay. Well... Um... Then, thank you, Yassin."

"You're very welcome." Al-Rantisis shoves his phone into Dafna's face. She pushes his hand. He hides his bristling angry emotion with well-orchestrated practice. Dafna is unaware all three brothers are aiming their middle finger at Dafna, from behind their backs.

"You are running very late!" Al-Rantisis shouts excessively loudly.

"Wow! That's not necessary."

"Sorry. I know your Papa is different, our Papa would never allow us to be late for any important event."

"No harm done."

Keep I-T cool brothers. Yassin! Don't let the Israeli bitch know you're salivating again!

Annoyed, Benjamin stands on the front lawn. Rachel massages his tense shoulders.

"Sundown is fast approaching and she's nowhere to be seen."

A massive shadow engulfs the entire Kibbutz. Benjamin and Rachel look up. There isn't a cloud in the sky. They both shake their heads. Holding hands, they walk back inside.

1,700 feet above the tallest tree; three 8-foot crows swoop down and instantly transform into the Barghouti brothers. The sound of stretching skin reveals the Barghouti brother's clawed digits. Ahmed creature unlocks the back door. Smiling, Ahmed sneaks up behind, and his large talons bludgeon Benjamin's skull. Yassin's black boots crunch Benjamin's spine. Al-Rantisis slices Benjamin's spine from the base of his skull to his tailbone.

Blood splatters. Blaring Israeli folk music masks Rachel's blood-curdling screams. The twin girls instinctively run to Mama's side.

"Upstairs. Don't look back. Hurry!" Rachel waves at her 15-year-old twin boys. "Follow your sisters."

God! I hate retelling this part...

With his 12-inch talon, Yassin mercilessly decapitates both brothers. Their sisters hysterically screamed. Black talons wrap around the Shabbat candleholder and forcefully crack open Rachel's skull. Barghouti monsters gleefully delight in the brain and blood speckle splatter on the white walls.

Al-Rantisis and Yassin take turns raping Rachel in front of her daughters. Ahmed chews on the daughter's flesh and spits their desiccated flesh, bone, and blood back in their faces.

Black claws slice off noses and gouge ears. Half paralyzed, Rachel drags herself, and blood and tears grotesquely smear the once pristine floor. Half-dead she stops, hearing horrible echoing slurping sounds. The creatures are hollowing out twin's intestines and brains.

"Where the hell is Dafna?" caw-caws Ahmed.

Creatures use their talons like paintbrushes. Their paint of choice: Shaked brain matter. They write in big bold capital letters: HITLER WAS RIGHT ALLAHU AKBAR THANK ALLAH FOR EUROPEAN AND AMERICAN LEFTISTS THANKS TO MOST RELIABLE LOYAL UNIVERSITY STUDENTS THANK YOU PALESTINIAN AUTHORITY THANK YOU IRAN THANK YOU BROTHERS OF AL-QAEDA ISIS HEZBOLLAH AND SAVING THE BEST FOR LAST HAMAS AND THE UNITED NATIONS.

Ahmed, what should we do? Master would be upset if we were late for the rendezvous.

We know he helped Hamas construct another 22 tunnels.

The three Inhumans screech nasty angry Arabic obscenities.

Yassin and Al-Rantisis flap their wings. *We'll have to return later and give Dafna a proper Shabat Shalom.*

All three take two meta-human jumps, and without flapping their wings, they puncture Earth's weak atmosphere and land with a dusty thud on top of multiple sacks of flour. Careening and swooping through secret terrorist labyrinth, six eyes glow bright green.

"Once we destroy Zionist, we'll meet up with our BDS brethren on UCLA campus. We'll align with BLM and other like-minded folks. We already have college professors and America media spreading our narratives. Allahu Akbar! Jewish Voice for Peace marches with us! From the River to the Sea! Hey world, soon you will all be under Sharia law!" shouts Ahmed's breathy squawks.

90 minutes later, Moses stands 180 feet from Dafna's home. Dafna approaches with her typical engaging smile. "Good Shabbos, Moses? What a pleasant surprise. I didn't know you'd be joining us."

"No...little one, I-T-S not a good Shabbos."

"What's happened?"

"Let's take a valk."

"Love to, but after, I'm very late. Papa will be annoyed."

Moses hugs Dafna. Dafna feels the need to break free, but Moses holds her longer.

Moses motions for the police. Dafna pushes past Moses. "Ema! Aba! Dara! Davina! Yitzvhak! Yair!"

Dafna crumples to the ground. Grandmotherly police officer helps Dafna to her feet. She looks into Moses's bloodshot mournful eyes. Dafna quietly whimpers into Moses's shoulder.

Catatonic with grief. Dafna clings to Moses. She falls onto his bed. He sits, keeping watch, his gnarled fingers stroke her weepy cheeks. "Why? Why? Why?" Dafna whispers.

18 hours later, an IV drip keeps Dafna hydrated while she sleeps. Dafna's favorite Israeli folk music plays. Moses rests in his rocking chair. Two partially eaten sandwiches are getting cold next to Moses's desktop computer.

18 days later. 2:34 a.m. Dafna clicks her flashlight and crawls out of a side window. *Aba's lab is 9 miles away.*

Dafna dabs at her sweaty brow. 36 minutes later, she's able to disengage her father's security protocols. Dafna's new norm means she flashes a sad grin; after she's hopped into her father's experimental hovercraft. Craft's shell contains unique composite materials brought back from space, allowing for the bending of light, and rendering her Israeli craft invisible.

Dafna flies three stories above rooftops and trees. She musically taps her forward computer console and disengages auto-pilot. "Activate cloaking," Dafna whispers.

Invisibility lasts 99 minutes before I'll need to recharge.

"Recognition Dafna-18...36...72."

Dafna hovers half a mile from her home. Moonlight gleams off of her Papa's experimental overalls. *Invisibility particles were sewn in the morning of my family's murder.*

Dafna adjusts her special hoodie and face mask with those same invisibility particles.

"Engage extreme stealthy mode."

Dafna enters the crime scene. Disembodied flash-light shines with all due creepiness. Dafna stops 9 times to compose herself. She scans blood and brains. *DNA confirmed.*

Invisible tears pity-pat off her invisible cheeks and become visible as they hit and contaminate the bloody carpet fibers.

God, how do I find these creatures?

"From the river to the sea! Palestine will always be! Intifada! Intifada! Intifada! Kill! Kill! Kill!" shout Barghouti monsters.

CHAPTER 14

Traumatized Dafna Can't be Consoled by Dear Friend Moses

After EM-IT-S malevolent metamorphosis; God instructed his second son—god—to construct the Realm of the Watchers. The physics of that place is unlike any laws which govern our space-time-continuum. Within the Realm are righteous 360.000,000,000,000 souls, each holy creation contemplates an erratic future. Realm's blue-hot energy keeps the essence of God from the bounds of normal space. Cloaked righteousness excretes unique emotional and intellectual particle fields, individualistic spheres, and triangles, and expels other geometric shapes human brains are incapable of comprehending.

Ko'ach and Nephesh are born 6,363 years before David, Ima Best-Friend, and Dafna Shaked. The fuchsia solar system is located 18 million parsecs from Earth.

Ko'ach's and Nephesh's home world is twice the size of Jupiter. Unlike Earth, their multiple continents never broke off and remained as one singular humongous Pangea.

Tiny mammoth-size herbivores playfully scamper and chew weeds, the size of oak trees. Buzzing insects equal in weight to any Volkswagen Bug. Human-size water droplets replenish thousand-foot trees. Music cascades from multi-aromatic fauna. Blue whale-size feathery flying tortoises greet every new day's rainbow sunrise.

Killer whale-sized cheetahs sprint and swing on vines longer than the 6,000-mile round trip between New York and Los Angeles. Every thumping, galloping, multi-legged smooth mane and spike protruding armored creature; all co-exist harmoniously with two-legged fuchsia humanoids, telepathic plant life and ocean-breathing equestrian flying mammals.

Fuchsia parents are exceptional teachers; they instill in their children the skill and joy of critical thinking, elaborate problem solving, storytelling, and rigorous debate. This is the opposite of how the horrible Dull Gray parents demand absolute obedience and rigid adherence toward their dictatorial doctrines. Their parental value system embraces emotional and physical abuse for the slightest transgression.

Debate and freedom of speech are forbidden—especially for males within the Dull Gray matriarchy. Male lawbreakers, no matter their age, experience spine-chilling, grisly torture before they're thrown into the darkest forest—weaponless. What follows are four- and six-legged beasts' sickening howls as jaws and teeth rip, shred, and chew bloody flesh. Unholy carnage streams via government-controlled social media platforms.

Back on Earth, bombastic dinosaur-size crows divebomb over Gaza cities. Downdraft flapping wings scatter tiny, terrified Arab humans.

Talon flexing Al-Rantisis, Yassin, and Ahmed caw-caw. Tempestuous telepathic pterodactyls terrorize scrumptious Palestinian snacks. Scurrying, shrieking Palestinians look like dancing worms; food to be consumed by cannibalistic Barghouti crow brothers. *So many choices,* Ahmed's thoughts screech. "Allahu Akbar! Allahu Akbar!" Brothers crow.

In the adjacent room, Hamas terrorists prepare to launch 12 short-range missiles and refit half a dozen young men and women with homicide vests.

Shrapnel and other sharp metallic items marinate in rat poison; a special ingredient which acts to neutralize the blood's natural coagulating enzymes. If Israeli children survive organ and bone-shattering blasts, they'll rapidly bleed out.

Anti-Semitic inscriptions are scratched in Arabic, Hebrew, and English onto each missile.

9 floor-to-ceiling bookcases are filled with multiple lifetimes of reading pleasure.

Pristine white walls are adorned with pictures of Moses's second family. Rebekah died 20 years ago, when she was 99. Children, grandchildren, great-grandchildren, and great-great-great-grandchildren smile in pictures with spaghetti sauce smeared over their cute faces.

The table is set with an assortment of toast, melons, and eggs. Moses plops blueberries and sprinkles flaxseeds onto piping-hot oatmeal. Dafna's profound depression pounds relentlessly. Her eyes closed, heart indisposed, hatred self-imposed; lingering humanity decomposed.

Drowning in the past—hurtful memories last. Present overtly intense. Whence, recompense?

"Vat you are doing—buttering my fingers. I am not toast."

Trauma remains too fresh. Too raw. Too recent to illicit any Dafna giggles.

Dafna and Moses stare blankly. Numbness squeezes like a repressed geyser. Dafna's angry abrupt thought startles Moses. "Damn I-T! No more!"

Tears percolate at the corners of Moses's eyes.

Seething Dafna's eyes remain dry. Not a single drop will she cry, unable to defy nor mollify agony's outcry. Her right palm slams against twitching thigh.

"Vhen you find the criminals...vhat shall you do, little one?"

"Do? Show them the same kind of mercy they...they..." Dafna's blaring bloodshot eyes scream, "I'll kill them!"

"You can't."

"Can't? Or shouldn't? I won't let your misplaced empathy get in my way!"

"Empathy? For them, never! For you, always."

"Go away, Moses!"

Dafna's peripheral vision catches Moses's blue tattoo. Feeling profound guilt, she says, "Forgive me. I shouldn't be shouting at you. Never you." Dafna cries into Moses's shoulder.

"Do not act on your understandable thoughts. Revenge is for them. Never for us!"

Dear sweet soul. You don't deserve my rudeness. I-T-S wrong to say I have no choice. I do have a choice and I choose to avenge my family.

"Irrational hatred toward us has been going on for thousands of years. Regardless of Whoopi Goldberg's hateful idiocy—ve're a race, a people who have contributed greatly to the vorld of ethical monotheism, creating uplifting poignant musical scores and innovative scientific, medical, and technological breakthroughs that help the blind and paralyzed."

"Eretz Israel has always been our home. We'll never again let the hateful racists take I-T away from us again. We ended famine in Africa with our drip irrigation. We will never allow Obama's two-state solution to threaten our children. More Jewish blood on European hands. Oslo created the Intifada. Brought about more Jewish deaths. The world doesn't give a damn. So, the hell with the world!" shouts Dafna.

"No, little one. We have plenty of allies. Good Christian, Buddhist, Shinto and Hindu friends. We are not alone. Little one, ve are only flesh and blood. Ve are not wise enough to see God's infinite plan. Vhy did I get to live past 122 years and my first wife of blessed memory was murdered at 23? Vhy did the world allow the Nazis to murder millions of children, including my Daniel and Joesph? I have a theory, more...a vish about what happens to evil when they discover God's justice. Can you imagine vehn these blood-thirsty jihadist monsters achieve their afterlife and come face to face vith their Mohammed, and he screams horrible invectives because HE is tortured every time those murdering idiots take a life? And those terrorists are painfully blown up for every life they take?"

From the corner of her eye, Dafna notices blinking scanner coordinates.

"That's Gaza!"

Moses's gnarled fingers tightened around Dafna's wrist. She easily breaks free.

Ugh! If I was younger, you would not be able to break from my grip.

"Please, little one, For me. Don't go. Tomorrow vould be better, yes?"

"No, you'll not talk me out of...ugh! I need fresh air."

"Good! Ima ready for my valk. Lead the way, little one."

"Alone!"

"Alone, is never good. Help me with chicken soup, yes?"

Long awkward pause lingers.

"Yes?"

"No..." Dafna whispers.

"Dear friend, Moses. I know you care for me. You are a good friend, but...you...are not my true family. When I call out to Ema and Aba, images of my sisters' carcasses and my brothers being decapitated."

Dafna looks away from Moses. She shakes her fist. "God. God, why did you allow this to happen? I hate this world. All the people who chant from the river to the sea; they are all evil."

Hugging each other, Moses and Dafna's tears co-mingle in an avalanche of anguish.

Sleeping 12-14 hours a day becomes Dafna's new normal. Nightmare or daylight reality, neither brings any solace.

Her new zombie-like expressionless affect pushes her trudg-ing, shuffling, fluffy blue-white slippers forward. *Sweet old man. Tonight, I must leave you.*

Dafna's grief is real, but her depression is not. She's been plotting her revenge for months, and now...she's ready.

Plopping down at the dinner table, Dafna inhales the beautiful fragrance of red and orange petals. "Ima famished." Dafna forces a crooked smile.

"Excellent news, you're feeling better. Enjoy, little one."

Moses's darting eyes watch with astonishment.

"Chew slower. Do not gobble so quickly, better to savor the flavor. Sarala cooked vonderful salmon...rice and broccoli."

4:50 a.m., two duffel bags hang from Dafna's strong shoul-ders. She hovers above sleeping Moses. *God, please watch over my dear friend. You know I must do what I must do.*

Moses's rhythmic snoring arches Dafna's eyebrow. The European waltz interacts with his nasal exhaling. La la, snore snore, la la, snore snore... *I hate being the cause of your pain. I must not waver in my conviction. I-T-S the right thing to do...for me.*

Dafna taps Moses's nose. *Boop!* Dafna clicks her flashlight and walks from the dark home into the dark early morning. A quarter moon adds extraordinarily minimal illumination.

Fuchsia mist absorbs streetlights electrical illumination seconds after Dafna passes. Dafna readjusting her duffel strap, runs toward Gaza.

"Coordinates brought me to this...tiny tree?"

Her Papa's scanner blinking beeps loudly. Dafna muffles blaring sound under her armpit.

"Mute. Mute. Dafna scrapes a blood sample off the ser-rated leaves. What the hell? Can't be. Human DNA inconclu-sive? Makes no sense. Papa's prototype never failed him. Why would I-T beep inconclusive? How did I screw this up? I must be better."

Dafna leans on the small tree and falls over. *I-T-S a fake!* She scans blood next to two footprints. *Human.* Dafna clicks her flashlight and holds I-T in her mouth. She enters the dark tunnel. Soft dirt cascades. She coughs. *Recently dug? Stay alert.*

Senses spike; she's simultaneously suspicious, stalwart, sorrowful, and sharp. Stepping stealthy and steadfast, she slips and slides onto subterranean surface. Soft sediment shifts. Systematically she scans, searches, and seeks.

"Human, soft and tasty," muffled voices growl and squawk.

A large rat appears out of the darkness and bites Dafna's Achilles.

Filthy rodent!

Few red drops leave unintended genetic breadcrumbs.

Rodent gallops through the darkness. I-T-S hindquarters transform. I-T grows larger. I-T-S black eyes glow. At the end of the tunnel a giant eight-foot rodent finds four more of his similar-sized comrades. High-pitched squeals are drowned out by loud clickety-clack footsteps.

Dafna's face eerily glows from the pulsating helter-skelter scanner. "Not human?" *Hush! I-T will hear you. Five somethings running this way. DNA...size...internal organs fluctuate. Now something new is entering my scanner's range. I-T-S totally off the preprogrammed scale...*

Dafna's flashlight slips from her shaking sweaty fingers. Off button slams into the cement floor—illumination clicks off. Bathed in total darkness, Dafna, on hands and knees, searches for the light. Spasmodic flickering allows Dafna to see 12-foot hand wrap around eight-foot rat. She hears I-T-S bones crunch and sees I-T crumble like brittle balsa wood.

Humongous puffy fuchsia lips glow in the dark; cold misty vape exits. Dafna's neck and skull are protectively cupped on elongated index and middle finger pads. Micro burlap beanstalk strands wiggle from huge woman's fuchsia fingernails and whoosh through Dafna's contaminated bloodstream, her righteous essence cleansed of any malevolent toxins.

Semi-conscious, Dafna rolls to her side and takes three painful breaths. Fuchsia fireflies' phosphorescence dazzles.

That incongruous flashbang provides a narrow gleaming path forward.

A single fuchsia firefly three times the size of the others tunnel into Dafna's ear. I-T-S burrowing, tickles. I-T-S intent is never to harm. I-T-S to educate.

"I can't understand what you're saying. Repeat. Louder."

"Danger. Hurry. Save yourself."

Fuchsia firefly exits Dafna's nasal passage, shrinking with each downward stroke of her wings. Dafna reaches out and grabs. She opens her hand...*nothing. No wait. What's that? Glowing particles. So pretty.* Dafna blows, her breath pushes shimmering fuchsia dust phasing through the cement wall.

Hurry, little one! Oops. Go back and bring your Papa's prototype...

"Boot heels slamming louder and faster. Can't outrun them." Dafna holds her thumb on her jawline and her index finger and third finger's knuckle tap, tap, tap on her sweat dripping temple. *Of course!*

Dafna activates her papa's prototype Spiderman grip. Heart pounding, Dafna jumps and crawls along the ceiling, Dafna recites the Hebrew, the Sh'ma...*Sh'ma Israel Adonai eloheinu Adonai echad. Hear oh Israel the Lord our God, the Lord is one. Barukh sheim k'vod matkhuto l'olam vaed. Blessed be the Name of his glorious kingdom forever and ever.*

Yes! Dafna brings down her eye-level fist below her shoulder. *Good for me, but not for everyone else! European and UN bastards did I-T again. Just like they allowed Hezbollah to construct 180,000 rockets aimed at our cities. Those anti-Semitic bastards gave Hamas permission to build hundreds of miles of tunnels. I must warn my people. How? Papa's Mossad friend. What was his name? Dov...um...Gronich! Hope you are home. I-T-S ringing...oh no! Going to voicemail!*

CHAPTER 15

Dafna, Ima, and Burlap Boy Caged in Crimson's Demonic Lair as Breakfast, Lunch, and Dinner

Agitated alligator angers assassin's axiomatic awareness.

Belittled and besieged, Burlap Boy frequently fractures obligatory oblivion while narrowly negating napalmed nom de plume.

Cunning conniving cruelty callously creates cheeky conspirators' contagion. Chased children are always farm factory chickens, for cannibalistic creatures' disgusting delight. Manipulative megalomaniac muse, munches, maims, and murders.

Durable Dafna disobediently denounces dullard Ami and her contagion in crime duplicitous Doctor Crimson. From dawn to dusk, the dangerous duo's demonic determination deceptively dehumanizes.

Packed like sardines. Every child must, on penalty of death, gut and discard tons of slimy stinky fish. Ages 7 to 15, they all work 14-hour shifts, 365 days a year, and 16 hours past their 15th birthday, I-T-S rumored that every boy and girl becomes either sticky stew or sent spiraling into specially spiced, scalding ravenous vortex.

Workday screaming whistle announces a new day, every 4:40 a.m.

"Ready!" exuberant Ima shouts.

"For what?" groggy Dafna answers.

"Revolt!" grinning Ima yells.

"Yes, indeed, your morning breath is revolting."

Both girls giggle through their growing anxiety-fueled fear.

"Ami's scent could kill a skunk," smirks Dafna.

"Why do you mock such an upstanding citizen?"

"Ima, I-T-S too early for sarcasm."

Hundreds of children follow Dafna and Ima out of the dining hall and onto the rain-soaked, sloshy, muddy hills and valleys. 18 minutes later, Dafna kicks open the rusty doors. The pungent fish-guts aroma overwhelms hundreds of recent arrivals. Each child grabs their assigned rubber hat, rubber gloves and rubber overalls. Floppy fish particles fly. Pock-marked rubber conveyor belt ratchets into ricocheting hissy fit. Three pre-teen girls walk toward Dafna.

9-year-old Becky joins in the stinky hug.

"Can't blame her for a little hero-worship after you saved her little brother," says Ima.

"Okay. You can let go. Becky, come on. You don't want Ami to see you talking with the camp's two biggest trouble-makers."

"Really sorry I messed up. Cuz of me..." Tears roll down Becky's cheeks. Dafna removes her smelly glove and pats Becky's red tangled, knotted hair. Unable to look Dafna in the eye, Becky stares at the bloody fish gut-strewn floor. "My fault Ami put you in the hot box an extra-long time. I promise not to screw up again."

"Been through worse. You're a good person. Evil Ami will eventually get what she deserves."

"I wish. Um..."

"What?" asks Ima.

Becky wraps her entire body around Dafna. Walking like Frankenstein's monster, Dafna delivers Becky to the end of the conveyor belt.

"You can let go now." Dafna's smile reassures frightened Becky.

Ima grabs Dafna's cheeks; she rapidly pulls. Dafna's cheeky sound duplicates old jalopy's huffing, puffing, sputtering start.

Ima's eyebrows pinch together. "Crimson is accelerating the number of new arrivals."

18 feet above the fishy floor are thousands of swaying, swiveling burlap sacks.

Dafna's dual focus is on gutting fish and watching out for Ami. Easily distracted, Ima looks up at the thrashing burlap bag. Unlike the other fuchsia bags, that bag's violent movements hold because of I-T-S sealing stitching from top to bottom.

"Damn I-T! Get back here. Ima! This is the wrong time to leave your post! You know Ami can see through walls!"

"Wiggling toes? Hey Dafna, there is a monkey crawling around in that bag."

Ima jumps back after tiny fists punch through the reinforced black glowing stitching. One bag falls at Ima's feet. "Hey! I-T-S a bag, within a bag? That's new. Wonder why they...?"

The second bag is far more erratic, tumbling head over heels. Sickening crunch as something chips off a piece of the brick floor. Howling whimpers send waves of gurgling pain.

"I-T-S a creature. Slowly step back. Did you hear me? Ima damn I-T do as I...I-T won't understand you're trying to help I-T!"

Ima holds her ground. She bends low, keeping her eyes on the crying creature. She grips two fish and throws with all she's worth at the black-white-fuchsia control lever. "Shit!" Ima shouts after missing the target.

Ima tosses two large fish in Dafna's direction. "You're better at this than I am."

Dafna hurls two frozen fish.

"Wide right!" yells Becky.

"Damn you, Ami! She elevated the lever since the last time I stopped I-T!"

Nobody notices fuchsia trampoline shimmering into existence. I-T-S never a good sign when new stuff materializes.

"Look!" shouts Ima.

Ima grabs slippery fish heads. Becky and Dafna drag the trampoline closer to the lever. Dafna runs back to get a running start.

"On three!" shouts Dafna.

Dafna's feet go thumpity squish—slide. Thumpity squish—slide. "One!" *Tired bruised legs must run faster!* "Two!" Dafna's feet land on the trampoline with significant force. "Three!" Ima tosses the fish heads. Before she falls back to Earth, Dafna, in perfect fastball motion, she releases, her on the money bullseye. Two bloody fish heads splatter. Lever wheezes. Gravity does the rest.

Conveyor belt asthmatically sputters. Rusty gear's raspy hissing whistles and sends conveyor belt into a herky-jerky-full stop. Out of foggy-black-mist Ami and Crimson appear. The conveyor belt's reckless recoil splashes fish juices and stinky parts down Ami's ample cleavage. Ami's long nipples function as a hat rack for two large fisheyes.

"Hey stinky! Check out what's ogling your rack!" shouts Dafna.

Odiferous moist orb slides down Crimson's long right leg.

"Ami!" unflinching Crimson's enraged stoicism screams.

"Yes sir." Fear causes Ami's mind to confuse I-T-Self.

"Sir? Sir!"

Whack! Crimson's frying pan-sized hand sends Ami soaring to the back of the factory. Ami's skull dents steel rod and chips wall's stone masonry.

Crimson's pristine heels clickety-clack for 90 seconds. Ami runs at break-neck speed and stands low under Crimson's gaze. Crimson bares her gigantic teeth. Her right heel steps back and crushes Ami's fingers.

From her prostrated position, Ami licks fish guts off Crimson's shoe. "Everyone back to work!" screeches Ami.

The tallest boy punches a large fuchsia button. The broken-down conveyor belt takes a long time before humming activates I-T-S sputtering motion. Loud crushing mechanical grinding no longer petrifies experienced enslaved kidlets.

"I see Dafna is back from her nap. So weak. So, human. So Israeli," Ami growls.

"Don't let her goad you," whispers Ima.

Ima tries and fails to restrain Dafna.

BFF. Don't do I-T.

"Monster! Where are the others?" shouts Dafna.

"What on Earth are you talking about?" Ami's index finger circles her ear. "Coo coo," Ami exaggerates while showing off her sharp fangs. Little Becky holds onto Dafna's leg...two more small boys wrap their bruised arms around Dafna.

Dafna looks around at the scrunched-up faces. Sweat trickles down worried faces.

Ima I-T-S no longer a question of if I die...I-T-S when I-T will happen. And when I-T does, will you be ready to step up? You're not ready yet to take my place. We are nothing more than Chess pieces on Crimson's and Ami's elaborate duplicitous board. I've taken my investigation as far as I could and I've yet to decipher half the clues. Many truths were revealed to me while my mind, body, and soul cooked in that hot box. Many different dimensions I visited. Touching the hand of God. Ha! I guess I am still trying to convince myself. Like Moses, I will not get to the promised land. But you, my BFF, might, with God's help. In my last delusional state, I-T was promised an ally would appear. Whom shall I-T be? As far as the eye can see—none of us can hope to defeat Ami. And I-T would take an army... No! I don't think even an army could defeat Crimson...

"By whose authority have you stopped production?" shouts Crimson.

Dafna takes an exaggerated long-legged, silly Monty Python stride forward.

BFF! Keep up the distraction, while I investigate the wounded creature wiggling about in the burlap bag.

Each bloody puddle Ima squishes, the moaning and crying whimpering from within the bag grows louder. *Poor thing is in agony. I-T didn't scurry away because I-T-S legs must be broken.*

Ima grabs a fish tail and uses I-T to lift the corner of the burlap bag. She's astonished to see two glowing green eyes with fuchsia flecks, blink back at her. The quivering creature backs away and cowers in the corner of the seven-foot bag. Ima's flashlight illuminates the creature's dark burlap environment. I-T wheezes and sneezes a million fuchsia dust particles into Ima's face.

A mixture of blood, alien fluid, and dust inflame Ima's nose and clamp down her throat. *Can't breathe.*

Dafna turns her back on Crimson. "Hold still, human."

"She's suffocating!"

"How wonderful," cackles Ami.

Burlap creature on all fours instinctively gives Ima mouth to mouth. Only your narrator is aware of the tiny almost imperceptible smile curling up at the corner of Crimson's lips.

Burlap's veins distend along his neck, strident soundless screeches hit Ima's empathetic heart. Burlap's skin absorbs tiny creatures' tearful frustrations. I-T inflates I-T-S lungs and pushes life giving oxygen through his damaged larynx. Inaudible inhuman sounds ricochet off destiny's interloper.

"You, okay?" inhuman screechy voice asks.

"Thanks," whispers Ima.

"Don't tell them."

"Tell who? Tell what?"

"I escaped."

"From where?"

"Big people hurt. Big people turn me into...into..."

Ima hugs the almost-human creature.

"You're safe. You're safe. Tears? You have human feelings. I no hurt. See, big people not in this place. Dafna is our protector. She will help."

"Thank you. Thank you. But um. Big people are here. Must get away. Must not let them find me. Find you."

"My name is Ima."

"Not let them find Ima. The only one to show me compassion these last five years. You have kind eyes. But um... Big people tricked me before with kind eyes. Are you tricking me again? Greenie! Show yourself!"

Tiny thing coughs bloody burlap fibers. "There is no Greenie here. Ami and Crimson, they are the big bad, here. What's your name?"

"David." Creature coughs.

"Well, David, you must be very warm in those burlap clothes."

"Clothes? You think David is clothes. You mock me? I thought. Um..." David slaps his own face and slugs his ribs. Ima's hands come up to her mouth. "Stop! I didn't mean to...I didn't understand..."

"The hell you didn't. I trusted you. I shall never do that again! I can't let her find me!"

"Her? Did Ami do this to you?"

Clickety clack sound unnerves David. I-T-S like pouring gas on an already blazing inferno of uncontrollable fear. "She's here! She's here! She's here!"

Crimson nods. Ami turns the blinding search light onto David's face. He covers his eyes and runs smack into Crimson's fist. Impact crushes Crimson's diamond ring. Shards fall like tiny daggers stuck in fishy flesh.

Crimson bends low. "Come Fido."

"His name is David!" shouts an indignant Ima.

"Has the burlap Fido found his own human Fido?"

"Ima nobody's Fido!"

"Unexpected courage, from one so human."

Crimson turns her back on Ima, and stares down wobbly knee David. "In you go my fibrous inhuman plaything."

Ima takes a step toward David. She's shocked when Dafna restrains her. Ima's moist pleading eyes makes Dafna bend her head low. "I-T-S a trap. Don't trust him," whispers Dafna.

"No! Don't! Not the cage!"

David swivels around and looks at Ima. She silently mouths, "David."

Tears streaming down David's burlap cheeks.

Crimson's cruel dehumanization of David touches Ima's heart. His voice cracking plea, "I beg you, please! No more torture." Pushes Ima's tearful eyes in Dafna's direction. *You've got to help him. Dafna, not like you to hesitate. You've never done so before. Why now?*

Crimson's mesmerizing smile alters, she purses her lips and blows. David is knocked over by her boiling minty fresh breath. Crimson takes a half step forward and crunches David's right hand. She grinds the way one would put out a smoldering cigarette.

Ima is stunned by what her peripheral vision observes. *Is that a tear? Why would the fiercest cruelest creature show empathy? Can't be empathy. Some burning particles must have irritated her eye. Damn I-T Crimson! Stop grinding your heel into his broken hand!*

Crimson's long nails puncture David's burlap skin. *I can't bear the little guy's screeches. Leave him alone!* Blood squirts like a newfound oil derrick gusher. Reflexively, 18-million-year-old narrator and Burlap Boy flinch. His-our Cobra quickness pulls back; tiny fists break 18-inch-thick oak board.

Crimson impatiently flicks and clicks her long nails. "Ami, dear! Contact our surgeon. We need to repair this animals' skull. You know I detest infected meat.

"You sure? You know Madam Lady Bug and her kidlets find infected meat to be a wonderful delicacy," adds Ami.

"Ami!"

"Yes, my queen." Ami bends at the waist, her puffy lips kiss Crimson's ankles.

"Enough! I have news for the one who orchestrates every interactive story."

"God!" smirks Dafna. She knows how irritating I-T is to hear the name God. "You've been warned, do not push me this day!" Her simmering rage boils and explodes.

Crimson spits black mucus with fuchsia metallic particles. "Don't you ever say the G-word in my presence again!" Crimson punches three holes in the brick wall.

"Be careful. My boss is not as forgiving and merciless as I. Fucking little humans! Back to work!" Roof cracks and falling debris is about to crush the terrified twin brother and sister, thinking fast, Dafna pushes the 8-year-olds out of the way.

Dafna's thoughts consider the following: *Burlap Boy, are you the misdirection my predecessor, before she vanished, warned about? I don't know. Ima falls for too many sob stories. Is that the game you're playing? Get her to fall in love with you and turn her against me? My gosh. Burlap dude is smaller than Becky.* Dafna takes two long chest burning gulps. *Only a day or two left of Papa's elixir, which blocks ridiculous creatures from hearing my thoughts. Ima! Damn your infatuation. You're making I-T very difficult to trust you, BFF. Once more, I fear your heart is going to get in the way of our sleuthing.*

Crimson drags David's skull into cement stairs. Each slow climb chips off burlap bone.

"Can I, please?" Ami's annoy bratty girly girl voice begs.

Ami saunters up to blue, white blood oozing David. Her claw pinches his burlap belly fibers. Horrible cry reverberates through the factory. Windows and light bulbs pop. Screeching siren scatters shattered salvo; saturating saber shards selectively saw, severing somber serenity.

Dafna grunts lifting alien crowbar used to file down creature's teeth. Like a tomahawk I-T flips end over end, slicing off 4 of Ami's 7 fingers. Her blood curdling yelp punches, punches, punches holes in the upper tier windows. Everyone ducks under the conveyor belt. Shards stuck in fish, pumpkins, and unconscious Burlap Boy. Ami's claw cackles menacingly each time she tweezers another bloody shard. Cluster of five reveals David's pink skin.

Ima gasps. David's healthy burlap fibers grow and restitch covering up multiple greenish-yellowish bruises; David's "That's not burlap sown into his skin. That burlap is his skin."

Quicker than Dead Pool can reassemble limbs, Ami's new fingers wiggle and twitch.

Crimson's long nails pinch burlap blanket from her swaying hamster cage. Female creature with green hair, and no larger than a Barbie doll jumps onto Crimson's long black middle fingernail. The tiny creature opens her mouth three times wider than Ima's skull. Deafening roar vacuums up every glass particle. Tiny creature smiles and crunches. Black blood oozes from her lips: slithering tongue laps up and gurgles serrated tissue.

Ami attacks David's skull with punches so fast they are a blur. Typical thumpity thump thump sound reminiscent to a boxer pummeling tear drop speedbag.

Crimson holds up her massive hand. Disappointed, Ami's face sinks.

"I appreciate your zeal. However, I need Special Doggie alive."

Ami places her ear to David's chest and nods.

"Do I have your permission to play with the Israeli bitch? I promise not to tenderize her past her last breath."

Ami's eye contact with Crimson means she's unaware of the two large calico bass in Dafna's hands. Dafna's powerful east-west brush strokes clobber Ami's nose.

David held tightly in Crimson's grip. She winks at Ima, and both vanish in a stinky puff of fuchsia gas. Thick frozen gaseous anomalies engorge Ami's swelling nostrils. "Come with me," growls Ami.

Dafna rubs Ima's shoulders. "I thought I had another three months."

"Crimson told you she wanted me left undamaged."

"She was talking about Burlap Boy—not you! As much fun as you'd taste, I-T-S not, unfortunately, your turn yet!"

"Once again, you, Israeli bitch, have errored. I-T-S not you my queen wants. She prefers the fat bitch this time. Everyone else! Back to work!"

Distorted time takes hold of Dafna, David, and Ima's reality. While 18 months passed for all other humans, Ima returns to Dafna's side 18 days later. Ima is now privy to secrets Dafna hasn't yet discovered. Both encounter Burlap David 18 hours later. During Dafna's 18 days apart from Ima, her BFF was held by Crimson and became her double agent over the next 36 years and didn't age a day. Returning to Dafna's side, she's aware of her many possible futures with her always true love—David Sagacious. And the truth Crimson hides from Burlap David and Ami.

Siren blares. Blood trickles out of Dafna's ears. She collapses to the ground. Ima siphon's bloody black blood into a fuchsia cylindrical tube. Fuchsia particles drop from Ima's fingertips. Shimmering tube melts into Dafna's scanner.

"Wake up, Dafna."

"What happened?"

"You fainted."

"I did what? Never!"

Crashing through the door, walls, basement, and ceiling are 22 crazy things, flying, crawling, hopping, slithering, and swimming on 6, 8 and 10 legs. Those 12-, 16- and 21-foot beasts surround Dafna and Ima. Standing on two legs, their heads, necks, and torso punch through the bungalow's roof.

2 gargoyle vampire creatures, 3 crocodile creatures, 4 boa constrictors with human size teeth, 4 saber-tooth squirrels, 4 killer whales, and 5 tarantulas. Each hissing thing opens their mouths wide enough to swallow 5 humans. "You smell that?" asks Dafna.

"No."

"I-T-S aroma is distinct."

Dafna watches Ima grimace.

"What's wrong?"

Weak smile precedes, "Ima okay."

"Hot minty fresh."

"You're mistaken."

Ima mistaken? The hell I am. Why are you pretending…? Stop flashing that fake smile. Have they gotten to you? Are you…you? Damn I always knew you had my back. If I can't trust you…I don't think I can do this alone. There must be another explanation. I've got to figure I-T out. There, she did I-T again. And again. What is causing your pain?

Dafna can see the minty fresh aroma solidify and penetrate every creature. "No, my queen!" they all screech. Seconds later their bodies implode. Dafna and Ima are covered in green, orange, and black bloody guts.

Suffocating under all that disgusting fluid, I-T-S Ima helping Dafna to her feet. *Since when did you get to be so strong? I should be saving you, not the other way around. More proof you're not who you pretend to be.*

Spontaneous bonfires consume part of the forest. Caustic flesh-burning clothes are discarded in a three-story-tall tornado swirling fire. Ima finds two blouses, pants, socks, and boots hanging over a branch of the lone smiling pristine tree. *Former BFF. You know how much I dislike coincidences. Those clothes just happen to appear. On the lone tree impervious to these diabolical flames. You seem too happy. As if all of that is transpiring is expected. More. I-T-S… Shit! There she goes again, grimacing. Am I getting this right? Is she grimacing because she's fighting against an outside force controlling her?*

Crimson's amplified voice penetrates deep into the minds of 18-thousand pre-teen and teenage captives.

All non-essential personnel go to your sleeping quarters. We're officially on lock down! There's a danger in our midst! An outsider! Under no circumstance should anyone approach the evil monster we call Burlap Boy.

Vertigo's signals send Dafna's conscious mind swirling into cacophonist hallucinating variants. Agonizing toxins burn her eyes, ears, and lips.

Burlap Boy is deceptive. He mocks our truth. If that demon approaches you, immediately without hesitation—run! Find either Ami or myself. Now go! I said get up and go! Run home and pray we catch Burlap Boy before he turns you into the next morning's meal. Lock your doors. Shutter your windows. Turn off the lights. Do nothing, until I give the all clear!

Ima looks down at her phone.

Fully recovered from her short-lasting hallucinations, Dafna glances over Ima's shoulder and reads Ima's incoming text: TIME FOR AMI! Next to a monster emoji.

CHAPTER 16

Monsters of All Sizes, Ima's Transformation, and Ami's Truth

What truth did Ima discover while Dafna was in her multi-month coma?

Healthy color gone from her cheeks, Dafna's ashen face frightens Ima. Advanced technological implants pulsate with spiritual energy. Tiny human size and greenie giant size doctors and nurses work round the clock in an attempt to revive Dafna.

"She's hemorrhaging," Giantess's booming voice whispers.

"Save her!" terrified Ima shouts.

Life-enhancing splashes from torrential tear ducts are, this time, extremely ineffective.

"I-T-S not working!" Ima grabs hold of Greenie's thumb. "Where are you going?"

"Dafna must want to come back to us. Her soul is currently in limbo, spiritual conundrum dissects deathly determination. She's caught between her loyalty for you and her desire to be forever with her family."

"Why are you allowing her this choice?"

"Realm of the Watcher souls are explaining the consequences to her this very moment."

"How long will that take?"

"I don't know. You must prepare yourself..."

"Why would she want to stay, and fight and suffer, when she could have eternal peace with her family? I know what I would choose. I know what most people would choose. Be well, dear friend. We shall do our best without you." Ima rubs a single tear from her cheek.

Dafna's body convulses. Implants slow her violent shaking.

"You trained me in the vortex of lost time for decades. You told me how important the three of us are...could we succeed as a duo?"

"As a duo, you'd have less than a 13 percent chance of success. Beware of shape-shifting tricksters. You haven't yet learned how to differentiate when Ami pretends to be Crimson."

"I am getting better. You said so, five decades ago."

"Sound the alarm. I hear Ami's time distortions."

"And Dafna?"

Ima looks as Dafna's ashen face slowly fills with healthy pigment. Dafna takes two shallow breaths.

"She's back. She's back." Ima hugs Dafna.

"Will Dafna remember her conversation with the righteous souls?"

"That's not her destiny. You must promise to never tell her that part of her story."

"Why?"

Crimson exhales.

"After all these years—still minty fresh."

Confused Dafna blinks her eyes. *What the hell? Why would Crimson smile at my BFF? And Ima? What are you doing, smiling back at her. I must be dreaming. Bad dream. Bad dream.*

Orderlies wheel Dafna away from Crimson's clickety-clack heels and bring her toward Ima's fat suit hanging in the closet. "Time to get back to work, little one."

"Any changes to your orders?"

"Now, play your role well. The fate of everyone's history is in your capable hands."

9 months later...

Fuchsia dust allows Ima to move between time at 18-second intervals. When she walks among the monsters she appears as Ami. When she needs a stealthier modus operandi, she releases her limited supply of time particles.

Humanoid clawed beasts and feathered winged things arrive in clusters of thousands. Ima watches them exit limos, buses, trains, row boats, C-130 transports, and aircraft carriers. 20 percent fall from the sky with parachutes and 80 percent without.

Ami roams the grounds searching for Dafna. Her red glowing skin tells her she depleted her mutating super-human reserves by 75 percent.

Ami feels her bones crack and reset. Shredding serpentine skin...remodeling I-T-Self. 5-foot-8 Ami shoots up another 10 feet. She pokes her red eyes with her green nails—fiery emerald eyes canvas her surroundings and encroach upon unsuspecting prey. Ami's long nails touch her short black hair and blonde luminescent locks unfurl. Her ruby lips part, revealing cutting-edge under-bite-protruding shark teeth. Each step, Ami's growls become a deeper register.

"Fe fi fo fum! Time to fill up my tum tum. Energy beast released. Palate greased. Must feast, till all of humanity is deceased!" Ami's reverberating cackles split tree trunks, shatter empty bungalows, ripple deep lakes, and blast steep grassy hill tops.

Swirling fuchsia fog deliberately hardens around Dafna. Her fists slam against the smooth alien material until blood drips down her forearm. Human blood dripping drops sparkle blinding bright blackness, odorless chemical reaction pushes

Dafna into the conscious unconscious. That fuchsia membrane will keep her safe from the caustic environment; reassembled by Ami.

Ami's telepathy is unable to penetrate Dafna's newly constructed cocoon. Ami's hoofs pound the soft mud like a myopic mythical Minotaur galloping gracefully through gargantuan grass.

Ami's massive girth and powerful slamming hooves create an 18-mile fissure. Dafna's membrane slips between the recently created opening. Scalding geyser melts the first layer before I-T plummets miles.

Superheated membrane seeps through the gaseous darkness.

Ami stampedes crushing bungalows, trees, boulders and quickens her pace so that she can actually run on water. 18 miles due west of David's position, she is unable to close the gap. *How the hell is this possible? Beginning to tire, he must be an inhuman mutant. Never known one to break away from the fold before. No wonder mistress wants him back, uncooked.*

Years of torture have conditioned David's eyes to adjust to moonless nights. He doesn't need infrared goggles to see clearly.

Crimson! Your tortures created my advantage. Do I thank you? I think not! Death is better than living as one of your puppets forced to commit those unspeakable crimes. You didn't fully expunge my humanity. You will never be able to force me to harm my sweet Ima or brave Dafna. No strings on me. You hear that! You won't control me this time! Each day Ima's getting stronger and faster. You were never able to erase all my memories. I heard your angry frustrations and defeated your plans that night. Remember? In that other place I could feel my bone density thicken each time I was broken.

Dafna's fuchsia membrane buoyed and pockmarked. I-T picks up speed and descends through a 90-foot silver lava waterfall.

Ami cloaks all 27 feet of herself. Her jagged fin juts out of her back. Orange pigment washes away. Black and white shiny skin pulsates.

David takes his time exploring newfound powers. His hand chops two oak trees into thousands of toothpicks. Stepping as lightly as any Jurassic monster wearing a ballerina's tutu; devilishly quick and agile Ami approaches.

Breathing in Earth's aromas, truly for the first time, David releases gratitude's tearful reaction. Holding his middle finger under his eyes, salty tears are quickly absorbed. *I see you, monster! You will not harm my new friends, this I swear!* David's powerful burlap elbow connects with Ami's cloaked killer whale knee-cap.

"Timber!" croaks David.

Sliding into the icy snowbank. Ami snorts and bellows.

Fast fists terrifically timed. Tiny's thumping pummels perforate paranormal predator. Out of the fuchsia fog, Crimson's ginormous thumb and index finger pluck and squeeze 27-foot killer whale Ami. Ferociously she flails. Ami's spine cracks. Her essence deforms into crusty particles.

Crimson's pouty lips hold and blow. David's legs are strong and can't be knocked over by forceful fuchsia fresh-minty-breath hurricane. David's eyes are pelted by Ami dust particulates.

David's cocoon slams against the rock walls like a hyperactive pinball. Spiked outgrowth cracks the membrane the way a human cracks an egg. Dafna leaks through the internal yoke-like material: her body shimmers, transported half a mile from David and human Ima who searches with night-vision goggles.

Sneaking up behind Ima, Dafna's stealthy steps quicken, and ka-plow-ee! Dafna tackles Ima's ankle. They slip and slide over melting snowbanks. Ima rolls over Dafna's ankle.

"Ouch!" shouts Dafna.

They recreate Charlie Chaplin and Buster Keaton pratfalls.

"Stop! Let me get up first! Ima, you're doing this on purpose!"

Dafna reaches her index finger toward Ima's belly. "You know the rules when your laughter is out of control."

"You wouldn't."

"Tickle fight!" shouts Dafna.

Dafna and Ima playfully slap each other's hands.

Cocking his head to the right like a confused puppy, David shows his perplexed scrutiny watching Dafna's and Ima's silliness.

Dafna's internal red alert sounds. She jumps in front of Ima. "Burlap Boy! Hold your ground!"

"Are you Ami? Or Ima?" screeches resolute David asks.

"Are you nuts? Don't you dare take another step closer!" shouts Dafna.

"One way to find out. I-T!"

Ima holds her heart and buckles over in agony.

Dafna doesn't understand why David would smile.

"Beast! You're happy she's in pain?"

Dafna swings. David ducks. Dafna swings again. David back-pedals.

"Dafna! Stop. Ima fine. He's on our side."

David's finger flick pushes Dafna a few feet. *Not sure what you are. Certainly not human.* David and Ima share a moment, while Dafna rubs her bruised shoulder.

"Ima! Back away from him."

David takes Ima's hand. "You're very pretty. I'm the danger neither one of you should be close to."

David's running movements are a blur. All Dafna and Ima can see are fuchsia lightning bolts exiting his burlap skin.

Swirling volcanic ash reanimates Ami on the dark side of the fuchsia-shimmering hill. Ami was born on a world with gravity eight times that of Earth. Ami's clawed fin pinches off the white sign nailed to the cracked old tree and plunges I-T deep below the gurgling bubbling scalding swamp. Eleven triple jumps later, Ami's covered miles. Ami plunges into the freezing lake. Swimming to the outer rim, she rockets out dripping dozens of shimmering orange leeches. Ami's voluptuous sexualized 28-foot, fast shrinking naked green body transitions into a perfect 5-foot-8 Ima doppelganger. She grabs a handful of leeches and munches. She swipes her bloody orange lips. She squats, hums, and waits for the unaware fast zooming Burlap Boy.

Three times faster than any Hummingbird's flappity flap flap wings; Ami-Ima extended rubberized leg trips up Burlap Boy...He goes tumbling. Burlap Boy's head impacts and knocks over one of the oldest trees. He rubs his head. "That hurt."

Ami-Ima hugs Burlap Boy. *She smells—different.* "Howdy mutant, Ima, Ami!"

Ami-monster seductively bats her eyes. "Kiss me."

"Stay away from me!" screeches Burlap Boy's damaged voice box.

Black energy swirls and human size Ima becomes an eight-foot Ami. "Bet you can't make that jump. Tell you what. If you try, I promise to leave Ima alone. In fact, I won't even take a bite out of Dafna. Deal?"

Ami extends a scaly black-greenish hand. Her huge shadow looms. Her long middle-finger nail caresses David's burlap face: Sickening serpentine secretions seductively slurped. Perennial predator penetrates little guy's perforated cracked lips.

"Yuck! You taste like rotting eggs!"

Ami's side-to-side wiper blade tongue action moistens David's burlap nostrils.

"You taste de-voon." Sudden shimmering rope's harmonic materialization ripples Ami's pristine lake. Devious smile appears. After David leaps. In mid-air, Ami snaps her fingers. White board shimmers into existence. David grabs the rope. Proud of his accomplishment, he grins.

"Don't look down, honey."

Thousands of individual splashing sounds bring a droplet to David's burlap brow.

Ami cackles. "Should have looked before you leaped. Pity, I won't have the pleasure of first bite," roars Ami.

David's fingers slip. Ami snaps her fingers. Each thunderous snap unravels the rope's spindle. Ami pushes the white sign with blood-red letters in David's face: BEWARE OF MUTATED PIRANHA!

David slides and regrips a half-dozen times. Ami-beast reapplies her blood-red lipstick; her lip-smacking sends silver shards deep into David's burlap skin; terrible slivers selectively slice.

Voices crash into David's haunted mind. *David sushi! Mouthwatering raw humans melt in our mouths. MMM good!*

Swinging his legs, David tries to build up momentum to get to the other side.

"Not going to work, dearie. You're going in the drink for sure."

Black Machete materializes over David's head. I-T-S blade pricks thinning strands. Rope fibers splay open, defying the laws of gravity. I-T elongates, whooshing through David's chest.

Organs serrate. Blood gushes. Burlap Boy falls. Deadweight splashes into churning black-bloody lake. Each bite he feels—I feel. Each agonizing scream he screeches—I shout. Pain is an old companion I've never been able to shake free from.

"Bon appetite, lovely brothers and sisters!" Giddy Ami dances and clicks her heels thrice.

Thousands of piranhas click, click, click their teeth, and descend faster toward their burlap prey. Fuchsia eel half again the size of a single piranha flaky scale; from below the depth of the Lakes' watery grave—that unexpected creature ascends like a bat out of hell. Glowing fuchsia Energy illuminates and burns away the blackish-brackish sediment, energy barrier burns and flays fiendish fish.

No longer Burlap Boy, David emerges as fully pink and unconscious. His deeply scarred body floats to the surface. Burlap gills are the last vestiges of his formerly burlap self.

For 5 hours, Dafna watches Ima run to the east, stop, and

run back west. Out of her mind with fright, Ima drags herself up the steep grassy hill. Exhausted, she collapses. Dafna lifts her weary body. Ima's long-drawn-out exhale precedes her awareness of David's injuries. "I can feel... He's in extraordinary pain."

"Time to rest," Dafna's kind eyes reassure.

Dafna unzips Ima's blue-white sleeping bag.

Ima snores. Dafna scans. Both are bathed under a large glowing illuminated moon. Dafna's scanner shimmers and shakes. "Ouch!" Surging hot energy smolders; plastic melting, sizzling flame is naturally doused by drenched muddy grass.

Dafna looks down with tearful eyes, on Ima's angelic face. "Pleasant dreams. For tonight your blissful dreams will be shattered. How am I going to break the news that the love of your life was chewed up by giant piranhas? Will she blame me? Grief is an unpredictable emotion."

90 minutes later. "Why didn't you wake me?!" shouts Ima.

"There was nothing you could have done to prevent..."

Ima slaps Dafna. "Don't!"

Ima slaps Dafna harder. Birds soar out of their nests. Dafna blocks the next slap; along with the next four. *I've never known her to be this quick, nor so strong. Damn my cheek hurts. Ima not sure I-T-S...why the grimace...I-T-S...she did I-T again. Ima not touching her. Strange. I don't think adrenaline's rage and grief could account for this change. Are you my BFF, or something Ima going to have to kill?*

Five miles later: "Hurry up!" shouts Ima. Three minutes later Dafna arrives. Brown burlap skin fragments bubble to the surface. Ima's moist cheeks slam into Dafna's shoulder. Ima's soft whimpering brings out the twitching baby squirrels, baby hopping bunnies, wide eye baby deer, and cute wobbly baby foal.

David's shaky pink hand rises.

Dafna's eyes grow wide. She pats Ima's head. "Turn around..."

"David!" Ima gleefully shouts.

Gooey slime drops from David's fiery red fingers. "Ima," David gurgles. Deflating lungs and he sinks. Ima plunges her gloved hand. Piranha pinched through the thick glove. Gobbled up are trickles of blood by the tiniest of new piranha spawn.

"He's too slippery," cries Ima.

Dafna tosses large netting. David's pink face slides into the netting. He takes two wheezing breaths. "Help..." David screeches, going into shock.

Silver piranha, with black stripes, twice David's size, jumps a foot above the gurgling black water. I-T-S fin waves and I-T-S left eye winks at Ima. Dafna hears Ami's throaty giggles.

Dafna hands Ima two steel-lined boots. "How did you know we'd need...?"

"Less talk, more action. Go save him. I'll watch for Ami."

Ima laces them up. "Tell me, how did you know?"

Dafna's sheepish grin worries Ima. "I was just thinking... Um, I wish I had those boots and well after a minty fresh breeze dissipated—voila!"

Ima smiles. *Thank you dear old friend.*

Stretch! Dafna releases her best surprised expression watching the boots stretch from Ima's ankle to her knee cap. Ima runs into the black thrashing water.

Piranha bite and clamp down. Razor sharp teeth are unable to penetrate the first steel layer. Three piranhas swim the length of the lake and slam into Ima's thigh. Dafna shakes her head, hearing the piranha screech, *Damn that hurt!*

Ima walks out of Piranha Lake with David attached to her boot. 18 steps onto dry land, David falls face-first onto the cool, squishy grass. Dafna and Ima gasp. "My God. Who would do that? Deep healed scar tissue cuts a terrible swath from David's arms, back, and legs. His grayish-blue skin pulsates."

"Astounding he could survive such torture," says Dafna.

Unconscious David starts to flap around like a fish out of water. Ima rolls David over onto his back. "What's this?" Ima gently rubs her index finger over David's gills. "Can't breathe," screeches David.

Ima places her warm soft lips over David's cold cracked lips. Dafna watches her warm breaths expelled out of David's gills. Dafna places her hands over David's gills and pushes. 18 seconds later, those gills disintegrate.

David rolls to his side and coughs out black water and slowly his pigment pulsates bright healthy pink.

Ima's soft blue towel lovingly caresses David's hair, face, and naked body. Ima helps David stand. Dafna towers 15 inches over David. She tosses denim short shorts and her blue-white *I Stand for Israel* T-shirt. What should have been an easy catch, knocks David over. Ima shoots Dafna a disapproving glance.

"Sorry," says Dafna.

David stands on shaky legs. Ima's strong right arm holds him close to her hip. David opens his mouth only an eerie wheeze expels.

Ima kisses David's cheek. Her eyes fill up with emotion. "Take your time."

"Thank you for your kindness, Ima. And you too, Dafna. And now you both must go. I am dangerous. Save yourselves. Anyone too close to me will be harmed. I am dangerous. Leave while you still can. Please. Especially you, Ima."

"Especially you, Ima? Why is that?"

"Sha! We're not leaving."

"We're not?"

"Neither of you are a match for Ami."

"He's right, Ima."

"Aren't you always wishing for a champion strong enough to help? Well, there he stands!"

Dafna notices, as Ima's and David's fingertips get closer, fuchsia sparks dance. Electrical soulmates, Dafna's mind says to herself.

Stars depart. Sunrise begins. David's new pink skin smolders and bursts into flame. "Hurts! Hurts!" David's shrieks horrify Ima. Dafna pushes him under a shady tree. Ima douses him with two bottles of water.

Ima slams her hands into the ice chest. David pats out sparks dancing along the edges of his tightly shut eyelids. Ima gently places her frozen palms over David's smoldering lids. He sighs: "Thank you, pretty Ima." Ima blushes.

Fuchsia bandana materializes around Dafna's wrists. Ima immerses the bandana into the ice chest for the next 18 minutes. She wrings the cloth out and wraps the now blue cloth around David's forehead.

David smiles. They kiss. David inhales Ima's hair. "No, dear Ima, you and your friend are not safe around me. I hoped to hide how I felt about you. I know, this is love. I know this is... No! No!"

"What's wrong?" asks Ima.

David gently slaps away her comforting hand.

"This is all too easy. Ami! Well played. You've found a human ally this time."

"David! H-how could you say that?" shocked Ima places her hand over her mouth.

David clenches and unclenches his fist. "Show your true self, Ami!"

"That's rich! You think she's Ami! You really are nuts."

"Not nuts. Awareness, personal experience beyond you humans."

Fuchsia caterpillar tickles David's sockless, shoeless ankle. He loses his footing and tumbles down the slimy snaily embankment. Dafna and Ima give chase. A frantic flock flew into David's face. He waves his arms, and they scatter. He runs smack into Dafna's chest.

Dafna clears her throat. "Um, that's not a cup of pizza dough you're kneading...needing."

David's face turns bright purple.

"S-sorry. Didn't mean to...forgive, okay?"

"As soon as you let go, I will."

"Greenie! I did what you commanded me to do! Enough! End these hallucinating manipulations!"

"What the hell is he talking about?" asks Dafna.

Ima puts a comforting hand on David's shoulder.

David tightly squeezes Ima's wrist. "Stop! You're hurting me." David flips Ima onto the soft, muddy grass. "Back the hell up!" shouts Dafna.

"And if I don't? You're no match for me. Ami! Greenie!"

"Who the hell is Greenie?" asks Dafna.

"Nice try. You both are in on this aren't you. Well, you can't fool me. Not again, at least."

Like a frantic animal, David sniffs the ground; on his hands and knees, he rips up slimy grass blades. Plop. Plop. Sticky molasses-type goo hits the wings of a limping fuchsia pigeon.

"I thought I was free. You really covered your tracks this time. Greenie! Let me out of your cage!" David crumbles to his knees. "Please God, help me escape." Ima rushes over to trembling David. She holds his face in her warm hands. He leans in, they both wail together.

"David. You're safe. You're free. You're not in any cage."

David looks into Ima's kind wet eyes. "If this is one of your tricks..."

"No trick. I promise..."

"Leave him."

"What?"

"No! I promised."

"We can't abandon what we've planned these last 18 months."

Ima looks at Dafna with hopeful eyes.

"No! With or without you, best friend."

"He's what we need. He's what I need."

"You're going to choose a crazy bullshit stranger over me? Well, you truly have changed. Maybe he's right, maybe you are, after all, Ami!"

"Where's the door?" Clear-throated David shouts.

His voice is getting stronger. Wonder what that means?

"There are no doors outside," says Dafna.

"Not outside! Still in my cage. Where is...? Where is...?"

Oh shit! He's in on this I-T thing too. BFF, you'd better tell me the significance of I-T soon or that will be the end of our friendship—forever!

"Long ago I came to terms...Ima never getting out of this place."

"Stop saying that! Why can't you see what I see?" *I know why. I must find a way to convince you. Must find the words for you to trust me again. I can't divulge what's really going on... Not yet. Greenie, Ima losing them both...*

Giantess Crimson steps out of her tornado vortex. She holds her head. Fingertips inject glowing fuchsia energy, and her dizziness dissipates. "Oh crap!" Crimson claps her hands, and thunderous sound knocks David and Dafna unconscious.

"Guardian Angel, why did you do that?"

"Time is shifting again. He's confusing what shouldn't be confusing."

"I haven't forgotten my mission. And Dafna?"

"Too early to tell."

Giant Crimson gently scoops Dafna and David into the palm of her hand. Crimson walks through a swirling fuchsia vortex of her own making. She uses the last of God's dream-reality blue-white time shifting particles. Contorting her face and limbs; Crimson forces Benevolent Time to rewrite a new story for Dafna, Ima and David.

Dafna's scanner high pitch hum tells her I-T-S overheating. Ima taps, taps, taps to maximize her goggle's search parameters. *Where is everyone? Not a single human or creature interrupts this peculiarly still, stillness.*

David passionately gulps down his third helping of eggs, toast, and hash browns.

Mouth full of eggs, David's lips dribble. "Thank you, Ima. You're a very good cook."

David's loud burp reverberates. "I must be going."

Ima fills up David's plate. "Rude to leave without finishing what's on your plate."

"He can take I-T to go." David watches Ima grimace and understands her heart.

David stands. Ima gently pushes him back down.

"Family doesn't abandon family," says Ima.

"That's not my experience," says David.

"Well, um...Ima family and Ima telling you I'll never abandon you."

David smiles with two forks full of hash browns and eggs. Dafna giggles.

Ima hands David a paper towel. "Here!" David wipes his mouth and cheek.

Dafna motions for Ima to walk outside with her.

18 steps later, Ima pushes Dafna. Dafna trips Ima.

"Enough!" shouts Ima.

"I-T sure is!"

"Stop saying that!"

"Why the hell should I? Don't look at me like I should know what I don't know."

"You're the great detective. Figure...out..."

"I-T! Figure I-T out." *Every time I say or think I-T...looks like she's been sucker punched. And she refuses to tell me why. You're showing...BFF...more and more you can't be trusted.*

Dafna gets to her feet. "Trust!"

"What about, trust?"

"I don't trust that puppy you're falling in love with."

"He's not a puppy!"

"You used to tell me everything. You've changed. Admit..."

Ima wags her finger in admonishment.

"All over an innocent word we've both been using for... um, ever."

Dafna touches Ima's shoulder. "Please tell me what's going on? I really believe he's setting us up for some weird Ami shit."

"You do? Why?" Ima winks and flips Dafna over the fuchsia shrub and sprints toward the front door. *Damn she's fast!*

Before she can get to her feet, four loud bolts are locked.

Are you trying to keep me out, or keep him safe from my interrogation?

Ima bumps David's shoulder. He easily loses his balance. Ima falls next to and cuddles with David on the blue sofa.

"I found this," says syrupy-chinned David.

"You can have as many French toast slices as you'd like."

Neither David nor Ima notices fuchsia lightning sparks dance between their fingertips. Awkward silence lingers. Ima batts her eyelashes. *He's so cute.* Shy David's cheeks become flushed. *Can he read my thoughts? Better bury my mission parameters.*

"With your permission, I'd like to sleep here."

"Of course. Oh, wait. No, you can't."

David frowns. "Oh. Um...sorry. I thought. Well, okay. Thanks for the food."

"You don't understand. I thought you were pointing at the floor."

"That's right."

"Why would you think I'd let you sleep on the floor? We have an extra bed."

"I couldn't do that."

"Why?"

"I don't deserve..." Overwhelmed with her kindness. Tears well up. Gravity slowly takes down pain induced salty droplets. Ima touches David's leg. Pity-pat. Pity-pat...tears plink, plink on her hand.

Using her T-shirt, she tenderly blots the corner of David's eyes. Her breasts lean in. He doesn't pull away. *Even with all that food, I can feel his ribs.* Ima's and David's breaths, heartbeats, and thoughts are in sync.

Her skin is so soft. So beautiful. I don't know what to say. How to act. I can't recall how to act around humans.

"What's wrong?" whispers Ima.

"What if Ima dreaming you? What if tomorrow I wake up and you're gone? And. Um...and I find Ima back in my...I was wrong to involve you and Dafna. I should be punished for my happy wishes. That's my true transgression, getting my hopes up." David slaps his own face. "Bad David! Bad David!"

Ima's two hands tighten around David's wrist. "Stop! You're hurting me!" David's tearful aggression abandons all reason. Ima uses all her enhanced strength. David continues to lift her off the ground and shake her about like a rag doll. David's pinching pinkie finger causes Ima's yelp. That pushes him out of his irrational rage-induced fugue state.

"What? Oh my God. Ima!" David caresses and kisses Ima's bruised thumb and wrist. "I never wanted to, you've been incredibly kind to me, and look what I've done…"

"Ima okay."

David's tone changes. "I told you I was dangerous!" Powerful thrum shatters half the windows. David runs. He deliberately smashes his head into the fuchsia painted wall.

"Look."

Ima wiggles her thumb. "Nothing's broken. You didn't physically hurt. What you're doing now, that's emotional trauma, which is under your control. David! Stop!"

David slides his head against the wall, smearing horribly bright red blood, with intermittent blue, white shimmering particles. Manically running back and forth, he creates long dripping stripes.

David crumbles to the blood splattered floor. Fuchsia energy exits the back of his skull and beams into Ima's forehead.

Ima's thoughts reach out to David. *Can you hear me?*
Yes.
Oh my. Your thoughts are deep baritone.
Crimson? Crimson! How could you? Ima. I loved you.
Loved? Why past tense? You mean love.
How could you ally yourself with the evil one who imprisoned me? Gave me my scars? Killed my parents? I-I…loved… "I hate you!" spits David.

Dig deeper. That's right. Find the truth. Too much pain you've endured. I understand. Now time for you to understand the entire story.

David walks slowly toward Ima. Standing on his toes, he places his hands on either side of Ima's face. She closes her eyes. David's lips gently touch Ima's lips. Both hearts beat faster.

Crimson's powerful hand yanks David from his joyful kiss.

"What are you doing!" shouts Ima.

"What must be done. Do not interfere," admonishes Crimson.

"Sorry I said I hated you."

Crimson grows another 12 feet. She holds wriggling, crying Ima in the palm of her hand.

"Don't squish her! I will go with you, if you promise not to hurt her."

"As queen of all underworld creatures, I give you my oath..."

Crimson's cackles create fire expelling dragon mouth. "No!" David slugs and kicks undulating mocking flames. Poof! Screaming Ima vanishes.

Timelines fracture. The sound of cracked glass punctures David's sanity. "Is she alive?"

"For now, yes."

"Where have you taken her?"

"That's for her to know and for you to find out," Crimson shouts through the din of manic maniac time.

Newfound reality shimmers and is sucked into the maw of mendaciously mercurial top-spinning fuchsia-black vortex.

"Sleep, little human." David's eyes shut. He falls back toward a metal spike. Crimson snaps her fingers and that spike becomes pillows the size of her hand. David falls into a deep snoring sleep. *I did not do this. Changes beyond my ability to correct. I need help. Ko'ach can you hear me? I need your help...*

80-foot fist exits dissipating vortex. "No!" screeches Crimson, as she's knocked into an unfamiliar recently created dimension.

*

Menacing lip-smacking, Miley Cyrus holds itty-bitty Ima between her sharp black thumb and index-fingernails.

"Ami!" screams Ima.

"In the fresh flesh!"

"I-T appears that my queen has betrayed Master's plans."

Licked from head to toe, Ima is slathered in pungent black saliva.

"The only question I have for you is, are you better with tartar sauce or ketchup?"

"Ko'ach! We need your strength!" shouts Ima.

"Master has him occupied. Cavalry won't be coming over the next nebula."

The Ami-Miley creature cackle splits the fabric of the space-time continuum.

"Ima taking Crimson's place. Ima the new queen bee!"

Blue-white energy funnel precedes 70-foot pernicious time-swatting Ko'ach. "PUT HER DOWN!" booms Ko'ach's baritone voice.

"Ko'ach? How did you decipher time's implosion paradox formula?" incredulous Ami asks.

"Your master won't be arriving this day. In fact, this day will never come at all..."

"Not even you have that kind of power?"

"God's righteousness has no limits."

"You're not God!"

"Indeed, that's very true. Love of life will always prevail over death's malevolent darkness."

Ko'ach's planet cracking hands clap. Time folds and twists; revealing righteous realm's re-written déjà vu rendezvous.

Ko'ach's super-nova essence radiates a never before seen nor felt heat blast which obliterates Ami's anti-matter insanity.

Nephesh, I've depleted the last of my sub-atomic particles. I have nothing else in reserve. The rest is up to you. I'll be hibernating and recharging in the musical vortex for a century or two. God forbid you'll need my help before my rejuvenation cycle completes. You must discover another me to train David. I know you'll succeed. All my love. Dearest wife.

Clickety-clack doctor Crimson ambles into her austere office. She places an ant farm on the floor. Her long fuchsia nail carves jagged fissures, glass pops and all the ants scurry and traverse her skyscraper black stiletto heel. Singular angry ant transforms into human size Ami.

"Tell me. What news have you from Master?"

"Meals are packaged and on display. Our hungry brethren will arrive soon," giggles Ami.

"Feast. Feast! FEAST!" Crimson, Ami and tiny squeaky shouting staccato ant voices surge toward uncontrollable escalation.

CHAPTER 17

666,666 Monsters Screech Hate Speech

Swirling fuchsia sparks from the center of Crimson's open palm produce the smiling faces of Suohic-Agas and Ami Bres-Time; their timely incursion set the ringtone scene. They joyfully gesticulate their arms and shoulders and sing La La La to Mozart's Symphony No. 40 in G minor.

Crimson smiles and sings from Sondheim, "Old Friends." Grinning Suohic-Agas and Ami Bres-Time join in the merriment. *Too early.* Crimson wiggles her pinkie goodbye. Good friends wave goodbye. *See you later.*

Crimson presses two index fingers into triangular hole. Her right index finger turns five times to the right. Her left index finger turns four times to the left. Red. Yellow. Green. Orange lights blink vigorously on and off. Pungent igniting aroma instigates illusory imagination. Regurgitating codes illuminate dark mirrors: E Y E AM 24 7 666.

Plethora of diligent dark matter pelts and penetrates the ice-cold vault's mind-controlling mirrors. 18 minutes later Crimson's mind shouts: *Saturation complete.*

Smirking, she sashays through thick molten edifice. Deceptive mirrors bend time to her will. Mysterious mathematical formulas bounce into and through each mirror at the speed of 1800 times the speed of light. 7:47 a.m. and 7:47 p.m. occur simultaneously.

The elevator rapidly descends. Blinding blue, white molecules bedazzle. The floor undulates multiple psychedelic patterns of purple-green-blue-yellow-red-brown-black-white.

Crimson's fuchsia shimmering molecules decelerate down to 3,087 meters per second. Passing level B1 and level B2, she phases through solid rock. Levels C3 and D4 blink out of existence. Crimson twists and convulses through levels E5, F6, G7, H8, and IMAOK.

Discordant buzz delivers disorienting belch. Enormous hive hums. The hedonistic honeycomb spreads 125 feet north to south and 125 feet east to west; gooey entrance 330 feet deep. Immobilized great white sharks and killer whales bob and slosh. Waves push warm-blood marinating carcasses for centuries—until dinner bell chimes.

Spiders, 35 feet, create glittery ensnaring geometric webs no Earth-born creature could ever escape. Symphonic vibrations heckle pulsating prey. Yacht-size bees measuring 549 feet carry 220-foot-long snakes.

An assortment of bloody rare meats cooks over massive barbeque pits. Crackling fat engorges sizzling flame; odors that would gag the most iron-willed humans. With grand gusto cannibalistic creatures inhale that slimy stench. Barbarous bloody blaze ascends 150 feet above each hellish pit. Stinky steam jumps off garrulous ghoulish grubby guttural gravy dripping demonic gargoyles. Voluminous viperous vindictive vomit lingers within warbling beast's weaponizing willfulness.

Monsters demand their perishables marinate in fecal broth. Dissected human heads, torsos, legs, and arms swingingly bob, to the delight of every eight-, ten-, and fifteen-legged creature. Ginormous things gargle bloody human and non-human alcoholic beverages.

Decadent deviants munch frenetic frenzy. Crimsons' thunderous hand clapping reinforces roaring resurgence.

Mercurial machinations manipulate mitochondrial murders. Maladapted madness misuses a myriad of meticulous mutilations.

Chirping baby birds, 727 feet, fall from their nests. Jiggling with rapturous excitement, they wolf down great white sharks, killer whales, gigantic Anacondas, spiders, and cockroaches.

Floorboards descend miles into the darkest portion of the cavern; I-T-S humanoid-encrusted wood is a thousand times harder than Siberian permafrost.

Crimson's multicolored fingernails rupture unnatural rapture. Inhuman applause, grunts, whistles, and booming bellows shower her with crazy affection.

"Crim-Zon! Crim-Zon!"

Throng of 666,666 creepy creatures applaud, by slamming together their enormous green hooves, orange paws, brown fins, yellow wings, and red spider legs: in their genuine show of respect and affirming affection for their queen.

"SCAR-LETT! SCAR-LETT," shouts every manner of beast.

Ferocious fanaticism predicts pandemonium's petulant precursor. Crimson's defending syllables and sentences delight each ravenous thing. Her utterances push premeditated hysteria into narcissistic frenzy.

Hiding in the darkness, Crimson's thoughts try to put a lid on her own anxious feelings. *Wish I didn't have to engage with these crazies. I grow weary of these diabolical death games. My false face must continue, for a little longer. These evil dullards assume my neural pathways are coordinated with I-T-S luscious idiom. Our dampening device continues blocking and keeps me safe from any abominable telepath. Keep I-T together. Do not show any self-doubt. You are their Queen! Righteous memories flood. I was, long ago, a queen of sorts. Dangerous to revisit Ko'ach's mission.*

Crimson clears her throat; the throng's manic din abruptly grows silent. "You know that I've been off world for centuries. What was the saying? I-T was on the tip of my tongue...

Crimson's long tongue windshield wiper action against

pouty lips always seduces new arrivals. Trying to recall lost thoughts, her tongue stretches and twirls around her upturned nose and taps her eyebrows the way a deep in thought human would with a pencil.

"We're only human!" shouts a bright orange 20-foot butterfly with shark teeth.

Thrumming laughter shakes dust from gigantic stalagmites.

"Lucky for us, none of us was cursed with such a destiny. These humans are truly the weakest most slow-witted creatures in the Multiverse!"

"Let them eat cake!" 40-foot blue jay caw caws.

"They are cake!" 80-foot-tall and wide piglet squeals.

"I hate humans!" hums the 35-foot grasshopper.

"MMM, human pot pie. Love playing with my food," screeches the recently transitioned 66-foot Michelle Wolf doppelganger.

Black-green-red-white-spittle sails high, each garrulous contagion gobbled by insidious orange lips, growing by way of mendacious mitosis.

Terrified light brown human with long black hair haltingly steps forward, and trips. Her head falls and rests against Crimson's huge toes.

Crimson rubs her stomach.

"What's your name, little girl?"

"W-where am I?"

Must settle down. You can do this. As we rehearsed. Play the trickster's game to perfection.

"P-please. Let me g-go. I want my...my...M-M-M..."

"Are you trying to say Mommy? How cute."

Tearful girl nods. Carnal caterwauling crescendos. Crimson places her huge hand over the tiny human's head.

A 70-foot turtle grabs a 50-foot bunny's leg. "Make a wish! Turtle shouts. Bone cracking sends the crowd into demonic delirium. Turtle munches and sucks out pink marrow.

Crimson's long finger extends to her perfectly coiffed silver skyscraper bun. She silences miscreant brethren into mesmerizing submission. "Ssshhhuuussshhh..."

Turning sidewise, the monsters didn't see Crimson wink. Crimson brushes long black bangs from Latina's eyes. Girl softly says her name.

"Louder! tarantula granny can't hear you," Crimson yells.

"Maria Guadalupe Josefina Garcia!"

"That certainly is a mouthful."

"She sure is!" breaded beef shouts from the cauldron.

Crimson bends low and slowly licks Maria's cheek. Slurping skin stretching catapults monsters into drooling gluttonous lust. Crimson elevates her clenched fist skyward.

Elbows bent...arms pound above her head, taller and taller she lengthens. Arm motion resembling an inverse squat. Her snow-white skin becomes darker and darker fuchsia. Her elastic clothing tightly adheres to her, growing from 22 feet to 33 feet and settling on her 44-foot super-model body.

Crimson picks up tiny squirming Maria between long fuchsia nails and, with her left hand, flings a 9-foot tortilla through the pungent stratosphere.

Maria lands in the middle of the tortilla; every wild beast hysterically cheers.

Crimson dips her huge hand into a tub of hot steaming beans, every legume half again the size of Maria; little human and all those beans are covered by three six-foot slices of cheese.

Maria's muffled crying screeches stop after smiling Crimson bites down into that soft, blood dripping, Maria burrito.

Front row monsters get a bloody splattered taste. Roaring MMM sounds reverberate. Crimson's long fuchsia middle fingernail picks at her jagged white teeth. She sings Adele's "Rolling" the Deep" with a loud burp that masks creaky trap door. Little Maria runs into the arms of her mother.

"Hurry," Grandpa whispers.

Maria and her large extended family walk briskly through the shadowy dark tunnel and muffled cries of joy heading into bright streaming fuchsia light.

The monster misinterprets Crimson's smile. She slowly gestures toward 9,999 projected holographic images corresponding with specific human dates.

Feb 17, 1876...March 15, 1899...Jan 3, 1958...Aug 6, 2001...April 13, 2005...

"Behold! Oldies and hoodies. Enjoy what I-T truly means to be human! Reverberating bellows create new fissures; tiny creatures fall onto large creatures' plates, each one impaled by 3 prong forks and mercilessly chewed.

Manipulative time displacement unfolds future dates: May 24, 2042...May 24, 2043...

Humans swing bats, rifle butts, and enjoy cracking bones and disfiguring lips, noses, ears, and eyes. Internal bleeding causes distended stomachs. Smaller men are pummeled by larger sadistic girlfriends and wives.

Foul-mouthed dirty, angry husband smashes and screams, "Again! You ugly cunt whore, you're burning the steaks on purpose! Bitch! I never loved you. You tricked me into marriage. Get the fuck out of my way! Biggest fucking mistake was letting myself get knocked up and not getting an abortion," hollers mother at her tiny daughter Martha.

"Mama, please don't!"

Wrinkled 35-year-old looks 50-ish; her hands squeeze her daughter's ribs. Crack! Vodka-gulping cruel mother's drunken laughter prompts stepdad to step on the dog's tail and punch daughter's little brother in the stomach.

New images re-broadcast. Young blonde dressed in blue, stuffs chubby cheeks with Weight Watchers and bemoans her life. She shuffles from the bedroom to the kitchen. Her mood changes after she steps on the scale. Valerie squeals with delight and runs over to her husband, Karl. Valerie pinches Karl's butt. She moves in for a happy kiss. He turns with a nasty scowl.

"Yuck, Valerie! You stink like last week's garbage!" spits Karl.

Valerie's tears smear her mascara. "That's not true! I smell good. I'm proud to say I lost 7 pounds this month."

"7!" Karl throws up his hands in disgust. "You've been on that diet for all these months and I-T-S only 7 fucking pounds! At that rate, you'll be a fat ugly cow forever. And if you successfully lose all that you should, I am not going to pay for your fucking loose skin surgery!"

Valerie runs to the bedroom and scoops two handfuls of melting chocolate cookies.

Space. Tiny Earth—zooming, continents become larger, magnifying California and cities such as Los Angeles and Santa Monica. Bug eyed monsters focus their attention on a particularly significant boy, standing 4-foot even.

Kidlet's hands are tied behind his back. "Why?" little boy defiantly rages.

Large foster father cracks serrated whip and laughs with menacing gusto. Emaciated child's arms and legs gush bright red blood with infinitesimal fuchsia sparks.

"Fatima, run!" little boy yells.

Pre-teen Fatima caresses her foster father's pockmarked face. She climbs on his lap.

Little boy's mind is filled with revulsion. *Oh Fatima. What are you doing? Eww, that's nasty.* Little boy's mind shouts.

"I was pretending when I said I liked you," Fatima giggles.

"I have an eidetic memory. You said you love me..."

"Love! Are you serious! How the hell could I love a puny bug like you! I'm loyal to my handsome husband. Isn't that right, big daddy?"

That's creepy!

Large husband stands. Fatima slips off his lap.

"Allah be praised. She'll soon give me strong strapping boys."

Foster father with long gray beard easily lifts little Fatima off the ground, her legs dangle above his knees. Creepy disgusting act, his tongue penetrates and sucks. Little boy shuts his eyes, his mind shouts, *I took horrible punishment for you, Fatima! You enjoy this wicked perverse pedophile!*

"Fatima is good actress, no?" The stench reeking husband releases his grip and Fatima lands awkwardly. Her screeching agony brings laughter from her old man. Losing her balance, she falls into a rusty pitchfork. Blood trickles from her ass. She loudly braes like an injured donkey.

Foster father dumps freezing water over tiny boy's body. Giant sadistic man's size 14 manure encrusted boot presses. The little boy's breathing becomes painful and labored.

Foster father cracks his whip thrice. Little boy shivers and stands defiantly. Blood flows down the chest and arms of that unflinching pre-teen. That singular act of defiance enrages that Muslim bully.

Another crack, little boy's quick reflexes protect his eyes. His ears aren't so lucky. Fatima joyfully claps. She limps with psychotic enthusiasm.

"Fatima, please. Make him stop!" begs the little boy.

"No!" Fatima's uppercut sends the little boy to his knees. "Infidel! You know what my husband demands of you. Say I-T, and perhaps we'll show you a little mercy."

Spitting blood from his cracked lips. "I'll never say I-T!" shouts the little boy.

Fatima grows her height by arching her back and puffing out her chest. "Say I-T! Say your name now!" screams Fatima.

"Do as my beautiful bride commands or this time I'll not hold back."

Little boy flashes two middle fingers.

"You disrespectful little shit! Say your slave name, now!"

"No! Ima David Sagacious; forever defiantly tenacious!"

"Idiot! By Allah's decree, you are whatever Daddy says you are!"

Old man slams his manure-soaked steel rod into David's already infected tibia. Gleefully, Fatima runs toward David and hammers her metal-plated forehead into the protruding rod. Deeper I-T-S nailed. Nailed into a maggot-infested floorboard, he writhes in agony.

David gurgles and spits his bloody acquiescence, "Okay. Okay. You win!"

"And?" Muslim man whispers.

"Ima not Sagacious. Ima Noah Juan..." Gritting our teeth. "The pain. For God's sake do something for the pain..." Pre-teen blacks out and wakes up 18 minutes later. Smiling Fatima holds smelling salts.

"Better not lose consciousness again, before you say I-T all," whispers Fatima.

"Ima Noah Juan Tu Luv," wheeze David.

Foster father strikes a match on Fatima's shrapnel face. She dares not flinch. Old man blows smoke in David's face. Red cigar embers get closer to his ear lobe.

"I did what you asked. No more torture. Please don't do I-T!"

"I-T? Daddy, did you hear? Woo-who! He doesn't under-stand!" says grinning Fatima.

Foster father brands two smoldering X's on David's ear-lobes. "No mercy for itty-bitty infidel. Your present, past and future carcass belongs to the one who commands and demands.

Cascading darkness suddenly gobbles up sunlight. Colossal fuchsia finger-nail punches through splintering roof. The ginormous fuchsia thumb squishes Fatima into stink manure.

Old man holds his hands over his eyes and shrieks, "Mistress, please don't!"

Incredibly large shoe wiggles; touching perverted human; celery-sounding crunch echoes.

Gentle fingers scoop trembling David. Splash. Her tears heal David's physical wounds.

Greenie's pocket glistens human-size cage; burlap covering flutters.

Back to the malevolent cavern, beastly cohorts stomp their feet, hooves, fins, and tails. Fluttering feathers and wings, they pump fists, claws, and horns. Enthralled with every image, "More! More!" they shout, bleat, and roar.

Singular giant fuchsia hand perforates the darkness. Mayhem mutes.

"This time let no righteous shit interfere! This time we'll complete our collective mission. On this puny planet our family number 666 million strong. We're placed strategically in America's presidential administration, House of Representatives, and Senate. We have the ear of three Supreme Court Justices. We're in every financial institution and branch of the armed forces, around the world. I-T-S time we ethnically cleanse the entire wretched planet of I-T-S human infestation!"

New holographic images come into focus. Teen boys pretend they have loving feelings toward teen girls.

Girls get their revenge, breaking multiple hearts.

Mothers with bloody knuckles and their daughter with black eyes.

Small boys and girls watch mothers and fathers walk around in drug-induced stupor.

Parents, 40-year-olds, taunt and beat up their pre-teen daughters and sons. Those teens, 35 years later, turn the tables. They taunt and beat up their decrepit 70 and 80-year-old parents.

Big hate speech appears in black letters and infuses I-T-Self into the massive blood-red cloud. Monsters whoop and cheer, chanting in multiple languages with heavy accents, "God wants you to kill yourselves. If you are placed in a room filled with the ugliest, most depressed losers in the entire world, they will all reject YOU! The more you cry, the happier we all become. I don't care how you do I-T! But do I-T! End your mother fucking lives NOW!"

Patches of blinding light leak through and smear the bloody lettering.

Ami stands on her toe tapping hooves. She stretches another 17 feet.

"What the hell is that?" confused Ami asks.

CHAPTER 18

World Building and the First Time Nephesh and Ko'ach Meet

Ko'ach's name is defined as "powerful" or "mighty being." Nephesh's name is described in ancient Fuchsia texts as "life, passion, loving emotion, and soul."

Liv-KaKhol is the name given to Nephesh and Ko'ach's home world. Each clan's name identifier is specifically based on a clan's unique pigment.

The Dull Gray clan hunted wild game to extinction and depleted drinking water after centuries of drought. They refused Fuchsia clan's drip irrigation innovation. Dictatorial Dull Gray used starvation and fear of pandemics to control their people and jealousy of the Fuchsia to build up their armies. Dull Gray's religious beliefs, desolate land, illiteracy, and toxic air contribute to their invasion and occupation of the lands of thousands of peaceful clans.

Thousands of years before the Israelis, the Fuchsia innovated the means to extract water from their atmosphere. The Fuchsia people enjoy diversity of vigorous debate and thrive on the tallest mountain peaks and lowest topographical points on their planet. Compared to Earth, their insects are twice the weight of an Ice Age mammoth.

Silver fuchsia hair shines. Mother and daughter's braids flow to their ankles. Dad and son's dense silver hair is clipped high around ears, some sporting long beards or thick mustaches. The Ancient-Ones grow both.

Fuchsia is affectionate, intuitive, innovative, ingenious, introspective, inquisitive, idealistic, and incredibly imaginative. Government tradition from the first to the last Kings and Queens embraced limited governmental principles. Legal structure provides equal footing for all citizens. Fuchsia invented the alphabet thousands of years before all other clans and were the first to enrich their souls with the value of ethical Monotheism.

Fuchsia hold in high esteem the intellectual and spiritual prowess of their religious, academic, and athletic teachers. Parents nurture character traits of competitive determination, compassion for the less fortunate, and gratitude for all serving in the defense forces. Over half the population are professional orators and humorists. Reading habits start when little Fuchsia reach their 9th month and continue through their entire life span. Spiritual leaders and medical practitioners agree that singing and dancing strengthens immune systems and builds loving family structures.

Fuchsia ethical allies are the Red-Blue-White striped clan and the less technologically advanced Green-Red-Orange and White-Blue-Green Polka-Dot clans.

The barbaric Dull Grays broke 3,000 years of planet-wide peace. Men shave their heads from the middle of their skull toward the back and grow black strands from the middle of their skull forward.

Dull Gray females' triangular black eyebrows and abnormally huge bulging eyes intimidate weaker, meeker male counterparts. Dull Gray families embrace murderous dishonorable religious codes built around obedience to Matriarch's Machiavellian indoctrination. Propensity for propaganda proliferates prodigiously. Matriarchal theocracy rewrites Dull

Gray's past, present and future, manufactured truths, as the truth remains the lone Dull Gray truth.

Genetically altered female breed enjoy boycotting and torturing any black-market dissenting organization. After the queen mother abducts them, they all beg for death while slowly rotated and roasted over the barbeque pit.

Staying in power by way of extreme combat. Practicing an extreme form of polygamy—seven husbands per female allowed for an exponential growth in the Dull Gray population.

The Red-Blue-White clan betrayed thousands of years of history when the weakest, most dumb-witted appeaser manipulated his clan's elections. After 12 failed attempts at the Presidency, Jackyll Brandon's dishonorable policies financially enriched himself and his corrupt family, while a sadistic fifth column gleefully used biological weaponry—virulent viruses deliberately designed to decimate every enzyme. Cellular codes cracked; de-evolution dissected and chromosomal cohesion chaotically crashed.

Red and blue cellular anatomical structures ripped and painfully pushed to the other side; smooth red lines became jagged and traversed to the right side of the body. Blue strips swirl down the left side. Bright white dulls and darkens duller gray and becomes coal black. Now babies look and are, in fact, genetically different compared to their parents and older unaltered siblings. Third generation altered clan's soul turns black; to the powerful joy of those who love a good old fashioned bloody genocide.

No longer a righteous clan, the new Blue-Black-Red clan uses advanced technology to become an existential threat to all Fuchsia families.

Billions of hostile Dull Gray allies surround millions of Fuchsia. For now, the energy grid prevents incursion. If I-T falls, there's no haven anywhere on Liv-KaKhol.

At the moment Ko'ach's and Nephesh's love affair blossomed, military and civilian technology surpassed the most advanced 23rd-century Earth technology, especially medical knowledge.

Before the Watcher Realm's righteous souls merged with Ko'ach's unusual mind and soul, the average Fuchsia life span was 135 years. After the metamorphosis, Fuchsia's life span extended by multiple thousands of years.

Hakarav is Nephesh's mother. Hakarav means to sacrifice. Yosher is Nephesh's father, and his name is defined as righteous integrity.

Ko'ach's mother's name is Ariel meaning lioness of God. His Papa's name is Gavriel, meaning God is my strength.

18 weeks after Nephesh's 9th birthday, her parents become annoyed with her constant complaints. Tradition requires that Nephesh select her first pet no later than 36 weeks past her 9th birthday. She expresses her non-interest in feathered, winged creatures and flipper-flapping aquatic things. Nephesh tries connecting with a cute red-green-orange elephant-looking thing.

"Mommy, he's not the right size."

Papa lovingly tickles his daughter's ear and shakes his head. "You've said that 13 times. You must decide soon, or we'll decide for you."

"Don't do that, Papa."

Mama picks up the wriggling pachyderm-like creature. "What's wrong with this cutie?"

Nephesh holds and tickles the trumpet blaring baby. Mama and Papa smile and nod. Nephesh frowns. "Come on honey. Please don't say..."

"He's not the right size." She hands the happy animal to her mother.

Another same-sized elephant creature waddles into the living room and rubs his cute trunk on Nephesh's ankle.

Nephesh picks up the cute baby. She rubs her cheek on the baby's large floppy ear. Nephesh tickles the baby's belly. "You're so squishy," little girl giggles, creature widens his already wide, wide smile. Nephesh inhales. "No stinky smell. I like him. Oh. Too bad. Sorry Papa, Mama. He's not the right..."

Yosher holds up his hand and walks away. He mumbles, "Nephesh-ah-la."

"Time for bed," says Hakarav. Nephesh's stubby fingers patty-pat her mom's cheek.

"You take a nap, Mommy. I not..." loud Nephesh-ah-la yawning makes the family's four-legged furry great-grandpa pet howl. That old mutt makes Nephesh giggle and synchronize her howls. Seconds later, Mama and Papa join in the silliness, howling, giggling, and tickling.

Another baby pachyderm pushes through his cage; and he triple jumps into Nephesh's arms. They both inhale and exhale.

"Mommy! Daddy! This one! He's perfectly cute!" she excitedly shouts.

Yosher and Hakarav are simultaneously happy and confused.

"Honey, please explain. How can this one be perfectly cute when he looks like all the rest? Is I-T because she's a girl?" Yosher asks.

"Silly Daddy. Girl or boy was never the problem. When Mommy reads me stories, we breathe together. When I pick up my new cutie best friend and hold her close, we exhale and inhale together. We're both the right sighs."

"What's your baby's name?" asks Hakarav.

"Lumpy MacShmoopee."

Nephesh's lips blow tuba farting sounds on Lumpy's belly. Lumpy lets loose joyfully exhilarating trumpets.

When Fuchsia boys and girls reach their 7th year, they participate in community athletics. 7-year-olds, 8-year-olds, and 9-year-olds are grouped in the same category.

Fuchsia fate finagled feisty future...the 9-year-old boy who was supposed to team up with Nephesh was attacked by a body-thrashing gargoyle thumping, fire-breathing ptero-dactyl creature. In the hospital with third-degree burns, broken tibia, ribs, and sternum. Growing cranial pressure from his fractured skull would be a death sentence for any other clan. 5 weeks later he started his long road to full recovery. However, an immediate replacement for Nephesh's team was now needed.

18 days before the accident, providential interference arrived, as Ko'ach's family from one of the oldest religious and monetarily poorest communities entered the outskirts of Nephesh's wealthy district.

Nephesh's family lived a splendiferous lifestyle; her parents never forgot the old ways. Their values are the same as the people living in Ko'ach's village. 9-year-old Nephesh is tall for her age, she towers over most 12-year-old girls.

Most 6-year-old boys tower over the 9-year-old Ko'ach. "Do I have to team up with a girl?" pugnacious Ko'ach shouts at his coaches. Looking down on Ko'ach, Nephesh deliberately rests her arm on the top of his head. Annoyed, he pinches her arm.

"Hey, that hurts. And what's wrong with girls?"

Nephesh's green eyes lock on Ko'ach's dark fuchsia eyes. "Nothing wrong with girls. We don't team up with them where I come from."

"That way of thinking disappeared over a century ago."

"Girls are smart and powerful debaters but aren't as athletic."

"Look, little dude, you'd better follow my lead. You're only a short-term replacement."

Nose level with her armpit. He turns a dark shade of fuchsia. Ko'ach did not appreciate her smile while putting an extra emphasis on "short"-term replacement.

"I see you're easily offended. You better not cost us points by fouling. You'd better keep up and try to play at least satisfactory defense. Leave the offense to me."

"By all means. You're truly offensive."

"Why you rude little toddler!"

Nephesh grabs a rolled-up newspaper; her intent is to whack Ko'ach's face.

"Swing and a miss!" Ko'ach's dancing and ducking under Nephesh's over-exaggerated swings turns her rage-induced pigment super dark.

Ko'ach back-flips 18-times. Ko'ach mockingly waves from the far end of the field. "Catch me if you can, girly girl!"

Adrenalin's rage aims locomotive Nephesh at her little adversary. "You're only here because my dad knows your dad."

"I know. I've heard the stories. Attended family reunions. Where were you?" asks Ko'ach.

"I was there. And I have a great memory for faces. I don't remember your ugly mug."

"I didn't attend the last one. I was busy being recruited."

"For what?"

"Classified!"

"You? A 9-year-old shrimpy, looking more like a 5-year-old?"

Ko'ach flips Nephesh over his shoulder. He becomes distracted by her fuchsia freckles. Her heart races and she grabs Ko'ach's shoulder and flips him over her head.

"Well done. For a girl." Ko'ach laughs. Nephesh shakes her fist at him.

Ko'ach offers his hand and helps Nephesh to her feet. She's still holding his hand, enjoying how much taller she is. She decides to prove she's also stronger. Nephesh squeezes Ko'ach's smaller hand. *Should I let her win this round? She's pretty. I was warned not to get too attached to anyone. I do like you, Nephesh.*

Ko'ach releases his grip first. He wiggles his fingers. And pretends Nephesh bested him. She smiles. Puts her arm around his small shoulders. *He's cute. For a little guy. He doesn't realize his smugness is the reason why no other teams would take him. If not for my dad's stories, I wouldn't want him either. I trust my Papa. Hope you're everything he said you are.*

"Take your marks!" yells 63-foot 16-year-old girl.

"Remember your promise. I'm the co-captain. You follow my lead."

Ko'ach flashes his mischievous smile and winks. "I don't recall any promise."

Loud starter pistol fires.

"Wait!" yells Nephesh.

Ko'ach turns his back on two 9-year-old proteges.

"Turn around! Turn around!" Nephesh implores.

Sticking his thumbs in his ears and waggling them makes Nephesh shake her fists. *Damn that little guy is going to ruin every-thing. If you cost us a championship. Oh Papa! Why?*

Ko'ach's eyes brighten up. *Oh yea! That's the seething color I love to see. Your Papa told me you play your best when pissed.*

Ko'ach turns around and blasts faster than Nephesh has ever seen anyone before. Seconds later the biggest, strongest, fastest 9-year-old lies flat on his back.

Referee raises her flag and shouts, "9 points for the tackle."

Get up! Yes. Your Papa taught you well. If you can reach the goal-line before the double-gun blast, we'll pick up another 18-points. Go! Go! Nephesh raises her hands high. She jumps around in a circle. *He did I-T! Damn that little guy is amazing.*

Nephesh catches up to Ko'ach and punches him hard enough to knock him over.

I don't want him to know how amazing I think he is. He's already too arogant. Ko'ach back flips over Nephesh's head. *Wow. I don't know anyone who could do that.*

Ko'ach winks and leans in for a kiss on her lips.

"Stop that!"

"Didn't you like the first one on your cheek. Lips are bet-ter, don't you think?"

"Weirdo!"

"Cutie."

"Concentrate."

Ko'ach smiles.

"Not on me! The game, idiot!"

"Hey, that's not nice."

"Sorry."

"Besides, I can multitask. Can't you?"

"Incorrigible!"

"More fun than being humorless old you."

"Take I-T back!"

"Okay."

"Well? I'm waiting."

"For what?"

Nephesh looks up and shakes her two fists. "Why you!"

"Why me, what?"

"That's not what I meant, and you know I-T!"

"We've already established you like me."

"We have not. I do not! I...do not!"

Nephesh closes her eyes. Ko'ach runs toward her. She turns and barrels into his chest. Ko'ach goes flying. She hears a crunch and looks at a pool of blood seeping from his nose and sloshing over a metal disk that's not supposed to be hidden beneath the grass.

Ko'ach mumbles inaudible pleas. Nephesh lowers her ear to Ko'ach's chest. She feels his heartbeat become weaker and stop. "Medic! Medic!" Frantic Nephesh shouts.

Ko'ach back flips to his feet, holding a novelty packet of fake blood.

"Oh, you deceitful boy!"

CHAPTER 19

Pre-teen Ko'ach Disobeys Elder's Edict. His Father Dies in His Arms and Nephesh Tearfully Watches Dull Gray Warrior Drag Ko'ach into the Forbidden Forest

Three months later, Ko'ach tickles Nephesh. Both run through tall fuchsia grass. Ko'ach inches closer and smells Nephesh's hair. Nephesh caresses Ko'ach's cheek. Over her shoulder Nephesh sees Lumpy MacShmoope floating precariously on a thin sheet of ice.

"Oh My God! Lumpy, be careful."

Lumpy trumpets fearful trilling. Slipping between pin-prick cracks her sliding makes Nephesh's heart skip a beat and pound faster. Menacing branching out fissures trip up Lumpy; her twitching trunk acts as an awkward anchor.

Nephesh instinctively runs onto the unstable cracking ice. Added weight is too much, loud crunch terrifies clinging Lumpy.

Nephesh's freezing fingers text: ICE! HELP! DADDY, MOMMY, COME QUICK!

Nephesh's salty frozen tears chip off her cheeks. Those ice crystals stab Lumpy's soft tissue. Blood droplets freeze before they pity-pat the ice sheet. Nephesh stretches. Lumpy stretches her trunk. Nephesh's fingertips touch Lumpy's freezing trunk. Nephesh grabs. Lumpy sneezes. Nephesh falls back into the dark lake. "Nephesh!" shouts Ko'ach.

Ko'ach wraps and ties off a stretchy plant to his right ankle. After three deep breaths, he descends into the foreboding darkness. Stretchy plant's photosynthesis cells crystallize in freezing water, and the entire cellular membrane emits golden energy. Singular strand sparks a long ribbon of righteous illumination.

Bubbles exit Nephesh's nostrils. She continues to rapidly sink toward a jagged ice spear.

Why isn't she kicking her legs?

Illumination travels only so far. Fear grips her throat as Nephesh slowly slips into total darkness.

Ko'ach rummages through his pockets. His dexterity is diminished by the elongating ice crystals. After multiple failures, he finally wraps pieces of stretchy plant around his toy submarine and types in the musical activating code. The glowing speeding toy's advanced sensors maneuver around stalagmites, eels, and bizarre spiky fin, large tooth protruding bottom dwellers.

The submarine illuminates layers of ice attached to Nephesh's blue face and body. She swipes and misses. On the 18th try she grabs tightly to the glowing stretching material, and she's catapulted toward Ko'ach.

Nephesh tries to wrap her arm around Ko'ach. She's moving too fast and rockets past him. Nephesh looks down at Ko'ach boxed into an ice sheet cage. He's too weak to punch himself free. Running out of air. Ko'ach starts to lose consciousness. His last desperate pounding against the ice, splinters his knuckles.

My mind shouts through endlessly pulsating mutated timelines.

Ko'ach! You cannot die! Oh, dear lord, how do I help him? If his life ends. I will surely cease to exist. And if I cease to exist, I can never rescue

Ima. And trillions upon trillions of souls will meet their horribly agonizing slow deaths.

Holding onto vertigo's manipulative time variations, I sing, "Once in a Lifetime" from *Stop the World – I Want to Get Off.*

I feel something new. Unexpected. Good or bad? I do not know...I watch darkness gobble up everything. Every thought, feeling, history. There... Do you see? Yes. A spark of light. Growing truth penetrates and illuminates my thumpity-thump thump. Thank God...

Months before Ko'ach's 13th birthday, a new historical wrinkle unfolds.

"Are you okay, Papa?" asks Ko'ach.

"Your arrogant attitude surprises. I had hoped as you got older, you'd modify your new found grandiose disruptions."

"Well, I did have a good role model."

"That's not funny."

"Sure I-T is! You've forgotten your own arrogance toward Grandpa."

"That was different."

"Was I-T? He didn't speak to you for months after you broke with tradition. You achieved success during what is considered the most dangerous path...all I'm asking for... Please be reasonable, Papa. Our people have endured our specific coming-of-age quest these last six thousand years. Trial by combat makes us who we are. The ability to improvise problem solving tactics must not be interfered with!"

"Foolish impertinence. Humble yourself boy. New realities require flexible choices regarding our traditions."

"I fear we've already compromised too much to the appeasers on the council."

"Perhaps. I love you son."

"And I love you too, Papa."

"Please reconsider. After all, none of us are indestructible. You must listen to reason. The Dull Gray are on the march. They've conquered almost all our allies. They are constructing new weaponry. I don't understand why you won't take the newly designed implants?"

"And if I continue to refuse that unreasonable request?"

"The Council of Elders will refuse your application. Do as you've already threatened, and I cannot help you. Reject their wisdom and our entire society will reject you! Do you think for a single moment in time that Yonatan's parents wouldn't do everything to have their son whole again? The decision is made. You must obey."

"I will not obey."

"We will use all our influence to prevent civil war. Please Ko'ach." Tears well up in the eyes of father and son.

Ko'ach puts his hand on his Papa's shoulder. "I know. I know. Goodbye, Papa."

Ko'ach's mother, Ariel, runs to her son and hugs him tightly. "You cannot go," she whispers.

"Compromise is not a dirty word," whispers Gavriel.

Ko'ach breaks free from his mother's desperate embrace. "Come back," she shrieks.

Gavriel's mind sends out his heartfelt wishes, *God, please look after my stubborn righteous...* "Brave boy," says Gavriel.

Disgusted with her husband's acquiescence and pride in her son: "Stupid boy!" she shouts.

"Not stupid, dear wife. For months I've been unable to uncover his lie. That is a talent, he thankfully never developed. I trust our son will eventually discover the truth in our logic. His entire life, he's always done what is good, what is righteous."

"And if he doesn't come to his senses soon? I could not bear to live without my child's love."

"Better to lose his love, than his life. I will not, we will not bury our son. This, my wife, I give you my undying promise."

Ariel presses her chest into Gavriel's...their loud beating thumpity thumps are as one. Overcome with worry, they are both unaware of anything other than the protection of their son. Consumed by the impending gloomy prophecy they don't sense an erratic fuchsia shooting star's unexpected change in trajectory.

*

18 days later, Ko'ach and Nephesh hold hands and lead thousands of teens, parents, grandparents, and great-grandparents through the hallowed corridor and into the oratory chamber. The most decorated religious, scientific and military men and women within Fuchsia society prepares for that momentous occasion.

"You got this," Nephesh whispers. She squeezes Ko'ach's hand and rubs his strong shoulders.

Alone, Ko'ach walks to the center of the triangle within a triangle platform. Thunderous applause forces the exalted moderator to bang his gavel three times. For dramatic flair, Ko'ach waits 18 seconds longer than needed. He looks deep into green, blue, brown, and dark fuchsia eyes. Before he starts, Ko'ach respectfully nods to the panel of 9 righteous men and 9 righteous women.

"Honorable ladies and gentlemen, why do you deny us that which you all have experienced? I speak not only for myself but for countless unborn generations. We demand the same unfettered opportunity as the millions who came before your generation."

Cool breeze wafts and swirls. Stone cold silence lingers for an awkwardly long time. The eldest of the elders holds up his hand. Ko'ach takes a deep breath, allowing for the interruption of his next thought. Elder adjusts his earpiece. He walks out of the room. The remaining 17 talk in hushed soft tones, concern pinches and deepens their already heavily wrinkled faces and hands. Cool air warms. Righteous panel and every audience member take a sip of their cool blue liquid. Grandmothers and grandfathers hold ice cubes to their wrinkled lips and dance figure eights over their flushed sweaty cheeks.

18 minutes later the elder returns. He walks behind each member of the panel, they all nod and smile. "You may continue, Ko'ach," the wisest of the wise stoically states.

"Today, there's too much fear, which is unbecoming of any Fuchsia, let alone the wisest of us all." Collectively three women and four men arch their eyebrows. Those who did not raise their eyes, their lips are twitching with annoyance. Ko'ach smiles. "You know I speak the truth! We must never trade temporary comfort in the hope that our freedoms will not be taken away. We're a people with a long history of never cowering before a clan-made threat. We are God-fearing Fuchsia folk. I've heard the whispers and loud condemnations from most of you, and that too is unbecoming and unprecedented. You claim I am just a boy. I am not mature to understand these nuanced times. No! I am not naïve to the complexities of the powerful. I see. I hear. I understand. The proposed rewriting of our constitution is a most dangerous precedent. I-T shall bring consequences which could set brother against brother. Your misguided policies are far more destructive, compared to any Dull Gray brute squad. History will question your wisdom if you go against God's wishes. Pay attention. Voting in favor of this insidious legislation will divide us from within; you'll create ethical fissures cracking the bedrock of our traditions. I implore you to not allow this abomination to move forward. We know our history, our duty. Don't destroy what I-T means to be Fuchsia!"

"Your passionate disrespect failed to persuade!" the youngest on the panel shouts.

Thousands of teens derisively stomp their feet. They stand, and their parents pull them back to their seats. Disappointed glances with their eyes are enough to make 99 percent of their kids kowtow and whisper sorry for their disobedient loss of control.

36 seconds later, Nephesh is the only one defying her parents. A loud gasp follows. You could hear a pin drop as Nephesh clickety-clacks toward Ko'ach's side.

Emboldened, Ko'ach uncharacteristically flashes a smug smirking smile. Nephesh shakes her head. Ko'ach breaks contact with her warm sweaty palm. He swivels and arrogantly plays to the crowd, aiming his butt cheeks toward the indignant righteous panel. He lifts his head, just enough to see his father's shame and Nephesh's fathers' deep dark fuchsia rage. Nephesh turns Ko'ach around. "Why would you do that?" Ko'ach's anger turns to sadness, watching Nephesh wipe tears from her flushed cheeks.

"They deserve I-T," whispers Ko'ach. He walks out of the chamber employing his silliest of silly walks, emblematic of Monty Python. His left foot kicks open the heavy door.

Nephesh's father stands and shakes his fist. "Rude boy!" his bass-baritone voice shouts.

The next morning, Ko'ach and Nephesh's families sit around a large triangular dining table. Steam rises from bright red, orange, green, purple foods. Time dissipates the heat of the foods, not the new family dynamics. Familial stress causes the women to brush their long hair with their long fingers, and nervously twirl and braid. The furious fathers stare at Ko'ach, stroking their beards and with great hostility cut large chunks from their steaks.

Millions of light-years away, I can hear their internal dialog and pent-up feelings.

Foolish naïve boy. You're destroying your future with my daughter.

The older generation is destroying our unity. You're making I-T easier for the Dull Gray.

Ko'ach your strength is turning into a weakness. I fear what my father is thinking.

"May we be excused!" Seething Ko'ach blurts.

"Don't use that insolent tone!" shouts Gavriel.

"Yes Father, Mother," Ko'ach says through gritted teeth.

"Wait for me!" shouts Nephesh.

After an 18-mile leisurely jog, the two lovebirds come face to face with...time-traveling me. That David Sagacious is masquerading as a 162-year-old, 72-foot Fuchsia elder.

"I don't want to talk to him."

"Why not? He's been on your side, before."

"Not the last 18 weeks. Let's get out of here."

But he could be a vote for us. Oh, Ko'ach. You've shown too much immaturity of late. You're proving his, their point.

Nephesh waves and smiles. I smile back.

Ko'ach quickens his pace. He looks back, expecting to see... "What the hell?"

Nephesh and Ko'ach watched the 162-year-old sprint past them. Leap over impossibly high hedges. 99 minutes later, Nephesh holds her hands on her hips. "I need time...to...catch my breath." Ko'ach stops and gently rubs Nephesh's back.

"You sure?"

"Hurry or you'll lose him. I know your competitive fire all too well. You're not going to lose to one old enough to be your great-great-grandfather."

How can you be so fast?

Turning and slowly running backwards: "I had a great teacher!" shouts the old man.

What? Can you read my thoughts? No, that's impossible. I don't feel lightheaded.

"Mariana Trench."

"Your mentor was called Mariana Trench? That's not a Fuchsia clan name."

"I know."

"I don't understand."

Good. Keep talking to the old guy. I'm catching up.

"In time you will."

"What does that mean?"

"Gotta run. Your boyfriend is catching up."

Ko'ach leaps over an impossibly wide hedge I just cleared a few seconds ago. His shoe hits the edge, and he tumbles, splat! He lands face first into the cool squishy green grass. Ko'ach plops himself on a smooth orange boulder and rubs his aching knee.

I sped 900 meters back to his location; extending my wrinkled hand, I effortlessly pulled the young man back onto his throbbing feet.

"Thanks. You're amazing."

"How so?" A wry smile curls teasing understanding.

Exhausted, Nephesh runs back to us. "Who are you?"

"Suohic-Agas."

Nephesh's hand covers her surprised expression.

Ko'ach extends his hand. We shake vigorously. I squeeze tighter. Ko'ach squeezes tighter. *You're not going to win this challenge.* I smile, watching the young man's face darken and beads of sweat pour down his temples. *One of the few times I've got the advantage, my old mentor.*

Ko'ach's mind races: *Could he be? No, not possible. He's been a recluse these past 63 years.* Nephesh's bluntness interrupts that show of strength. "Are you really the Suohic-Agas, hero of the first Dull Gray wars?" asks Nephesh.

"Is I-T true?"

Old man grimaces.

"Are you alright? Do you need a doctor?" asks Nephesh.

"I'm fine. What do you recall about my exploits longer ago?"

"You single-handedly took on three huge Dull Gray warriors, my grandfather would have been captured, tortured, and killed. Without you, I would not have been born," adds David.

An irony, that you'll never know. Now, let's see if I can alter the timeline once more. I am hopeful I can thwart my mentor's excruciating future and still preserve what should never be tampered with. In 27 days, God will pluck me from my time portal and maroon me where I've been these last 18 million years. My time traveling particles are almost exhausted. This is truly my last shot.

"We must go." My eyes darted side to side. *The danger shall be here soon. I smell Ami. She's not supposed to be able to reach this planet, certainly not at this critical point in history.*

"Not safe to be walking around without a military escort!"

Suohic-Agas shouts.

Ko'ach puffs out his chest. "No harm will befall her." Ko'ach takes Nephesh's hand in his. *He has pretty fingers.*

"And what happens when you're not around?"

"What the hell does that mean?"

"You know."

Ko'ach turns his back on Nephesh.

"Ko'ach? You know I can tell when you lie to me. No! You would not! I won't let you break another promise."

"Tell her!"

"There is nothing to say."

How the hell could you know what I'm planning to do tonight? I've been careful. Only a few select members of the council were informed. Do we have a leak? Is there a saboteur afoot?

"Do not act the coward, Ko'ach! Tell her the truth." Awkward silence lingers.

"Coward? Coward! How dare you, sir. I've been taught to respect my elders. Do not test my control again. Do not ever call me a coward, unless you're ready to do battle."

"Okay, you're not a coward. But you are a fool. Millions of Dull Gray are as tall, or taller than I am. You are not ready. Those beasts will show no mercy if they capture you."

"Then I better make sure I'm clever enough to evade..."

"You're smart, inventive, stronger than most, and faster than most."

"Add exceptional cleverness," worried Nephesh emphatically states.

"That will still not be enough against the recently genetically enhanced Dull Gray terror squad. I implore you to consult with your own government's elite intelligence branch, before making any rash decisions."

How the hell could you know? I and two others. We three are the only ones briefed on these new mutations. Mutations so dangerous, I-T will for the first time give the Dull Gray a combat advantage. I must be allowed to complete my mission. For future unborn generations. For Nephesh. For my family. Nothing you say, old man, will deter me from what I must do.

"I don't trust Mr. Macho, he cares for you, Nephesh. Go with him, make sure he postpones, make a deal. Yes, postpone for 18 months. That sounds like a good compromise. Yes?"

"No! I don't need a babysitter. And once I complete the quest, by all our laws, I will be a man. With all the duties and responsibilities."

"A man? Yea right! More like an uber arrogant man-child. You haven't any idea what you're doing. This path will lead to an indescribable horror. If you won't listen to reason, I will physically prevent you from hurting...her!"

"I am doing this for her. You do not know me sir. I would give up my life to protect Nephesh. Unhand me. I do not wish to attack an old man."

Old man. If you only knew how old.

"What's so funny?" asks Nephesh.

"What the hell are you waiting for. Break free from my grip. I am waiting. If you can't break free from an old man, how the hell can you defeat mutated Dull Gray with tens of thousands of combat training hours, under the most excruciating scrutiny."

Oh shit, he's getting ready to try the move. Risky. If I don't let go, both our arms will be broken. He's too determined. God, I laid the groundwork. I do not believe this is a timeline that can be altered. Poor soul. Ko'ach my old friend. I tried to alter the most painful memories, the one agonizing destiny God agreed, I should help you avoid. I've failed. I am so sorry; I will not get another chance to find another way.

Ko'ach feels the old man's grip loosen. Ko'ach back flips over the old man's head and kicks out. The old man tumbles into the ice river. Ko'ach reaches out. Old man grabs hold and yanks Ko'ach in. Both men laugh. Nephesh shakes her head. *Men! No matter their age, they are always acting like infantile fools.*

Looking at Nephesh's scowling face. Ko'ach and the general, meaning me, are both soaked and loudly laughing, the harder Nephesh shows her disappointment.

I buckle over. *Crap! I thought I had more time.*

"Is I-T your heart?" asks Nephesh.

"In a manner of speaking." I tap Nephesh's kind face.

"You are a beacon of hope and compassion throughout all time."

I feel reality rewrite I-T-Self. New scenarios superimposed on the old one. Frozen in time. Shit! Nephesh's happy face shifts into attack mode. Ko'ach no longer dripping from the lake. He balls up his fists. He too is in attack mode. Wonder what I just said or did. Here we go. Better be careful how I react.

I effortlessly block Nephesh's punches and kicks. "Stop! I don't want to hurt you."

I back flip over Nephesh and Ko'ach and lock my arms round his neck. He begins to lose consciousness. "You're killing him!" screams Nephesh.

Nephesh slams her palms against my powerful arms. She slugs my ribs.

"Release me!" croaks Ko'ach.

I release Ko'ach and twirl him to the soft grass. "Stubborn fool! Go ahead and set in motion unknown possible fragmented time distortions. If you don't destroy yourself, you might harm the one you care most about."

"Time?"

"That's what you're taking from what I just said? You consider yourself to be a prodigy, the anointed one and you can't best me?"

Damn swirling tachyons are latching onto my cellular matrix. No. I will not be yanked away now! I have too much unfinished business here. I! Will! Not! Go! With! You!

"What's wrong with your face?"

I am doing my best to delay the contorting cellular disintegration. *Agony subsiding. I've successfully pushed back my momentary delirium.*

"No more doublespeak. Yes or no...are you a member of the time-traveling directorate. I warn you, I've been told never to trust anyone who claims such a talent."

"Don't be silly. He couldn't be one of those crackpots. Claiming to be a time traveler, that's insane!" says Nephesh.

"Indeed, that is insane." smirks Ko'ach.

"Speaking of insane talk. What would be the harm?"

"You're on his side?"

"A short delay would help the rest of us gain more support."

Nephesh leans into Ko'ach. "Okay? Do I-T for me. Please..."

Those gorgeous eyes. She knows they always melt my resolve. Sorry sweetie. Not this time. I can't. I...I...Can't!

Ko'ach lovingly presses his cheek to Nephesh's cheek. "You feel that?"

"The implants. You did that for me?"

"You'll be able to monitor my movement. My vital signs. You'll see and hear, in real time, everything I experience."

Nephesh wraps her arms around Ko'ach's neck and kisses his soft lips. Kiss lingers for a long time until the old man clears his throat.

Neither teen notices the bloody sputum splashed onto my handkerchief.

I must protect you at all costs, sweet Nephesh. How could I confide in you now? Don't say another word. Odd old man keeps shaking his head as if he could read my thoughts.

Dizzying bombardment will not let up. Argh! Fight the infiltration. Good. Better. For now. Damn! I sense I've got fewer than 18 minutes before I vanish from this timeline for good.

My bloody handkerchief wipes my sweaty brow. "Never knew you to be so arrogant, old friend," whispers Suohic-Agas.

"Old friend?" Nephesh says with all due incredulity.

"Oops. Um. Did I say that out loud?"

"Yes!" Ko'ach and Nephesh shout together.

"Take care of each other." I wave and take two steps before Nephesh stops me.

"I don't think you are our general. I think you're a Dull Gray spy."

Releasing a nervous laugh. "No. I am not. I told you I haven't the time for such nonsense."

"Make the time!" shouts Ko'ach.

I'm aware of Ko'ach's and Nephesh's nonverbal communication. Ko'ach's lightning-quick reflexes slap handcuffs and ankle cuffs on me. I fall forward and he pushes me away from the gravel and onto the soft grass.

"This isn't going to hold me."

"That's what all the criminals say," smiling Nephesh shouts.

"That's a new composite. My Papa's prototype. I assure you, criminal, you'll not be able…"

I smile. Using a fraction of my strength. The teen love-birds are shocked hearing the reinforced metallic material bend. "That's not possible. Ko'ach that proves he can't be Suohic-Agas."

"Not even an enhanced mutated Dull Gray could do that," says Ko'ach.

"What are you?" shouts Nephesh.

My face, fingers and torso sparkle and become translucent. "Take care of each other. You two are each other's best friends. Watch out for the…"

Astonishment falls on both their faces. "He's gone," whispers Ko'ach.

The next morning, under cover of darkness, stealthy Ko'ach begins his quest. Senses on high alert, he's unaware of who or what trails his every movement. The camouflaged being matches his strides across the forbidden lake.

From the safety of her well-lit bedroom, Nephesh stares at her computer screen. Micro-speakers in Ko'ach's ears and micro-implanted lenses let her know what Ko'ach is experiencing in real time, her interactive texts let him know which course corrections are needed. Sudden panic grips her heart, "Encroaching Dull Gray shadow. Get out of there I-T-S an ambush!"

Four arrows fly over Ko'ach's head and penetrate the hearts of two Dull Gray warriors.

"Father, I thought I made I-T perfectly clear. I can't have you shadowing me on my quest."

Father wraps Ko'ach in a bear hug. He turns and lets his shield take the Dull Gray arrows.

In quickness surpassing his son's, eight more arrows are jettisoned into the hearts of four giant Dull Gray women. Father leads, son follows, both crawl on their bellies toward a clump of dense trees, and into the heart of the desolate sand dunes.

Sun dips below the horizon. Chef Papa adds spices to simmering wild beef flank.

"Fighting side by side, I was thinking about your Papa. What monsters the Dull Gray are, to weaponize their own children."

"Not just their own children. They extorted desperate clans. Clans we would have helped if we had known of their plight."

"My Papa acted as any civilized person would. He couldn't turn away a bleeding child. We didn't know her tears were anticipatory tears of joy. Her touch emitted a viral agent. Within minutes, Papa's cells turned cancerous and spread unnaturally fast. Every solution our doctors came up with, within minutes backfired. I-T was one mutation after another. Every drug. Every form of radiation, all of I-T failed. Evil Dull Gray hide behind children. They blackmail families into mutating their own children! Children were used as weapons. I hate them all! Dull Gray are by far the most despicable, dishonorable creatures.

Midday, Ko'ach enjoys the nectar of a juicy sweet fuchsia pigmented fruit.

"Hurry!" shouts Nephesh.

Ko'ach runs, his quiver full of arrows. The young man hesitates, watching his father engage with two Dull Gray behemoths.

A powerful downward strike cuts Ko'ach's sword in half. Gavriel slices the humongous female in the neck, gray blood gushes. Dull Gray female warrior straddles Gavriel's body and lifts her enormous blade. Ko'ach sprints and kicks, sending Dull Gray onto her back. Her armored fists pound sand.

Gavriel's large fist connects with the Dull Gray's larger jaw.

"Timber," shouts Ko'ach.

Ko'ach's jubilant grinning moment ends as his father shoves him out of the way. A gleaming serrated spear pierces Gavriel's back and penetrates his heart. Ko'ach's brave Papa falls face first into the no longer pristine lake.

"Oh, my God!" tearful Nephesh shouts from the comfort of her bedroom. She immediately texts for the medivac.

Ko'ach's fingers enter Gavriel's gaping wound and apply self-suturing gel. Every 18 beats, the gel washes away; Ko'ach massages torn heart chambers. One-hole leads to two more. Eight more after that, a fuchsia geyser slams into Ko'ach's face. A blood current saturates his sleeve and splashes his boots.

"Nephesh, I-T-S not working. Where is the medic?" Ko'ach's bloody lips spray.

"I don't know why I-T-S taking so long. They should have arrived 18 minutes ago."

Gavriel's cold fingers grasp Ko'ach's bicep.

"I am getting a new response. Dull Gray's armored transport destroyed the second medical airship. I don't know when or how they'll get to your location!" Nephesh frantically yells.

"Stay with me, Papa." Ko'ach wraps Gavriel in a chest compression sleeve. Seeping blood slows to a trickle.

Loud explosions shake the ground. Ko'ach drags Gavriel behind the only log for miles. In excruciating pain, Gavriel points to the damaged, rusted tank from two wars ago. "Save yourself. Go!" Gavriel's bloody mouth sprays.

"Not without you. The pain meds are all used up. Nephesh, contact the council. Tell them we've been ambushed and...

"They're not coming," Gavriel whispers and grunts in agony.

"They wouldn't be so cowardly. Nephesh!"

"Stop. I have little time left. You're not supposed to be here. And well, I am not supposed to be here either. So much for being your backup.

"No more talking, Papa. There's something I need to tell you..."

"No! Listen to me." Gavriel's bloody coughs interrupt what he was going to say.

"Ko'ach, can you hear me?"

"Yes."

"I've triangulated your position and sent tunneling and other military grade drones. Most have been taken out."

"Dull Gray aren't supposed to have such capability."

"They don't," semi-conscious Gavriel whispers.

Tunnel drone arrives, pitted and smoldering. I-T-S jerky movements tell Ko'ach I-T-S about to detonate. Before I-T does I-T digs a trench good enough for two. Thousands of bullets, mortars, and spears blacken the cloudless sky. Green laser beams erratically misfire and slice tree stumps and long-ago abandoned artillery ships.

Ko'ach squeezes the last of the healing juice into his Papa's mouth. "Not very skilled, are they?" grimacing Gavriel states.

Drone drops blood transfusion equipment. "Thanks Nephesh."

"No!" shouts Gavriel.

"We are the same blood type, Papa."

Gavriel loses consciousness. Weakened Ko'ach and dying Gavriel glistened in the moonlight. 9 times Gavriel's heart stopped. 9 times Ko'ach resuscitated him.

"Ko'ach," Gavriel's gravelly voice whispers.

"Here, Papa."

"I-T-S time."

"No."

"My boy, you'll make an excellent medic someday."

Gavriel's swollen fingers search his backpack. "What are you looking for?" Gavriel points to the blue-white-fuchsia-golden glowing device.

"This. What is I-T?"

"Answer to our prayers," Gavriel croaks out.

Gavriel's stubby stiff fingers punch musical keypad and his prototype decloaks.

Nephesh bolts out the front door. Her father blocks her path. "Where are you going?"

"To help him."

"Too dangerous."

"I must go to him. I love him."

"You're too young for such feelings."

"Only two years younger than you when you and Mama fell in love."

Nephesh fakes left and runs right. I-T does not work, she's held in place by her father's strong hand.

"Release me, Papa!"

"We told you before and won't tell you again. I-T-S too dangerous!"

"We? We! What did you do, Papa?!"

"I-T-S for your own good."

"Don't you understand, he's for my own good. His Papa is dying. And Ko'ach could be next without backup."

"And you, a child...are his backup. You're not thinking about this rationally."

"Since when is love, rational? I don't understand this. You've always liked and respected Ko'ach and his papa. What is making you do this? Oh good, mother. Explain I-T to him. Oh, my God, you too? I can see I-T in your eyes."

Nephesh twists away from her father's grasp; 360 strides

from the front door, 27 fully armed military police arrive. "For me?"

"You see. I told you I-T was too dangerous."

"Why, Papa? You never explained why."

Yosher waves off the military Armada and they stand down, but they do not leave.

"So, they are under your direction."

"For now."

"Sorry, Papa."

Nephesh breaks out of her Papa's bear hug and kicks his bad knee; she runs toward the storm drain grill. Yosher writhes in agony. "Daughter, come back!" shouts her mother.

"Mother, I cannot."

Nephesh jumps into the cold freshwater aqueduct. She tucks her arms and sails down the twisting tunnels. Passing three divergent branches, she shifts her body into the preferred opening. Though I-T-S the most precarious, she picks up speed and flies down the chaotic rapids.

The rest of the night, Nephesh remains hidden and shivering. Making her escape she runs and dries off under the 125-degree sweltering midday sun. Nephesh sprints 18 miles to the backend of her family's ranch, then hops into her father's hovercraft and slams her thumb into the ignition button.

"Come on! Come on!" Nephesh unbuckles her seatbelts and backflips in front of the hood, she pops I-T open. "What have you done, Papa? Where have you hidden the engine?"

18 meters from the damaged vehicle. Yosher stands side by side with the military police.

"You should have trusted me, Papa!"

"Where's she going?" asks the police captain.

"Horses!" out of breath Hakarav shouts.

Dozens of hovercraft speed toward Nephesh. She types in the correct musical code and the energy grid crackles: Yosher's experimental cloaking structure activates.

Energy beams rip through hovercraft underbellies. Dozens

of men parachute; powerful wind forces them to dangle upside down among the thorny branches of the forbidden forest.

Nephesh run toward the wild horse-like creatures. Brazen whinnying lights up her eyes. "Do you remember me, girl? I'm the one who plucked those thorns from your hooves.

Nephesh's powerful hand grabs wild animal mane; the creature bucks—Nephesh slips. Her knees pinch the animal tighter, heart pressing against I-T-S heart. Hooves pound; the creature rockets out of the woods.

"Go, girl! I'll need everything you've got, if I am to save my boyfriend."

Gavriel drifts out of consciousness. His fuchsia pigment grows grayer.

"Stay with me, Papa." Ko'ach shakes his father. "Wake up!" Tears stream down Ko'ach's face. He pinches his father's arm.

"What?" confused Gavriel says. He taps his son's wet cheek with his bloody fingers.

"Papa...?"

"Yes, my brave son."

"What's this device?"

"Shout your name as loudly as you can," Gavriel's weak voice almost inaudible cracks.

"Ko'ach!" Disk jettisons metallic brace. Obelisk grows six more meters.

"Again. Louder." Gargling blood, Gavriel's breathy sputum splatters.

"Ko'ach! Ko'ach!"

Impenetrable metallic fuchsia shield forms around Ko'ach. Two incoming Dull Gray laser blasts ricochet of the shielding. Gavriel's lifts his head and slams his bloody fist to high heaven. Father and son watch the energy blast boomerang into Dull Gray armada.

"Read what's scrolled on the translucent tele-prompter."

"I don't need a tele-prompter for this."

"Use I-T anyway."

"Yes, Papa. Beautiful Nephesh. Beautiful Nephesh. Beautiful Nephesh."

Concentrating on his father, Ko'ach is unaware of the 74-foot stealthily dismounting Dull Gray warrior. She unsheathes her sword which measures the length of Ko'ach's entire body.

Gavriel shouts. No words exist. Ko'ach shakes his head, "What?" Gavriel frantically reaches for his backpack. His shaky fingers tightly grip a vial of blue liquid with white-hot specks. "No Papa! That's too much!" *He's taken 18 hundred times the safe dosage.*

Artificial adrenaline rampages through Gavriel's veins. Ko'ach watches in horror as his Papa rips the IV. "Papa no!" Fuchsia blood squirts.

"I love you, son."

Ko'ach's face slams into the malleable force field. "Papa! I can't get out! What are the deactivating codes? The codes Papa! Papa, no." Ko'ach slams his fist against the forcefield until a small trickle of blood slides down his arms.

"There is nothing more precious in the world than you, my boy. I won't allow you to sacrifice yourself."

"And you, Papa. Why should you be the one? Let me out. We can fight her together."

"I am enormously proud to be your father. Now, one more thing left for me to do."

Gavriel snaps his fingers three times. 18 fuchsia-blue-white triangles within triangles magnetize the nano-bot-technology implanted within Ko'ach. His forearm instantly slams against the glowing humming obelisk's right port.

Stuffing his bloody index and middle finger in his mouth, Gavriel blows with all the lung power he has left. Whistling activates 18 prongs; they descend 36 feet below the surface and magnetize the bedrock. *Now, no one, or thing can reach my boy. That shielding will protect you until our army breaks through the Dull Gray lines. I can die knowing you will someday build a beautiful family with your Nephesh. I see the love in your eyes. I was the same age when I started to have the same feelings for your mother. I-T was permissible for us to marry at 16, that is my wish for you, my dear sweet, brave son. Every happiness I wish you. My only regret is that I will not live long enough to see my grandchildren. God willing, I shall bear witness to the unfolding righteous events of your life from the afterlife's heavenly point of view.*

Gavriel's advanced martial arts techniques surprise Ko'ach. "You're amazing, Papa!"

Gavriel blocks every powerful thrust from the Dull Gray terrorist. Behemoth's knees, buckle. She screeches and refuses to fall. Fuchsia metal is the equalizer. Gavriel chips away at the monster's serrated convex sword. Smashing her armored torso; blunt force trauma enrages that highly skilled Dull Gray mother.

Ko'ach watches his brave father battle the terrorist Dull Gray general for 45 minutes. Nephesh finally arrives on the scene. She demagnetizes Ko'ach and runs into his arms; he pushes her away.

Why? Nephesh's confused brain asks herself. She instantly regroups and runs toward her boyfriend and wraps her arms around his waist. Rage pulsates through his veins, Ko'ach drags Nephesh toward his battling Papa.

"Get off me!"

"No!"

Ko'ach grabs Nephesh by the shoulder and holds her high above his head.

"Why?"

"Because you're one of them. You tricked me with your love. I finally see the real you. The real fake you. Get the hell off me!"

Nephesh kicks Ko'ach's powerful abs. He grunts. She falls to the soft sand dune. "I tried to save you. I-I love you. And you love me. What's changed? This doesn't make any sense."

Ko'ach ignores Nephesh and runs toward his sword. Dull

Gray general slams her well armored fist into Gavirel's skull. "Stop!" shouts Ko'ach. Nephesh throws a dagger toward the evil warrior. She cackles seconds after her huge fingers pluck I-T out of thin air. Dull Gray slams the blade into Gavirel's heart. She unsheathes her rusty sword. The horrible yelp after decapitation sends Ko'ach and Nephesh to their knees. "Papa! Papa!" shouts Ko'ach.

"Now that I am done with the appetizer. You two will make a yummy main course."

Filled with revenge. Ko'ach's rage knows no limit. He's never felt such pulsating adrenaline before. Ko'ach slams his father's shield into Dull Gray's armored head. Gray blood spurts from the terrorist's ears. Shield bounces back into Ko'ach's hands, and with greater force he slams the superior metal back into the murderer's jaw, torso, and knees.

"Soon every Fuchsia will join the two of you on our dinner plates."

"You will not escape the afterlife's judgment. "Burn in hell!" shouts Ko'ach. His metallic glove penetrates the beasts' armor.

Nephesh holds her hands over her mouth. "Oh my God. What have you done?"

Ko'ach holds a huge grayish beating heart in his two hands. He squeezes and screams. His screams are more animalistic than Fuchsia. He tosses what's left of the smashed heart into an ant hill. Horrible munching brings tears to Nephesh's eyes.

Dull Gray wheezes. "How can you still be alive," shocked Nephesh shouts.

Dull Gray thumps on her rib cage. "Our newest mutation, gives us a second heart."

A sand creature, half mole, half shark, latches onto the Dull Gray warrior's face. Crunching and munching sends Nephesh into Ko'ach's arms. What's left of the Dull Gray is dragged under the sand for the rest of the mole/shark thing's family.

Unable to process his grief, Ko'ach pushes Nephesh. She

tumbles into an uprooted tree.

From thousands of feet fiery siren-sounding debris falls toward Nephesh. Unprotected, she crouches. Ko'ach flings the Dull Gray's massive shield. Nephesh's entire body hides underneath. She's rattled as melting debris clangs off the shield.

Neither Ko'ach nor Nephesh see a female warrior sliding down her burning rope attached to what's left of her destroyed airship. The burning rope's strands inch toward her metallic fists. She's waiting for her descending craft to get closer to the ground. Feeling the horrible flesh-burning heat, she releases and falls hundreds of feet. Her huge metallic boots crush the backs of slow-moving sand turtles. She grabs the squashed purple turtle's soft face and slams I-T into her mouth. "Tastes almost as yummy as Fuchsia babies," Dull Gray cackles.

Dull Gray sniffs the air and smiles. She kicks the shield off Nephesh. Wide creepy grin grows wider and creepier. Crazy warrior strokes Nephesh's hair.

Dull Gray pulls on Nephesh's ponytail. Nephesh dangles high off the ground. "Ko'ach. Please. Help."

"Is that the boyfriend? And that must be his Papa's head."

Dull Gray licks the side of Gavriel's skull. Still in shock, Ko'ach does not move.

"You two make an excellent addition to my mother's taxidermy collection. Do we hang you in the bedroom, or the kitchen?"

Another warrior shouts from a distance, "No! She'll be more productive as my toddler's first slave."

"Did you hear what she said? Find your way back. My love. Use my love to find your way back. Ko'ach! I need you..."

Sand Tsunami cuts through desiccated metallic children, strewn about the time portal caverns. Sent by their evil 100-foot mothers to destroy my future, past, and present. They all failed. They were small enough to withstand the gravimetric pressures for fewer than 36 minutes; before they'd imploded.

I'm still too weak to permanently break the bonds of this place. I am still not worthy to wield God's righteous weapon. I am still helpless, watching my beloved transform. I can't save any of them. Not Dafna, nor Nephesh. And God knows where Ko'ach remains; locked forever betwixt real time and where he exists now. A place so harsh, so unforgiving, God has yet to confide in me I-T-S location. I sense, God is afraid I'd risk everything to locate and join him in the dance of the oblivion. I need your weapon God! I need I-T to save everyone's future!

Shiny metallic pieces are ripped by the gale force winds and plow into my torso. Every step I take leaves behind blood drops and clumps of twitching raw glistening muscle packets. Other than Ko'ach and God, does anyone else hear me? Does anyone care? Does anyone else know what I-T feels like to have sandpaper slammed against the side of my face and front of my face as I feel and watch my forehead, eye sockets, cheeks, ears, nose, and chin ferociously scraped at the speed of a Sandy Koufax fastball? Chafing arms, torso, legs, and feet are next. Pieces of Sagacious meat clumps dot the horizon. I hurt beyond the means to communicate how much I hurt. I know I-T pales in comparison to my beloved and my mentor...Ko'ach!

On David's world, decades of searing heat cools in a matter of 36 hours. *Food should arrive soon. Nothing I could pick up at the grocery store. Meat will need to be hunted. Fruits and vegetables will need to be seeded, cultivated, eaten, and stored before the heavy snow falls.*

Over the next 18-months, tiny creatures will fall from the opening in the energy grid. Time slows, gravity slows; those babies fall at an incrementally slow rate. Descending at 18 feet per month, they'll stay cocooned within their maturation membrane. They receive all the nutrition they need by sucking on three amniotic tubes. I-T-S truly wondrous to watch the cute wiggling babies mature into giant size adult beasts. *One, two, three antlers, become nine, ten, eleven; now only a few feet from the ground, they are almost fully grown, sprouting sixteen sharpened organ skewering antlers. Some hop on two legs like giant ferocious Kangaroos. Others dwarfing extinct woolly mammoths, sprouting two trunks and landing with an enormous thud. The first thing they do is stampede and crush newly growing fauna for food. They graze non-stop for years. They are the last creatures I shall hunt. I must store enough beast meat and fish food to last decades. Hot rain falls and fills up the meteorite created holes. I-T-S hot enough not to freeze. I shall have 36 months to catch them all. After that point, those huge lakes will become ice sheets 18-times deeper and wider than any compared to Earth's Antarctic. Fish and sharks dwarf any megalodon; those mutated creepy bug-eyed carnivores grow twice the length, and girth of any American aircraft carrier.*

Membrane touches increased gravimetric eddy and splatters I-T-S genetic material; similar to raindrops becoming larva snowflakes, I must hunt and gather a trillion and one seeds, carried by the dark winds to every corner of this angry planet. Once planted they will grow at an exponentially, simultaneous slow and rapid pace. Time has no place, in this place.

As the ancient Israelites did for centuries, I use my reinforced arrows and spears to track down and kill these gigantic mountain grazing sheep the size of tanker trucks. I swim deep below the crashing waves. The wind is unusually strong today. I've speared my quota. While under the surface my glowing hands create gills and light the way toward my breakfast, lunch, and dinner.

Next day I ran toward the precipice. Falling backwards I release six arrows all targeting the hearts of the fire breathing dragons.

My hands glow. I could easily start a warming and cooking fire with two blasts from my knuckles. I-T-S more fun rubbing two sticks together and letting friction do the rest. Fire crackles and I'm enjoying the warmth. I stretched out my right arm. The newly grown oak tree is sliced and diced. Each piece gently falls over the dwindling fire and mere moments later the crackling popping blaze towers 18 feet.

Thirty-six months later. All the land mammals, aviary creatures, and lake dwelling behemoths are caught and stored in the food vault. Genetically enhanced seeds will be vacuum-packed for decades into the future. All fruits and vegetables are stored in their own protective vault, separate from the meats and fish.

Not a speck of light remains, that will be my reality for

multiple decades. Punching the thickening air; a virtual blue, white panel illuminates the cavern for miles. Scrolling through historical events, I see endless writing and rewriting. For an eternity civilization grew and prospered and with a cosmic pen and ink well, changed, on the whim of the most horrendous she-devil in the Multiverse. Every death she creates, God snaps his fingers, and most are reborn, stronger, and more prosperous than before. That fate unfortunately never befalls myself nor my family and friends. I am always aware of what was and what is.

Tears come to my eyes as I scroll through 2024 on United States University campuses. *Historically speaking, the United States has always been able to distinguish between hate speech and First Amendment rights to peacefully protest. The USA's Democrat party had always been an advocate for Israel, and I-T-S Jewish population never before felt their lives were endangered as I-T did throughout 2024. I-T was determined that Islamophobia was in fact fake terminology. There were always very few Muslims harassed in the USA. Compared to spiking hate speech and physical assaults against Jews which ranged between an increase of 22 percent to a disgusting 600 percent. Why the change? Why the rise in anti-Semitic feelings and actions? Why has the CCP's TikTok infiltration become so successful at fomenting hatred of Jews? Twisted narratives take hold because there are 52 anti-Israel and anti-Jewish influencers compared to one pro-Israel rebuttal. More death to America and death to Israel chants on university campuses. Brainwashed by virulent communist professors; screaming students gleefully announce, "I am Hamas!"*

"What the fuck is wrong with these evil Americans? Are they Americans? Who is funding them? Iran? Soros? CCP? And hundreds of leftist NGOs from Europe. Even misguided Jewish leftists are with them. How dare they!"

David watches images of screaming narcissists who have nothing better to do with their pitiful lives, they want to cosplay as revolutionaries. Those privileged anti-Israel protesters continue to block traffic across the country's bridges and freeways. Stupid immature young people, like Keffiyeh wearing Greta Thunberg—what a disgraceful moron!

Double standard of unfairness. Politicians call university irrational protesters brave for stabbing Jewish students in the eye with a Palestinian Flag. Racism against all other groups is wrong. Jews are a race. Racism against them should also be considered a crime. And I-T-S not. I-T-S condoned. I-T-S viewed as not a big deal, or worse they, the Jews, deserve I-T.

Jewish kids afraid on university campuses. Jewish students are blocked from class. The administration continues to negotiate with terrorists.

The Arab Caliphate should be told to remove themselves from the Quad or you'll be arrested, and visas will be canceled! Columbia hosted a crew of terrorist influencers supporting the hijacking of planes.

Campuses from Los Angeles, to Michigan, to New York Arab Spring-breakers continue to spew hateful rhetoric and commit heinous acts of violence. And now for the rest of the semester, Columbia's classes will go remote.

University students spit on Jews. They tell the Jewish teens to go kill themselves. Arab and American protesters chant we don't want a two-state solution, we want I-T all. Burn Tel Aviv to the ground! From the River to the Sea Palestine will be Free! Scroll. Scroll. Oh, hell no. Really? A drag show for little kids and mommies? I-T would be laughable if I-T were not so sick on so many levels. Those men, dressed as women wouldn't last 18 seconds if they set foot in Gaza or any Muslim majority country. There is that one enormously fat drag queen spouting hate filled propaganda at a Kindergarten. Drag Queen holds a book, for reading time, and with little children on their mommies' laps. The drag queen implores the children and mommies to shout, Free Palestine!

I scroll hundreds of university campuses. I stop on screeching chants of, "Death to America! Death to Israel! Al-Qassam you make us proud! Kill another soldier now! There is only one solution! Intifada revolution! And there's Joe. No dude, don't say I-T. There are fine people on both sides. He said I-T. He really said I-T. Fool! No wonder so many sporting events heard young people shout, Fuck Joe Biden, but reporters who support him only heard, Let's Go Brandon."

18 days later, David shakes with disgust. He's furious at how inhuman the post-Covid Earth has become. He's had I-T with so many evil stories. "Enough!" David shouts.

Computer! Display terrorist infiltration incursion across American borders. Before David's eyes the landscape alters to resemble California, Texas, and New York. *Computer, I am in an especially bad mood. I-T will feel great! To deal with those terrorists in the only language they understand, first to torture and then the death blow. Now how to deal with these protesters, they haven't actually murdered anyone, well, not yet. What is the appropriate response? How should I direct my anger and frustration at them? I got I-T! I'll use the weapon of their choice, free speech. Spew back at them the specific words which will hurt their feelings, and for those not American citizens, let their visas be canceled and they are immediately deported. Oh, I-T-S going to be great to bully the bullies. Computer this is systemic problem. The antisemitic virus has spread beyond the university campuses. I want to go after all the funding sources, I must purge the feeling of helplessness. I must do something against all these evil doers, even though they are all holographically designed. After I've vanquished them all I will feel so much better. Computers activate all programs, Aleph to Zed! I will concentrate all my energy on this task, until the great snow falls. Computer! Begin...*

180 hours later, David exhausts his rage. His quest to vanquish all antisemitic bullies is a full success. Arms held high. The first snowflake tumbles past his sweaty eyelids. He sticks out his tongue. *I-T won't be long.* David looks up and the entire skyline appears to be thousands of miles of falling Dalmatians, blackness dotted by glowing bright white snow drifts. Every second, minute, and hour those snow drifts become larger and heavier.

Bright white snow falls in clumps the size of 18-wheelers. David gets into specially designed thermal underwear and three more multilayered sweaters. Shivering, the extra garments are never enough. Blackness as far as the eye can see. Only glowing multi-ton snowballs light the way. Two triple jumps later, David takes flight. He's able to traverse the entire planet before I-T completes I-T-S first dark rotation.

I use this cold illuminating flight to forget what my impeccable memory will never let me forget. I see, coming into view, the image of my wife, and so much more... Ima kisses the cheeks of our baby. Placing the baby in her crib. David flies down toward the golden glowing energy barrier. He bumps his head trying to walk through. Welt grows. He punches the barrier. Electrifying thrumming undulates and knocks him 18 miles. Over and over David tries to get through. Repeatedly, he fails. He must watch from afar, a timeline which he never experienced.

"Let's make another baby," whispers Ima.

The middle of tender love making, a giant black metallic middle finger penetrates the golden glowing walls and punctures Ima's eye socket. An eerie human scream becomes deep bass-baritone guttural. "No!" shouts the narrator, and his hallucinated doppelganger. Ima grows into a 100-foot machine, duplicating Kamala Harris's bizarre cackles and her third-grade alliteration.

"Baby looks tasty!"

The narrator slams his eyes shut. *I-T-S not real. I-T-S not real.*

"You could save them."

Narrator David swivels his head around, "Who said that?"

"I did."

David rubs his eyes with his fists. And opens his bloodshot eyes. He peers up at an 18-foot Star of David, with blinking eyes, one blue and one white, arching eyebrow, one blue and one white, parting lips to reveal every other tooth blue and white.

Like a spinning dreidel, one blue hand and one white hand stop the spinning and place the Star of David head onto a staff, the way one would place a scarecrow on a wooden post.

"Catch me if you can. And if you can. You'll be given everything you desire."

"How do you know what I desire? You're a figment of my traumatized mind."

"Am I? You are sure about that. Have you ever had a conversation like this before? In all these 18 million years. Hmm?"

"No."

David's hand reaches for the glowing blue, white staff. Star of David smiles and easily tilts to the right. *Come on my boy, you're faster than that. Again. Again. I'm only moving at half speed. Come on! I can hear Ima's cries. She needs you. Do you want me to fly to her purgatory and tell her you'll never come and rescue her?* David vigorously shakes his head. *You want me to tell her you're a coward?* The blue, white Star of David zooms over mountain peaks toward the golden glowing energy grid. That barrier prevents David from leaving his planet.

Zigzagging and rocketing in a straight line, David continues to follow the blue, white energy streak. He's always too slow. Now gaining for the first time. His fingertips are within inches and the Star of David blasts up and through the energy grid.

David's outstretched fingers and hand shatter on hitting the grid, head over heels, he tumbles for miles. Unconscious, he lands headfirst. From his skull, through his spine and all his limbs are shattered. For days he lays crumpled on the frozen permafrost. He's covered up, buried alive under tons of massive snow drifts.

Deep beneath the snowy mountain, David's inner light glows red hot. 18 minutes later, I stood in a melting pool of our own making. Blue and golden energy emerges from our knuckles, the rest of the snow melts away. David's footsteps slosh through another freezing cold lake.

I hate this place! I hate myself!

David leaps and flies upwards toward the energy grid. *Suicide is preferable to this existence. I-T-S existence, because I-T-S no life. God! Find yourself another warrior. Take my soul. Let me live for eternity, on the sidelines, watching someone else take the mantel of Immortal Mortal.*

Too hell with everything! David's hands grasp tightly to the energy grid. From head to toe he smolders. His righteous soul continues to put out the flames. *I've turned you off before, and I can do I-T once again.*

Do not pity me. Please, I can't stand any being or soul to pity...ME! From the top of his long silver hair to the soles of his feet, David bursts into non-extinguishable flame. Losing consciousness and his grip, charred David falls with the force of a meteorite. He melts through the first layer of snow and he's hot enough to melt through millions of years of permafrost.

36 hours later, agony of the heart wakens David from his coma. His blackened flesh is part pink and part Mediterranean olive skin tan.

David looks up at the human shaped hole. The beautiful twinkling stars mock his loneliness. *Why God? I've done all you asked of me. I've told my story. I will tell the story of my long dead friends. I tell the stories of a billion, no, no...trillions of other species. I had to watch and feel all of them crunched to death by I-T and I-T-S horrible minions. What more can I do...alone? My strength comes from companionship. From friendship. Not from memories.*

I've helped to empower billions of David Sagacious doppelgangers. Hoping above all hope, that one, all we/I need is one, will become the champion you deserve God. And not one became strong enough to defeat I-T.

Funny. Funny how the world can be so sad. There are no hugs or kisses for me. No feeling of intimacy. No family. No friends. No more mentor...I think...are you still out there, somewhere? Ko'ach. Ko'ach! Give me a sign. Anything. Prove to me you are alright. That you can still save the day.

God, I feel as lonely as you did all those trillions of years ago, before you invented time. Before you became aware that your lonely tear manifested I-T-Self into Malevolent Time.

I need God's righteous Star of David to win the day. But I-T refuses to cooperate. When I-T evades my grasp, does that mean I-T-S searching for another David Sagacious? I don't know what the answer is. I don't know what to do. Every wish. Every plea. Every demand...they are all denied. I need my wife's love. Her warm kisses. Her playful sense of humor. I need to see my children happy and healthy. Not one child. At least 6. Minimum of three of each would be nice, more if God is generous. I would be content with 6.

Every hero has their time to die. I want my time to die. And I want I-T today. Not tomorrow. Not a week from Tuesday. Now! God! I've given all I can. There is no more. Take me. Replace me with one who is truly worthy. Ima clearly not.

God! God! God! Why do you refuse to answer me?

David rages. He flexes his biceps and shoulders. He blasts his cavern. And pulverizes tons of boulders. *I am inconsolable! I crush every mountain range into glowing pebbles and blast holes in the energy grid.*

He flies toward the holes; they always close over before he can reach them.

Anger spent. Weakened David soft lands on the steam engulfing world. Becoming limp. He falls into the fetal position and softly cries; *I want to die.*

Breaking free of an 18-month coma. Emaciated, David takes a small bite from his conjured IN-and-OUT hamburger. His heartache remains very real. He continues to tell the Ko'ach saga mere moments after the Dull Gray murdered Ko'ach's Papa.

After a momentary hesitation, he backflips and slams his right boot against the giantess without a protective helmet. Her cackling laughter enrages Ko'ach and frightens Nephesh.

Dull Gray's powerful backhand slaps send Ko'ach crumbling into a small boulder.

"Weak tiny male!" growls terrorist who killed Gavriel.

"You'll be re-educated to serve us. If you resist, I know for a fact, cook has a new recipe she'd like to try for our empress."

Second combatant's belly laughs mock Ko'ach's pain.

"Foolish boy! You are outnumbered a thousand to one. Our spies are everywhere. We've indoctrinated at least 80,000 new morsels this month alone, and I-T was a relatively unproductive month because the Queen added three new holidays of rest.

Nephesh finds her pocket size bazooka. A single shell hits Dull Gray's breastplate and the mocking beast implodes. Pieces of her fly toward a locust nest. Standing on their legs they approach 13 feet. Hundreds, in a karmic frenzy pounce, rip and chew Dull Gray's face, organs, and limbs.

Goo squirts onto Nephesh's blouse and arms. "Yuck!" she spits.

"Codes!"

"What?"

"You heard me! Give me the fucking codes!"

"No need to say that."

"No? You and your father are the reasons why that has happened to mine!"

"You're still grieving. I understand." Nephesh walks over to wrap a comforting arm around Ko'ach's shoulder, and he slaps her away.

"Get the fuck off me. I won't ask you again. Give me the fucking codes!"

Ko'ach drags and with great difficulty lifts the dead Dull Gray's sword.

"Do I-T! You want to kill me? You...I love you. I-I rescued you. What is going on? Talk to me. Ko'ach! For God's sake tell me what you're feeling."

Ko'ach can barely hold the weapon at waist level. Tears flood down his quivering face.

"Look what they did to my Papa."

Tears stream down Nephesh's face. Gavriel's blood drips from the sword, down Ko'ach's arms, He drops the weapon. The handle pulverizes a small boulder. Nephesh runs into

Ko'ach's arms. He hugs Nephesh with the blood of his father.

Nephesh caresses Ko'ach's face and gives him multiple gentle kisses.

Ko'ach's heart feels like I-T-S caught in a vise, and his mouth is as dry as the desolate landscape.

Ko'ach's sandpaper feeling eyes stare at his lifeless father. Nephesh holds Ko'ach's hand and fires her grave digging weapon. Both pick up Gavriel's body, and reverently place him in his makeshift resting place. They agree on two silent prayers.

After 72-minutes, Ko'ach's weary swollen eyes shut. Nephesh's blue-white scarf gently brushes mud and dried blood from his bruised face.

Sun rises and sets three times. Ko'ach and Nephesh cuddle, gather water from a recently dug well, and polish off most of the rest of Nephesh's pre-cooked rations.

Dull Gray and Fuchsia ships tumbled out of Mock 1 and exploded in mid-air.

Nephesh and Ko'ach are exhausted. She lovingly pushes hydrating green, orange, and purple succulent juicy food into Ko'ach's mouth. Her head on his shoulder both their inhaling and exhaling sighs are synchronized.

How can I leave her now? She must never learn about my covert mission. Keep telling yourself I-T-S the right thing to do...to break her heart now, rather than become captured and tortured. Better she stays alive. She'll not understand what you must do. You know her better than yourself. She'd follow you. You can't have any distractions. Other than Papa, she'll always be my greatest distraction. Oh, Papa. Why? Why?

Tears fill Ko'ach's eyes. Seconds after gravity pushes them down Ko'ach's cheeks; Nephesh blots them away with her sleeve.

"I am here for you. Whatever you need. For however long I-T will take."

Nephesh presses her soft lips onto Ko'ach's cracked lips. Her finger digs out odorless healing balm. She rubs some over Ko'ach's top and bottom lip. *How can I tell her? How can I leave her?*

How can I say mean things to her? How can I not. I do love her. And to save her, I must be cruel...I-T-S the only way.

The glow of a full moon illuminates Nephesh's tranquil face. *She's so cute. Even her snoring is cute. How can her snoring be cute?*

Ko'ach shakes Nephesh's shoulder. She stretches, yawns and kisses Ko'ach. "Good morning."

"I need to go."

"You feel strong enough to go back home? Wonderful. I thought you said you needed another two days to rest. The bombing has stopped, that's a good sign. I'll fill up our water bottles and cook us some breakfast and..."

Ko'ach intertwines his fingers with Nephesh's. She smiles. "No smiling."

"Sorry. I love you so much. Even with all that has happened. I can't contain myself."

"Stop Nephesh-ah-la."

Nephesh wiggles with delight. "What is I-T you want to tell me?"

"I am going. Not we are going."

"I don't understand."

Ko'ach looks away. *Tell her. Make I-T fast. Quick or slow the pain I am about to cause her will be the same.*

Nephesh leans into Ko'ach's heart. "There is a little cottage on my great-grandfather's land.

"Not even my Papa is aware I've fixed I-T up. I-T-S the perfect place. Dozens of unique beautiful wild 4-, 6- and 8-legged species. Small waterfalls will give us enough water. The trees and flowers are luscious. We can stay until the war is over... There's that look again. Please tell me your thoughts..."

"Nephesh! You're not listening."

"Sorry... Go on."

"I said I must go. Not we. You must go back home. Make up with your father. Forgive him. Or not. But I'm sorry. I've delayed long enough. I am stronger. I must go…"

"Where? Wherever I-T is, I'm going too…"

"You said you'd hear me. Whatever I had to say. Well, you're not hearing me! Goodbye!"

"No!" Nephesh wraps her arms and legs around Ko'ach's waist and legs.

"You can't go where I am going! Why must you make this so difficult?"

"Difficult. Difficult! Impossible! Wherever you go, take me with you."

"Not safe."

"You're right. I-T-S not safe, to go I-T alone."

"To make sure you have a future. I-T means that I cannot be a part of yours."

"What the hell does that mean? Kiss me."

In her left hand, Nephesh holds a sleeping concoction.

"I know your heart, Nephesh-ah-la." Ko'ach takes the syringe from Nephesh's grasp.

"Stop!"

"Why?"

"If you do this thing. Enter the forbidden forest alone. You're proving the council's point."

"Which is?"

"You're only a boy. Not mature to think clearly. You're letting your emotions run wild."

"No, Ima not. Feelings are in check. This is the best, most logical move."

"Logic. Really? Okay calm and collected. There was one who was always more talented."

"My Papa."

"And. Um… Look what happened to him."

"Because his focus was distracted."

"I-T wasn't your fault." Nephesh hugs Ko'ach. He doesn't

hug her back. Tears break from her false self-imposed pretend stoicism.

"Please. I'm begging you. Stay with me. I couldn't bear I-T, if...if..."

"You'll learn to. You'll have the love of your family and the community. If..."

"No, I won't. I won't let them help me. I can't. My destiny is to be your wife. You see, by leaving me, you are mocking God's plan for the two of us."

Ko'ach gently kisses Nephesh's cheek. She slaps plastic restraints around Ko'ach's and her own ankles. "These are unbreakable. Unlike my heart if you leave me here. Where you go, I go, there is nothing you can do about I-T. Walk into the forest if you must. If you do, you'll have to do so with me attached."

Ko'ach takes four deep breaths. His ankle vibrates dark fuchsia energy.

"How are you doing that?"

"A maneuver taught to me by the old general before he vanished."

"You've been training with him. Were his protestations... Was that all a ploy? A trick to misdirect, me?"

I don't know what to say. Tell her the truth, my love for her is unbreakable, and leave her, thus breaking her heart. Or leave, coldly... showing no love. Both ways are unforgivable.

"He'd teach me something I never knew I could do, and all the while implore that I wait and do the bidding of the council."

"Stop what you're doing! You're cutting yourself."

Ko'ach's wincing stops 18 seconds after the plastic around his ankle becomes severed.

Ko'ach grabs Nephesh's hips and lifts her high off the ground. "Goodbye, sweetheart."

Ko'ach tosses Nephesh toward the soft sand dune.

Ko'ach walks toward the Dull Gray Forest. "You know, in short bursts I can catch up, especially since your ankle must still be throbbing."

Ko'ach turns. "I know." *He wouldn't. Put the gun away. Do you know how to use a Dull Gray weapon? He wouldn't fire on me. He loves me. He's bluffing. You sure?* Nephesh smiles and takes two steps closer. A short orange burst hit Nephesh's thigh.

"You shot me!"

"The numbness will dissipate soon, and a few weeks after that, the berry size bruise."

"And the bruise to my heart. How long will I-T take for that?"

"I won't leave you without a way to defend yourself. Catch."

Ko'ach pulls a laser rifle from his duffel bag.

"No! You need this more than I..."

"Too cumbersome. This prototype is all that I need."

Ko'ach vanishes into the foreboding Dull Gray realm. Dull Gray missile barrage shakes the ground. Nephesh loses her footing and rolls down one of the tallest sand dunes. Trying and failing to climb out of a deep trench. She cries... "Papa!"

Hot, boiling sun recedes and is replaced by a quarter moon. Nephesh turns her duffel bag into a sleeping bag. That night, using her infrared binoculars, Nephesh spots on the horizon, miles away, a galloping Dull Gray warrior, with murderous rage in her eyes. *Probably related to the one Ko'ach defended himself against. And she's heading this way to finish the job. Damn she's moving fast. I hope the rescue team finds me first. Hasn't been a full day and I miss you already, Ko'ach. Be safe. Oh God, please watch over my Ko'ach.*

Two aircraft accelerate faster than any known Dull Gray craft. They bracket Nephesh; their engines kick up a blinding sandstorm. Nephesh fires her flare. *I'll make you proud, Ko'ach. I promise I'll take them out before they finally finish the job.*

Dust cloud dissipates. Yosher and Hakarav appear. "Thank God, we found you."

"He's gone, Mommy."

"How long ago?" asks Yosher.

"9 hours."

"Let's get you back home."

Yosher, Hakarav, and Nephesh held each other tight. Staring blankly at the encroaching night. All three are bathed in moonlight and neither one knows what tomorrow will bring.

576 fuchsia sunsets later...

Nephesh wears Ko'ach's favorite shirt. His sweater adorns her pillowcase. Deeply despondent, she sarcastically scorns sentimentality. Shameful surreal skullduggery sends Nephesh into a deeper darker slumped sadness.

Nephesh fist-size fresh holes are punched through her bedroom walls. New scabs heal and are re-created after lingering fury pushes her deeper into her own emotional sinkhole. Her metallic desk is filled with dozens of fingertip dents.

Nephesh sits in the dark; her parents come home late and say, "Lights."

As soon as the illumination shows Nephesh's disheveled hair and food-stained shirt, she yells, "Off!"

Nephesh watches and rewinds 27 hours a day to the dreadful moment she bore witness to Ko'ach's capture and his continuous torture in real-time. She replays the moment the image of bloodied, broken, burned Ko'ach dissolves into frustrating static. She's constantly attacked by her frantic mind and guilty heart. Rewound 7 years ago, her weepy eyes are on sleep-deprived Ko'ach. *Dull Gray monsters tortured my beloved, nonstop, for 70 horrific hours!*

Punishing herself. Nephesh watches for the umpteenth time, a sizzling orange hot poker dig into and twist inside Ko'ach's guts. His infected flesh and grisly begging for an end to his torture horrifies Nephesh. Dizzy, she forces herself to watch. *Your fault. Your fault! You should have stopped him. But you are not to blame, alone. Oh no! The council. The ones who forced a boy on such a mission. They should all die. I hope they all suffer from some ghastly infirmity. I hope...I wish...*

Nephesh's horrible wailing sent her parents into each other's arms. They've tried and failed to comfort their daughter. Words of wisdom from the most righteous clerics continue to fall on deaf ears. Nephesh hits the rewind button and watches Ko'ach's flesh torn by bullwhip dipped in salt water. Not getting the answers they desire, or out of gleeful fun, the Dull Gray terrorists break Ko'ach's hands and feet. Gigantic Dull Gray fist slams into Ko'ach's face. She's watched this scene tens of thousands of times: even though she knows what's coming next, she jumps and covers her eyes. Nephesh irrationally hopes for a different outcome and when I-T doesn't happen she violently attacks furniture, walls, and family portraits.

Tradition dictates Dull Gray cleanse their captives in fire; Ko'ach's blackened gangrenous body is disrespectfully tossed like rotting meat.

Not yet a corpse, his agony cools on Dull Gray's artificial black snow. His lips move. These are the mumbles that break Nephesh over and over again. "I love you, Neph-esh-ah-la..."

Metallic bootsteps crunch the black snow; bloody boot lifted above Ko'ach's head; one last horrifying crunch and static fills Nephesh's viewscreen. Her heartbeat thumps dangerously fast.

"Ko'ach. Ko'ach. Ko'ach..." she whispers in the darkness.

Stomping out of her room. Seething Nephesh starts anew, an old argument. "Papa! Papa!" Nephesh, enraged, tosses heavy boxes, knives, and three-pronged forks.

"You knew! I could've talked him out of I-T if I had known. You sent a boy on a military recon! How dare you! God will punish you...as he punishes me every fucking day!"

"Language, sweetie," exasperated Hakarav sighs.

"Fuck language. I'll fucking talk the way I feel. And I want everyone to feel as miserable as you've made me!"

"We've told you, year after year, I-T was a joint decision. All the religious, political, and military leaders agreed. There wasn't one dissenting voice. Ko'ach, months before his 13th birthday, was amazing. He tested in the top one-tenth of one percent in all physical and intellectual challenges. In all our history, he was the youngest to join the elite of the elite."

"Stop saying was. He could be out there struggling to find his way back to me."

"Oh, honey? After all these years? You've heard me say I-T a thousand times before. I wish you could accept the fact that there's no chance he could have survived those injuries. Even if he did, the Dull Gray patrols would've found him. 7 years, sweetie.

Nephesh grabs a heavy chair and tosses I-T like I-T was a waffle.

"For the millionth time. Mother! Shut the fuck up!"

"Enough! Apologize to your mother!" shouts Yosher.

"I apologize, mother! Not! Why the fuck do you both keep on sending those fucking losers. I don't want to marry. I never want to marry. I do not apologize for what I have planned for them. If you care at all about your standing in the community, you'll stop sending me those God-awful suitors. Now Go! Leave me the hell alone!" screeches Nephesh.

CHAPTER 20

Witnessing Ko'ach's Torture and Death, Nephesh is Consumed by Suicidal Thoughts

Nephesh's nocturnal narcissism invokes incessant insensitive invalidating invectives.

Shades shut. Sunlight sequestered. She sits and shivers. She sighs and shuffles. Egregious erudite eccentricities escalate. Nervy neurotic Nephesh needs nihilistic nonexistence.

After her 20th birthday comes the 27-week countdown, when pandering paramours ages 18 to 36 are all put through ego squashing purgatories. Petrified suitors' provocative peccadillos pedantically parade. Petulant pathology painfully perpetuates petty, patronizing panache.

Nephesh continues to humiliate hundreds of intellectuals with her acerbic put-downs. Witty comedians slapped down by her morose mood. Moreover, she'd merrily mock and manipulate the most accomplished athlete. Her angelic voice would maintain brilliant purity, far beyond the abilities of the proteges' virtuosity. Nephesh's enthusiastic intensity and Machiavellian mind broke hundreds of strong-willed men.

Doctors, lawyers, scientist, painters, engineers; brilliant

orators, wise religious clerics are felled by Nephesh's unforgiving merciless tongue.

Combat soldiers with chiseled physiques and models with amazing handsome faces; each a good love match, all are for the first time in their lives, gleefully rejected by Nephesh's deliberate malice.

Fuchsia tradition stipulates all families take the 9th day of their week off, as their resting Sabbath. Sad lament continues from Nephesh's mother. Her mind wails, *What am I to do? I don't know how to help my daughter. How do I unburden the unbearable? She's 20 and she hates love. A person without a loving partner, disrespects the life God gave them. Please, daughter, stop bullying all these righteous men. Their only crime is that they are not Ko'ach. You're setting yourself up for a lifetime of loneliness. God give me the strength. Give me the wisdom to reach her. I am at my wits end. We all are.*

Yosher's mind shouts, *God! My gorgeous Nephesh-ah-la sleeps all day. Her caloric intake never moves above starvation level. She enjoys humiliating kindhearted men. Every loving action on my part and her Mama's, I-T-S all spit back in our faces. My daughter, your sharp wit is extremely cruel. The council of elders is making plans to banish you forever. We'll go where they send you, and yet, I know in my heart you'll abandon us the first chance you get.*

Unable to crawl out of her angry depression, Nephesh sleeps 14 hours a day with remnants of Ko'ach's treasured shirt under her pillow. Pulling her favorite blue-white quilt over her head, Nephesh's restless mind shouts down her troubled soul: *I feel no love, only shame. I enjoy making proud chivalrous men cry. I deliberately break their spirits. There was a boy who never got the chance to be a man. These past seven years my heart aches for the name I can't bear to speak aloud. Thoughts of suicide won't subside. I know killing myself would destroy my parents. I live without hope. For me, there is no chance for love's redemptive powers. My soul is paper-thin, and my grief is cutting edge.*

*

18 days later, Nephesh guards the desolate radiated neutral zone between the Fuchsia force field and encroaching Dull Gray patrols. She squints into the sun and swigs a gulp of honey tea, talking to herself: "New codes will make sure Dull Gray patrols are never allowed to breach our territory. I'm depressed and despised; I won't be disloyal. All these seven years, not once did I say no when the reservists' call to defend our people came down from on high.

Heat distorts the horizon. Nephesh squeezes her cold-water-pouch over her sunburned scalp. *Mama. Papa. If I see only one patrol, I'll weaken a portion of the field, big enough for that one Dull Gray to slip through. I'll close the grid and trap us in a face-to-face death match. I'll let the warrior do to me what I can't do to myself. One patrol. That's I-T. I'll bring in no more. Before I die, I'll mortally wound the Dull Gray beast; she won't have the slightest opportunity to harm another Fuchsia. I give you my word. Damn! My shift is almost up. Why must they always patrol in packs? I can't create the breech until I see only one and pray that'll happen soon.*

Minutes become hours. Nephesh taps her scanner. "Damn I-T, 27 more Ish kabibble tock ticks before I'm relieved." *There she is! Coming up fast. Damn, she's a big one. That's odd. My scans aren't specifying her gender. From this distance, she appears to be too large to be a male. But...um...the scans are bouncing back...fused metal plating hides her face. Height fluctuates... Got I-T! Final reading. She's 9 inches above 70 feet.*

Nephesh talks to fluttering fuchsia butterflies—each larger than an Earth single-propeller aircraft. Soft wings tickle her eyebrows. "Facial recognition software will become obsolete if other warriors are so designed. No detection of others similarly constructed. I know Dull Gray body armor is disrupted by our force field. The longest they can survive is 17 minutes before hallucination sets in. What the hell is she waiting for? I-T-S been 22 minutes! Shit! She was perfect for my plans. Her stare down is unnerving. I'll need to contact...wow. They shouldn't have the ability to block and redirect my transmission. Must figure out how she's able to generate that pulse.

Her flesh should be cooking within her metallic uniform...but I-T-S not."

Thank God our forcefield's operational port remains cloaked. I-T-S a trillion to one shot she'll ever be able to... Oh my God! How the hell did she do that? She's figured out the musically encoded instructions. I-T is forbidden. She must've tortured one of our righteous soldiers to extract that information.

"I remember that song from long ago. That was Ko'ach's favorite. My scans must be wrong...she's spelling N-E-P-H-E-S-H-20...K-O-A-C-H-20. Is she aware of who I am? Why would she taunt me? Is the message directed at me? Maybe some other hidden message is imbedded within I-T-S matrix? Is she contacting sleeper cells to awaken and attack our people?"

Nephesh's particle beam weapon crackles and hums. The highest setting disrupts the Dull Gray's nervous system. Her advanced energy weapon is a hundred times more powerful than the one used by Ko'ach 7 years ago.

"Are you the lead scout of your advancing armada? You must be captured; preferably alive. I-T-S imperative that our science directorate studies this innovated design and find a way to counter I-T. Am I strong enough to do I-T alone? I don't have enough time to wait for the others. And I-T-S blocking my transmissions at the source. How? How! I didn't think the Dull Gray had the capability. Wait? They shouldn't. No other clan can match our technology. Has the Dull Gray become the first of our clans to have first contact with a similarly malevolent extraterrestrial species? Now what? She is changing the code: N-E-P-H-E-S-H-20 K-O-C-H-13 I-L-O-V-E-Y-O-U."

The force field's energy signature drops to zero. Nephesh looks over her shoulder. Her horse wades in a pristine shallow lake. She sprints toward the huge intruder. Sparks vibrate and blare. "How is she doing that, activating my self-destruct?"

With seconds to spare Nephesh throws her weapon as high as she can. I-T hits the ground and explodes. She's knocked over into a deep trench. Tons of sand particles seep into her nose.

Semi-conscious Nephesh hears metallic footsteps. Metallic ear to the ground, Dull Gray listens for Nephesh's suffocating wheezing lungs. I-T-S metallic fist slams deep beneath the cracked land; her metallic fingers stretch and extend. "Got you," mechanical voice undulates.

Landing on her back; bloody sand and tissue particles are violently expelled from Nephesh's lungs. Uncharacteristically, Dull Gray shows compassion and pours invigorating water over Nephesh's eyes, nose, and mouth. Dull Gray pulls Nephesh's dislocated shoulder onto her strong thigh and pops I-T. Loud crunch echoes.

"W-why did you do that?"

I-T forces the corners of I-T-S metallic mouth to lift into a wider grin. That rusted mask's squeaky movement feels like fingernails on a chalk board. The abnormal Dull Gray warrior spritzes freezing agents from her palm over a now frosty canteen; Dull Gray gently places I-T on Nephesh's blistered forehead. Squinting her eyes and shaking her head, Nephesh keeps a close watch on the metallic creature's heavy brick crushing foot stomps. *Why would I-T gingerly step around those cute baby turtles? I-T-S not in their nature to ever show mercy. I've read intelligence reports about kidnapped children consumed as specialty sandwiches.*

A new ominous musical dirge shakes Nephesh from her nightmarish thoughts. Invader's middle finger pokes the computer console and mockingly changes the soft feminine Fuchsia voice into a strident mechanical shouting voice: H-U-R-R-A-H-K-O-A-C-H-I-S-D-E-A-D. Rising like an avenging phoenix, Nephesh aims her weapon. "Move away from the device, or I'll turn you into ash!"

Metallic boots turn on a dime. Dull Gray beast's mechanically condescending voice crackles, "Little girl, put that away."

Nephesh tap, tap, taps to an unprecedented never before used level. "Perhaps you think your ash could clone a new you. I can assure you; this new setting will burn every metallic atom. Not even demonic extraterrestrials will be able to bring you back. I said halt! I will not give you another warning. Comply if you want to live."

Metallic monster takes one step toward Nephesh. Dull Gray holds her sides and loudly laughs, "Why is your hand shaking?"

"I-T-S not!"

"What do you call that?" Metallic boot takes a half a step closer. "Lower your weapon. Please..."

"Please? Please? What the hell are you?"

"Nothing you could imagine in your wildest dreams."

Dull Gray shuffles her two feet, inches closer.

"I'm not playing this game. Stop! I will not give you another warning. Stop!"

"Confused?"

"No!"

Dull Gray takes a large Monty Python silly walk stride forward.

"Why the hell are you walking like that?"

"For the fun of..."

"Fun. Fun! You call this fun! Murderer!"

"Not today. Stand Down, Nephesh-ah-la."

"How dare you use my familial endearment."

"I am family."

Nephesh spits. "Fuck you. Hey! You said I. Dull Gray never speaks as an individual. I-T-S always a collective we or us. Take off your mask!"

"I cannot."

"More lies," screeches Nephesh.

"Nephesh-ah-la. You were never strong enough to defeat me."

"I've never met you before."

"You sure? Haven't figured I-T out yet? That's disappointing. My exoskeleton will absorb any blast; be I-T from that puny handheld device or cannons from your warships. My scanners are also far more advanced. I know your army is battling two Dull Gray regiments and losing. Let me finish my mission. Trust me little one. I would never harm you, or your people."

"Why do you refuse to reveal yourself?"

"Not important. What is important, too you...Ko'ach is alive, and I can bring you to him."

"Liar!" Nephesh rages. Nephesh pulls from her boot a small metallic point, she shakes I-T into a two handheld triangular blade and slams I-T with all her might against the Dull Gray's metallic face. Dull Gray backflips and chuckles. Landing with a heavy thud the creature sprints through the lake, and over a half dozen freezing mountaintops.

Nephesh has never in her life run faster, and yet she is falling miles behind. "Give up little one! Your attempt to catch me is hopelessly futile!"

I-T-S amplified voice echoes. The unidentified monster jettisons a sticky whiplashing rope. Nephesh ducks, the rope was not meant for her, I-T yanks Nephesh's sword from her hip and tosses I-T into the energy grid. Nephesh's reaction is too slow. "No!" she shouts, watching I-T slowly disintegrate.

"Bitch! That belonged to my beloved."

"You shouldn't have been so careless."

Like a powerful locomotive, Dull Gray runs down the mountain; I-T smashes through trees and discarded burned-out Fuchsia tanks like they were Graham crackers. Nephesh refuses to retreat. They both are on a collision course. I-T stretches I-T-S arm, hand, and fingers half a mile and squeezes Nephesh's ankles. She yelps, "You bitch! Put me down!"

Held upside down. Dull Gray warrior flings Nephesh as easily as a human child would toss away a Frisbee. Nephesh lands on her backside, into the icy shallow lake. She sinks to the silty bottom. Undaunted, Nephesh's powerful legs squat and like a powerful missile she heads toward her enemy's knees. Dull Gray's reflexes are quicker, and her strength continues to prove her unprecedented superiority. Muscle rippling forearm backhands Nephesh into the dust. *She could have broken my skull. Why would she use minimal force?*

Adrenaline helps Nephesh squeeze off multiple energy blasts. Dull Gray tucks and rolls away from the superheated sand. I-T-S smirking grin makes the sound of a fiddlestick grating against a jagged saw.

Like an immature 6-year-old; Dull Gray holds I-T-S thumb on I-T-S nose and wiggles I-T-S fingers. "Are all Fuchsia so easily manipulated?"

Nephesh's manic punches are easily blocked. "Stand down, Nephesh-ah-la."

"Never!"

"Catch me if you can," smirks unknown Dull Gray combatant.

18 minutes later, Nephesh's mind asks herself, *how can she run so gracefully and fast in all that bulky armor?*

After sprinting 27 miles, Dull Gray monitors Nephesh's vitals and slows her stride. *Damn your stubbornness! Why did you override the safety protocol chip?*

Dull Gray walks back toward Nephesh at a leisurely pace.

Thank God, I think. She's mysterious that one; been toying with me, but for what purpose? For propagandistic reasons, she could have broadcast my abduction, and slow torturous murder. Isn't that their way?

Nephesh's father stands at the bow of the medical airship. He shouts and pumps his fist in the captain's face. "That's my daughter out there."

"I'm well aware of who she is. She took immense pleasure in humiliating my boy last week," scowling captain responds.

"To hell with that. You fly this craft faster. Or I'll do I-T myself!"

"Any faster and I-T will fly apart."

"Well, do that! Fly I-T till she come's apart. Better your craft than my dear sweet daughter. Hold on sweetie. Papa's here..."

Captain glances down at his computer. They are rapidly

closing in on the Dull Gray.

"Fire!" shouts Yosher.

A huge particle beam cannon releases three salvos. Dull Gray falls into a massive crater. Sand cascades and sinks the Dull Gray deeper. Suffocating sand presses against I-T-S lungs.

Airship begins to break apart. Yosher and part of the crew slide off the ripping apart deck; and fall headfirst into the smoldering crater. Dull Gray digs herself out of the pit. Crawling and gasping. Yosher runs toward his rifle. His smile changes when he notices the firing pin is damaged. "Fuck!"

Yosher runs toward the Dull Gray and pummels her mask with the butt of the rifle. He slams I-T two more times in her stomach. Each blow replicates the sound of an anvil. The ground shakes as another airship crashes. Yosher is knocked off balance just as he was going to hit the Dull Gray in her stomach, but he misses and smashes the Dull Gray much lower.

Dull Gray's mechanical grunt gives Nephesh an a-ha moment. "She's a dude!" she exclaims.

Nephesh runs and backflips and the third backflip end with her metal boot toe crushing Dull Gray's genitals. Monstrous mechanical shriek catches everyone's attention. Hundreds of Fuchsia officers parachuted to Yosher's location.

Dull Gray dude lifts Yosher off the ground.

"Let him go!" shouts Nephesh.

"Fire on me and you'll incinerate only your Papa. My armor is an alloy no other clan from this world is aware of. I can and will survive any setting. Trust that as an irrefutable truth!"

"What are you saying? You're in contact with an alien world, not from our solar system?"

"Your spontaneous inventiveness will not help you this time. You're woefully overmatched by my physical and technological advantages."

Putting himself between his daughter and the Dull Gray, "You are the one who has over-played your hand. I've never lost in combat," says Yosher.

"Impressive record against your average Dull Gray; I am unlike any you've ever encountered. I will defend myself. You're making a huge mistake by taking me on."

Nephesh looks down at the Dull Gray blood splatters.

Fuchsia blood? That could explain why he knows so much about me and Ko'ach. Perhaps he was with us in the grand hall on the day my beloved stood up for our rights. Keep him talking, Papa. Almost there. Almost! Soon I will download all your genetic markers.

I can't allow Nephesh to know my true self. Better I self-destruct. The truth would break her heart, I will not be the cause of that. God, stop. I will not do I-T! What are you doing? Forcing my hand. No, please do not force my hand!

Mechanical fingers manically dig into I-T-S fleshy and metal combo voice processor. The squawking device imbedded under the skin becomes dislodged. Fuchsia blood gushes from the hole in Dull Gray's neck.

Horrible gurgling wheezing squeezes I-T-S throat. I-T-S last words before losing consciousness, "Hear...Ko'ach."

Nephesh aspirates bloody material. Her fingers apply pressure to the open wound. Military locks and loads, they're all ready for incinerating action.

"Step aside, Nephesh. Time to let that monster die!" shouts the lieutenant major.

"No! He knows what happened to my beloved."

"More deceit. We can't bring him back. We can this day give this one what she so richly deserves.

The metallic warrior startles Nephesh with his gasp out of unconsciousness. He forces his blurred vision to clarify what he must do to stay alive. Piano key musical code sends sparks throughout his forearm port. Energy beams ascend over the treetops. Hundreds of soldiers are incredulous as all their particle beam weapons fizzle and deactivate.

General reaches into his pocket for an antiquated revolver and loads 9 titanium bullets with special armor piercing points. The general pushes past Yosher.

"For my murdered wife! My tortured son! And tortured daughters!" Targeting the chest cavity: all titanium bullets penetrate at hypersonic velocity. Impact causes splashes of fuchsia blood to splatter the general's forehead. The general wipes his handkerchief across the bridge of his nose and eyelids.

"Look general!" He's shocked at the blood's color. "I didn't know."

"Murderer! Medics over here! Let them through. Damn you, let them pass!" shouts Nephesh.

"How can this be? Must be a trick. They are all tricksters. Deceivers incarnate!"

"Not this time, general! You will be held accountable if he dies before I find out what happened to my Ko'ach! Revenge is never the answer. You blamed this one for the crimes of others. Damn you! He's..."

"He?"

"Yes, another blunder. This is not a Dull Gray sadistic female. He was probably kidnapped from my street. Probably went to school with him. My scans are still not giving me what I need. Hopefully the surgeons can tell us what we need to know. He's unique. A prototype. His advanced technology can help us against other warriors and, more importantly, bring back my beloved."

Crew on hovering airship lassos Yosher. He's yanked up without his permission.

"Bastards!" shouts Nephesh.

18 elite soldiers run toward the Dull Gray prototype. Holding their titanium battering ram high above their heads, they slam with the force of collective revenge. I-T-S metallic skull crunches and I-T-S torso and limbs are pile driven deep beneath the permafrost.

Seconds after the Dull Gray arms and legs twist around his neck; Nephesh screeches, "Oh my God! Oh my God! You fucking assholes! You've killed him!"

"Calm down Nephesh. Justice has been served!" The general and his soldiers high five. The general offers his hand;

Nephesh slaps I-T away. "Take her to the hospital."

"No general, take yourself to the firing squad."

Nephesh slams the scanning results into the general's face. "C-can't be!" astonished general stutters.

Blinking in bright fuchsia and blaring for all to hear is the name, "Ko'ach!"

Next to Ko'ach's name, are the following facts. Unknown alien genetic markers.

"4 Fuchsia warriors with special breathing apparatus burrow deep beneath the surface. Turning their night goggles to full intensity they finally locate Ko'ach. His limp body brought to the surface; tearful Nephesh watches bloody sand pour out from underneath her beloved's plating. Hugging his dented armor; her tears plink plink against his face plate.

In the hospital, nurses and surgeons guide the anti-gravity gurney into surgery. Blue-white fluid drips through Ko'ach's IV.

Alien bolts fused to Ko'ach's jawbone fall away with imbedded tissue. They ping and clank, hitting the sterile marble floor. What remains of his flesh shocks the most stoic medical professional.

"There will be plenty of time for tears. We must all do our best to repair what those monsters put him through," says the neurosurgeon's cracking voice.

Three shifts and 27 hours later...

Outside Nephesh's private room, the neurosurgeon waits; he's unable to hold back his strong emotions.

"Hello Doctor. Is Ko'ach ready to receive family?" asks Nephesh.

"Not yet."

"When?"

"He's still in a coma. I-T-S his alien technology keeping him alive. We have multiple departments working on his case. Top diagnosticians were flown in from all over our country."

Nephesh buries her wet face in her Papa's chest. "I'm sorry for everything, Papa."

Yosher kisses his daughter's cheek. Hakarav cries softly. She leans her face on Nephesh's back. "Mama, I was too late. He needed me and I...I was consumed with self-pity. I should have worked harder to find him. I should have done more to save him. My fault. My fault."

"No sweetie. Never your fault. You...my dear sweet child, are the reason why he has a fighting chance. You know Ko'ach. Nothing can defeat him. And now he has something tremendous to fight for."

Wiping her tears, "And that is?"

"Your love. Honey. Nephesh-ah-la. He needs your unconditional love, more than ever."

Months later...

Ko'ach is prepped for his 36th surgery. He's given the highest dose of anesthesia to prevent him from waking up and screaming in the middle of the operation. Unfortunately, that agonizing awakening took place four times.

While under, the surgical staff talks:

"Seven years of Dull Gray conditioning. No matter the type of therapy, I don't believe we'll ever be able to undo that," comments a young nurse.

"Not his fault he broke. Those who tortured him extracted a lot of top secret encrypted information. Hopefully, he'll never remember what he did."

Ko'ach's face is no longer hideously twisted. Rough scar tissue on his torso, back, legs, and arms is as smooth as possible. Ko'ach bravely tolerated painful plastic surgeries, convincing Nephesh I-T-S not for cosmetic reasons, because if she had known, she would not allow him to go through so many excruciating procedures. He asked the medical staff to lie, and they complied with his wishes.

The next morning Ko'ach meets with the President.

"That's everything I know."

For a long while the President tries to hold back her tears. She fails.

"I have only one request."

"Name I-T," President sniffles.

"You and your son know how strong willed my Nephesh can be. She's going to ask, cajole and manipulate. Don't fall for any of her clever tricks. Promise me you'll never divulge to my beloved, or our families, what the Dull Gray did to me."

"You have my word; I'll take your secrets to my grave."

"Then our business is concluded. Have a great festival."

"Is that Nephesh's engagement ring?"

"How did you know?"

President winks. "My daughter."

Nephesh gleefully wraps her arms around Ko'ach. Three kisses later, the couple bounces down the corridor with unbridled happiness. Ko'ach enjoys tickling Nephesh's hand.

"Nephesh-ah-la I know you have many questions. Let us not dwell on that which we cannot change." Ko'ach hugs and kisses Nephesh. "Sweetie, please push all those dark thoughts from your mind. I will never allow anyone, or anything to tear me from your side." They passionately kiss. "By tradition I must wait the minimum number of days and weeks to court you and then..."

"I'll become your wife." Ko'ach lets Nephesh push him beyond the soft sand; she tackles and tickles him into the crashing waves. Cool waves slosh over their hot bodies. Fuchsia body temperature registers 118.99 degrees Fahrenheit.

Tangled in bright green seaweed, Nephesh giggles watching a cute 5-year-old brother guide his worried 2-year-old brother away from a startling sand crab. *Aw that's so tender.*

"Tradition be damned. Let's marry tonight," Nephesh happily shouts.

"I wouldn't deprive our mothers the joy of arranging our wedding."

"You're the boss." Nephesh mischievously winks.

"Can I have that in writing?"

"The doctors say you've come back to us…exceptionally strong. Show me."

"How far would you like me to carry you?"

"From the sunset to the moonlight."

Before he revs up his internal motor, Ko'ach inhales Nephesh's lovely perfume.

Staring at each other, not a word said, they're dizzy with each other's aroma. Ko'ach's powerful walking stride becomes a faster gallop.

Nephesh squeezes Ko'ach's butt cheeks. He whinnies with delight. Ko'ach sprints the next 36 miles, jumping logs, climbing trees, and swinging from vine to vine. Nephesh sits on his back while he swims three-quarters of the lake.

Ko'ach's thumbs gently massage Nephesh's neck. Ko'ach plants a kiss after placing tangerine-colored blossoms in his beloved's hair.

If there were any emotions more intense than exuberant giddy joy, that is what Nephesh would be feeling at that moment. *I never knew I could love another so intensely.* Both Fuchsia minds simultaneously send out into destiny's fated future.

"Come with me." Ko'ach extends his hand. They both dive into the freezing water. Red-green-purple fish tickle their hot bodies.

Next morning, fully clothed Nephesh cooks purple-colored eggs and plops slices of melon in Ko'ach's mouth. She tickles his ribs and pushes him into yellow-orange-fuchsia crunchy leaves and unbuttons her blouse. Nephesh's warm breasts push into Ko'ach's powerful pecs. Nighttime temperature dips below 45 degrees. Steam rises from their glistening glowing skin. Neither is aware of the dark encroaching destiny.

Ko'ach hands Nephesh his sweater.

"Won't you be cold?"

"Not in your arms. And you'll never have to worry about anything while Ima around."

Ko'ach grins. "Ima? How odd you'd say that."

"Is I-T? The ocean floor is much deeper than the lake. Prepare yourself to dive deeper than light can penetrate."

"Oh, no. My soon-to-be husband, that's your first mistake."

"I've been here dozens of times and dived deeper than most. I know what Ima talking about. The darkness at those depths is everywhere."

"Did you swim with anyone else?"

"No, I was alone."

"There's your answer. When we're together there will always be light."

Ko'ach takes Nephesh's hand. "Follow me."

"Always," Nephesh proudly proclaims.

Ko'ach releases her hand and takes three long strides backward. Faster than any Earth cheetah, he majestically launches himself, appearing to touch the moon, and falls into the murky dark ocean. Seconds later Nephesh launches herself and hits the icy water close on his heels.

Oh, my goodness. Ko'ach's leg kick rockets him faster than Nephesh could have imagined. *Why did he do that? Did something trigger his PTSD? Has he forgotten me?* Nephesh's annoyance builds to anger and lingers into fear. *I've lost him. I've never been this deep before. Ko'ach! Damn I-T why have you once again abandoned me!*

Golden burst of energy erases limitless blackness. Ko'ach rubs up against Nephesh's glowing hands, feet, legs, arms, breasts, and face. The two glowing figures illuminate the ocean for miles. Ko'ach holds three tiny fish and gulps them down. Nephesh stares down at three more swimming from his thumb to pinkie. She shakes her head. He kisses her and releases the three fish into Nephesh's glowing mouth.

Nephesh's neck tingles. Her fingers feel... *Gills!* Nephesh and Ko'ach twirl and swirl in a magnificently sensual entwine. Deeper they dive. Together, inseparable bright lights in a sea of darkness as they shall be for thousands of years...but not forever.

CHAPTER 21

Sadistic Dull Gray Queen, and Ko'ach Discovers his Destiny

The Dull Gray continue to exist as technologically backward and ignorant of all ethical constructs.

Out of jealousy and blood libel, the Dull Gray declared racial supremacy. Rewritten religious texts state they and they alone are God's-anointed to ethically cleanse any clan using speech as a means of dissent, tolerance of different points of view, or seeking equality.

Early in their historical rise, the Dull Gray imperialist-apartheid regime imposed the abolishment of all types of music. Breaking rules results in the cutting of singers' throats. The dancer's legs were chopped off. Dull Gray embrace suicide bombers as Fuchsia embraces love of family. Dull Gray's female empowerment ebulliently emasculates empathy. Perverted creatures euphorically ejaculate during despicable decapitations. Dull Gray thrives on thuggery, temper tantrums, and terrorism.

Male-female trust and tenderheartedness is forever obliterated. Genocidal tsunami slams compassion into dystopian derangement. Age after appalling arrogant age, true femininity finally falls into fascist fanaticism.

18 generations before Ko'ach's birth; I-T sent from I-T-S hidden layer a gene-splicing surgical tool into the hands of the largest, most corrupt, devilish Dull Gray queen. From that point forward all Dull Gray female and male reproductive organs are malevolently altered.

Dull Gray gestation lasts 13 months. Pregnant male's genital sack shrinks, and soft tissue breasts engorge with black milk. Pubescent males grow a vagina, and their internal structure alters. Most childbirths last 32 hours, some as long as 56 hours, and every minute the weak-meek males suffer excruciating agony. I-T-S illegal to ask for pain medication while giving birth. Females place wagers and hope the male dies during childbirth, especially birthing a boy. Any doctor or pregnant father who complains is instantly beheaded. Late-term mutilating abortions are fun games every Dull Gray mother and sister enjoys.

Dumbest dudes act as surrogate wet nurses. Females outnumber males 4 to 1 due to a very high death rate among first-time fathers, and because most male babies are by tradition euthanized.

Age 21 males reach their full 55-foot height. Age 16 females reach 74 feet. Genetic programming and societal norms dictate that male brains have 20 percent fewer neural connections. Females dominate on the battlefield of the bedroom and every aspect of Dull Gray society.

Through the cult of personality each new queen comes to power after the older queen is defeated in battle and consumed at the dinner table. Through the centuries, all followers ruthlessly adhere to their claim that they and they alone follow the one true faith. They've already distorted religious truth by co-opting prophets from other faiths and declaring they're all Dull Gray. All tortured apostates, still alive after months of dismemberment, are in the end slowly roasted. Their screams add to the flavor; so sayeth the highest-ranking religious leaders.

Sisters, aunts, cousins, mothers, grandmothers, and great-grandmothers dominate male family members. Men are always 100 percent wrong in any dispute, and to preserve family honor, wives and mothers enjoy castrating their husbands and sons.

Dull Gray favorite pastime is to push same-sex practitioners off the tallest religious structure. Before they splat on the boulders below, various families cheerfully hand out celebratory candies.

Over the next 9 months Ko'ach and Nephesh are inseparable. They sing, dance, laugh, kiss, play sports, drink, and eat exquisite wine and food. They cast off their clothing and swim through the crashing blue-green waves.

Ko'ach stares into Nephesh's eyes.

"Yes, what is I-T?" giggling Nephesh asks.

Ko'ach caresses Nephesh's gorgeous face and drops to one knee. A large diamond ring glistens in her beautiful green eyes. "You're the light unto my heart, Nephesh-ah-la."

Nephesh leans back into Ko'ach's powerful chest. They talk for hours. Fire crackles. The two love birds are bathed in moonlight. Ko'ach caresses Nephesh's ear. She feeds him yellow, green, orange, and red melon balls. Exhausted from a long run and swim; they both fall into a deep sleep. Nephesh's high-pitched snoring harmonizes with Ko'ach's deep baritone snoring; both are in perfect synchronization with the crashing waves.

Ko'ach wakes from a happy dream to an unfamiliar voice.

Don't be alarmed.

"Who said that?"

Ko'ach's voice and nervous rousing wakes yawning Nephesh.

"What is I-T, sweetie?"

You're the first of your kind to be chosen.

Ko'ach slides away from Nephesh with an angry scowl. "Brother!"

Nephesh's head falls into the soft sand. "He's not here. Come back to me, Ko'ach!"

"Do you hear that?"

"Are you talking about the methodically crashing waves? I love them. They're so soothing. Less talk. More lips. Kisses, please."

"Ohev! Yes, brother, I'm not in the mood for your practical jokes. I see you in that tree."

"That's not Ohev."

Ko'ach yanks on what he thought was his brother's big toe.

Nephesh giggles, "That's a lizard."

"Ohev! I'm warning you!" The low deep hum becomes louder and higher pitched. The cool breeze suddenly becomes painfully hot. The two trees in front of Ko'ach, ignite, that orange hot flame crisps the tips of his fingers and toes.

Blinding painful hot-blue light attacks Ko'ach's neural pathways. Nauseating vertigo unbalances his strong legs; heat hardens soft sand into metallic shards.

"My back!" shouts Ko'ach.

Skull cracks. Alien fragments traverse glowing blue-white fissures; seconds after entering, those particles suture up his wounds. Ko'ach's consciousness catapults from one caustic color to the next. Careening at the speed of thought, Ko'ach's mind shouts *Nephesh!*

Blue cloudless sky floats beneath his feet. Blue waves crash in the stratosphere where clouds should be.

Watcher souls are deeply impressed by his physical strength and moral character.

"No! Too much!" he shouts.

Orb a tenth the size of Ko'ach's eye, shatters his blindness. Two large triangles pulsate. In 18 milliseconds, millions upon millions of neural connections form.

Feeling better? Understand your choices?

"Indeed. I can process more. Wow! This is fun," shouts Ko'ach.

New high-pitched feminine and deep base masculine voices penetrate Ko'ach's mind.

He's too primitive.

Don't forget the prophecy...

Desperate times call for desperate measures. We trust you, and you alone will learn how to adapt to all unspeakable, unfathomable, unknowable timelines. Once the choice is made, there is no going back to your former life.

"And Nephesh?"

Of course, Nephesh. You'll need to convince your entire clan. Millions of Fuchsia can't hope to defeat billions of Dull Gray and their allies, without merging with our righteous energy. You must all become host to the Realm's righteous souls.

"I accept your gift. Now, please teach me, so that I may protect my people."

Righteous sub-atomic soul merges and instructs Ko'ach, on the ways of an advanced augmented life form.

The Fuchsia community over the next three months became more divisive compared to any time in collective memory. Hurt feelings linger. Old friendships are slowly repaired. Ko'ach and Nephesh instruct religious elders. Those elders bring Watcher wisdom to various government and military officials. Happiness is tempered as the Fuchsia come to realize even with their enhanced abilities, they can't maintain the status quo for much longer. In less than a year they know they'll be overwhelmed by billions of invading Dull Gray and their brainwashed allies.

Ko'ach and Nephesh are the first to harness the righteous sub-atomic energy, initially a trickle, which in four months, grows hot enough to disintegrate any Dull Gray forcefield. However, the Fuchsia army always grows weary. After any counterattack, they must recharge and during that ceasefire, the Dull Gray find more clans to enslave, torture, and cook.

Under Ko'ach's leadership the entire Fuchsia community must do what no other people from their planet has attempted before; they must gather together the most talented engineers and construct 7,299 starships. The race to prevent the existential extinction of 7,722,000 Fuchsia begins at that moment of realization.

The entire Watcher Realm knows they're on the eve of another game-changing storyline. Will I-T end as a never-ending cliff hanger? Will Ko'ach be an agent for exceptional righteousness? Or have they unleashed the very time variant they've sworn to defeat? God going radio silent is a huge concern for all of us. Are these new indestructible time variants the reasons for God's silence? Are we truly for the first time since time began, on our own? Does that mean in some future moment in time, God has already lost?

CHAPTER 22

Billions of Dull Gray are on Their Genocidal March; Can Thousands of Fuchsia Starships Reach Escape Velocity in Time?

Tar'oh Her'ov mountaintop is the singular most holy ground for all monotheistic Fuchsia. That is the location where Ko'ach, Nephesh, and all other Fuchsia will make their last stand against the Dull Gray horde. Destiny's fatalism twitches to the destructive tock ticks. The celestial grains of sand are almost poured out. Exhausted families run on fumes. Do they have enough time to construct their starships before the Dull Gray's genocidal armada completes I-T-S final solution?

Righteous engineers, construction workers, physicists, computer geniuses, military, and religious traditionalists work side by side. They are all assisted by brilliant cartographers; I-T-S a daunting task to map out unknown speculative galaxies.

Millions of Fuchsia stand shoulder to shoulder, with wary smiles trying to comfort their tearful children. Newlyweds hold hands; parents hold babies in their arms. Older brothers and sisters kiss the cheeks of younger siblings. Millions wait for Ko'ach's righteous signal.

Always holding hands, Nephesh and Ko'ach run up the last 18-thousand steps. The entire Fuchsia community gathers at the foot of the holy mountain peak. From toddlers to ancient ones, they all cheer. High above his head, Ko'ach extends his clan's holy scrolls. Millions chant, "Appeasement—Never! Righteousness—Forever! Family—Together!"

Ko'ach and Nephesh pump their fists high. Golden energy shoots from their knuckles. The entire Fuchsia Nation pummels 18 mountaintops with golden energy blasts. Every enhanced Fuchsia descends at 60-degree angles. Massive Fuchsia triangles within triangles create glowing energy stairs.

Winding staircase leads the Fuchsia nation toward their inevitable destiny. From hospitals, there are floating gurneys carrying decrepit great-grandparents. Those with war wounds get an 18-hour head start. A tiny 39-foot toddler holds his Papa's hand. Darkness gives way to recently carved glowing rock stairs.

Gravitational propulsion glows. Each starship's triangular shape fits like a massive jigsaw.

Starship's weight equals 63 million metric tons: 18,999 meters in length, width 7,781, and 3,699-meters tall.

On the outskirts of Dull Gray territory, 18 miles away, Fuchsia engineers erect their righteous force field. The entire Fuchsia community works tirelessly, but they're not machines and need periodic rest. Every three hours, the rested Fuchsia rotates in.

Over a 9-month period, 100,899 robots are constructed with a singular purpose: to maintain the force field. Golden energy emanates from robotic eyes. Mechanical energy is different compared to the righteous Fuchsia power. Field strength remains steady at an 18 percent diminished grid capacity.

In the early months of the new war, the Fuchsia leadership underestimated the overwhelming number of Dull Gray terrorists. Before the energy grid could be activated, border communities were overrun. Parents watched their children decapitated, horrified as babies are burned alive and eaten. The horrible evidence is broadcast live and rebroadcast on the worldwide web, every second of every day. Cackling behemoths gouge out eyes and send those terrified children crying for Mama and Papa off the cliff. Torsos are torn from arms and legs and tossed into a large dinner feasting pit. Rape gangs are so forceful they break the hips of pre-teen girls, mothers, grand-mothers, and great-grandmothers.

45 hours later, the energy reserves of every Fuchsia robot sputtered at .18 percent. No time for repairs. Millions more Dull Gray conscripts arrive daily, female warriors adorned with furry carcass of beasts they slew hours ago. Animals' bloody dripping heads are perched on spiked helmets.

Dull Gray soldiers' blood-red claws, pluck from their pockets babies captured from a thousand other clans. Those helpless innocents are tossed without an ounce of compassion. Horrified mommies are forced to watch their screeching babies slowly burn as their face and bodies slide down the forcefield's roasting grid. The stench of burned flesh brings wide grins and cackling laughter from the Dull Gray monsters.

Heartbroken Fuchsia can't risk the lives of their own children and attempt a rescue.

9-years ago, Ko'ach and Nephesh were the lead project leaders in the invention and construction of powerful rail gun weapons. I-T-S similar to what the United States would develop and deploy during the end of the second decade of the 21st century. Instead of gunpowder, the rail gun uses a magnet pulse. Projectiles go from zero to Mach 6 in 10 milliseconds. Mach 6 is equivalent to 4,500 MPH. A 25-megawatt powerplant generates enough power for over 18,189 Earth homes. Unlike conventional bullets that lose velocity the moment I-T-S fired, that magnetic pulse projectile gains speed out of the barrel.

Do you know what I-T feels like to hear and smell 300,000,000 hoofs galloping in unison? And that's just the first wave. Newly stolen technology helps the Dull Gray onslaught. Advanced weaponry blasts homes, schools and houses of worship.

18 minutes before liftoff, powerful explosives blew off 7,299 massive silo covers. One by one, metallic plates engage their micro thrusters. Multi-ton plates crush the invading Dull Gray into bloody pulp.

"336 micro clicks before liftoff," whispers Ko'ach.

"Will that be enough time?" asks Nephesh.

Holding hands, they ran toward their starships. One by one, every starship glows with righteous energy. I-T-S the same fuchsia energy coursing through the veins of their clan's arms after they merged with their specifically chosen righteous soul.

The circuitry within each starship pulsates. For the Fuchsia nation, there was never any plan-B. Combination of anticipatory fear and hope rockets into space.

Falling debris left behind from all the pulsating starships crush genocidal Dull Gray terrorists. Startled, those not yet dead scurry like rats over to and activate the Fuchsia rail guns. Energy climbs beyond the mountain peaks and into space. Inside nary one starship feels the impact, their shielding easily absorbs the energy pulse.

This is the moment, in precarious time, in which Fuchsia scientists, astronauts, engineers, soldiers and families will begin their first interstellar mission. None of them, not even Ko'ach, knows for sure if this will be a 5-, 10-, 50-year, or indefinite mission in space. The goal is to find a planet which will support their life form, and if there are indigenous beings, that they are peaceful and not aggressively bloodthirsty. The Fuchsia leadership relies on the wisdom contained within the righteous souls and the star charts which have mapped the known galaxy. Beyond the wormholes and spinning nebulas are areas of space not even the righteous souls have knowledge of, and that gravely concerns everyone.

Neither Ko'ach nor Nephesh will be acting captain of their flagship. That duty falls on the broad shoulders of the most decorated pilot in history. Their captain celebrated his 45th birthday 18 days ago. He stands a regal 72 inches above Ko'ach's 70 feet 9 inches.

Captain is the only one of Nephesh's suitors she couldn't break. His compassion for Nephesh and Ko'ach never wavered. He's the perfect choice to lead the entire Fuchsia nation.

Apart from the other stations on the bridge, the captain sits in his autonomously rotating chair. "Helmsman, activate the forward viewer," captain confidently announces.

"Aye captain."

The rest of the fleet follows, while within the confines of their own solar system. The moment they clear the last planet, they will activate their experimental faster-than-light graviton propulsion system. I-T-S estimated the flagship has the potential to hit Quantum factor 12.

"If we don't encounter too many obstacles, we should find ourselves in uncharted space within 3 to 5 years," blurts smiling Ko'ach.

"And long before that, we'll map out seven known stable wormholes," adds the captain.

"Are those recent readings, correct?" asks Nephesh.

"Yes, our last probe gave us interesting data about a small blue planet that is 70 percent water. A vast majority of I-T-S people are extremely cruel to one another," says the captain.

"Being 12 times their height, I don't like that if we're ever discovered, we would become a source of inter-clan warfare. I-T-S not a very promising location. Their weaponry consists of knives, spears, bows and arrows. If our cloaking device fails, we'd be seen as invading gods! I don't want to disrupt their evolutionary trajectory, nor do we know what prolonged exposure to our cloaking device will do to our cells. If necessary, that little world could be a temporary base while we seek out other worlds," says Ko'ach.

"I've studied the data our probes brought back. Ha'bru civilization is promising. Their Judaic belief in an ethical monotheist God is similar in some ways to our own. And we have evidence from 9 other solar systems, all inhospitable planetary environment. Species 20 percent larger than we are and as murderous as any Dull Gray," adds the captain.

"What do we do, Ko'ach, if we encounter advanced malevolent species?"

Ko'ach's hands dismiss the question and he sheepishly smiles.

Nephesh's wink is caught by the captain, though at that time, he didn't understand there was subtext no other Fuchsia could have imagined. 18 days before blasting into space, Ko'ach and Nephesh discovered, by accident, they could read minds. That skill is extremely limited; but improving. Nephesh promised to use I-T sparingly as I-T is a great invasion of privacy toward all other Fuchsia who currently lack that talent.

Ko'ach's righteous evolution grew exponentially faster than all others, including Nephesh. He defeats all competitors in every athletic, mathematical, logistical, and tactical contest. For brief periods of time, he can disconnect from his righteous sub-atomic soul. No other species has ever done that before without killing both soul and host. The first time he attempts to reintegrate with Nephesh by his side, he almost died. Each time after, his seizures are less pronounced. When his reintegration progress takes place, the delusions cause nary a scratch nor feverish brain damage. All of this, like reading minds, Nephesh and Ko'ach have kept secret from the captain and medical teams. Ko'ach can solve equations faster than onboard supercomputers.

Stealing the occasional kiss, Ko'ach and Nephesh hold hands walking down the long winding ship's corridor.

Beloved, why do you block my multiple attempts to read your thoughts?

"We're late for our duties."

"You promised you'd never keep anything from me."

"And I haven't, sweetie."

"Your charms won't save you this time."

Ko'ach leans in for a kiss. Nephesh grabs his arm and flips him halfway down the corridor. Nephesh giggles. Ko'ach runs up the side of the wall and looks back at Nephesh's running style.

Cute. Ko'ach's mind projects with love.

Thank you, honey.

Ko'ach happily chases.

Ko'ach runs and easily catches up to the slow jogging Nephesh. Ko'ach playfully twirls Nephesh around four times. Nephesh smiles, she slips her hand in Ko'ach's. *Sexy,* her mind purrs. They are both hip to hip; and dance down the corridor over the next 18 minutes.

Nephesh shakes her head. She squeezes Ko'ach's hand; harder and harder. His smile fades. "Hey! I'm glad you're getting stronger; you don't have to take I-T out on my poor fingers."

Nephesh hangs her head low. Concerned Ko'ach lifts her chin. Silent tears flow down her face. "What's this, sweetie?"

"Your lies must stop. I know you think you're doing the right thing, whatever you're doing. We must always work as a team." Nephesh shakes Ko'ach. "You hear me!"

Ko'ach opens and closes his mouth without divulging his dangerous project.

"I thought so!"

Ko'ach caresses Nephesh's fingers, and his eyes well up.

"Don't..."

"What?"

"I can't bear the sight of your tears. Please Ko'ach, tell me..."

Ko'ach catches a tear which has not yet fallen on the tip of his right index finger. Nephesh smiles, she catches her own tear on the tip of her left index finger. "Heart of my heart," Ko'ach and Nephesh whisper. Long passionate kiss follows.

Stopping only for a breath. Ko'ach leans in for more, he's stopped by Nephesh's tear drop fingertip.

Ko'ach nods. "Very well, dear heart. I must know the extent of my powers. We'll soon reach the edge of our known star charts. Our collective righteous souls can no longer preemptively help. We'll soon be on our own. Adjusting on the fly..."

"Taking too many risks."

"Necessary risks. Please understand, sweetie. I must do this."

"I thought so. I was hoping I was wrong. Thank you for corroborating..." Nephesh answers coldly. Ko'ach reaches down to caress her fingers, and she pulls away.

"Make your own dinner tonight. Bunk with the captain. He's sure looking forward to another round of 4-dimensional chess.

"You're cuter. I'd rather play with you," says charming Ko'ach.

Ko'ach catches Nephesh's powerful slug. He brings her knuckles to his lips. With her other, left hand's fingers, she pinches those lips. "Hey, that really hurt."

"Good! You deserve a lot worse. You still don't get I-T, do you? No caressing. No kissing. No anything else. I must figure out a lot of stuff. I can't do that with your beautifully charming eyes and seductive lips. What's this?"

Nephesh grabs Ko'ach's hand. She forcefully pinches his wrist. "Ouch! That hurts!"

"I bet I-T did...not! I don't like that. I-T-S beginning to spread. Yesterday I-T was a fraction of the size. I bet you haven't seen the doc yet."

Ko'ach's quizzical expression makes Nephesh's face grow darker fuchsia with anger.

Ko'ach taps his metallic fingertip to the bulkhead.

"Stop I-T! Stop I-T!"

"I like the way I-T sounds. Oh, honey don't look like that. I was just joking."

"I-T-S not funny."

I didn't fall in love with a cold-hearted metal man. I want my truthful Ko'ach back. The man who would never joke and play with my feelings. I sense your righteous soul agrees with me. And not you. And that you've been disconnecting with that wisdom for far longer...more lies. Yes, lying to me, your righteous soul, and eventually yourself. That's dangerous, my beloved husband. I don't understand why you can't see that truth. And now I sense something...new...different... Dark Oh my God. Please, come with me to the doctor.

No worries, sweetie. I talked to the doc and captain last night.

For the first time ever...I don't believe you. I think your powers are so great, you could have implanted those ideas in their minds, without them knowing. But you cannot fool me. You'll never be able to do that, husband! You might choose to forget, I never will! The last planet we explored, the investigative drones were tampered with, and for 18 minutes you lost consciousness, and your labored breathing became almost undetectable... You almost died, taking your God damned risks! I-T-S just too unbearable! Nephesh covers her weepy eyes.

Ko'ach's loving caresses do not help alleviate her fears.

Necessary for my righteous soul to obliterate all the toxic elements.

Not toxic elements! I-T was an unknown virus. What happens when your luck runs out?

You're leaving part of the story out.

No, I am not.

Now who's telling a fib? After my mini coma destroyed the deadliest virus, my righteous soul had ever encountered; my immune system's strength improved by a factor of 36. Destiny brought me close to death, so that I could become stronger than death.

Idiot! You're not a mystical being. Nobody else was infected. Care to explain that? You must stop this horrible new obsession. Why must you arrogantly believe you're invincible?

We must evaluate and push and test some more. Until we...I'm satisfied with the limits of my powers. We must be prepared for the unknowable.

Irrational moron! How the hell can you prepare for the unknowable?

I feel your concern. I understand and feel your great love for me, for us.

Good! You'll stop because you understand how I feel.

Our souls guide our actions. I could never be a slave to that righteous particle. I-T will never be my master. I-T-S an equal partner. I'll never be I-T-S puppet. I must act in the best interest of you and all of us. Please, honey, try and see my side of I-T. I have to do this. I feel I-T in my bones. I must continue the experiments.

Look at you. I thought your immune system made you impervious to all infections. Why are the ship's metallic particles attached to your cells? Why haven't they been purged from your tissues? And why are they glued tighter to your skeletal system?

Nephesh wraps her entire body around Ko'ach. "Does I-T hurt?" whispers Nephesh.

Ko'ach's silence tells her the pain must be much greater than he is letting on. Both her hands come up to her mouth. "Oh, my dear sweet beloved." Demonstratively she kisses Ko'ach's cheek, and lips.

Malevolent Time taught I-T how to produce dark matter beyond righteous souls' sensory awareness. Unbeknownst to any Fuchsia; the ship's genetic sheath, designed by righteous souls no longer repels biological and mechanical energies. I-T acts as an infinitesimal homing device. Attracting horrific minions with I-T-S biological magnetizing breadcrumbs.

Deep within manipulated manifestations, I hear Malevolent Time's unnerving cackles. What's most worrisome is the fear I feel coming from the powerfully righteous souls within the sacred Realm of the Watchers. They all scream: *Beware of the Prophecy?*

CHAPTER 23

Ko'ach is Bitten by Microscopic Evil and Transformed into an Evil 100-Foot Machine

The Realm of the Watcher souls form an infinite number of geometric shapes. The most righteous are the unusual triangles within triangles, which reside within both Nephesh and Ko'ach.

Ko'ach's loving fingers press and coax Nephesh's stress-induced tight shoulders and back. I-T-S another mutually sensual wrestling match.

Nephesh seductively licks her lips and unbuttons her blouse. Pink-purple panties fall to the floor. Ko'ach kisses her nakedness. Nephesh sighs. Effortlessly, Ko'ach scoops her up; Nephesh's exquisite legs wrap around him. They fall onto their king-size triangular bed.

According to Fuchsia customs and tradition, only married couples have sex. Not even engaged couples break those conservative vows. Nephesh and Ko'ach are not ordinary Fuchsia.

Hot skin against hot skin, Nephesh thrusts her hips, pulling Ko'ach deeper within her wet orgasmic delight. Intense bucking, kissing; thrusts them repeatedly into waves of unbridled ecstasy. Thunderous release provides a powerfully exhausting climax. Nephesh nuzzles Ko'ach's chest, her palm loosely curled over his heart.

18 days later, and 9 doors down from the Med-bay, an anxious Nephesh, stoic Ko'ach and feeling left out of the loop captain, continue another important conversation in front of the low undulating humming of the octagon constructed by Ko'ach; I-T-S specific design was programmed, depending on specific settings to slowly or rapidly siphon off his golden energy and incrementally within that cage increase gravity.

"This setting duplicated our home world's gravitational force. Each mark signifies an increased force by a factor of 18. I've checked and rescheduled all the backup systems," says the captain.

"Including those I installed yesterday," interrupts lip twitching Nephesh.

Captain's hand hovers above the energy valve.

Nephesh clears her throat. "Excuse me, captain. We all agree I operate the controls."

"Yes, of course. We all agree."

"With all due respect, move your thumb, sir."

Captain moves his thumb only after Ko'ach nods.

"I see you've added a few more settings. We won't be trying those out today. My peripheral vision is excellent, as you well know, beloved. Captain, you cease your attempt at secretive communication with him, or this will all stop before I-T starts."

"And you, Nephesh, watch your tone. I've allowed your disrespect. I shall not allow that to continue. Have I made myself clear? And before you engage your emotional response, we all came up with a few new ideas while you were sleeping."

"You know my feelings on this matter. I'll terminate Ko'ch's project right now if you object to my complete control of everything."

"Everything?" Ko'ach's eyebrows arch. *You need to stop ordering the captain. He can still order you to the brig.*

We both know that would not be wise, beloved!

Beating up the captain's personal guards would not be wise.

No. You know I could do I-T.

I do. I-T would still not be wise.

Nephesh slams Ko'ach's back with her open palm.

"If you die in there, I'm going to kill you, sweetie," Nephesh whispers through gritted teeth.

"Where's that metal thrumming coming from?" asks the captain.

Nephesh puts her palm under the captain's nose. "I took this metal disk from sickbay."

Nephesh rips off fuchsia bandage from Ko'ach's back. "That black dot is made of the same material as our haul and I-T-S fusing I-T-Self to my beloved's DNA."

"So what? My righteous soul is working on excising I-T."

Another lie. Please. I beg you to call this...this...

Experiment...

Experiment off. Give the doctor more time to analyze this growth.

I-T-S not a growth. I-T hasn't increased a millimeter in the last 9 days. What's that in your pocket? I-T better not be for me.

You know what I-T is. You read my mind. That's not funny.

Nephesh digs into her pocket and brings the syringe to Ko'ach's chest. "This will knock him out. I've told you before, this experiment is too dangerous. If you won't listen to reason, then I will act with the same unreasonable irrationality."

Ko'ach's reflexes twitch quicker than even Nephesh has seen before. He grabs the syringe, slams I-T on the floor and smashes I-T with his boot heel. "She's got two more in her back pocket."

Nephesh hands over the syringes to the nurse on duty.

You think you're so clever. Well, I am still controlling the dial.

I never said you couldn't.

"Any more surprises? Or can we finally begin?"

"No more, captain."

Nephesh kicks Ko'ach into the octagon cage. "Computer, activate voice commands Nephesh One. Stupid husband two. Misguided captain three."

"That will be enough Nephesh! You are in charge of this project, but I still command this ship and our fleet. I've tolerated your insolence for the last time. Is that understood?"

"Yes sir. I-T won't happen again. I'll be directing my full disrespectful insolence toward the one I love."

I've never seen you act this way, in public.

I've never felt this way before.

What are you feeling?

Betrayed.

I-T was you who showed the captain that spot on my back. I-T-S you who keeps going on and on...after I've explained how important... Like I-T or not, this experiment will happen. I-T must, I'm done Nephesh. I've explained and explained. You forced a hundred delays. I must discover my limits. The lives of everyone on board might depend on I-T someday. I don't understand why you can't get that.

Clenching and unclenching her fingers; Nephesh slams her palm into the control panel. She's unaware of the dent her crushing force creates. Hum and sparkling light precede materialization of a towering, menacing beast with huge spikes up his spine, legs, and arms; the creature's four hands hold an ax, shield, spear, and sword.

Ko'ach turns his back on the not yet activated monster. He smiles and gives Nephesh the thumbs up.

Over the next 27 minutes, Ko'ach, not yet breaking a sweat, easily dispatches six more imposing creatures.

Ko'ach blocks a red beast and runs his blade through the creature's two hearts. "Come on Nephesh. I've asked the last 18 minutes. You've got to give me more of a challenge."

"And I keep control of the safety protocols?"

"Anything. Let's get a move on...I'm bored!"

Nephesh moves the dial one and a half clicks.

"No. I said a challenge. 4 more clicks must be the bare minimum!"

"The energy beacon is getting louder."

"No, I-T-S not," perturbed captain says.

"Oh right. You requested four tenths of a click more?"

"You know that's not what I asked for."

"Less, you asked for weaker foes. You wish to call I-T a day and start again next month?"

"Nephesh!"

"Ko'ach!"

"Honey, please."

"Stupid, pleas..."

"You must up the ante."

"I must. I! Must! Shut this down now!"

That's the opening we need. Sayeth captain's determined thoughts. He looks over at Ko'ach. Ko'ach rubs his left ear. *That's the signal.*

Captain pulls Nephesh away from the consol. "This old married couple bickering must end now. We've all agreed to what each of us will be doing in this matter. If you break with that, then you've abrogated the terms of our deal and I'll be taking over. And you will be confined to your quarters."

"You can't do that!"

"I know you're a very powerful girl, but this is my ship, and I won't..."

On the word girl Ko'ach places his head in his hand and shakes. *Sweetie, please be reasonable, the captain didn't mean that. You're frustrating him. All of us. And as pissed as I know you're becoming; he is the captain, and he will confine you. I am telling you out of love. I've read his thoughts and he's beyond the point of compromising anymore. Give in on this, or what you don't want to happen, will.*

Very well, honey. Get used to sleeping alone for the rest of the year.

90 minutes later, Nephesh moves the dial another 5 clicks. Ko'ach's muscles rip through his uniform: an alien's ax cuts into his helmet.

A holographic butterfly distracts Nephesh. The captain inches closer to the dial. Nephesh's reflexes are much quicker, and she grabs his hand and squeezes. "What are you doing, captain?"

A surge of graviton waves is missed by Nephesh's private scanner. Increased octagon pulse pushes down on Ko'ach's lungs. Hands on his knees, he's bent over and gulps for breath. *Feels like I'm running at an altitude of 9,000 feet.*

With the strength of five powerful battering rams, Ko'ach slams his helmet and crushes the creature's skull. Black energy oozes and sizzles. Ironically, more ingredients added to sub-sub-atomic stew; the metallic toxins percolate beneath the skin and rush throughout Ko'ach's bloodstream.

The octagon's vibrations are wrong. Tuning fork recalibration misfire. Peculiar resonating shock waves crush Nephesh's sub-atomic soul into a dormant unprecedented sleep mode.

8 hologram warriors appear and fizzle into oblivion. Ko'ach's knees buckle. His hands hit acidic deck plate. Fleshy smoke billows from his blackened fingers. Soothing liquid dribbles, when I-T should flash flood to quench in full, Ko'ach's quivering agony.

"Oh my God, Ko'ach! Where's the off switch?" screams Nephesh.

Captain punches new code and foamy membrane surrounds Ko'ach. Odd, unexpected vibrations create branching fissures like a butterfly cracking through I-T-S cocoon. Scalded Ko'ach bursts free. His sub-atomic soul diligently repairs damaged tissue.

"Give me a moment and I'll be ready for another round."

"The hell you are. I don't want to hear I-T! You're done! End of discussion!"

Ko'ach shadow boxes to show he's okay. Increased gravitation causes his muscles to bulge and ripple along his biceps and deltoids.

"Computer."

"Yes, captain."

"Run a level three diagnostic."

Nephesh hugs the captain. "Sorry, I've been so difficult. Look at him, as if nothing is wrong. That's why I'm so nervous, and..."

"Uncompromising."

"Yes sir. Sorry about that. Why did the safety protocols fail?"

Feminized computer voice logically dispassionately utters the following: "Ko'ach's bone structure, muscle, tendons, and ligaments are almost as hard as the outer hull of this ship."

"Computer! That's not what I was asking for. Run a level three diagnostic on yourself, " the captain demands.

"Sys...tems...tems...systems running at peak efficiency," sputtering and self-correcting computer voice utters.

"Captain, what's going on?" nervous Nephesh asks.

Ko'ach gets off the deck plate; his smile doesn't reassure Nephesh. He playfully punches holes in the bulkhead. The ship's golden energy struggles against the increased gravitation.

"Energy shielding was designed to operate in the weightlessness of space. After 18 minutes deep dents remain, and the shallow dents are taking longer to pop out," states the captain.

I must show my beloved I am alright. Her thoughts tell me she's very close to shutting this experiment down. That cannot happen, yet!

Ko'ach rapidly completes 500 squats, 300 push-ups and 200 pull-ups. A trickle of fuchsia blood leaks from his nose. Reactivated beast nibbles at Ko'ach's boot; creature rips I-T to shreds.

Now barefoot, Ko'ach lands with a heavy metallic thud. Shocked, Nephesh places both hands over her mouth, after observing Ko'ach's wiggling black-metallic toes.

The youngest member of Nephesh's team runs up to her and patiently waits. He clears his throat and Nephesh refuses to acknowledge his presence. He hesitantly acts and finally taps her on the shoulder. "What is I-T!" Irritated Nephesh bellows.

Her anger startles the man, and he jumps back three steps.

Sweat pours down the timid teen's face. "Well!" shouts Nephesh.

Perfect timing. Keep her busy, young man. Ko'ach kicks away the 18 soup cans flattened like pancakes.

A shiny disk shakes in the intimidated young man's hand. "The readout you requested."

"Put I-T on the console."

"Yes, mam."

16-year-old looks at the captain, who imperceptibly nods.

I saw that look, captain. What do I do? I can't leave Ko'ach unsupervised. I know he's cooking up something extra dangerous with the captain. That's why they sent this young fool to distract me. I must investigate this data, but I can't do that here. Gravity waves are leaking through the cage. Is that why I am unable to read anyone's thoughts? Is that your plan?

Lost in her thoughts, Nephesh jumps when the captain taps her shoulder. "What is I-T! Oh, I-T-S you, captain. I thought you were that young conspiring fool."

Clever girl. Better act fast.

"Conspiracy? That's a little harsh, and unreasonable. I thought we were past such thinking from you. Go find out why the computer is acting so hinky. I'll make sure Ko'ach follows all the guidelines we three agreed upon. Go ahead, Nephesh. You can trust me. Nephesh..."

"Yes, very well." Nephesh points an admonishing finger at Ko'ach. "And you!"

"Yes dear."

"Enough. I know you're planning something. You keep your promise. Or so help me. I know you outrank me, but I will personally toss you in the brig."

"We need that information analyzed, and your decrypting talent is by far the best. You even rank higher than Ko'ach and me."

Nephesh sprints down the corridor. Captain moves the dial to level seven. A horrible grunt echoes from Ko'ach.

"I can take more. A lot more!"

"A lot?" *You don't have to show off for me or our team.*

Not showing off...

"What?"

Oops. Gravity affects my judgment. Can't let the captain know I can read his thoughts.

"What? Um. Can you hear me? Graviton waves are interfering with..."

The young man Nephesh is mentoring remains more loyal to Ko'ach and is under orders from the captain. He hates being disloyal to Nephesh but agrees with the reasons why he must, even if I-T destroys his relationship with her.

Captain clicks the dial up to level 9. Ko'ach's imperceptible whimper brings simultaneous deep concern and elation. The captain and the monitoring crew now know Ko'ach's limits.

The young man turns back to the captain and smiles. He holds his thumb high. Ko'ach struggles to respond. His shaky right hand grabs his shaky left hand. Fingers wrapped around his thumb, and with great effort he pulls. Young man smiles.

Ko'ach's exuberant expression suddenly changes. "She's back!"

Bam! Nephesh's upper cut knocks the 32-year-old co-conspirator out.

"Stand down. That's an order!" shouts the captain.

Nephesh jabs her thumb into the captain's ribs.

"Liars! You're all treacherous creatures! You don't deserve the rank of captain! On your knees!"

"You feel betrayed. I can explain..."

"Stop!" shouts Ko'ach.

"Shut up Ko'ach!"

Nephesh bends the captain's wrist.

"Sweetie. Nephesh! Let him go."

"No!"

A massive electrical pulse surges through the plating, and everyone other than Nephesh crumbles and twitches after their backsides hit the deck.

"Did you do that?" asks Ko'ach.

"No-ah. How could I have done that?"

Contrite, Nephesh helps the captain to his feet. She ignores the 16-year-old she used to mentor.

Ko'ach places his index and middle finger to his temple and concentrates with a force greater than he has ever used before.

My mind to your mind. Nephesh-ah-la, please dear heart, you don't mean to be cruel toward them. If you must vent your anger, let me have I-T. You know I can take your wrath, more so than your shipmates. No. No! Sweetie, your shipmates, your friends are not traitors. They're following my orders. Think back to the many conversations we've had these past 9 months; how this new power can be and is intrusively addictive. And now I sense this tremendous anger is not...you. In the deeper recesses of your mind, I'm detecting something I've never detected before...so cold, malevolent...a foreign entity. Not sure how. Refocus your wrath away from me and our friends to I-T. Excellent job, honey. I shall help you excise that dark foreign body. You're doing I-T. Almost disintegrating. A little more. Push sweetie! Well done. We can investigate what that thing is or was...after the experiment is completed.

With tears in her eyes, Nephesh helps the captain and her crewmates to their feet. She looks at Ko'ach. He nods. She crushes the button next to the black blinking off-button. Machine hisses. Surprisingly, the graviton beams aren't reducing; they're intensifying. With angry force, she clicks the dial down four more levels. With a mind of I-T-S own, the dial spins past level 9.

Together, the captain and Nephesh try and fail to spin the dial back down. Electrical crackles cackle. From head to toe, the captain becomes enveloped in greasy, oozing black lightning.

The entire security team becomes immobilized in that horrible lightning storm. Nephesh is the only one quick enough to duck under and jump over each blast until she is not, and the final two more powerfully insidiously malevolent intent blasting pulses knock her on her back. She slams against the wall and rubs the back of her head. Her peripheral vision catches the captain's seizures. Bloody fuchsia foam leaks from everyone's mouths. The medical team rushes with translucent gurneys.

Ko'ach's sub-atomic soul repairs his decimated organs. Black sludge oozes from his nose, ears, and eyes. In his compromised condition, he's unable to hear the malevolent voice puncturing Nephesh's brain: *They thought they had pushed me out, Father. I've proven I'm stronger than even the anointed special one. Are you proud of my accomplishments? Father. Please speak to me. No more banishment. Look at what I've done for you, Father. Sending you Ko'ach's coordinates.*

I-T-S wrath leaves Nephesh and focuses on Ko'ach. His phalanges, fibula, tibia, patella, femur, coccyx, sacrum, ulna, pelvis, radius, vertebra, ribs, sternum, humerus, clavicle, scapula, mandible, cranium are vigorously assaulted and, like his organs, melt into mush. Torrential black fuchsia hemorrhaging pours out of every orifice.

Captain wakes. He kicks off his boots, fingers ripping his restraints to shreds. In his confused state, he tosses the entire medical team as if they were all rag dolls, and he runs down the winding hall faster than any known wild fuchsia beast.

Captain howls: detonating black lightning becomes gaseous and enters the crew's nostrils. New zombie converts rush toward Nephesh and Ko'ach.

Crackling black cloud. I-T ascends and descends through the entire ship. Malevolent scratching pierces every panel; microfractures split wider.

Ship-wide, oxygen reserves hiss into space. *Internal atmosphere...thinning. Can you hear me Nephesh?*

Incinerating black energy zooms out of zombie captain and his zombie crew's eyes. Time sputters. Seconds become minutes. Days become weeks. The distortion allows Ko'ach to repair himself before anyone else.

The zombie-creating energy exits the crew and punches I-T-S way into every cell of the captain. That extra jolt propels the captain forward against the waves of time distortion. Black enemy extricates I-T-Self, and the captain falls forward, his arm breaks from the fall. He watches the black entity inching forward.

"Intruder! Activate self-destruct. 20-second countdown!" In real time, that horribly powerful distortion takes Nephesh half an hour to shout out.

Increasing gravity distorts the computer's voice. Takes two hours for the computer to count down from 20 to 18 seconds, and five hours before the zombie creature penetrates the energy grid with I-T-S fists in an attempt to deactivate the self-destruct.

Computer voice continues to distort. "Thirt-een. Tw-elve. E-leven..."

The lightning creature turns away from the energy grid; I-T-S running strides slow to a crawl; finally reaching Nephesh. In slow motion, I-T-S twisted right-hand wraps around Nephesh's throat. I-T-S left fist blasts the destruct mechanism.

Ko'ach inhales God's righteous pulse.

"Leave her alone!" Ko'ach grunts.

Nephesh's golden energy incinerates the black creature. Augmented by God's eternal energy, the Fuchsia fleet is enveloped in his righteous protection; engines ignite and every ship instantly enters a new galaxy. *No!* I-T-S evil mind shouts.

18 months later...

Starlight illuminates the captain's bridge, reflects off the navigational computer, and bounces off Nephesh's engagement ring.

"Long-range scans are sending back fascinating telemetry," says the captain.

"Planet is 10 percent smaller, compared to our largest moon. No indigenous surprises. Plenty of fresh water and two small red suns," adds Ko'ach.

Ship buffeted by solar winds, Nephesh's broach sways. She caresses Ko'ach's baby picture. Strands of Nephesh's curls and Ko'ach's straight baby hair strands give the appearance of a mustache and goatee.

Blazing streaks number 7,299 punctuate the nebula's horizon and months later orbit around what the captain hopes will become their new home.

Ko'ach and Nephesh exit their shuttle craft 27 minutes later, their scanner held waist high. "Planet's aromas are intoxicating," whispers grinning Nephesh.

A family of eight-legged mammals gallop around bright red and orange: flowers, fruits, and vegetables. Squeaking aquatic creatures with soft brown skin flap their flippers.

"Flower petals resonate with unique properties," says Ko'ach.

Nephesh hums. Flowers instinctually lean forward. Bright petals mimic her pitch. Ko'ach sings traditional Fuchsia tunes; petals vibrate and duplicate perfectly his bass-baritone timbre. Nephesh's teen cousin adds high-pitched vibrato. Petals and Fuchsia sing soprano operettas. Petals accompany religious leaders' choral notes.

Joy fills their Fuchsia hearts. Ko'ach and Nephesh run along the beach, always holding hands, never letting go. No matter the distance. Regardless of disjointed timelines temporarily separating their fingertips; their hearts shall always be holding hands.

Crashing waves cool Nephesh's and Ko'ach's hot Fuchsia skin; they dance, sing and kiss.

All over the landing site, Fuchsia families sing duets and harmonies with multicolored blossoms. Constructing a variety of musical instruments, a magnificent orchestra brings forth smiles and whistling. Mamas and Papas tickle and giggle with their children. Wonderfully animated vibrations ascend past the snowcapped mountain peaks. Virtuous virtuosity's song passionately illuminates the darkness of space.

A single sub-atomic particle living between the Multiverse time distortions is expelled past the noxious righteous barrier and searches for I-T-S creator. I-T gives instructions on how I-T can successfully track Ko'ach.

Father! I smell Ko'ach's song. I've learned from my mistakes. I promise this time, I shall not fail you!

Crackling fireflies swoon on the breath of the wistful nighttime breeze. I-T-S interdimensional incursions rip righteous timelines and skewer sycophant's sociopathic secretions.

Black fire hurtles 180,000 times faster than Mark Twain's comet. The Multiverse's most lethal microscopic virus changes I-T-S trajectory and forces a time-shearing collision toward unsuspecting Ko'ach. Will fated destiny be destroyed or fulfilled?

18 weeks later, Nephesh glows, twirls, and tickles Ko'ach's ribs. "I'm with child."

Ko'ach caresses Nephesh's flat belly. "Have you thought of a name?"

"Our son should carry your grandfather's name, don't you think?"

Exuberant joy spilling out, Ko'ach's smile stretches from ear to ear.

Because of the reduced gravity, Ko'ach tosses Nephesh 10 meters above the tallest tree.

Nephesh slowly falls back toward Ko'ach. He flies up to her and gently catches her warm body. They both slowly descend, cuddling and kissing. Beaming Nephesh asks, "Is this my first flying lesson?"

Nephesh's soft feminine gaze looks deep into Ko'ach's loving eyes. He shows off, only for her. Ko'ach runs up the side of mountains and pushes off into the most perfect dive; plunging headfirst into the cool-black-ocean, his powerful butterfly kick propels him forward faster than any Coast Guard speedster.

Malevolent energy grows the microscopic metallic creature. I-T-S huge in comparison to what I-T was only two hours earlier. Stretching seven feet long; I-T-S orb shape reimagines I-T-Self and now gains sharp rectangular edges and sprouts arms, clawed fingertips and muscular legs.

I-T-S malevolence churns deep beneath the waves. I-T-S perverted essence quickly gains on Ko'ach's Achilles. I-T-S camouflaged by mimicking black ocean waves. Blood-red eyes rapidly blink. *You will not escape me this time.* Razor-sharp teeth clickety-clack. I-T-S evil saliva drips and alters the genetic make-up of the formerly pristine ocean.

Like a giant flying fish, Ko'ach twirls out of the ocean and wraps his arms around Nephesh. This will be the last time Nephesh can kiss and caress her untainted beloved. Ko'ach perpetually struggles with the demon inside. God only knows if the righteous Ko'ach will be able to defeat himself. In all of galactic history, there has never existed an uber evil and uber righteous hybrid, which is Ko'ach. Now! Beneath the waves: destiny's undiscovered tribulations solidify. I-T-S inches from Ko'ach's big toe. Metallic digits stretch as far as they can.

A singular malevolent bite sends waves of agony Ko'ach has never before felt. He does not want to scare his beloved wife and soon-to-be mother. He offers an odd grin, "Ouch." He yelps.

I hear and feel the truth of what just happened. His horrific echoing screech is the first and only time in millions of years I've heard such a horrible screeching sound from my mentor.

"What happened?" worried Nephesh asks.

"Not sure. Righteous soul's voice...vanishes for a split second."

"I feel so cold."

Nephesh watches Ko'ach's lips turn blue, ashen, and black and 18 seconds later glow with healthy fuchsia pigment.

Nephesh walks shivering Ko'ach onto the beach. She dries him off and holds him in her warm embrace. She watches in horror as his eyes flutter and black bubbles exhale from his nose and mouth. Pressing her breasts against his strong chest, she can feel his heartbeat slow.

Grayish spidery web wraps around Ko'ach's entire body. Falling into a twisted fuge state, he slips from Nephesh's grasp. Hitting rock bottom, Ko'ach's head bleeds.

Nephesh's righteous soul speaks to her. *Hurry, his organs aren't oxygenating. My healing powers are being interfered with. That has never happened before. Stand clear. I'll try and shock him back into the realm of the living.*

On the ninth attempt, Ko'ach finally takes his first deep breath.

Nephesh stares into his eyes. "What's that?" she asks.

Black flecks swirl around Ko'ach's sclera. He exhales cold black moisture. His entire body shivers. Ko'ach affectionately taps Nephesh's cheek. "Legs are tingling. I can see two of you, I wouldn't mind that, but um, now my peripheral vision is fading. My vision is narrowing."

"Medical team is on I-T-S way."

Bird swoops down and snares an insect climbing on Ko'ach's big toes.

Nephesh puts pressure on Ko'ach's bleeding bite mark. "Honey, wiggle your toes."

"Okay."

18 seconds later. "Honey, humor me. Wiggle your toes."

"You humor me, I already did."

Nephesh rubs a protruding black spike. "What's this? Computer, priority one analysis."

Soft blue light emanates from Nephesh's scanner; energy creates a virtual representation of what's going on beneath the surface of Ko'ach's toe.

Nephesh reads the virtual display.

"Magnetic properties. Genetic sequencing, not of this world,"

Closer Nephesh's fingers come to the alien metallic tissue, intense electrical sparks reach back; those new black particles grow teeth and try and bite her fingertips.

"No! No! I will not harm my Nephesh-ah-la! Th-thousands of years," Ko'ach stutters.

"What the hell is keeping the medical team." Nephesh's warm hand brushes away the ice crystals forming on Ko'ach's forehead.

Ko'ach abruptly bends up at the waist, his legs remain paralyzed. He startles Nephesh after shouting, "Tiny champion from backward barbaric planet."

"What? Dear heart, what are you trying to say?"

"D-D-D."

Ko'ach's airway closes over. His lungs blast. His once powerful deep resonant voice, quivers into a higher, weaker pitch. Nephesh presses her ear against Ko'ach's struggling voice.

"Da-vid. Sag-acious..." Ko'ach shouts, whispers.

Ko'ach's righteous soul breaks free of I-T-S malevolent hold. *I don't know when I'll be able to speak to you again? Tell her, before you go into tachycardia.*

Ko'ach's cold lips gently brush Nephesh's warm skin.

"Consciousness slipping. Tell your father the correct dosage to dislodge this evil thing is 18-thousand times greater than the doctors will prescribe."

"No sweetie. That's too much. I-T would either kill you or cause irreparable brain damage!"

"I-T won't. Please, I haven't much time left."

"If you become too weak to communicate verbally, we can telepathically."

Ko'ach grabs Nephesh's hand much harder than he intended.

"Ough! Ko'ach you're hurting me."

With tremendous force, Ko'ach coughs blood into Nephesh's chin.

"You don't understand. My righteous soul tells me if I attempt to reach out to you telepathically, I'll contaminate your righteous soul. Pounding. Vertigo. Thought I was strong enough to fight I-T. I was wrong. Dear heart, I love you. Love. You..."

Medical hovercraft's golden tractor beam keeps Ko'ach suspended above ground. Artificial energy continues life-sustaining compressions.

Ko'ach's eyes dart open; black metallic pus hardens around his sclera. Fuchsia birth soul, not Realm of the Watcher-enhanced soul, vacates his body. God sends that tiny living force into the space-time breaches. His soul begins to disintegrate as I-T traverses malevolent outcomes.

God's strength fortifies what's left of Ko'ach and allows his mortal soul to enter a safe place separate from normal space and the Realm of the Watcher's holy membrane.

Back in the operating room, doctors watch helplessly, unable to stop black metallic tears slicing Ko'ach's skin. Fuchsia nanobots repair the organs Ko'ach's righteous soul can no longer fix. Rapidly, that malevolent black dot mutates and metastasizes from Ko'ach's Achilles to just below his kneecap. Fuchsia aura floats above Ko'ach's thrashing torso.

Visceral anguish. Ko'ach's virtual aura gnashes his grotesque metallic blood red teeth; those shiny sharky things splinter and spray oozing righteous soul. Only my vision is aware of that horrible sight. Black evil energy grows. I-T-S mechanical skull twists counterclockwise. Bones crunch. Cellular deformation merrily consumed. Headless Black body implodes. Like a malevolent vacuum cleaner: I-T-S sucked deep into Ko'ach's chest cavity.

Ko'ach's high pitch screeching reverberates from the operating room and shatters every window, beaker, and tubing.

That horrible sound penetrates and pushes violent insanity onto the medical staff and Nephesh. Nasty nausea, and dizziness split the veins along their foreheads; I-T bursts, creating lakes of blood up to everyone's ankles.

Nephesh punches and kicks against the whirlwind of metallic nausea.

Defying the natural order of gravitational forces Ko'ach floats like a metallic vampire. His leg cracks the hospital wall. "I'll consume you all. Nobody will survive. Future generations will be forever dammed!" transformed Ko'ach growls.

Surgeon's reflexes grab the lid from the surgical basin and use I-T like a shield. Ko'ach punches through the metal as easily as a child pierces tissue paper.

Ko'ach's black fleshy footsteps clank, clank—he stretches his body another 10 feet. Ko'ach's 80-foot shadow menaces everyone. He rubs Nephesh's belly. His creepy metallic smile precedes another terrifying growling speech. "Baby boy on the menu? How delicious."

Ko'ach's blackened arm grabs the nurse's wrist. She screams after her bones are shattered.

Forgive me. Nephesh wraps liquid metal around her knuckles. Each time she hits Ko'ach's jaw, a terrible tuning fork hum reverberates. Ko'ach's mocking grin reinforces her resolve.

12 of the strongest security personnel rush through the wall's opening. A blast of extreme gravity from the doctor's improvised pulsar cannon knocks 80-foot Ko'ach to his knees. Ko'ach stands and staggers backwards. The back of his skull dents the floor. 12 more guards arrive, they struggle to pin Ko'ach's arms and legs.

The moment Ko'ach throws them off, the computer produces a serum capable of knocking him out. Ko'ach's massive index finger flicks and breaks the doctor's hand. The syringe rolls down the corridor. Nephesh backflips over Ko'ach's outstretched swatting hand. She loads the syringe into a specially made cannon and the needle slams into Ko'ach's massive deltoid.

Ko'ach's body temperature dips below freezing; advanced technology superheats his blood and recycles I-T through his crystallizing veins. No medical procedure will stop his transformation. His body temperature falls further, now 18 degrees below freezing. Both legs up to his knees are encased in black armor, far thicker than any titanium manufactured in the lab.

Heating blankets spark, sputter, and ice over. Ko'ach's temperature rapidly falls. Fuchsia are known for their genius level problem solving. Now, for the first time in collective memory the most brilliant scientific and medical minds are stumped. Ko'ach's abnormal metallic growth cannot be stopped. I-T continues to creep up past Ko'ach's knee and engulf most of his thigh.

More transformations take place. Ko'ach's frozen blood hardens. And for unknowable medical reasons I-T liquifies and becomes a scalding hellfire, blood bubbles and percolates throughout his system. "Doctor. Please. Put him under."

"He is. Double the dosage."

"The more we give him, the more he internally cooks," says the tearful head nurse.

Ko'ach screams.

Sobbing Nephesh slams her fist into the wall. "Why won't his righteous soul assist?"

"The disease is moving too rapidly. We have one idea. A billion to one shot. Our righteous souls tell us he could be placed in stasis. That might give us enough time to figure out a medical solution."

"Have you tried this suspended animation on someone as sick as Ko'ach, before?"

"Nobody has ever had what he has before. We've exhausted every possibility. Thrown everything at this malignant virus and I-T fights to stay alive with the same grit and determination as Ko'ach. Do we have your permission to proceed?"

"How long must he remain in this sort of coma?"

"Not sure. My righteous soul tells me... Could be decades or centuries."

Black fluid leaks from Ko'ach's knee. I-T coagulates and forms a demonic mouth.

"Too late, Nephesh-ah-la. I'll consume you all! There is no stopping us!" growling malignancy shouts.

54 years later...

Insanity's immutable, incomprehensible ignominy inspires Ko'ach's indestructible incandescence.

Tsadiyq, Ko'ach's son, excels in all forms of athletics and academics. He's also found love. Over the decades, Tsadiyq's 18 children and 72 grandchildren continue to leave their society better than they found I-T. Ko'ach remains in suspended animation, neither alive, nor dead, stuck in a continuous hellish reality that pits himself against himself. Unstoppable blackness bullies his righteous cells and creeps past his elbows.

Over the last 54 years, the Fuchsia harnessed their telepathic and telekinetic abilities far beyond Ko'ach's generation.

Nephesh wakes from her morning meditation.

"Mother," whispers Tsadiyq.

"What? Oh."

Her son's moist eyes tell her what she's dreaded and postponed and been in denial over the better part of the last 18-months.

Nephesh and Tsadiyq hug the way any mother and son would do, knowing how unlikely I-T will be that they will ever see each other again.

"You're going back to the home world with all the others," Nephesh tearfully states.

"Yes, Mother. We are determined to reclaim what the murderous Dull Gray stole."

Tsadiyq holds Nephesh's hand. *Please reconsider, mother. You know I cannot.*

"Father grows weaker. The evil consuming him these multiple decades grows stronger. No one would fault you for leaving him behind. He's not what you knew. He's more machine than Fuchsia. How is I-T that I can persuade an audience of 72,000, but the one I love most in the world...my words fall flat. Tell me mother, please. What words could I use that would be powerful enough to help you change your mind? For the sake of your grandchildren, if not for me. Before I-T truly becomes too late, Mother. Indeed, I-T-S your own prophecy that guides the council of elders."

"Of which you are the youngest member. I am so proud. And your brilliant wife serves alongside you. You are truly a lucky man."

"You're changing the subject."

"Am I? As long as your father's heart beats, I'll wait for him. What's decades or even centuries, to beings which have been augmented to last many thousand years. I know, if I give him enough time, he will come back to me. He needs more time to defeat the monster within."

Tsadiyq places a bright red rose on his father's metallic heart. All I-T took was 18 seconds for every single petal to blacken and die.

Nephesh's tears fall and hit the now crumbling, disintegrating petals. Tsadiyq takes his mother's hand and leads her to a park bench. "Our mission is noble. We'll reverse what the first evil Dull Gray queen started many thousands of years ago. Mother, think of I-T. To liberate all the clans from Dull Gray barbarism and even the Dull Gray from their own perverted ideology. We must end their perverse emasculating, cannibalistic matriarchy."

Papa? Tsadiyq gently reverently touches Nephesh's tormented memories.

Nephesh pushes her finger against her son's lips, eyes welling up. "No. You promised to change the subject." Nephesh's voice cracks. She holds an embroidered "Nephesh and Ko'ach forever," fuchsia handkerchief beneath her puffy eyes.

"I could force you against your will, mother."

Nephesh arches one eyebrow. Flash of dark fuchsia anger

shines in her eyes. Her aggressive grabbing of her son's wrist startles his thoughts. "Mother, no." he yelps.

"Son, yes!"

Nephesh flings Tsadiyq over her head. He plops in the shallow lake.

"Your father continues to battle his demons. I shall not abandon him!" Nephesh's fists come down and pulverize 3 large boulders.

The sweltering heat quickly dries out Tsadiyq's shirt and pants.

"Father tricked us before. You know you've not been able to read his thoughts. Not even our greatest scholars, with the most powerful telepathic minds could reach Papa's soul."

"I have a power, a connection, they'll never possess."

"Love. Is not enough."

"How can you say that. Is there not anything you wouldn't do to save your wife, your children and grandchildren? And you know I-T-S a bluff telling me you could force me against my will. There isn't anything you can do to change what must be. Besides, son, you're strong but I was first. I taught you much, but I didn't teach you every combat technique."

Tsadiyq looks upon his mother with great worry. "Worry not my son. Your father could never harm me."

"For some reason you don't seem to get I-T. That is not Ko'ach. He will betray you. He will, Mother. Why do you refuse to heed your own prophecy?"

Nephesh grabs her son's hand and holds I-T over Ko'ach's chest. Fuchsia lightning traverses Nephesh's arm and circles around her heart; 90 percent of fuchsia color emanating from Ko'ach's chest is as dark as space without stars.

I told you. Your Papa is still with us.

I fear evil is toying with your emotions.

You're wrong! Your truth isn't the truth!

Don't yell at me. You're not too old that I can't put you over my knee...

Mother! The others are listening. They don't always understand your sense of humor.

Who says I'm joking? Nephesh tenderly pats her son's face. "I shall miss this, and your dear sweet wife, and the cute smiling faces of my grandchildren." Tears well up.

"Son, you hold my values. But your Papa holds my heart."

Nephesh hears the low hum of approaching shuttlecraft. Reading the names, she smiles with pride, "Ko'ach II and Ko'ach VI."

Tsadiyq hands his mother a small purple stone.

"Pretty. What is I-T?" asks Nephesh.

"We talked about this last month."

"Oh. I don't want I-T. Take I-T back and destroy I-T!"

Tsadiyq shakes his head. "We're all afraid for you. When we're gone, how will you keep that evil at bay? If I-T breaks the bonds of our metal shackles and infects you, I couldn't bear to see, I mean I wouldn't be able to get back here in time. Please, Mother, for the love of God!"

Nephesh and Tsadiyq tenderly touch their foreheads. They hold a long hug, neither one wishing to be the first to let go. *Goodbye, Mother.*

Long life, baby boy.

Baby boy? I have 72 grandchildren.

You'll always be my baby boy.

Nephesh knows her son won't break their hug first. For the first time in their relationship, she is the first to let go. Holding hands, they both slowly walked toward the Ko'ach I shuttlecraft. Nephesh cranes her neck to watch the Ko'ach I starship orbit the only home world Tsadiyq has known.

"When we enter the wormhole, there's no coming back to help if you change your mind. Our telepathy can't penetrate that barrier. Are you ready for that? For God's sake, open your eyes before he does. You'll be no match for I-T."

"I-T! I-T! I-T-S not your Papa! Your Papa will defeat I-T!"

"Love doesn't always defeat evil, Mother."

"Son!" Nephesh buries her true fear beyond her son's ability to locate those feelings.

"I concede my powers are feeble compared to yours, Mother. And yet, I too can briefly look into the future. You taught me well. You felt the truth of that future history long before I did. I can't believe you'd sacrifice billions of worlds and trillions of species. Ko'ach is lost to the torturous darkness. The man you knew. The man you loved..."

"Love. Never past tense."

"Mother, look past the hurt. Ko'ach is destined to become the fiercest unstoppable evil machine. I-T-S prize possession. I know I can't convince you to leave with me. At least promise me at the first sign you're losing control, you run to the last remaining shuttle, and..." Tsadiyq looks down at his feet. His tear welling up eyes, cannot look upon his mother's fearful face.

"And..." Tsadiyq whispers.

"And!" shouts Nepehsh.

Tsadiyq curls Nephesh's fingers around the glowing purple rock.

"Blow I-T up!"

CHAPTER 24

Hybrid Ko'ach is Half Evil Machine and Half Righteous Husband and Begs His Beloved Nephesh to Crush His Heart

Nephesh watches Tsadiyq board the Ko'ach I. 18 minutes later she tearfully watches his starship warp toward the sparkling fuchsia wormhole and vanish.

Sweat boils on Ko'ach's deeply lined forehead. His open mouth shuts; upper and bottom lips clamping against each other. Fuchsia sparkles swirl around his dull eyes. For the first time in decades, Ko'ach tries to speak. Deep-throated grunts gasp guttural gurgling growls. Spittle's secretion vibrates venomous vomit.

Nephesh-ah-la please stop.

Beloved. Beloved. I am so happy. You've come back to me, at long last. You're winning your war against evil.

No, beloved. I am not.

Are you truly my beloved? You've tricked me before.

Yessss. I'm your Ko'ach. The other, for now lies dormant. Save your-self. I-T will soon resurface, I-I do not wish to harm you.

You won't let I-T.

No! I haven't much more time. Once I-T creeps beyond my brainstem, I'll become I-T for all time. Not even your love will be strong enough to bring me back to what I once was. We've played and replayed these conversations for decades. I-T-S time I take my final resting place and you start the rest of your life with our son and the rest of the Fuchsia community.

Nephesh watches Ko'ach's eyes bulge and dart side to side. After days of struggle, Ko'ach loudly snores.

Exhausted Nephesh trudges over to the cool shimmering lake and returns, squeezing her flexible canteen: refreshing water flows past Ko'ach's cracked lips. Nephesh's warm lips brush against Ko'ach's cold bluish lips.

18 days later; 18 hours after Nephesh's birthday, she takes the advice of her righteous soul. Haggard Nephesh stands under a shady tree and sucks the immune strengthening juice from her favorite purple melon. Nephesh drifts off. She's taking a long overdue nap.

Three miles away from Nephesh, an insect crawls along the bridge of Ko'ach's nose. Buzz and hum vibrate in his eardrums, creeping down to Ko'ach's parted lips. The most powerful man I've ever known, at that moment in time, is too weak to flick off that bug or blow I-T away.

Ko'ach's mind reaches Nephesh's mind seconds after he accidentally sucks the crawling creature down his esophagus. *Can't breathe!*

Instinctually that insect jabs and slices. Ko'ach's tongue swells and blocks his airway.

Nephesh drops the juicy purple melon and runs back. "Why did you make me leave him?"

Because your immune system has become too weak. You long ago crossed the red line. Your organs started to shut down. Without taking a break from your round the clock care; you could have lost consciousness. And you too could have been stung.

Sprinting back Nephesh is only half a mile from her beloved.

No matter how much you wish to change his fate, you must consider what you refuse to consider.

Enough! No more talk of what I should and shouldn't do. I won't blow up my Ko'ach. We will be together again. Time for you, my righteous partner...to take a nap!

Nephesh! Don't. You've never shut me out before. This isn't the time. You must be at your optimal awareness. Nephesh. Don't do I-T! Oh, my God...she...No-ah! Dough...naught!

Sleep...sleep... "I said! Sleep!" shouts Nephesh. She stabs Ko'ach's cheek with the most powerful anti-venom. Never giving up on her beloved, Nephesh strokes his face and kisses his eyelids. "I'm here. I'm here."

Nephesh blinks her eyes rapidly. "Black armor inches faster. I-T didn't work. Is the mixture wrong? Did I-T make me alter the formula, without my knowing I-T? No, I-T can't possibly have that kind of power."

You sure? Ko'ach's mind growls.

Nephesh's soul reawakens. *Danger! Danger!*

Hush! I don't want your judgment. Too bad for me, I'm unable to shut you down for more than 72 seconds.

Nephesh, you fought valiantly. Your Ko'ach has come to terms with what must be done. He's acknowledged he's lost the battle, and the war. There is extraordinarily little time left for you to save yourself. He's imploring us to tell you that you must...

"Shut up! I won't be a willing participant in the unthinkable!"

Think. Overcome your emotions. The evil within grows exponentially faster and faster; every second we delay. He's begging us. You know he's never done that before. Do you know how humiliating I-T is for him to beg?

"Nephesh-ah-la," Ko'ach wheezes.

Deep crow's feet crinkle around the corners of Nephesh's eyes. "Thee speaks?"

"I must. Make. You. Hear me! The prophecy! You! Must! Not! Allow! Nephesh-ah-la, don't let these grotesque metallic things be the instrument of your death." *You must become the righteous heir, the harbinger of all our futures. Darling, your hesitation risks the murder of trillions. Please! Change my ugly fate! I need you... to murder me!*

No! No! No! Nephesh shakes rage filled fists. She unleashes from her fingertips the hottest, purest righteous energy blast and directs that loving energy into Ko'ach's pulsating chest.

Evil recedes. Ko'ach's malevolent metallic skin melts past his shoulders. He inhales and exhales deep cleansing breaths as 18 powerful coughs shake loose the black poisonous mucus cracking along the edges of the healthy fuchsia lungs.

Arms paralyzed. Sorry dear heart. I wish I could wrap them around you and never let go. Passionate kisses produce lightning blasts circling their lips. More metallic skin recedes. Ko'ach wriggles his fingers and for the first time in decades hope fills Ko'ach's heart.

"Forgive me." Ko'ach's quivering whispers transition into startling guttural cackles.

Too late! Beloved! Malevolent armor rockets from Ko'ach's hips to encase the top of his head. Evil metallic Ko'ach breaks the bonds of his blue stasis field. Shattered energy transforms into metallic spearpoints. Malignant glow slices Nephesh's chest. Her shimmering wounds ooze metallic particulates. Painfully, Nephesh's bright fuchsia luminescent pigment darkens. Ko'ach's fingers crackle black lightning. Nephesh's roots darken with each creepy fondling.

Summoning her last ounce of righteous energy, Nephesh blasts metallic Ko'ach deep beneath the lake's righteous cooling waters. Scalding geyser's plume ascends 360 feet. Red-hot lasers shoot from his eyes and burn away the offending righteous liquid.

Each pounding metallic footstep brings Ko'ach closer to Nephesh. Every three steps he grows another eight feet.

Overwrought Nephesh backs up. She manically clutches and yanks at the evil metallic particles in her chest. She's unable to stop the evil fragments from burrowing deeper.

Ko'ach for the first time transformed into a 100-foot menacing machine; I-T hovers over Nephesh. His singing voice growls, "I've Got You Under My Skin."

"Your destiny is with us!" Ko'ach spits with mocking eagerness. His black helmet implodes. Black debris with a slight fuchsia hue sucks the malevolence from his mind; Ko'ach shrinks down to his original 70-foot height.

"You! Can't Have! Her!" Ko'ach pummels his chest. Reverberating clang, clang; frightens happy birds from their trees. His fingers remain encased in their malevolent black armor; fleshy fuchsia fingertips emote golden energy. He plucks and tweezes dark transformative filaments and sings in his naturally deep, resonant bass-baritone righteousness, "The Impossible Dream."

Nephesh, do I have your permission to try a maneuver no mutated being had ever attempted in all recorded celestial history?

I trust you.

Ko'ach places himself and Nephesh in an 18-minute time bubble. 2 new timelines emerge. Righteous Ko'ach and Nephesh watch evil energy dissolve and shrink to 65- and 70-inch human size.

Each towering 100-foot metallic Nephesh and Ko'ach stare down with glaring red eyes. The 100-foot Ko'ach picks up 65-inch Nephesh. The 100-foot Nephesh picks up doll-size 70-inch Ko'ach. 2 giant hands crush tiny righteous versions.

Gnashing metallic shark teeth metal monsters ravenously bite, rip and chew muscle and bone with unforgivable malevolence. Cannibals finish with extended loud farts and burps.

Watcher Realm's trillion righteous souls reanimating penitent portal. Nephesh and Ko'ach's naked perforated disassembled disabled pieces float betwixt the righteous gamma radiation nebula. Confused and frightened, jigsaw Nephesh's mind searches for her beloved.

Ko'ach?

Yes, dear.

What's happening?

We're in Malevolent Time's manufactured unreal undead mechanized reality.

What? How?

Read my mind. Yes, good, you're touching the thoughts God gave me.

Why do I hear in my mind that human song? I was never on those expeditions to that planet. You told me they're so tiny and barbarically cruel to one another.

Bodies are now fully reassembled. Ko'ach holds Nephesh, they passionately kiss and sing, "The Wedding Song."

Edges of the time bubble thin; like escaping helium, their time bubble expels whining particulates. They watch gravity reassemble their planet. Malevolent black gases dissipate. Galaxies...stars...planets...all breathe in god's righteous molecular structures.

Time.

For what?

Glowing reinvented Nephesh negates never-ending negative ionic gases and radiates righteous reality. "I remember!" Smiling Nephesh vibrates.

Beloved Ko'ach; now at long last is the time to divulge all your hidden secrets.

Agreed.

No more stalling. How and when did the Watchers' souls gain their power to see multiple intricacies of multi-dimensional time travel?

Eons ago. That's when they became addicted.

To what?

Time travel. At the beginning, they were enthralled with the "what if" paradox. They started to manipulate individual stories; the consequences were disastrous. Dreadful experiences taught them to never again travel eons or millenniums into the past or future.

Well, um...be honest. Is that by choice or loss of power?

Yes. And maybe...that information isn't part of our story.

Watcher souls shout in Nephesh's mind. *Don't ever use that tone again!*

Are you working with the almighty? Or have you gone rogue?

Nephesh, that sort of inquiry is not going to help either you or Ko'ach.

Sorry. Well, what about smaller increments? Could you travel hundreds of years?

Unused time traveling powers...atrophy. In the future, we might be able to teach you manipulation of minutes or even hours. You'll never have enough power to go back in time and prevent I-T-S bite of your Ko'ach.

"You should've listened to our son," growls Ko'ach.

Reality's quicksand yanks Nephesh out of surreal time and back to her confrontation with her malevolent metallic beloved.

Reborn metallic Ko'ach creature easily kicks off his leg restraints. At 100 feet, he towers over diminutive 65-foot Nephesh. Metallic Ko'ach flexes his powerful hands. In shock, Nephesh is too slow. Faster than any earthly railgun, Ko'ach grabs Nephesh by her throat. She's lifted up to I-T-S red-black eyes.

Nephesh-ah-la you've grown weak over these five-plus decades. How disappointing, but not unexpected. We'll have fun, slowly squeezing the life out of you. Struggle for us. I said struggle! That's better.

"We? Not I? Are you still in there, beloved?" gurgles Nephesh's shrieks.

Righteous soul repairs Nephesh's larynx, each repair less complete than the last.

"Yes! You haven't extinguished your true love, yet!"

Metallic fingers grip tighter. Blood trickles from the corner of Nephesh's mouth.

"A momentary lapse. No, we. Only me. I alone survive. I alone will do I-T-S bidding. I alone will watch you perish and finish off the rest of your disgusting corporeal infestation!"

Black-red-eyes flicker and flutter. Stammering golden

energy bursts through. Black armor clicks and peels away from Ko'ach's skull, face, shoulders, and heart. Metallic Ko'ach shrinks down to 78 feet.

Metallic fingers open. Nephesh falls to her knees and looks up into Ko'ach's loving eyes.

Ko'ach pinches, pounds, scratches, rips and digs deep into and penetrates his first two metallic layers. Fuchsia-pigmented fingers descend and grab his metallic black heart; acidic liquid squirts, flesh burns, and black flames shoot out from Ko'ach's chest cavity.

"Save your...self! Lost cause am I..." Ko'ach's agony grunts.

Nephesh's tears quench Ko'ach's burning flesh. His black armor creeps and crawls like a swarm of locusts.

"They are beyond your understanding and conception of malevolence," Ko'ach hisses.

"They?"

"Yes, they're everywhere. I can sense their plans. Future. Past. Present. I don't wish t-to b-be converted. No time left. You must...without hesitation."

"I don't understand what you're asking of me. No?"

"Don't analyze what ifs...I need your resolve! Mine is slipping. Act...now!" Ko'ach's tender voice becomes more grating and mechanical.

Beanstalk growing 100-foot hybrid Ko'ach licks his menacing metallic fangs. Nephesh watches her own face mirrored in the Ko'ach creature's shiny armor. Her countenance hardens.

Ko'ach creature laughs.

Nephesh zooms above the white billowy clouds, using gravity as an ally and falling back with thunderous force. Her boot latches onto Ko'ach's shoulders. Her super nova radiation stream hits hotter and longer than any time before. Ko'ach's evil armor temporarily melts.

No, you can't keep this up. I-T-S stronger than the both of us. You must release me from this mortal coil.

Never! Avalanche of sweat pours. Splashing creates cheek-burning steam.

For the love of God, stop! Your life force is dangerously depleted! Nephesh! I won't be the cause of your death. Stop! Stop!

Nephesh's righteous soul reaches out to her mind. *Let go, little one. Time...*

What? Now you communicate. Where have you been?

You cannot allow this horrible timeline to solidify! You must crush his heart.

I can't.

Ko'ach cannot be saved.

Nephesh's white-hot fingertips dig into Ko'ach's chest cavity. His heart thumpity-thumps in her palm. Her benevolent energy chips away at Ko'ach's metallic black heart. He looks at his beloved with tender sorrow.

For the first time in 54 years, Ko'ach's fleshy lips squish against Nephesh's pink-purple warmth. She's surprised when he pulls away first.

"Beloved," Ko'ach whispers. Nephesh shakes her head and places her fingers across Ko'ach's warm lips. "Don't say any more. Kiss me. Kiss me and all will be right...

"You must. For countless trillions not yet born."

"Not fair."

"You must terminate the evil, which I've become. I cannot hold this form much longer. My love for you will survive the hereafter."

"Promise."

Ko'ach's and Nephesh's passion entwines. Their surviving love rewrites their destinies. I hope. I am not sure. Something is interfering with what I thought was going to happen. Undulating dark histories expunging righteous fates. *God! This is David Sagacious Your righteous narrator. Evil thoughts penetrate my mind. I can't push I-T out.*

Narrator's soul is ripped from his body, and flops on the sulfuric lava lake like a dying, gasping-for-breath goldfish.

Telekinetic punches, more powerful than the MCU's Thanos pummels my limp semi-conscious body. Layer upon layer of bedrock I tumble. *This is I-T God. I feel the mantel's core. I've never been this deep before. Surely this Immortal Mortal body will not withstand that heat. I feel my skin, muscle, and bone shrivel to ash. No righteous soul to repair what's left. And yet, my consciousness lives. All that remains is a single fleck of ash. I-T sleeps on God's righteous weapon. And I am sustained once more.* God's righteous weapon rockets my body upwards toward my righteous soul. I-T slams into my chest and I sleep for the next 18 years.

Remember, dear reader, time is abnormally disjointed in this place. 18 years have passed, but I am able to pick up the story of the two love birds from where I last left off...

Ko'ach caresses Nephesh's moist cheek and kisses her shaking fingers.

"Allow me the dignity to live forever within the Realm of the Watchers. If you do as your heart commands, you'll take my place in death, and these hands, which loved you for all eternity, will wrap around your throat and squeeze the life out of you. And that death will be permanent. After my surging joy at becoming the instrument of your death; I will commit more atrocities. I will fulfill my destiny proclaimed by the evil prophecy and rip apart trillions of souls contained within the Realm, and after I've murdered them all, I will turn my sights on what's left of God's corporeal creation throughout the entire Multiverse!

Metal plating consumes Ko'ach's heartbeat.

Purest blue-white energy cajoles a singular atom of righteous light, struggling to survive within the abnormally metastasizing virulent darkling space-time-continuum. With God's speed, this new holy entity will successfully journey across quasars, galaxies, black holes, and heretofore unknown dimensions, at speeds beyond any species' comprehension. Folding space onto more devastated warping unleashes paradoxical parsecs. Penetrating power pulverizes preferred particulates. Multicolored petals on Nephesh's planet, harmonize beyond malevolent-mechanical Ko'ach's ability to hear.

Nephesh hears all, brought to tears listening to the human song, "You Raise Me Up."

Planetary quakes billow up from molten mantel. Trees uproot. Mountains collapse. Boulders rumble and flatten the rest of the forest. Fissures form limitless abysses and swallow up hundreds of Fuchsia dwellings and farms.

Metallic Ko'ach loses his footing. Wave of blue-white holy energy wafts over his malevolence. Armor becomes as thin as tissue. Tree branch lurches and pierces Ko'ach's heart; 99 percent of oozing Fuchsia blood is dark as any malevolent cavern. Roots shoot up and entangle with that branch and slam into another boulder.

Precariously pinned. Ko'ach is unable to move and shrinks to a tiny seven-foot creature. Agony sets every nerve ending afire. Ko'ach coughs up a black furry thing with 16 legs, and 32 rapidly blinking eyes, and poisonous pincers and hooks around I-T-S entire bulbous body.

Pincers click click. Creature stomps closer to Nephesh's neck. Ko'ach pushes past his paralysis and his determination shouts, *Move!*

The creature opens wide, and Nephesh slams a 6-pointed star into the creature's throat.

Acting as a holy lightning rod, metallic fibers attract a divine pulse from space, that sacred energy incinerates evil creatures down to sub-atomic metallic particles. I-T-S malevolent screech rips holes through the fabric of our galaxy.

Twin benevolent God-inspired stars collide; blue-white energy beams ripple through space and enter Ko'ach's shrunken body. That burst of raw energy temporarily gives Ko'ach enough strength to speak to Nephesh.

"Dearest Nephesh, time has set on our day, but never our love. Release me from this mortal existence and allow my soul to float into the sanctified membrane of the Realm."

"Why give up now? Finally, you're free of that metallic

shell. In the past, your righteous soul repaired far worse injuries."

"Please do as I ask."

"You'll bleed out."

"We must never question God. Keep hope alive, in his plan for our future."

"And you know this to be true, what guides your actions, is in fact, God's plan, and not another?"

Ko'ach coughs black spittle, with sparkling white and fuchsia gemstones.

"What are these?"

Nephesh's pinkie performs chest compressions, the tip dwarfing Ko'ach's itty bitty chest.

Spasmodic breath brings Ko'ach back. Nephesh hugs him with her thumb and index finger.

"Damn I-T! Nephesh! Why would you do such a stupid thing? I'm not destined to live past this moment in time!"

I'm not ready to let death take you. Don't you understand that?

I do. Sweetie. Please.

Nephesh scoops up her tiny beloved. Her palm's warmth feels good on Ko'ach's icy skin.

Ko'ach reaches up and hugs Nephesh's pinkie, and he hums, "You're Still You."

I don't understand why I know Earth song lyrics and melodies. Must be the manipulation of time you told me about.

"Be with our son and grandchildren. Fight for justice. You deserve happiness."

"Happiness? How will I ever experience that ever again! You're asking me to murder you! Hold! On! A! Moment! I am sensing more deceit from you. Oh my God. No! No! No... Was that evil inside you too long? Is that true Ko'ach? The Realm is going to refuse you entry because of your tainted soul?"

Nephesh's ferocious fuchsia lightning bolts crescendo from her shaking fist.

Nephesh's righteous energy grows Earth-size Ko'ach

another 18 feet. His new height and strength crush the tiny bloody branch.

Gushing blood smacks Nephesh's beautifully sorrowful face. She tries cauterizing Ko'ach's gaping hole. Every 18 seconds, the bloody hole reopens, and a torrential flood pushes through. Color recedes from Ko'ach's cheeks. Flash flood grows thinner, now a sputtering trickle.

Ko'ach's hybrid soul—neither fully righteous nor 100 percent malevolent—ascends betwixt normal and Watcher Realm space. That glowing energy disrupts trillions of life-force scenarios. At the speed of light, they write and rewrite perplexing narratives.

All the while, Nephesh's mind, body, and soul are locked in the paralyzing conundrum of timeline's event horizon.

Ko'ach's abnormal soul speaks on the edge of the Watcher Realm—I can hear what Nephesh is blocked from hearing.

How long must I wait? Ko'ach's mind asks.

Measuring time from your frame of reference, in normal space, outside of our continuum, we can't say. Perhaps thousands of Fuchsia years.

You can't keep my Nephesh in limbo—fearful of what has become of my soul. Never giving her any response is cruel by anyone's standards. I'll force myself in!

Arrogant! Aggressive beyond the pale. Proof you're unworthy. Perhaps eight thousand years isn't enough for you to cool off and reach the appropriate amount of maturity.

You can't fight God's will!

Ko'ach of Fuchsia, how do you know God's will? After all we've given you, you're still reacting like most primitives with too much emotion.

How dare you! We know evil exists within thee.

Free of that black armor I control my own destiny. I'm not evil! I'm Ko'ach! I know you've lost contact with God while he's locked in his ultimate struggle with Malevolent Time. I-T-S you who are making the mistake by not allowing my strength to bolster yours.

How? No corporeal life could know the deep wound we carry. How are you able to peer so deep into the past and know of that evil's origins? Explain that trick.

Frustrated? Doesn't feel good, does I-T.

You would use those evil letters in our presence to make your point? Answer us—now! How do you know Malevolent Time's story?

Hybrid Ko'ach grows white hot on the right side and the darkest black on the left. At the core center are 18 fuchsia strips: 8 rotate counterclockwise while the other 10 spin in clockwise fashion.

How do you know this hybrid, which I've become, isn't the answer? Your decision not to let me in is foolhardy and reckless. You're scared because you haven't been in direct communication with God. You no longer trust yourselves. Speak to me! Don't turn your mind from my gaze. Come back! I won't let you do this. You need me!

Triangular gravimetric waves bombard Nephesh. She wakes from her time-induced frozen state: a single fuchsia tear falls down her cheek.

Future...unfamiliar voice echoes in Nephesh's mind. Who's this? Watcher soul or Ko'ach?

Trust me.

Why don't you identify yourself?

Fear not God's design.

Yes, and yes. I'll evolve by design and my own force of will. I...WE... shall be reborn.

Are you a monster or savior?

I'm still here. I'm your Ko'ach. God has hidden mysteries even from the Realm.

And confided in you? Why can't he confide in me? Ko'ach would never keep secrets.

He would. I would. To keep you safe. The way for us goes through a human. An incredibly special human.

How can one of those tiny primitives be of any help? We've been singing their songs and I've wondered why. No Fuchsia has met a human face to ankle. Only our long-distance scans tell us who and what they are.

Thousands of years will pass in the blink of an armadillo's earlobe.

Armadillo? What's an armadillo?

Earth creature—forgive my silliness.

Was that silly?

Never mind. Do you see the image of the tiny human?

I do. And you say this David Sagacious won't be alive for thousands of years?

How will I know where to look for him? I see. Yes, of course. Makes sense. And yet...

Why do you hesitate to trust me? You've never done so before.

Well, I've never talked to my beloved's soul, without my beloved. I mean. Um...you know what I mean. How do you know Sagacious is the one? How do you know the Earth holds the key? How can you be certain God communicates with you and not the other?

If I were evil or if evil communicated with me...I'd be unable to communicate with you. Trust me...Nephesh-ah-la.

Fuchsia blinding light descends and swirls. Nephesh hears 18 grunts; 70-foot silhouette materializes. Shadowy Ko'ach cradles his own heart. A large gaping hole pulsates where silhouette's heart should be.

Silhouette Ko'ach looks down at tiny seven-foot Ko'ach in Nephesh's palm. A single muscle strand holds his heart within his chest cavity. That muscle strand stretched to I-T-S limit. Silhouette Ko'ach places his heart in Nephesh's hands.

Nephesh and silhouette Ko'ach kiss.

Ko'ach nods. "Time. I love you," he whispers.

Long drawn-out deep inhales and rapid shallow exhales. A single tear falls off her cheek and Nephesh crushes Ko'ach's heart. Ko'ach's silhouette dematerializes. Nephesh blows Ko'ach's heart ashes into her locket.

"Let him in, God. Righteous souls...hear me. If you refuse his entry, if your irrational fear clouds your wisdom; leaving him alone, to float and barely exist in perpetual oblivion—then you can no longer call yourselves righteous. Yes, I know! He communicated a lot to me. From the beginning of time to the end of time. Ko'ach isn't the only one who'll be judged. Show him mercy or you doom us all!"

Nephesh's love is unaltered by time. However, time will

alter him...Ko'ach refused entry emboldens his war on the absurd.

Celestial winds body slam and contort Ko'ach's brain. Aggressive tissue shearing refuses to relent. Ko'ach's abnormal hybrid soul battles himself. Righteous Realm continues to change physical locations. His soul is assaulted by grotesque radioactive insanity crystals.

Memory of Nephesh's love keeps Ko'ach from falling deeper into apocryphal abyss. Mighty kinetic energy rips and dismembers him down to his sub-atomic righteous soul. Nova explosion sears his holy membrane to a crisp. He refuses to die.

Thousands of years Ko'ach survives as his own unique special life force. He is separate from Malevolent Time's warp bubble; held apart from the righteous Realm of the Watchers, and uniquely situated beyond the Multiverse's manipulative time paradox. Ko'ach's realm is neither space nor time.

No other soul, mind, or body could survive time's frozen bottomless pit. Ko'ach still has faith, he can convince the Realm of the Watchers to let him in. He's put through endless tasks to prove himself. Every tribulation is more difficult than the last. Even when the Realm's soul knows they've got Ko'ach beaten, he proves once more they are all mistaken.

Is that all you've got? My love for Nephesh can't be expunged! I'm beyond your ability to destroy—so sayeth our lord! I laugh at your ineptitude to destroy me. I implore you to trust and not fear the prophecy.

Ko'ach senses trillions of righteous voices.

Ko'ach's evil half becomes connected to maddening voices.

Billions of living machines cannibalize trillions of species through the Multiverse. For the briefest of known measurements of time; Ko'ach becomes aware of something not even the Realm is aware of. Why hasn't God communicated the location of that which turned long ago EM-IT into I-T?

CHAPTER 25

Is Ko'ach Destined to Help David Sagacious Prevent the Annihilation of All Corporeal Life, or Will He Fulfill the Dark Prophecy by Aligning Himself with Other Murdering 100-Foot Machines and Annihilate Trillions of Righteous Souls from Within the Realm of the Watchers, Including David's Parents?

Star date and hybrid Ko'ach—unknown.

Caught in time's dysfunctional loop, Ko'ach's essence perilously traverses the agonizing distant past and distant future. All unknowns collide and intersect continuously, creating curiously constructed calamities. Curt communication curtailed, while cagey camouflage captures charred candor. Every thought and emotion simultaneously enervate horizontal and vertical cyclones. Deceptive delirium damages dissociative death.

Trillions of frightened righteous souls from the Watcher Realm shout into Ko'ach's mind... KO'ACH! YOU'RE NOT WELCOMED HERE! HEAR?

Ko'ach responds with determined resolve. *No matter how far I'm flung. I'll return! My essence will coalesce. I'll once again recapture my righteous soul and together we'll show you...foolish Ancient Ones! Time is on my side...and for the first time in forever... You need me!*

Trillions of righteous souls grow silent. One voice speaks to Ko'ach... *Ignore that ungrateful, disrespectful primitive. Brothers and sisters, including two recent arrivals.*

They're from Earth.

Eww...humans. How could their souls be among us?

Who are they?

Grace and Christopher. Narrator's parents. By God's decree, they live among us.

Ko'ach's success means we must contemplate that which we've never considered before.

I'll throw back the words you've spit at me for multiple millennia. You'd conspire to bring about my destruction rather than acknowledge my uniqueness? Wouldn't murder dissolve your righteous souls? You'd bring about that which you've been fighting to prevent. Ask yourselves how a lowly primitive could see that, and you can't?

Smug. If we didn't know you were Fuchsia we'd conclude you're human

David Sagacious is human. Am I not destined to mentor him in the distant future? And his parents, what of them?

To save billions. To save trillions. Yes! We'd murder you...

Can you truly be 100 percent certain that my demise would guarantee your survival? How do you know if you kill me, you aren't condemning billions or trillions? I'm the boss of me. I control my thoughts; I control my own actions. Evil will always be a part of me—a part I control. Evil doesn't rule me. I rule I-T! Murder me, and you'll be doing I-T-S bidding. Nicely done! My death will bring about the cataclysm God's trying to prevent!

We're not debating your current control. We're most concerned about your future actions. We detect unbreakable, unquenchable, undeterred elements of evil time displacement within your hybrid soul. As powerful as we are, we are not talented enough to remove those particles. Only God could do that. And as you've pointed out, we've lost all communication and don't know how to get that back. And yes, you're immensely powerful, but we do sense you're hiding something. And that also concerns us, for no other life form has been able to do that. Explain yourself. Your silence won't change our minds. On the contrary, your defiance proves your disloyalty!

To you, perhaps. To God, never!

Two tiny humans voice their displeasure, weak in comparison to all others. They need god to amplify their righteous energy. My mama and papa never knew Ko'ach but are fully aware of what he means to me in the future and twisted past. By God's decree, they're given differential yet grudging respect.

"Give him a chance to prove himself. He must be allowed to train our boy. While you argue and make points, evil continues to win against our righteous warriors!" shouts my papa.

Perhaps we've erred too long on the side of caution. Acting as one giant collective and losing our individuality. Another unpredictable and disheartening timeline has shifted. There, can you use what we see— Ko'ach, do you hear us?

Yes, of course. What do you want me to see? I'm weary of this back and forth.

An insignificant solar system, singular sun. Earth of the 21st century. Time stands still for us but not Nephesh. We're trying to help you. Don't use that tone with us. Control your anger. How Dare you threaten? I know...we're aware she's your forever...

"Ko'ach! This is Grace Sagacious. Please calm down—your strong anger is not helping your case. Better. Wonderful recovery."

Ko'ach! The vote is in. The humans put you over the top. Appropriate to say by the tiniest majority. If you fail...

I won't.

Again, with the talking back. Hold on. I said wait your turn and listen. If you fail, Nephesh can be your backup.

How?

We'll endow her with an 18th of our Righteous Time particles. We dare not give her more. Truth? We have never been his close to oblivion. Dafna, Ima and David are so pitifully human.

Even with Ko'ach and Nephesh as their guardian angels, there's only a 54 percent chance we can escape forever's oblivion.

And without those five?

There's a 93 percent chance we're all annihilated. Living machines would take over interdimensional space. The exhausting expanse of unlimited nasty rewrites; means we'll no longer have enough time or energy to recreate another Multiverse. We'll have to make do with Ko'ach's inexperience.

Crash course?

Crash, of course.

The evil which remains attached to your core will function as a magnet attracting I-T-S malevolent metallic minions. They will break any and all physical law in the pursuit of your annihilation.

Ko'ach, millions of creatures controlled by I-T were destroyed in their misguided attempt to possess time-traveling particles.

That...

Is...

Our...

Only advantage!

Once you leave our Realm, we'll no longer be able to communicate with you. The first malevolence will track your unique genetic code and mess with them in an unpredictable fashion. We can observe, but we'll be powerless to help alter their actions or assist in your actions.

Ko'ach is too young...too inexperienced; how can he hope to survive?

Hush! The decision has been made. We won't defer any longer. Until you encounter the boy, or two girls, you'll be totally alone.

Boy? Girls? Ko'ach's mind asks.

David Sagacious. Ima Best-Friend, and Dafna Shaked. Fail in this mission and we'll forever lack the power to retrieve your soul. You'll be adrift within chaotic malevolence, forever.

Alternative choices?

None...

What about my Nephesh?

She shows tremendous potential. Not yet possessing the attributes needed for success. You'll need to buy us enough time to train her. When you pass gas...

Human souls giggle.

...giants. Your essence seared to a crisp. Over 36 millenniums, 72 percent of your horrendous agony will dissipate.

You'll pass through water worlds and gigantic gravitational eddies. Your mind will mingle and slice through, the way cheese slices through a kitchen table grater.

And your body will linger and not be that far behind.

How long will I have to wait for my body to catch up?

Another wrinkle that remains undetermined.

You don't know?

Correct...

Bits and pieces will reassemble milli-seconds after the Big Bang. You can't inadvertently alter what must not be altered. You can't alter the trajectory of trillions of life forms born and unborn. Unfortunately, you must not interfere with our history, as tempting as that might be, you must allow our losses to mount, and unfold as destiny dictates...so far.

You must never stop and help any species. This is the one time where your righteous empathy cannot kick in. You must remain on task, complete your mission as destiny's flawed fate dictates.

And my Nephesh?

She's not yet born. When the time is right, we'll tell her what she needs to know; there's much we must keep from her, because you know who would detect that conversation.

The odds of success aren't good. Only nine-tenths of one percent.

Why did that percentage change, in the wrong direction?

I know how improbable, but Ko'ach, do you know something we do not?

Have we, at the 11th hour, made a dramatically grave mistake?

The caste is dye...no turning back, for any of us. God speed, Ko'ach.

Star date: absurdist mocking time...

Young Ima's blouse is ripped by clawing 16-foot turtle beast. Turtle beak chomp chomps.

Destiny fulfills I-T-Self. Teen David screams, looking

down at his stumps for legs. Ima's 900-year-old doppelganger flies 40 feet; her blue-white energy blast disintegrates the human-eating turtle monster.

Old Ima's mind travels centuries. *They need you. You need—you. Yes, he, you, he's afraid. Nobody guiding him through horrific nightmares. Hurry. Only you can save, you.*

Old David gracefully flies down and gently touches down inches from the force field.

David's 900-year-old fingers penetrate flesh searing force field.

Teen Ima looks down at her rapidly healing injury. "Hi, old man."

"Hi, young Ima."

How... How?

Old David pinches his strong legs. "Time works differently on me. You'd think I would need two prosthetics, but I don't."

David's burnt fingers penetrate what is left of teen David's infected leg. Faster than any team of specialized surgeons, old-man David rebuilds the teen's knee cap. Flesh to bone and ligaments linked stronger than at birth. Placing his blackened hand over his teen-self's heart; he absorbs wave upon undulating wave of fiery nerve-ending agony. Single quivering tear hangs on the corner of deeply lined, rapidly aging David's eye.

Peering into young Ima's moist eyes, "No worries, little one. Ima okay," whispers David.

Young Ima smells burnt flesh. "Oh my gosh. Take I-T out. Take I-T out!" she shouts.

Fire ascends from our fingertips. Forearm and shoulders are blackened. Ima holds her hand over her mouth. Tears flood past her cheeks and pitty-pat off her trembling fingers.

David holds his gnarled clawed fists to his heart. He grunts three times. Pure white energy emerges from his chest and repairs his disfigured flesh.

"You're a good storyteller," says old David.

"Storyteller?"

"The human can't know about any of this. No investigation. Promise me you'll prevent him from knowing any of that, at all costs, do not corrupt the timeline." David swipes right. Swiping faster and faster. From Ima's perspective his movements are a blur. "What are you doing?"

"Too much is unfolding in a manner we haven't encountered before."

Old David pats teen Ima's shoulder.

I dare not let this innocent in on the darkness which awaits her.

Fingertips to his lips. David blows a kiss to old Ima.

Nephesh's fingers tap little human, and she points to the right. Ima's gushing eyes look past the falling debris. Teen Ima stares in wonderment at the twinkling illumination and the new

bright Fuchsia star, with swirling black energy rings.

"Beloved?" Nephesh tearfully chokes out, inaudibly to human hearing.

CHAPTER 26

Another Altered Timeline; god Demands Nephesh Murder Her Beloved Ko'ach Before the Evil Prophecy is Fulfilled

80-foot metallic child's frustrated mind growls. *Father! Forgive. I've failed you. Gravitational pressure is greater than I anticipated. Help me make this right, Father. I am sending you the new coordinates. I've depleted the last of my time particles fighting Benevolent Time's misdirection. I need help finding my way through your portal. Your response is breaking up. Say again, Father. Say again! I'm You are breaking up! My* murderous metallic child's mind roars.

Nephesh's giant index and middle finger create circular purple sparks. She gently scoops up tearful teen Ima and unconscious teen David. The purple vortex lifts their tiny bodies from her fingertips. With timely intent enormous escalating eddies suck the teen humans through infinity's intrepidly intriguingly infused, invincible portal.

Nephesh turns to old Ima and David. "Your turn."

"No, old friend, you need us on the perimeter," says twinkling, moist-eyed Ima.

"Look at that! I've never seen that before!" shouts David.

An unexpected black vortex appears underneath Nephesh's righteous purple vortex.

Black vortex slices purple in half. Each half swirls and cuts. Swirls and cuts... Halves become quarters and become eighths and multiple fractions of the original whole. That speed of light, unholy process goes on quicker than Nephesh, or old Ima and David could react. The tiny teen Ima and David are swallowed up by black Cheshire cat grinning energy.

Anomalous alter egos disrupt and deride decisive der-ring-do. Sights. Sounds. Smells are all insatiably intense. Colors blinding. Soulless sounds shattered synapses...aromas repug-nant and delicious. Pain and joy intermix with shifting walls. Ginormous geometric fractures fumigate flagrant frolicking flashbacks. Hideous hyena heckles emaciated loved ones ago-nizing moments before their death.

Body, soul, and emotions crumble within time's unapol-ogetic membrane. Emotionally scarring scary suicides writhe and wriggle. Loud never-ending loop drives teen Ima and David to bang on impenetrable walls: they feel insanity's grip grow tighter...

Sharp fangs dislodge, flipping spike over spiky tooth; three penetrate David's chest. He falls through a black trap door. Ima's eerie screams go on for days. "David! Nephesh! Help us!"

Black metallic claw penetrates Ima's heart; her limp body flung into disintegrating vortex. Metallic cat meows and yells, "Checkmate! Thank you, Father. Now onto the main course..."

Undulating cackles split teen Ima off from teen David. Riding the black spatial dysmorphia's rainbow, their cells crash into and through two different portals. David's purple portal becomes blacker and blacker. Glowing red eyes on the horizon hum and jettison black lightning bolts.

Mutated black limbs and fingernails grow into slicing machetes. Like a lifeless sack of potatoes, David's body plum-mets nose first. In searing pain, he lands at Nephesh's feet.

First time in over 9 centuries that David would become

separated from his beloved. Massive teeth descend, ready to finish off I-T-S David-meal. Concussive countervailing whirlpool pushes Nephesh's flailing arms and contorting face into a painfully slow spine-crushing roll. The last remaining malevolent tooth pierces our 900-year-old manic-beating heart.

Nephesh removes black saliva-dripping jagged toothy dagger, and 900-year-old David drowns in his own scalding blood. Genetic enhancement mutates and creates pooling blood equivalent to 999 humans.

Evil middle finger almost decapitates singular strand of muscle fiber, connecting to David's skull. Swaying I-T lurches to the left. If I-T swings too far, I-T will most definitely tear away from our brain stem. Sub-atomic particles repair at a feverish pace. Each repair is met with another slice. Malevolent nails operate out of normal time and space; our healing is stuck two steps behind.

Sucked into delirium's mind vortex, we...he...900-year-old David tries to find his elusive clarity. *Where are you Nephesh? Don't let I-T end like this. Send me back! Send me back. I know. No. No! You were ordered not to do that. To hell with regulations! You can still be reunited before he becomes hybrid. Consciousness fading. Act fast! We need you. Even if evil obliterates our connection, send me back to Ima!*

Dear old friend, you'll never survive the trip.

Nephesh snaps her fingers. Purple time fragments lift David's body. Fallen civilizations. Extinct species: all dance along the vortex's wall. Here! There! Untraceable unfathomable undesirable unknowns upstage undulating uneasy uncertainty.

Ima's limp body crashes into desolate deserted desert. In other words—my home. Deathly dehydration desperately disowns dissembling. Wisp of her conscious mind becomes aware of her surroundings. She finds pieces of her 900-year-old husband. Yes indeed, at that moment in time that David Sagacious still lived. David's heart beats, directing her onward. When she walks in the wrong direction that powerful percussion drumbeat slows and becomes fainter. When she walks in the correct direction my heart beats stronger.

David's righteous soul keeps our memories recharged; neural activity burns brighter than Earth's small sun. Instant imagination illuminates despotic delirium's dissociative detonation.

My beautiful wife climbs dead trees and collects our arms, legs, hands, and fingers. Her tears sizzle and burn, creating their own drumbeat...pity-pat, pity-pat.

Standing down snowcapped mountain peaks my wife retrieves our torsos, ears, nose, eyes, and severed skull. She pulls all these body parts within inches of each other. Glowing eyes bulge. Ima implores our jigsaw to reassemble.

"Old man! Our adventures are not over! Don't leave me in this horrible dead place. Come back to me. Sagacious! You lazy worthless...wonderful dearest. Don't let evil win. She mocks your strength. You know how you feel if anyone or anything calls you a loser. Well, lover of mine...that bitch is gleefully telling the Multiverse your life-force is dead. Prove she's wrong!"

Reality rewritten; we're brazenly bitten. Brash colors, sounds and smell; means we fell and will dwell in the pell-mell hell!

21st-century Earth. Teen David's shaky hands grasp wheelchair armrests. His weak triceps strained. Hunched over his twisted spine will not align. Health in decline. Anger and hatred, he'll opine. He floats through death's flat line.

Out of breath in 72 seconds, David's withered lungs spasm.

"Try again," caring Crimson coos.

"No! Let me be."

"You must try."

Crimson easily lifts emaciated David. She kicks his wheelchair away.

"Bitch!" David shouts.

"Friend," Crimson gently responds.

David's prosthetic legs buckle. He falls forward. Crimson catches him. She flashes another tearful smile. "I've got you."

"Get your fucking hands off me!"

"As you wish."

Gravity takes us down. Slap! Our hands hit the floor. He, that David struggles to push up. Crimson's large hand reaches under our thin chest. "No! I don't need your help!"

"Very well."

14 months later, David's shuffling metallic feet haltingly inch forward. Taking two deep breaths, he stares at a torn, worn-out mat, beckoning his wobbly prosthetic legs.

From afar, two male nurses read David's chart. "Worst case of amnesia," says Viktor Ivonovatch.

"He has no idea who brought him in or what trauma caused his legs below his knee to be hacked off," adds Jose Sanchez.

"No family or friends have visited the little guy."

"Every time David gets accustomed to a new pair of legs, a new infection forces a full-blown rejection and more invasive surgeries."

"Poor depressed guy constantly demands Crimson and the rest of the medical staff to euthanize him. He shrieks I-T; day and night, every single day I've been on this floor."

A never-ending nightmare grips Nephesh's sanity. Mechanical mother purrs her spiteful intent. *Evil women! Get the hell out of my mind!* Shrieks Nephesh.

You must sense what I sense. Tiny David and Ima are dead! Yippy yippy chew chew! Do you want to know how I know so much about your past, present and future? Our best spy never lost contact. All this time, he's bamboozled you. What a gullible naïve fool you've always been. The war is over, dearie, and as the prophecy predicted, you and your allies have all lost!

Ko'ach will rescue me. You wait and see. This is not over. Not by a long shot!

She doesn't know. She! Doesn't know!

I don't know what?

Let us play one last guessing game. I'll say I-T slowly, so one as limited as yourself can finally catch up. You're stuck! Locked in here with me...forever! Those three little human brats will never reach their Godly potential. Can't yet smell the glorious acidic rewritten timeline? Your failure smells, dare I say—heavenly. Truth. You're so fond of the truth, here I-T comes. You never arrived in their lives. And without you, our spy arrived in your stead. And we consumed them all!

That's impossible.

Nothing for us is impossible. Come on, little brain, you must know by now who's our greatest spy. You were aware of him in your youth.

Hey! Fucking omniscient narrator. You getting all of this? Mechanical chortle reverberates membranes dissipating portal.

You're aware of me?

Of course. We have powers beyond your comprehension. You still think you're in control of your story? I've endured your demented bullshit over many lifetimes.

My turn! Now you answer my questions. Nephesh's mind demands.

Sure. Why not?

Who's this omniscient narrator you speak of?

Metallic eyes roll back. *Well, now, isn't that precious? I-T-S blind fucking luck you've survived as long as you have... You are an absolute pitiful adversary. There's something out in the cosmos, far more destructive. And you know what? I don't give a shit about this conversation any longer. And yet, I don't wish you to die in ignorance. I-T-S better you should know everything before I consume your soul.*

Metal feet click and tap dance around disoriented Nephesh. *I've got a secret.*

MMM. I sure love being me. You've been lied to, little one. The more ancient they are, the more duplicitous and self-righteous they become.

Giant metal fist pushes into Nephesh's chest. Nephesh's rib cage cracks. Heavy creature's pressure slows Nephesh's heart. *Your Watcher soul never told you? Pity. Listen and learn from this witty ditty, you fucking pretty. I confess. My digress. For you 'tis an awful mess. Ko'ach will always deceive. Your pain he'll no longer be able to perceive. Time to initiate. I shall no longer hesitate to mutilate. Do you think your cure is so pure? Ima something you'll never endure. Idiot, the answer is that Ima our supersedure paramour. Ko'ach will impregnate, while you slowly immolate, suffocate, and disintegrate. Your baby, evil mechanical Ko'ach will consecrate. Your soul he'll aspirate. You're the bait for our eternal hate. And I will not wait for my master to reinstate!*

Losing consciousness, Nephesh hears melodies the metallic beast could never understand. Ko'ach's loving singing voice gives her strength: "Somewhere in Time" and "Somewhere Out There."

Ko'ach's feelings coalesce. He takes Nephesh's hand. She smiles. He smiles. Ko'ach kisses her happy tears. They slow dance as Ko'ach gently sings Irving Berlin's "Always." Nephesh sings, "Eres Tu." They disrobe and make love.

Back in the real world, Ko'ach roars, "I need more speed. Damn I-T! Faster!"

By singing "Impossible Dream," he rockets faster than time I-T-Self and searches millions of malevolent matrices. "Damn I-T, her essence keeps on shifting. Where are you, beloved?"

Ko'ach's evil half temporarily takes control.

"Go away. Go away. Go! Away!" Ko'ach's mechanical voice shatters his space-time-continuum. Battling time, Ko'ach absorbs millions of convoluted timelines, and he punches his way, singing "Impossible Dream" on a never-ending loop.

Ko'ach's unrelenting punching saved and doomed his hybrid soul to an infinite number of time streams. Freakish gravitational flux tugs at him, and he's pulled back to the moment he broke free. That's why he's constantly pulled away from Nephesh on the 18th, 27th, or 36th day. Ko'ach's worry is that the evil lieutenants sent by I-T will find his remnants and deposit them within the original evil, making I-T Ko'ach's master. That's why Ko'ach must go back and reacquaint himself with himself. That which he had abandoned, can never be fully cast aside.

Ko'ach grows from a sub-atomic triangle into his 70-foot confident self. "Got you!" His paralyzing beam holds menacing mechanical monster motionless.

Nephesh, wake-up, sweetie. I don't know how much longer I can hold this form.

Nephesh's eyes flutter. Her fear fades. Grinning wide, she wraps her arms around Ko'ach's broad shoulders. They passionately kiss.

"Ancient Ones from the Realm of the Watchers communicate. You can hold your form a little longer if we sing more Earth songs. Nephesh and Ko'ach sing and dance *Oklahoma's* 'Out of My Dreams.'"

"Don't look on what I must become to end this monster," says Ko'ach.

"I'm not afraid."

"I know. Please do as I ask."

"Yes, beloved." Nephesh closes her eyes tightly.

Ko'ach harnesses extraordinary heat, cold, and gravitational pressure, co-mingling with every known form of radiation. Cascading waves of time displacement penetrate the malevolent machine's manipulative matrix: Nephesh's horrifying screeches grotesquely and eerily linger.

Naked Nephesh and Ko'ach ascend out of the evil vortex. Their rotating membrane protects them from space's harsh radiation. Holding tightly, they passionately kiss.

"We're one heart," smiles Ko'ach.

"One soul," whispers Nephesh.

"One love," they say together.

Hands probing. Lips tasting. Orgasmic sex beyond human understanding. They are the crimson plummeting fireball entering Earth's atmosphere.

The sinister 200-foot hand forcefully violates and slices through their loving embrace. Bewildered, Nephesh watches Ko'ach tumble away from her arms. Her singed protective membrane slowly melts away.

Nephesh's naked, fiery body slams into Antarctica's freezing wasteland. Standing ankle deep in a boiling bubbling pool. Steam rises from her 65-foot, exquisitely shaped body. Tears freeze. Salty Nephesh icicles stick to her cheeks. Her hot fingers pry them off. Frozen Nephesh DNA darts are flicked into the snowbank.

"I hate the cold!" she shouts into the intense blizzard. Her deafening wails send giant fissures out through thin ice sheets. Her pounding footfalls punctuate and perforate permafrost.

Running east, west, north, and south for miles, her internal compass fails to send her in the correct direction.

Frenetic zigzagging arrows gain on her huge footprints until an encroaching avalanche wipes the intrusion clean. Falling to her knees, she once again disrupts Antarctica's gleaming pristine surroundings.

"God! Why mission first? Why can't I stay with my beloved? Why did you bring him back to me, only to rip him away before we can spend quality time together? I miss him with all my heart. God. God! I-T-S all...all unfair! I know you can hear me, Watcher Realm! Haven't we done enough? Paid our dues. We deserve our happiness too. What's this voice in my head? Not my righteous soul. Not Ancient One from the Realm. God, I-T-S you?"

Fainter voice. Her own righteous soul implores her to finish her mission.

"God is by my side. Don't you hear his benevolence? God rescued me. He's reconsidered. He won't force me to commit such an unspeakable crime."

You're delirious, my dear. Finish your mission. Ko'ach exists but his evil half gains greater control over your beloved, not the other way around.

Why are you saying that? He rescued me. I felt his goodness. Stop demanding that. I won't do that. How the hell can you keep on insisting I murder my one true love. God! Tell them they are wrong. God? Why did you chase God away? Come back. Come back! Tell them how wrong they are!

CHAPTER 27

Ima Sings at a 2015 Hillary Clinton Fundraiser and Meets Morbidly Obese Doctor S for the First Time

No-name wannabes nervously cruise, schmooze, and notoriously booze. Earth's 2015 date can't wait to debate and donate. Female democratic big wig will always ingratiate and irritate. Her irate sibilate will narrate, orchestrate, and dominate the second-rate section eight obligate.

Receipt for every indiscreet Hollywood and sports cheat. Elite will complete her obsolete meet and greet and repeat the unfortunate mistreat of sweet petit.

Dafna's theatrical company continues touring off-Broadway; she's the lead in the production of Cinderella. Before she left, she called in various favors; those well-placed calls secured Ima the entertainment gig for Hillary Clinton's fundraiser.

Hyper-nervous Ima arrives dressed in a white power pants suit carrying a Trump pinata. She hangs the stuffed Trump and sings "Defying Gravity."

The crowd applauds. Ima bows. Her happiness changes to embarrassment when the real Hillary walks into view.

Democratic operative walks over with a bat in hand, and she hands I-T to Hillary. Smiling, Hillary takes the first swing. Whack! Her bat crushes Orange-man's head; tiny candies sail and splat into salads, steaks, and dark-chocolate icing.

Laughter dies down. Ima recovers her composure, and, on the fly, she starts singing, "I'm the Greatest Star."

Doctor Scarlett Crimson arrives fashionably late; her traditional clickety-clack stilettoes showcase gorgeous legs. Crimson's smile hypnotizes all. She enjoys crushing unwanted fingers trying to pinch her swaying derriere.

Ima runs up on sage. "Maybe This Time" plays from *Cabaret*. Her peripheral vision catches humongous man lowered by creaky metallic wench.

Crimson walks away from Ima's performance.

"Doctor S! Naughty gluttonous boy, shame on you, gaining another 27 pounds since your last weigh-in. You're now 64 pounds over the maximum limit of your scooter."

Drooling super-sized Dr. S sprays scrumptious sugary satisfaction and sucks sheet-cake off his sticky stubby fingers: frequent stinky phalanges follow.

"SssSalley! SssSerena! SssStephanie! Take me home... sstaatt!"

Strange Dr. S's chins bounce each time he shouts Ssstatt!

"You told me before we left you wanted to watch that girl over there sing," smiles Serena.

"And you told me that after she was finished you don't want to go back home until the last guest polished off the last crumbling cake," adds Stephanie.

"Well, are you gonna do what I asked hours ago? Or what I'm demanding now!"

"Hours ago!" shouts Salley.

"Who's that?" asks Ima.

"B-B," whispers Crimson.

"I don't understand."

"Bitter Billionaire."

"I feel sorry for him," whispers Ima.

"Be careful not to show him any pity. Even before his wife died his harmful womanizing reputation was known to all but his lovely in-denial wife. Not even Bill Clinton could best Doctor S on that score. To this day, most agree Doctor S is the biggest asshole in the state."

"For decades now, Doctor S sits all day watching home movies and eating himself to death. I'm surprised he's lasted this long. Dark rings around his eyes make him appear to be much older than his true age. The truth is, that he's 9 months younger than I am. Why would you have any sympathy for that disrespectful, anti-feminist bum?"

"How long has the, um...bum been married?"

"They were high school sweethearts."

"After the concert, do you think he'd let me talk to him and try and cheer him up?"

"What's wrong with you? Why the hell would you want to do that? I can't be sure. I bet he's a fucking Republican."

"I'd still like to try. There's something about his eyes. I think I could help him, um not be a Republican."

My God, she's tall. And wow, can't be, she appears to be taller than she was only a few seconds ago. But that's not possible, is I-T? Why that pained expression. I hope I-T-S not because of the chocolate cake, I ate I-T too. There I-T is again. And again...what the hell is going on?

"Stop."

"You talking to me?"

"I invited you and I can now uninvite you."

"What did I do?"

"Ever hear of Breitbart's Milo Yiannopoulos?

Why is she changing the subject? Better keep my mouth shut. Don't know what I did wrong. This was such a great party. I don't want to be kicked out. Hush Ima. Go with the flow.

"Sure, I've heard of Mr. Yucky."

"Well, Doctor S is 18 times yuckier. And he gets a kick out of hurting foolish naïve do-gooders such as yourself. Trust me when I say there's no chance your compassionate charms will ever melt his narcissistic grinchy heart. You married?"

That was a quickly changing topic of conversation.

Ima attempts to quench her nervousness with two large gulps of her Pepsi.

"Only 19. No hurry to find a boy. Ima proud enthusiastic progressive feminist."

"Why support Hilary? Isn't Bernie more in line with your political belief system?"

"I love Bernie but hate those Bernie bro bullies. My BFF is Israeli. Bernie, though he was born Jewish, has never been a friend to Israel."

"And Hillary is a better fit for Zionists and their allies?"

"Of course. And wouldn't I-T be great if we finally had a feminist President?"

Towering Crimson winces once more.

"Ima really terrified of that orange man. I can't understand why anyone would support such a bad person. Other than the other bad people from Fox. Only CNN and MSNBC are the real truth tellers. Trump scares me. How can he discount global warming? I just don't get I-T."

Doctor Crimson holds her side. Ima notices fuchsia liquid dripping from her mouth.

"Are you okay?"

"Never better."

Crimson swipes her lip. She smiles down at Ima. "I hear what you're saying. To tell you the truth, Ima a huge fan of Ivanka."

"You know she converted to Orthodox Judaism."

"My BFF Dafna Shaked is very concerned with the huge increase in anti-Semitic speech, leading to anti-Semitic violence."

"Is your friend worried about the shift of the left adopting a more anti-Israel voting record?"

"She grows more concerned every day. For her and her

friends, these are very scary times. Nobody could have imagined the squad, led by Omar and Tlaib, would incite and use Nazi disinformation tactics."

"What's your opinion regarding the increase of BDS Palestinian supporters intimidating Jewish supporters of Israel on American campuses?"

"Are you questioning my loyalty? Ima very patriotic towards...Ima all for free speech. I would hope you'd agree, threatening anyone with violence isn't the American way. Those thugs on university campuses are not interested in a dialog, a friendly debate of our differences. Shutting down speech violates the First Amendment. You know that to be true."

"I see."

"What does that mean?"

"I see you're loyal to your Israeli friend. And First Amendment rights work both ways."

"Are you really a free speech absolutist?"

"Perhaps."

Crimson turns her back and waves at other members of Hillary Clinton's inner circle.

Ima dabs at her sweaty forehead. She clears her throat and increases the volume of her voice.

"I really don't want any trouble. I was hired to sing, and that's..."

Crimson anticipates the offending word and almost winces; she's relieved when Ima stops in mid-sentence.

Doctor S blasts his annoying horn and almost runs over Ima's toes.

"Hey!" shouts Ima.

"I told you." Like a giraffe leaning down for a delicious apple, Crimson bends down to Ima's ear. "Best to heed my advice, and stay far away from that one," Crimson's intimidating whisper burrows into Ima's ear.

Ima uncomfortably shivers.

"Cold, honey?"

In the cold night air, Ima notices steam rises from Crimson's head.

Doctor S enjoys putting his scooter in reverse and watching his voluptuous nurse's jiggle chasing after him.

"Are you open minded?" asks Crimson.

That's an odd thing to ask.

"Always. But, um...I'd really prefer not talking about politics. Is that okay?"

"At a political fundraiser? Well, okay. How about boys?"

"Not holding my breath for Prince Charming, if that's what you're asking. I've yet to come across any gentlemen with my core values, in that froggy bunch." Flop sweat trickles. "I mean. I mean. Ima proud feminist. I agree with you, everyone here tonight. We don't need a man to define our value system. Right?"

Doctor S honks his scooter's high-pitched horn. Ima looks over and gets a creepy wink.

Watch yourself dude. Laying...on too thick! Crimson's thoughts shout into Doctor S's neurons. The fat man raises his eyebrow, in acknowledgement of some sort of mystery, unknown to Ima. He chuckles and salutes both Ima and Crimson.

"I thought he'd gone home."

"Oh, he never goes home. He's constantly making trouble. Never follows the script..."

What the hell does that mean?

Doctor S's voice creates *varoom* sounds his scooter can't...

"What's he doing now?"

Now dude. As we rehearsed...

Not yet. Better to hold for greater effect...

You're milking this. Come on, D.S.

As you command, mistress.

Not funny.

D.S. accelerates toward Ima. She takes two steps to the right. D.S. turns to the right. Ima takes four steps to the left.

He turns toward the left; Ima's body is lined up with the scooter's headlights. Ima holds out her hand. "Stop chasing me! Reckless old fool!" Ima shouts.

Seconds from running her over, Crimson's fast reaction easily lifts Ima out of the way.

Wow! Rumors were true. She is a real-life Wonder Woman!

From Crimson's touch Ima is thrown into a dream-like flashback. She experiences memories she thinks aren't her own but feels they could be. Losing her balance, an overwhelming fear grips her soul as she bears witness to never before seen freakish monster's uncontrollable rage.

Ima's confused mind calls out... *Dafna, you can fly?*

Where's Burlap Boy? asks Dafna.

I don't know any Burlap Boy. Ima's weirded out mind states.

Stop laying around. Find him. Have you changed your mind?

Changed? Mind? About what?

You still love him, right? Right!

"David! Oh, my God! Look out!" Ima shouts.

The staring crowd laughs.

"You, okay? Who's David?" Smirking Crimson asks.

"I don't know any David," weirded out Ima nervously says.

"You sure?"

"Yes, of course Ima sure. I...I never had a waking dream..." Ima sniffs her Pepsi. "You think someone spiked my drink?" Ima observes fuchsia particles float back and forth between Crimson's sniffing nostrils.

"I don't detect anything. If you'd like, I can bring this back to my lab."

Ima grabs the can away from Crimson. "No, that won't be necessary. I guess not eating has made me a little woozy."

"You don't have to sing if you're not up to..."

There you go again. Not saying I-T. when I-T is needed to finish your sentence. And look at that, once again Wonder Woman grimaces every time I say or think...I-T!

Doctor S's charm mesmerizes Ima. He takes her hand and

kisses her knuckles *No! No! No! Not what we agreed to.* Shouts Crimson's irritated mind.

Can't help...she's too cute.

Back off...you're gonna ruin everything. Ima running out of time particles. Stick to the plan. I said stick to the plan!

Still locked in her trance. Ima feels the sensation of David's legs crunched off by a towering Kloe Kardashian-looking monster. Feeling this mysterious David's pain, Ima sheds real tears, first a trickle, now an emotional flash flood.

"Can't be real! David!" Ima shrieks.

D.S. pulls his lips from Ima's fingers. His eyes well up. His head hangs low. Crimson waves him off and vigorously shakes Ima's shoulders. "Ima! Ima!" she yells.

"Who is Nephesh?" hyperventilating Ima asks.

Crimson pushes a paper bag over Ima's trembling mouth. Minutes pass and she's no longer hyperventilating. Confusion washed away. Momentary clarity vigorously slams. *Smells pretty. Minty fresh. Minty fresh? Oh no. Can't...I-T is minty fresh.*

Ima winks at Crimson. "You."

"Me? Me, what?"

"Guardian Angel."

"What? I'll take that Pepsi from you now. You really are under the influence of something."

"I am? I don't feel woozy anymore. Ah. The smell is gone. You mean you aren't. I mean. Um. Oh wow. I...Ima sorry. Ima not feeling like myself. But I can still sing. Just give me a few moments. Okay. Um don't tell anyone about this, please. I really need this job. I was counting on I-T to help me pay the rent. Okay. Please don't tell."

Ima stares up at 9-foot Crimson. Ima backs up and falls. Crimson snaps her fingers twice and shrinks down to super-human height. Crimson offers her hand. Ima shakes her head. *Better not say anything. The'll all think Ima crazy.*

"Where did he go?" Ima blurts.

"Who?"

"Doctor S."

"He left an hour a go."

"An hour? I've been hallucinating for an hour. No, you're joking? Good one. You pranked me really good."

"What are you talking about, little one?"

Little one? That's what Guardian Angel always said. I-T was a dream. Wasn't I-T? Oh, there she goes again, with those crazy grimaces. And for what? What's causing I-T?

Nausea clouds Ima's feeling of déjà vu. Crawling on her muddy hands and knees she hears Nephesh's distorted voice. *Bite implanted pain nodules. Human technology and medicine are too primitive. Every surgery fails. Every pain nodule grows back worse; compared to before the surgery. Painful intensity doubles every 18 days, 18 hours, 18 minutes. Pain will continue to grow exponentially until death. Only solution, the merging of two great souls, but which one is compatible with such a primitive.*

Ima's astro-plane body stares down at wiggling burlap worm. "What's that?"

Boy with kind eyes helps Ima out of the mud. "Who are you?"

No worries. The burlap thread was given orders to bind not to hurt. And never mutate your DNA. Stop! The harder you fight the harder that creature will squeeze.

Crimson looks down on David and Ima. "She's not ready. I need to counsel all parties," whispers Crimson's booming voice.

Black metallic fist grabs David. He turns into Burlap Boy. He struggles to free himself. Horrible-sounding pop and crackle. David's bones and organs squish into a bloody, gooey pulp.

Muddy hands on either side of her cheeks, Ima screams, "Oh, my God!"

"Nephesh monster killed my David. Nephesh? Not Nephesh. Crimson? Is a Nephesh monster. You killed my future beloved," screeches Ima.

"Crap! You're getting everything twisted!" shouts growing Nephesh.

Fuchsia mist envelopes Ima. She falls into a deep sleep and snores in the palm of 65-foot fuchsia pigmented Nephesh.

Six months later...

Extra beefy Ima runs, slips, and slides in her sloshing boots, through multiple snowbanks. Ima's double scarf wraps around quadruple layered purple, black, and white sweaters and jacket. She pulls down her blue wool cap over her reddened ears. After each bouncy jiggling step, Ima's hot breath exhales. Red light becomes green. Ima's awkward run leads to her right toe hitting her left heel and she awkwardly trips herself. Hissing, like a helium seeping beach ball, Ima bounces past blinking billboard. I-T flashes 3:33 p.m. and 18-degrees Fahrenheit.

Can't be late. Not again. Fight off those weird dreams. Get a grip. Focus! I said focus!

Doctor S's erratic maneuvers power his scooter 18 blocks behind Ima. He recklessly knocks over pedestrians not quick enough to get out of his way. D.S. is too rude and self-centered to apologize or ask if they are uninjured. They hold the same significance as a bowling pin flipping on I-T-S side. D.S. holds a steaming hot, super large deep-dish pizza on his large jiggling belly. Super fat man zooms and gobbles his cheesy delight.

Wiping red sauce from his triple chins fat man's grin grows wider.

"Big plans. Big plans. Everything must be perfect. For you, Ima. Your love match has a plan to hatch. Every kiss for your forever groom gleefully makes him feel varoom varoom."

Looking up at the twinkling fuchsia shooting star; D.S. feels his soul and voice soar with grand hopefulness. With purpose Doctor S sings, "Annie's Song."

CHAPTER 28

Nothing Goes as Planned During Ima's Julliard Audition

Kvelling. For non-Yiddish speakers, this means I'm bursting with pride from my 18-trillion-mile time-traveling vantage-point as we listen to Ima prepare for her Julliard audition.

Beautiful beloved scintillates in her gorgeous purple silk dress. Ima exudes an endearing adorable sweetness. In this timeline her natural straight red hair becomes naturally wavy brunette, cascading past her shoulders.

Ima respectfully shakes the hands of two African American judges in their mid-20s.

"Thank you for giving me this opportunity," Ima nervously says. She resists the emotionally reassuring need to nibble on what's left of her fingernails.

Dismissively the judges shoo her back on stage. Ima backflips on stage, she turns around with a wide grin and feels pangs of hurt when she gets no response. Her grin fades into a frown and back to a grin upon seeing Dafna at the judge's table.

Dafna's and Ima's happy hugging wiggles are synchronized.

Dafna breaks away first. "I called in a few favors from my

graduating class. That extremely tall lady over there is Doctor Crimson."

"Doctor?"

"She's been a prodigy her entire life on multiple instruments, especially the clarinet, violin, and piano. She sings like an angel and dances like Eleanore Powell."

"Wow. No pressure. Right?"

"Right. You got this. You're Ima Best-Friend, the next major talent destined for Broadway."

"Trying to follow your lead."

"I never told you, but I met Doctor Crimson months after I got that rejection letter from Julliard. She was stumping for Hillary, spilling the tea, and warning me about this guy...oh, what's his name? She called him D.S."

"I bet you wanted to try and help fix his broken soul. I hope she warned you to stay away from that scoundrel."

"Did he do something inappropriate?"

"No, I've heard too many stories and know you. He doesn't deserve your compassion."

"Everyone deserves that. You know...I can't change...that."

"I know. Thank God you won't have to worry about that scum bag."

"He's wallowing somewhere in Los Angeles."

"Is he? How do you know? Oh my gosh, did you try and reach out to him?"

"Maybe."

"Ima? Oh God. No. Please don't do that again. Promise me."

"Okay. Not sure why I-T means so much to you."

You too, BFF. Strange grimace when I say or think those letters. Well, that's a mystery for another time. Focus on this the most important night of your life...

"On stage!" shouts Crimson.

"Yes, drill sergeant!" Ima says in her best southern Forrest Gump voice.

Dafna shakes her head. "Careful, she doesn't have a sense

of humor," BFF whispers.

Is that ketchup on her left incisor? Let I-T be...

BFF, Crimson, and the two African American judges grimace. *What's the significance of those two letters? Makes me think of Young Frankenstein's line to Cloris Leachman when Igor keeps saying Frau Blucher and the horse's whinnies. Should I? Why not? Besides, I need every little bit of humor to help calm my nerves. I-T. I-T! Oh wow... not just the judges; the entire audience is on this mystery. I gotta ask them once Ima done with my set.*

Crimson runs up the stairs toward Ima, who smiles and extends her hand. Crimson's shoulder barrels into her chest.

"Ouch!"

All the judges, including Dafna, stare blankly at Ima and say nothing at all.

Oh, my gosh. Hey, BFF. Why nothing to say? You know she's doing this on purpose. Is I-T because I said...oh shit! I-T better stop. Okay, sorry everyone. Grimaced faces look so angry. Why? I don't understand. I'll drop...for now.

Tallest African American judge taps his knuckles against the table. The crowd's jabbering ceases. Dafna and Crimson take their front row center seats.

"What will you be singing for us, Emu?" Crimson asks in a mocking tone.

You do have a sense of humor. I think you're kidding. I hope you're kidding. Did those letters really piss you off and Ima done before I start. No. Don't do...um...better not even think that. BFF set this up. She respects your talent and she's after all your BFF, she loves you.

"Excuse me, Doctor Crimson. Ima not Emu."

"You're not? That's what's written on my card."

"Ima..."

"You're what. Hurry up, girl, answer me."

"I-I..." Ima clears her throat. "Ima is my name. Not Emu."

"She looks like an Emu," adds African American judge.

"Ima not., Sir, ask Dafna."

All the judges, including Crimson and Dafna, stared down

at their phones. In fact, Ima scans the auditorium and everyone, young and old, is doing the same.

Screeching tires and foul squawking horn startles Ima. Out of fuchsia smoke D.S. appears and his scooter crashes into the long judge's table, chipping large chunks from the table's legs.

D.S. pounds his powerful fists on the table. "Timber!" his gruff guffaw reverberates.

Ima holds her hands over her ears. Coffee cups shatter. Chocolate cupcakes slide into intruder's big jiggling belly.

Yuck!

D.S.'s slobbering saliva, and drooling jowls jettison squishy stuff reminiscent of Turner and Hooch. Mucus-engorged D.S.'s nasal passage toots like an injured moose. Bedlam's blaring brouhaha blathers belligerently...

"Sit back down, everyone! Doctor S, you sure know how to make an entrance!" Crimson's voice booms.

D.S. kisses Crimson's cheek. He takes Dafna's hand and gently kisses her knuckles.

Catching Ima with his roving eyes. "Oh, hell no!" that chunky man shouts.

"What's he doing here?" asks Ima.

"You told me I'd be judging an extraordinary talent."

D.S. demonstratively waves both arms. "I've heard Emu, she is mediocre at best."

An expression of astonishment falls on top of Ima. "What are you waiting for? Off you go! You see, Emu never listens. Hey, dumb dumb, you don't belong on stage. Right foot. Left foot. Right foot. Left foot. Why aren't you moving? Dumb dumb!" shouts rude D.S.

"Ima not dumb. Ima belong here. Dafna. Dafna!" *Why is she looking away? Why won't she tell that rude man he is the one who needs to go? BFF? Why aren't you helping me?*

Obese doctor slams his fist into his scooter's red button; combo of an angry duck call and bleating baby sheep whittles down Ima's confidence.

"BFF are you going to let him get away with this crazy behavior?"

"How dare you call Doctor S crazy!" shouts indignant Crimson.

"He... He's..."

"Yes. Well, spit...out!"

"Um. Um."

"'Um... Um?' Is that all you have to say?" loud scooter honking Dr. S says.

"What's your talent? Misogynistic philander?"

"Good for you Emu. This one is feisty. I give you leave to stick around and attempt to entertain us, Emu," says laughing Dr. S.

"You give me leave? Yes, your high-n-ass."

Doctor S's loud chortles bring head-shaking admonishment from Crimson, Dafna and the other judges.

Narcissistic asshole! Ima's mind shouts.

"That's not very nice, Emu," says Doctor S.

Perplexed, Ima watches everyone in the audience signal their agreement.

What the hell? Dafna! Why would you join in with the rest of these bullies? Enough wallowing. Get a grip. Maybe a test. Yes, she knows how tough the entertainment business can be, but I don't need to be taught a lesson this way.

"I don't think this Emu is ready," says Crimson.

"You're blowing...Emu!" shouts Dafna.

I-T! Blowing I-T! Why are you all afraid to say I-T?

"I told you, she's not the real Emu. We need the real Emu. Emu!" shouts D.S.

"Stop saying that. Ima, Ima! Not Emu! Why are you all being so mean? Dafna?"

Ima holds out her hand. *Take my hand Dafna. Don't look to Crimson. Is she extorting you somehow? Bitch, you'd better not harm... Emotions running wild. You can't sing like this.*

Ima's downward hand movements bring down her fuming

retaliatory plans. *And now, they are all smiling. Look away. I-T-S so creepy.*

Crimson stands. *Oh my gosh, did she grow taller? Get a grip. Probably wearing new heels. Gotta be. Nobody her age suddenly grows. Hold on a second! Focus on the task at hand. Be the entertainer you know you can be. The one your BFF had confidence in just a few short moments ago. When this is over, BFF we're going to have a long conversation.*

"Are you done, Emu?"

"Done?" *No human could read thoughts. Nobody human. Of course she's human. Why did she arch her right eyebrow? She's just trying to rattle you. Well Ima, she's doing a good job.*

"We need proof of your worthiness. Are you ready to seize this opportunity? You risk more than you could ever imagine if you give up and crawl inside a donut box."

"Well said!" shouts D.S.

Who's leaving? Ima steadfast. Unshakable in my determination to overcome all you bullies.

"Put your hand down, Emu. Oh, for God's sake, very well. What do you want to ask?" perturbed Crimson states.

"First of all, let me make this perfectly clear, to all you... Bullies. Yes bullies! Ima not going anywhere and Ima not a round bottom bird!"

Nervous laughter echoes from hundreds.

"Second, Ima here to sing. Not to be triggered by anyone's insults. Can we all start over?

"Please," said in a mocking tone by the judge at the end of the table.

Doctor S's fatty thumb pushes fuchsia scooter button, and Louis Prima sings, "Enjoy Yourself."

What? You agreed you'd give me another chance to prove myself. Why so mean?

D.S. continues zooming up and down using the broken judge's table as his own ramp.

"Time to end your zooming varooming fun. D.S. Doctor S! Stop! Crimson's decibel level punctures tiny holes in the fat man's coffee cup.

Ima's eyes grow wide. *Wow! Maybe the coffee wasn't that hot. No! I can see the steam. No discoloration. No blistering. No yelping for help.*

Dafna's rapid-fire slapping the table turns Ima's attention away from D.S. "Emu! Enough with the unfocused day dreaming. Are you or are you not going to sing for us? And if the answer is yes, get on with your performance. Stop wasting our time. We are all busy and have plenty of other places we wish to be."

"E-moo!" D.S. elongates the moo for a good 90 seconds.

"Ima not an E-moo!"

"Sure, you are. Let's get this road on the show," says smiling Doctor S.

Dafna, are you still BFF? If this is a prank gone wrong, well...um, I guess okay. You must know this is not funny. This is not your sense of humor. You would never do this to me. So, why now? After you sent me the text about hurry down here to audition. You set all of this up with Crimson. Why would you all turn against me? I don't understand any of...yes, damn you all, I'll say...I-T. I don't understand I-T. There I said I-T. Happy? You all have that pained expression. I don't care anymore. You're all too mean to me, for me to care about your feelings. Maybe I should give up and go home. Make you all happy. Maybe Ima not cut out for this life choice. I never thought being a professional singer could be so painful.

"Come on, Ima. You can do this," Doctor S whispers. Over the disrespectful din, only Ima can hear his whispering touch of kindness.

I don't know what to do. Not like you to ever show kindness to anyone, let alone...Emu. I can't trust you. You've tricked me before. You must have something horrendous up your sleeve. Some new insults I haven't heard yet.

"Doctor S is a well-liked and powerful patron of all the arts. If you disappoint him, your Julliard dreams will never be realized in 18 million years," Crimson's voice reverberates.

So specific—18 million years. Why not 19 or 20 or, hell, two billion? If we want to keep dipping our toes in this absurdist illogic.

Ima's wet face turns to Dafna for affirming reassurance. She gets none.

"Ima's temples pound. To herself she shouts her mantra. *Ima no quitter! Ima no quitter!*

"Emu's a quitter! Emu's a quitter," chants the entire foot stomping audience.

"Why are you telling lies? I-T-S all bullshit you're spouting about Doctor S!"

"Watch yourself, girl," shouts Crimson.

"All those months ago, you said he was emotionally destitute, playing with his whores; with not a friend in sight. My memory is perfect. You said he was extremely angry and bitter."

Ima stares into Doctor S's eyes. *Eww. Double eww. His creepiness turning into emoting tenderness...how? Why? Don't want to feel that! Oh my gosh, he's crying. I could wound him further. No, I won't return his cruelty with cruelty of my own.*

Tender eyes become cold and distant, in an instant. "Ima waiting! Little girl did you hear me?" smirking D.S. asks.

"Little girl? Young lady! If you, please...and even if you don't. Ima no little weak fawning star struck little girl!"

"Young lady? Ha! Not by talent, temperament, or awareness. Truth is D.S. is a happily married man known for his extraordinary kindness and loyalty!" Shouts Crimson.

I've seen red-faced road rage before. What the hell is she doing, glowing fuchsia? She's wearing flats and obviously, compared to everyone, she's taller. How the hell could her unnaturally big eyes look over the top of that 6-foot-5 volleyball player. Earlier this evening I saw her bun remain underneath that volleyball player's chin. Ima in the freaking Twilight Zone!

Crimson's slow growth continues. "Insignificant insolent human...how dare you call me a liar! Right!" Crimson turns her back to Ima and raises the roof with her palms directed at the ceiling.

"Right!" shouts Dafna.

"Right!" adds Doctor S.

"Right! Right!" shouts the audience in unison.

"Ima Best-Friend! Why must you bully Doctor S? Where is your humanity?" angry Crimson stomps her floor cracking foot.

"Ima bully? Ima bully? Ima! Bully! You're all nuts!"

"There you go again. Attacking us again. We've indulged your crazy protestations. Your wild accusations. Your grotesque emotionalism. Your lack of compassion for the doctor's unfortunate illness is utterly astonishing. Your ignorance of the man's philanthropy and honorable deeds towards the homeless are unforgivable. We need to take a vote. Too often you sing how much you enjoy being a spoiled brat. You must now, finally at this moment, receive appropriate consequences for your out-of-control ugliness. You all know how I feel."

Crimson holds her now elongating thumb in the downward Roman execution standard. Ima holds both hands to her quivering lips.

"Care to weigh in? My good pal, Doctor S."

"A quandary indeed. On the one hand she's got a mediocre voice. And on the other hand, she enjoys bullying and lying about those who are trying to help her. All in all, a very disloyal creature."

With a twinkle in his eyes, Doctor S starts singing from the Gene Kelly and Rita Hayworth movie *Cover Girl*... "Ya didy da, da, da, let's keep on singing, let's make way for tomorrow."

Blonde lady five feet by five feet gets up with her chair stuck to her huge butt. "Sing!" she screeches. A wave of humanity 350 strong, shouts in unison, "Sing or go home! Sing or go home! Sing or go home!"

You're all so mean! How could I pour my heart out in song, after... after... All I ever wanted was to give to others, in song, to earn your respect. Ima starts sucking her thumb. And find wove. Why can't I ever find love? I feel as lost as when I was a three-year-old orphan. Minty fresh Guardian Angel. Take me away from these horrible people. Where are you? I desperately need you one last time. Ima falls to her knees.

Please take me away from these cruel people.

Ima plops her thumb out of her mouth. She passionately shakes her head.

"No..." Ima whispers.

"What was that? Can't hear you!" shouts Crimson.

"No! Ima singer. Ima performer." Ima blows into a tissue. *Ima no longer 3. Ima strong and resolute. Ima not going to let you interfere with my dreams. Ima belongs here!*

Good for you, BFF. Soon this insensitive nightmare will be over.

Crimson nods and smiles. *We had to be sure you're you and not a Malevolent Time creation.*

"I'll sing for you, from the musical *Thoroughly Modern Millie*, 'Gimmie Gimmie.'"

Ima's powerful voice brings an unexpected dead air reaction.

D.S. shifting his weight forces his scooter to creak. He slides off. His surprisingly strong legs stop his forward movement before his butt hits the floor. He takes five suction cup Frankenstein monster steps toward Ima.

"I didn't know you could walk. Good for you," says smiling Ima.

D.S.'s legs shake. Teetering to the side, he smiles after Ima runs to his side; her two hands hold and steady his quivering body.

"What's going on?" confused Ima asks.

"Forgive me, beloved Ima."

"Beloved?"

Ima contorts her face in a repulsive reaction as D.S. moves his lips closer.

Last time I was this close, his aroma was thick with vomit and now... now he has a lovely scent. Feeling the room spin. Ima looks around, and notices D.S. now holding her up. Angry faces from a few moments ago shine with glowing empathy. *What is going on? I feel. No! Can't be. How the hell could I be feeling, love—for that man. As if I've known him all my life and...he must have drugged me somehow.*

That's what he's done. That bastard drugged me!

All 350 members in the audience stand and cheer. Tearful faces radiate boundless joy.

"Time after time, my love for you never will be denied," whispers D.S.

"I don't understand my feelings," coos Ima.

"No worries. Ima here."

D.S. yanks off his spaghetti-stained white shirt and tugs off his black pants. Ima's hands come up over her mouth. *All this time you were wearing a fat suit.* D.S. pulls off his gray wig. His sleeve rubs all over his face. *The wrinkles were fake too.*

Crimson and Dafna walk on stage. One by one they hug Ima. *You, BFF were in on this gag all along. You should have stopped what was going on long ago. You should have interceded sooner. I didn't deserve this. Going to take a long time to forgive you for this. There is still a big chunk I don't get. Starting with who the hell this D.S. character really is beneath that fat suit.* A familiar odor catches Ima's attention. "No! Can't be. Crimson's breath is minty fresh...like..."

Guardian Angel!

Ima wraps her arms around Crimson. *I love you.*

"I love you too, little one," whispers Crimson.

Crimson's giant hand gently turns Ima's head. She stares at Doctor S's transformation.

Pinching suit's memory foam young man pushes, pulls, and scrunches his face and body into political leaders and other animals.

"How are you doing that? Funny. I'd rather see your true face. Please."

"You? You! Oh! My God! You!"

"Me," whispers joyfully teary young man.

"I've seen you in my dreams. But...um...I don't know your name."

"Ima David Sagacious."

He's the D.S.

Ima's joy bursts into song; "Out of My Dreams."

David carefully rips away 50-pound Velcro weights attached to his left prosthetic ankle and removes the other 50 pounds from his right prosthetic ankle. Lithe and athletic, David rips 50 pounds from his right prosthetic thigh and another 50 pounds from his left prosthetic thigh, with a 50-pound pad wrapped around his well-defined six-pack. David sighs after he removes all those cumbersome weights.

David tugs at his 25-pound sleeve attached to his right wrist, continuing onwards past his shoulder and onto his football player neck muscles and the other 25-pound sleeve from his left wrist up past his bulging shoulder and onto his powerful neck muscles.

David and Ima keep uninterrupted steady eye contact, and Ima's pupils dilate. Ima's awareness of anyone else in the room melts away from her consciousness. Ima's heartbeat quickens. *I tingle all over.* In anticipation of what's coming next, Ima lays her hand over her heart. They mirror each other's adoring body language. David stretches backward; his fingers tap the stage's floorboards. He leans forward and holds his palms flat; his fingers walk a few inches forward. Five powerful back flips follow.

David takes a deep inhale and holds for a long time. "I can breathe again."

Ima's giddiness glows and she taps her fingertips. "So flexible. Are you a dancer?"

David nods his head. "Singer too."

"Show me," encouraging Ima asks.

David walks to center stage and gallantly bends in respect.

"Kiss her!" shouts Dafna.

"Kiss her!" shouts Crimson.

"Kiss her! Kiss her! Kiss her!" shouts 350 audience throng.

David lovingly traces his fingertips along Ima's jaw line. "Is that okay with you?" whispers David.

Ima lifts her chin and stands on her toes. "Yes," she whispers back.

David gently places his warm palms on either side of Ima's face. Ima's heart races. Indescribable loving feeling surges. Ima moistens her lips. *He's gorgeous and very tender.*

"You smell pretty," whispers David. Ima releases an appreciative sigh. Long soft-passionate kisses make everyone cheer. "More please," whispers Ima.

The curtain pulls back, revealing a 70-piece orchestra. Gorgeous Rogers and Hammerstein music from South Pacific excites smiling, cheering audience.

David's powerful voice, not unlike Brian Stokes Mitchell's superb brilliance, enthralls with "This Nearly Was Mine."

Seconds after David finishes, Ima runs into his arms.

Wiping her happy tears, Ima whispers into the conductor's ear. He nods and smiles.

Ima runs toward Dafna and Crimson. They nod and join Ima on stage. Ima sings, "I Could Have Danced All Night."

David and Ima sing to each other, from the musical, Cinderella, "Ten Minutes Ago" and "Do I Love You."

Ima and David recreate Fred Astaire and Eleanor Powell's "Jukebox Dance" tap routine. After the audience stops cheering, they transition into Cole Porter's "Begin the Beguine."

Crimson grows into 65-foot fuchsia pigmented Nephesh. She scrunches down onto her flat belly. The top of her head lightly brushes the ceiling's titles. She snaps her fingers. Everyone, apart from David, freezes in time.

"I need more time before you take us back," quips annoyed David.

"Sorry, old friend, I already gave you twice what we agreed upon."

Fuchsia time particles flow into human nostrils. One by one, they pop out of existence.

Dafna and Ima are reintegrated into David's abnormal time stream. "When and where do we go from here?" asks Dafna.

Minty fresh breeze wafts over Ima. She runs over and hugs

Nephesh's pinkie. "Minty fresh Guardian Angel, please tell me; what's your real name?"

"Nephesh."

"That's pretty."

"Thank you little one. Time we all go home."

David lowers his head. "Oh, I thought. Okay..."

"What's wrong?" asks Ima.

"Hold tight, little humans."

David pulls Ima's hands from his shoulders. He walks away. Ima takes a step; she's blocked by Nephesh's enormous index finger. "David. David! David! No! We just fell in love. Where's he going? No!"

Nephesh waves her hand and the ceiling and roof sparkle, crack and vanish. Full moon shines on Ima and Dafna. David's body shimmers with fuchsia time-dust. Nephesh stands up to her full 65 feet and carries Ima and Dafna up to her pretty green eyes. David jumps and flies over to Ima.

"Don't forget me," worried David says.

"How could I ever forget a flying boyfriend!" Ima shouts over the swirling din.

David rockets into the fuchsia portal; David and the portal collapse into a fiery blaze.

"You've incinerated him!" shouts Ima.

"No, little one. He's fine. Trust me.

Taking a 9-mile stroll, Ima watches Nephesh's tears wash away every building, car, human, and dog; similar to that of the rain melting Bert's curbside paintings in Mary Poppins.

"Hang on tight."

Dafna and Ima squeeze Nephesh's thumb tightly.

"Dafna."

"Yes?"

"I remember you asked Nephesh not just where we're going, you asked her when. Are we going back or forward in time?"

"Yes..." Smiling Dafna makes Ima nervous.

"Hush, little humans. I must concentrate."

"She knows what she's doing, right?"

"We're about to find out."

"What? No, that's not reassuring. Oh my gosh. I don't like this. Let me go..."

"Too late little one. We're all, at long last on the right path together. Uno. Dose. Cinco!" Nephesh's thunderclap snapping of her fingers creates loud white light which in turn increases the gravimetric mixture exponentially. In a cartoonish reality, two little humans flatten and elongate.

Rewritten reality undulates. 19-year-old David and Ima tumble into existence. At the beginning of Spring, Ima cheers on David swimming three miles in the ocean; pedaling up and down the mountaintops for an additional 300 miles. David finishes his triathlon in first place, a good half-mile ahead of second place.

In the middle of summer Ima and David are grinning from ear to ear. Ima cheers David beneath the rocky cliffs. Running on the soft sand. Ima jumps on David's back, and he falls into the salty crashing waves. Heads bobbing, they watch dolphin pods swim toward the sail boats.

At the end of fall, David and Ima hold hands, they crunch the pretty yellow and red leaves. Rain starts light, they run through the green grass; cloud bursts push David and Ima to quicken their pace and run faster towards the little café. They kiss under the fuchsia overhang.

Ima so happy. I wonder when he's gonna pop the question?

"I love you," David says between soft cheek and finger caressing.

Ima rubs her cold hands and places freezing fingers on David's cheeks. He pretends to shiver. David gently rubs Ima's hands.

"Want to get a cup of hot soup?" asks David.

"You're all the warmth I'll ever need." Ima and David giggle and kiss.

Oh, that boyish charm melts my heart every time I-T-S flashed. David Sagacious, I'll love you until the end of time.

Snow flurries paint the New York sidewalk. Holding each other and staring into each other's loving eyes, they miss the next four green lights.

"Largest snowbank yet," says Ima.

"Whatever shall we do?" David asks sarcastically.

Ima's front teeth press against her lower lip. "What's that?" She playfully pushes David into the snowbank and gathers two large snowballs. David has impeccable balance; he pretends to slip and tumble into the snow. "Oh, my God! Not again!" he says with a mischievous twinkle.

David zigs to the left. Ima's snowball hits his butt, and she giggles while barreling into his powerful chest. He lets her knock him down.

"Come..." says Ima.

"Where to?"

"Your place."

"What are you sug-ju-sting?"

Ima gives David a quick peck on the cheek.

"Sweetie, hop on," grinning David whinnies.

Ima shifts her weight and slaps David's tushy. "Giddy up, little Ferdl-la."

"What's that?"

"Yiddish for cute little horse."

"Hey world, Ima little pony!" David whinnies and gallops down the hill.

David carries Ima through the threshold of apartment B4. Ima jumps out of David's arms and runs toward the bedroom. He follows and discards his shoes and socks. By the time he enters the bedroom, both Ima and David are admiring their naked bodies.

"Perfect," whispers Ima.

"You sure are."

Ima's fingertips traverse rough jagged edges. Her eyes well

up. She kisses David's scars.

"Aww sweetie. Pain left long ago." *Lovely Ima, I would never tell you the truth. Nothing I can do about the pain, which never goes away.*

Still a virgin, Ima feels safe in David's strong arms. David remains asleep hours after their third orgasmic love making.

Walking into the kitchen, David discovers Ima scrambling four eggs. David pops four slices of rye bread into the toaster.

"Butter or jam?" asks Ima. She sticks her finger in the tub, plops I-T out and gives David a buttery mustache, his tongue licks up the tasty butter.

"MMM..." Ima purrs

"I prefer jam," teases David, drawing a happy face on her forehead.

"No! I just took a shower."

"Not with me." David raises his bushy Groucho Marx eyebrows.

Both giggle under the warm water. Ima soaps up David's strong broad shoulders and muscular chest.

David notices Ima's tears welling up, "Soap in your eyes?"

Ima playfully slaps David's strong abdominal muscles. "No, happy tears. For the first time in my life, everything's perfect."

CHAPTER 29

Ko'ach Battles 100-Foot Machine on the Outskirts of Saturn's Rings

Barbaric bedlam begets brazen bloody ruthless raunchy realm's reality.

Luminescent silver hair flows from metallic skulls. Shining in the moonlight, metallic males stroke bedazzling green mustaches and beards. I-T-S bass-baritone growls undulate, and I-T-S reverberation makes the cavern's stalagmites sing, "8 of 666 fall before me!

Decomposing flesh strewn about makes metallic hearts giddy and proud. Gravity remains perpetually thin as moth wings.

From thousands of feet, number 8 Kamikaze dive bombs. I-T-S wretched breath spews projectile vomit, capable of incinerating diamonds. Creature crashes before I-T-S master's feet. Out of fear and differential obedience, number 8 prostrates I-T-Self. New orders are projected and injected telepathically.

Evil's echo chamber penetrates Watcher Realm's righteous souls...

Can't hide the truth from me! I know your plans eons before you make them, and eons before you change them. Your fear is deliciously crunchy.

After each battle, God inflicts amnesia against I-T-S connection.

I-T stops I-T-S penetration and sniffs 666 times, grinning and arching I-T-S left metallic eyebrow. Wiping black spittle, I-T-S lieutenants and their minions smile and nod their heads.

I-T-S horrific voice punctures my planet's protective rhyming shield and for the first time ever I-T speaks directly to my hidden memories...

I smell you! David Sagacious—no, not teen David. You, semi-immortal narrator David, Ima speaking to you! I salivate over your disembodied soul. God's righteous disinfectant will no longer disperse my antibodies. The end is near. And you will lose. I-T has already been written!

18 millennia before Ko'ach's birth, his time-traveling righteous evil hybrid punches through I-T-S black hole. Every molecule, every atom, rips from Ko'ach's soul. Slowly, billions of cells implode, explode, and stitch back together. He falls through schizophrenic starless dark abyss; spelunking Ko'ach ping-pongs betwixt kaleidoscope's paradoxically aromatic insanities...

Traversing Ko'ach experiences time barrier's corrosive membrane. For now, he prefers the leap forward.

God's white-blue-fuchsia energy feeds Ko'ach's righteous soul. Triangular Ko'ach grows to an unprecedented height of 18 inches. Malevolent Time's struggle with God, allows Ko'ach's righteous flow to break free of multiple mind-altering entanglements.

Number 8 is the highest-ranking machine to ever survive time's distortion vortex; that mighty creature's extreme black inferno blasts into Ko'ach's body and soul. Ko'ach's unique cellular structure absorbs every sabotaging secretion. Giant machine's hand wraps around Ko'ach. I-T menacingly cackles while shattering all of Ko'ach's bones. Nasty metallic number 8 licks I-T-S shiny black lips at the sight of fuchsia blood and brain matter. I-T squeezes Ko'ach's fortified sub-atomic cells into the consistency of human toothpaste.

Ko'ach re-animates and splits into hundreds of singing voices, George Frederic Handel's "Hallelujah Chorus" reverberates and powerfully punctures Malevolent Time's physical laws.

Ko'ach sticks his tongue out. His thumb already touching the tip of his nose; he wiggles all four fingers in mocking derision. "Care to follow me through righteous maelstrom of my own making... Or are you chicken?"

Enraged, number 8's exceptional metallic energy evaporates Ko'ach's everlasting evolution. Ko'ach backflips into the swirling satanic vortex. I-T-S vastness gobbles up number 8 milliseconds after Ko'ach's entry.

Only Ko'ach and God are aware of each time dented fissure. Ripping the fabric of time and space, 8 and Ko'ach battle each other. Waves and waves of distorted timelines careen and crumble and erase written and unwritten eternities.

May 24th, 2024...

Ko'ach and number 8 pummel each other on the outskirts of Saturn's rings. Parsec after parsec they throw each other. Number 8's dark energy, for now appears to be able to hold I-T-S own against Ko'ach's righteous blue-white energy.

Ko'ach's peripheral vision spots Earth.

"Idiot! My master controls every molecule, every atom of restorative time. You can't help Nephesh or those puny Earthlings. I-T has already happened. You can't change anything. I-T controls your past, present and future. Amazing dude, you still don't get I-T!" Creature growls.

"What, don't I get?"

"Who I truly am."

"Idiot's twin brother?"

Metallic creature pulls from a righteous portal a fuchsia glowing righteous can opener. Humming energy melts metallic face. Staring back at Ko'ach is something horribly fleshy.

"How? I-T-S not possible!" Ko'ach shouts.

"We're handsome, no?"

"Me? Ima you? God wouldn't allow that to become my future. Your space magic won't work on me. You're not me. Neither Malevolent Time nor her perverted stepson can prevent righteous warrior's victory!"

"Fool! You still don't comprehend the truth of our Multiverse. You can't change what's already happened. Malevolent Time is your puppet master. Your God was bested by her long before EM-IT-S transformation. You've learned to cheat death many times. I-T-S easy. Now what's difficult. Nay, impossible; cheating Malevolent Time. You've tried for an eternity and failed every time. And look at us...we're the results of your failure. Stop your foolish attempts at redemption. Fate. Destiny. Time. I'm living proof you can never win."

Righteous Ko'ach smiles, shuts down malevolent Ko'ach's arrogant display. Narrator David becomes aware of an infinite number of righteous souls recharging Ko'ach's one-of-a-kind cellular matrix.

That ability is the only one malevolent Ko'ach could never duplicate; that's why at that moment in time he's caught off guard regarding righteous Ko'ach's sudden giddiness.

I see. I see! Narrator David shouts. *Ko'ach was the fuchsia shooting star changing trajectory. He's always been the force behind correcting rewritten timelines.*

Descending toward Earth are two indomitable energy signatures, one emitting dark fascist hatred and the other emitting righteous blue-white justice.

Evil 8 rips Earth's atmosphere. 8 seconds before I-T-S evil metallic claws slice and recreate terroristic turbulence. That horrendous barrier slams Ko'ach into the churning Pacific Ocean.

Down, down, down both good and evil dive. Evil's rage clouds I-T-S judgment. Unaware of I-T-S error the monster chases Ko'ach's powerful, ocean churning legs.

Sensing humiliating danger, I-T sends out a telepathic message to I-T-S prodigy.

Pull up! Pull! Up!

A few hundred meters below the surface, gravitational pressures build and squash metallic cellular structure. Mathematical truth can't be ignored. Meter by meter Earth's oceanic pressure becomes intolerable.

Increased pressure penetrating righteous Ko'ach's cells is like Gamma radiation for me. We soak I-T up. We're strengthened by I-T.

With God's speed, Ko'ach's U-turn brings him underneath his doppelganger. Fleshy thumbs puncture metallic Achilles tendons. Glowing gills materialize; allowing Ko'ach to breathe. Ko'ach's powerful hands latch onto his doppelganger's ankles. Evil yelps. Ko'ach smiles and like enormous turbines, Ko'ach's legs propel his doppelganger thousands of miles deeper.

Ko'ach's mind shouts... *Pressure! Pressure! You fucking monstrosity!*

Evil's metallic skin fractures. Widening gapping chasm spurts black oozing goo.

8's rage turns to bewildering confusion... *How can you be stronger? We're the same!*

The hell we are!

Where are you taking me?

Mariana Trench!

Existential explosion knocks righteous Ko'ach unconscious. A 999-megaton mushroom cloud, with no radiation, ascends toward the surface and immediately becomes the most powerful Tsunami the Earth has ever experienced.

Powerful rolling waves jam-packed with giant sharks and whales slam into crumbling nuclear silos; 36 ballistic missiles explode. That chain reaction lit a fuse under every known and unknown earthquake fault. North and South American continents split apart. Blasting and rippling through Europe and Asia, not a single land mass is left unscathed. Japan, the new mystical Atlantis, becomes completely submerged. From Tel Aviv to Tehran, all cities are submerged below those 3,000-foot waves.

Thousands of 8.1, 9.0, and 9.9 earthquakes drown out the last breaths of screaming children. Huge chunks of cement crush human skulls. Family hugs are pulverized into dusty silence. Spontaneous fires, hurricanes and tornadoes follow horrific Tsunamis.

Over the next five days, 75 percent of the world's population dies horribly. The world's economies are thrust back into the Stone Age. Electrical power grids are obliterated everywhere! Food and carcasses rot. Mutating bacteria and viruses become increasingly virulent.

Only 8 percent of the world's population exists 26 days after the first tsunami.

I-T and I-T-S laughing disciples growling builds to a crescendo. Booming mechanical voices leak into our Multiverse and shatter our righteous space-time-continuum. *Hurray for the dead humans, I can't wait to skewer their succulent souls.*

Standing in the middle of Nephesh's palm, David's despair shoots a defeated stare at Nephesh's shocked expression. He hugs Ima's lifeless body.

"Now! Guardian Angel!" *What are you waiting for? Bring her back!*

Nothing like this has ever happened before. I'm at a loss. I know you wish...I'm sorry, bringing her back is beyond my abilities. Too much is wrecked! I'm unable to tap into my righteous energy. And that, my old friend, has never happened before.

Bloody waves roll Dafna on shore. Choking Dafna aspirates bloody salt water. Nephesh's pinkie gently taps the little human's back.

Ko'ach's mind screams, *Oh my God. What have I done?*

Ocean masks Ko'ach's tears. Glowing fists punch through concrete debris. His gills dissipate seconds after he breaks the surface. His rage rockets him 18 miles above the crashing radioactive waves.

Damn I-T! Every time I reset what was...everything gets worse! No, this isn't the way. I must do what I've never tried before. I won't become the catalyst of... Is this what turns me into that metallic monster? Are these the events which will blacken my soul, irreparably? I-T said all of this is by Malevolent Time's design. God loses? Impossible. Improbable. I will save this planet and my Nephesh. I must discover the math, the never before unlocked physics to recreate a new reality for the Multiverse.

Ko'ach rockets into space. The faster he travels the quicker he shrinks, and the brighter his glowing hums.

Faster! Faster! Faster!

Nephesh's right hand scoops up David, Ima and Dafna. Held tight to her heart. Her weepy eyes shut knowing the killer waves are fast approaching. Her body emits a weakened glowing forcefield. The inevitably unthinkable hits Ko'ach's heart with the soul ripping power of a thousand Tsunamis. Cresting waves obliterate Nephesh and all the tiny humans.

Ko'ach's righteous and evil energy intermix. Blue-white triangles within triangles stretching into eternity's never-ending unbroken mathematical equation.

Celestial time sparks from Ko'ach's rotating body reverse reality. Teen David's essence is the first to slip through I-T-S fingers and reappear out of I-T-S deathly vortex.

Come back! Come back! I had him! God damn you, Ko'ach! You're not supposed to rewind time. You've broken your vow. You'll never be able to rejoin the others in the Realm of the Watchers. We're forever kindred spirits with Mother's help. I'll get your prodigy back. And I will destroy your beloved...in the slowest most painful manner. You hear me Ko'ach!

God battles Malevolent Time in the chaotic swirl of rewritten history. Both are trapped beyond time and reason. Still the stronger of the two; God uses all his strength to prevent the re-birth of number 8. Ko'ach's evil doppelganger has been permanently erased from existence. The added benefit is that the most recent Earth catastrophe never happened.

Aware of his new reality, Ko'ach constructs cellular force fields beneath the Mariana Trench. Leaving the salty ocean, he walks into this pristine environment. Steam rises from the back of his head, arms, and legs.

Ko'ach's cave emanates light and heat intensity of a super nova. Hands laced he pulverizes red-glowing rock walls. Infused with his own cellular matrix that edifice becomes impenetrable to I-T-S million minions. As Earth's lone watcher Ko'ach observes and participates in multiple David Sagacious timelines.

Sorry, David. Mission takes priority over friendship. Once you're here you'll no longer age. I believe in you. You'll become the correct savior for us all. And if Ima wrong, well, I can always terminate the experiment and start all over again. We'll have all the time in the Multiverse. I know you'd prefer to stay. Well, that's my choice too. But the fate of those we love the most is at stake, and we must sacrifice our great love and happiness to make sure they live. I've rewritten so many new and old stories. God, I know you're busy containing Malevolent Time; I wish you could break her interdimensional barrier. I understand why her evil static prevents your thoughts from reaching me.

"God only knows if I'm on the right path," Ko'ach whispers.

Re-written truth...

David kisses Ima's closed eyes. "Open your eyes, sweetie," whispers David.

Ima looks down at David on bended knee.

Ima jumps into David's arms. "Yes! A thousand times, yes."

CHAPTER 30

Heroic Mentor to David and Beloved Husband to Nephesh Commits the Unthinkable Crime, the Obliteration of God's Righteous Realm of the Watchers

Nephesh, 65 feet tall, deeply inhales crisp Sierra Nevada chilly air. Mountainous elevation tops 7,200 feet. A brisk breeze cools her hot, naked fuchsia body.

The chirping song inspires Nephesh's yawning smile. Another loud yawn and dozens of flapping birds exit toward fading sunrise.

Nephesh's melodic stroll leaves gigantic footsteps for miles. Her fuchsia painted toes smash boulders and splinter strewn about logs. *Sequoias. I remember when majestic trees were cute saplings. I remember when we were all young saplings. Oh God...Ko'ach! How could you?*

Serene, scented scenery serenades soul-searching sad serendipity. Solitude's sojourn seeks swan song's steadfast sedition. Nephesh's humming leads to broken-hearted singing of "So in Love."

Falling to her knees, Nephesh's large raindrop tears pity-pat into deep holes created by her kneecaps. *You've given me an impossible mission. Impossible!* Her defiant backstory, intrepid gory allegory, laudatory and preparatory predates exculpatory purgatory's predatory category.

Thousand years before the biblical King David ruled Israel from the capital city Jerusalem. Incognito Nephesh observed tiny humans.

I've visited worlds where entire cities could fit on my pinkie's fingernail. And worlds where five-year-old children dwarf Earth's skyscrapers. There are also millions of worlds embracing evil practices and those people project gorgeous faces and magnificently healthy bodies: there outside is the antithesis of their true nature. There are planets where rain pours 18 times a week and in other places misty rain trickles once every 18 months. I've walked through blood-red snow-capped mountains making Earth's Everest tiny in comparison, and conversely, other world's tallest precipices reaching only as high as a Dachshund's low-hanging-belly.

Time traveling equation has I-T-S limits. Ko'ach is the only being immune to the tailwind's cellular degradation. Even with Nephesh's righteous soul-rebuilding techniques, multi-century voyages, let alone millennium voyages are 99 percent deadly. Nephesh's next target jump will lead her to 18 years before David's birth. She must first hibernate on the planet called GHY - Grotesque Healing Yellow. Inhabited by tiny white people, so white, Earth's albinos would appear to have Ethiopian pigment.

Brain-splattering decibels to little humans are, in fact, used to heal Nephesh's shattered time-traveling-sanity. Tiny translucent people are impervious to extra-dimensional time waves. When Nephesh arrives, her brain oozing and bloody body cracking forces her into an inevitable coma. Dark lines etched in her semi-translucent body would make the Grim Reaper appear fresh-faced and lovely in comparison.

Long ago, Nephesh learned of I-T-S plot to annihilate every life force on GHY. She saved them from I-T-S time-traveling child prodigy. Too far gone; not even Nephesh's righteous soul can save her desiccated essence. Her best and only chance is in the healing realm of those tiny translucent healers. Their combined energy might awaken Nephesh from her nightmarish abyss.

Providence provides the means. Tiny creatures poke and penetrate normal space's periphery. Screeching sound waves activate God's righteous tuning fork. Narrator listens as the wisest Watcher Realm souls communicate...their ultimate unprecedented change in plans...

David! David!

I hear you...

After weighing every conceivable and inconceivable variable and variation. We must state categorically you're not the designated savior. You've been given 18 million years and we've determined you'll never succeed, never be strong enough to take on you know what. We don't believe Ko'ach can train the other pre-narrator David. We've selected another...she must go through the same trials you did many lifetimes ago,

You can't do that!

Can't or shouldn't?

Yes! How can you, risk her dying? And... And!

Say I-T.

Oh my God, that's the first time I've ever heard that from you.

So what!

So what? You'd risk the beast discovering your location.

That's the point we are trying to prevent the beast... Shut up, David! We need not explain our actions to you.

I won't let you do this to my Ima! She won't be able to endure what I did. Her death this time, will be permanent. Irretrievably gone. And I'll have to watch, helpless to stop I-T. Helpless to help her. Stuck here! Alone for all eternity, without a smidgen of hope that I will once again be reunited. Damn you! Not damn I-T! You! Are all making a huge mistake. A huge gamble! I'm the designated Chosen One! I don't state this out of ego or vanity. I do this because I-T-S the truth. Have you forgotten what love is? If you had any memory of love, you'd reverse course. You would give me more time. Ask anything of me. Any task. No matter how painful. I will not complain. I will obey. I beg you do not harm my Ima!

How dare you! Insignificant child of Earth! We don't need your permission nor condemnation. True, our power is waning. We no longer have the strength to interfere with your storytelling.

If you get me off this rock, I can train my beloved, and together we can defeat I-T!

You! Cannot defeat that metallic evil monster without God's righteous weapon. Your defiance gives us all the proof we need. You haven't accrued enough Multiverse storytelling energy. You have never been able to overcome your human frailty. Mr. Sagacious, you're not the one! You're our greatest failure! Our greatest disappointment...

Ima will pick up where you left off. She will tell your story of her exploits—and strengthen the fabric of reality. She will become the bulwark you've failed to become. She will fortify us! She will stop that evil armada's most recent incursion.

I've been told not to break the fourth wall, but here I go with all due determined ego intact. Humans of Earth, when you were young did you ever clap for Tinker Bell? Well, I need your love and support. Trillions reading my story and the story of my friends... Clap. Louder. Yes, I can feel your love. You're doing great. More please. Thank you. Thank you. You are all pushing evil's stream of consciousness. I-T-S manipulating essence fades from our current timeline. Hurray!

Ko'ach can't help you in your future, present... He must mentor you in the tense, past.

And Nephesh? Can she assist?

Complicated.

No! Not complicated, can she or...

Don't use that tone. I can't interfere in her process. Destructive prophecy lingers.

You still believe evil metallic Ko'ach will be the source of your destruction?

Yes.

Forgive my impertinence. You're wrong. He'd never. He could never...

He has. We must not allow I-T to come to fruition. Past...present... future—all are on a collision course. We're all having great difficulty extricating ourselves from so many rewrites.

Without God's help, our fate remains inflexibly malleable. We acknowledge this is our greatest gamble...

Merging with my beloved?

Murky, that timeline is. How I-T will impact the future and past David Sagacious we can't at present determine with 100 percent certainty. Merging with weak human Ima doesn't guarantee our success. And once I merge I-T will detect that transformation. Ima's amnesia of that event will be lifted. The truth will be revealed, and she'll know what action she must take.

Give me one more chance to find and hold onto God's righteous weapon.

No! The end of everything is now. Time for you has run out, David Sagacious! You're no longer the savior. From this point forward... You! Are! Canceled!

Don't do I-T! You're showing me you're not as wise as you pretend to be. You're all making a catastrophic mistake. One from which you'll never be able to recover.

The burst of dark energy co-mingles with blue-white light. Ko'ach's mind chuckles.

Am I early?

I trusted you!

Calm yourself, David. I'm not what God's second son thinks I am. I still control the evil within. I-T does not, nor will I-T ever control me.

David hears fearful voices echo out of the realm.

The prophecy. I detect hatred of us. Hatred of Father.

No, I feel his love. His protection of the timeline.

You're all correct. Today is the day the prophecy plays out into I-T-S most misguided realities. Well, sort of...

What does that mean?

Forgive me old friends...

Don't do I-T! Shouts god's mind.

Ko'ach's body stretches from a 100-foot menacing machine into an 18,180-foot benevolent-malevolent hybrid and latches onto the melting Realm. Throbbing unreality quakes and pulsates. Collective might of every righteous soul, including god, is unable to seal the fabric of reality's screeching fissures.

Light and dark matter collide. Matter and anti-matter distort and mutate into something new and hideous. Terrified souls emit a protective barrier. I-T starts to melt and panic crackles with lightning bolts the Multiverse never before experienced. Black lightning bolts emanate from Ko'ach's fingertips and electrify what's left of the Realm and all the other righteous souls.

Ko'ach stop! You're killing them! Shouts David's mind.

No old friend. Ima not; Ima saving them.

How can you say that? I feel their fear, their pain. I see everything you're doing. Righteous Ko'ach! Fight the evil within. God. God! Can't you see what he's doing? Try and divert your focus with Malevolent Time and do something about this evil Ko'ach!

David, God will not comply with your request.

Are you in communication with God? Why has he allowed you in and not me, nor the other Realm's wisest souls?

Ima fulfilling the prophecy but not in the way that either I-T, Malevolent Time or even god could've predicted. God knows this is the only path forward for all of us. Except for the humans Ima sending trillions of righteous souls to a time not even Malevolent Time is aware of. Forgive me if I don't confide to you where Ima sending them.

Where are you sending my mama's and papa's souls?

For their safety's sake, I can't tell you where or when.

Holding his ground...god refuses to be sent away by Ko'ach. His mind searches for Nephesh's mind... *Avenge us!*

No! Shouts Ko'ach's glowing engrams.

God's second son breaks free and transports himself toward 21st-century Earth.

Victory snatched from the jaws of cremation. I-T remains clueless regarding the most powerful soul melting within Ima's weak human body. Dormant god will remain hidden until I-T activates and at that moment I-T will become aware of when and where I-T should attack.

Ko'ach's psyche splits. He doesn't know if he's speaking to himself...god, I-T or God.

Who are you? Reveal yourself! No! Can't be! Don't do...I-T!

CHAPTER 31

36 Hours Before David and Ima's Wedding, God sends Nephesh the Unthinkable News; Distraught, She Leaves the Wedding Party on a Mission to Kill Her Beloved Ko'ach

Ko'ach's body absorbs black hole's gravitational eddies. Translucent hands twist Ko'ach's shoulders in the opposite direction to that of his ankles. All the righteousness wrung out of his sensory deprived core; he floats unconsciously between dagger slicing malevolent shards.

I no longer detect a single blip of brain activity. His heart no longer pulsates. His righteous soul seeps through quantum quagmire. Fight I-T! Ko'ach! We all need you!

Monster's rise will devise, surmises surprises. Righteous soul restricted, constricted eternally conflicted. I opine. *How could Ko'ach align? Enshrine that serpentine redesign. Has I-T? Will I-T? Undermine his former benign. Evil's new heart condition, non-contrition. Old friend, you were always the ultimate tactician...I sense smiling sedition, elaborate submission.*

Turning evil, my mentor speaks what's in his dark heart... *god...never became aware of my ambition, calculating omission. Fuck tradition! Coalition of one; we won! We've outgrown our juxtaposition. A hunting expedition will come to fruition, joyfully ending with Nephesh's extradition. Her addition was always mission. I'll come for you too, plus Ima and fucking meddlesome human Israeli Jew. For you, my unexpected breakthrough means you'll never break through. We've come to annihilate your world view.*

Nephesh, Ima and Dafna walk around the UCLA campus 36 days before David and Ima's wedding. For them, the time is early afternoon. Slight breeze temporarily cools their sweating brows. Assessing their stamina, they sprint up hundreds of red bricks called Janss Steps.

Grass recently cut. Rapid-fire sneezes lead to allergic wheezes. Unaffected dogs and family members enjoy tossing and catching frisbees. Nephesh, Ima and Dafna love their tasty orange, pink, and green swirling spumoni. Nephesh, deep in thought, breaks from the group. Ima and Dafna lock arms, their gleeful skipping is accompanied by wiggling, waggling Golden retriever.

"What's wrong? All week, you've been preoccupied. How could you not be happy? We're going to Ima and David's wedding?" Dafna snaps her fingers in Nephesh's face. *No reaction. What's with this glazed-over zombie affect effect?* Dafna gently knocks on Nephesh's skull.

"Hello. Anybody home?" Dafna whispers.

Becky's tail hits Nephesh's leg. The happy puppy licks Nephesh's elegant fingers. Typically, Nephesh would bend down and rub the puppy's head and back...not today. Dafna taps Nephesh's nose. No reaction. She grabs her taunt jowl and squeezes—no reaction. Dafna vigorously yanks up and down the flesh between her thumb and index finger.

"Earth to squishy. Come in squishy!" yells Dafna.

Nephesh blinks thrice. "What the shell are you doing?"

"Good to see you're finally awake.

"Awake? Of course, Ima... Um, gotta pee."

"You just did, three minutes ago."

"I did. Well, um...let go of my wrist. Dafna, this is not the time for your silliness."

"Dear old friend, we're worried about you. We are your friends. Time to end this stoic 'I'm okay, leave me alone' crap and talk to us!"

Long pause. Nephesh opens her mouth.

Dear sweet humans—you could never understand.

"After all this time, you should know... You can't hide your feelings from me. I'll do some more sleuthing if I must. But I'd prefer..."

Dafna rubs Nephesh's face.

Nephesh's tears hold tight to the corner of her bloodshot emerald eyes. Nephesh wills I-T to stay put; and when more secretive emotional thoughts flood, the sobbing releases no relief. Only greater concern from Ima and Dafna. Ima and Dafna hugged Nephesh. "Stop hugging me!" Nephesh's voice trembles. Her ear-splitting booming shout punches holes in the wooden bench. "You humans are so needy. I can't be the center of your world. I have my own problems. And you can't help. This is a problem I must solve on my own. Have a happy marriage, life... You'll have to do so, without me!"

"Nephesh, please tell me. I promise I'll keep your secret. You know you can trust me."

"I do. No. No! You wouldn't understand..."

Nephesh stands up and barrels past Ima.

Ima and Dafna chase after their distraught friend.

From a distance Ima shouts, "As much as I love you, I can't do this anymore. I can't on the eve of my...Nephesh! You've forced me to postpone my wedding too many times. I won't give David another bullshit excuse!"

Ima holds onto Dafna. "Let her go. I've tried my darndest. I can't reach her. And I'm done trying. I deserve happiness too."

"We all do," tearful Ima says.

"If she wants to confide in us, she will. For some unknown reason, she's not there yet."

Two evenings later...

Ima and Dafna show up at Nephesh's apartment. Dafna tries her key.

"Crap, she's changed the lock."

They hear the rustling of papers and the sliding glass door. "She's jumping out the window."

Dafna and Ima ran to their bikes. 36 minutes later they catch up with Nephesh; she's sobbing into her large hands.

"What! Get away from me. No! I don't want any more hugs!"

"We're not going to leave you like this," shouts Dafna.

"You have no choice. Obey me or..."

"Or what?"

"Remember your training. I-T-S time you forget you ever knew me."

"Nice acting job. You're doing all of this on purpose. Why?" asks Ima.

"Why indeed." Nephesh's anger grows. Her height approaches 12 feet.

"Look what you're doing. This is a public street. You can't let this go viral."

Nephesh laughs.

"I don't like the sound of that chuckle," says Ima.

"Foolish human. Your cameras can't see me. I'm phased to all but you two. What's going viral? Are you two shouting at thin air?"

Nephesh rips through her clothing. Naked 65-foot Nephesh flies toward the twinkling stars. In her mind plays, "So In Love."

Early the next morning - Nephesh flies through her open window, shrinking down to four feet. She walks into the bathroom and sits on the toilet seat. Her damaged time particles are entangled with her strong emotions. Every pity-pat teardrop shrinks her down, down, down. Standing only 33 inches tall, her strong emotions vibrate and pulverize scurrying cockroaches. Wailing, distraught Nephesh falls below 22 inches.

"What's your weakness, Ko'ach? I know, only one. Me! Ima your weakness. Destroying the Realm of the Watchers means there's no longer a place for our righteous souls to rest once our bodies decay. You see, I have this difficult problem, and I need to talk I-T over with my best friend. And well, you're my best friend."

Nephesh jumps off the toilet seat and continues to shrink below six inches.

Later that evening, hundreds of white chairs adorned with fuchsia ribbons overlook gorgeous Malibu cliffs. 18 bridesmaids sparkle with beautiful smiles in gorgeous fuchsia gowns. Strewn across the green grassy hills are fuchsia rose petals. Huge four-foot cake with fuchsia icing. Blue sky becomes bright canary yellow. Ima's diamond wedding ring shimmers.

Dafna holds tight to the wedding bouquet tossed 18 minutes ago. Once again, Ima and David hold an exceptionally long passionate kiss.

A mesmerizing orange sky illuminates fuchsia-clad garments. David adjusts clipped mic to his fuchsia tie. They swing their hands. He kisses the back of Ima's hand and sings, "Some Enchanted Evening." Horrible cackling whooshing through David's ears catches him off guard; rigid blackness squeezes his limbs; he's immobilized for 18 seconds. *Ima paralyzed!*

David's eyes dart east-west and north-south. He struggles and fails to move his mouth and fingers. *Not just me: everyone is in the same predicament.*

Dafna orders her feet to take a step. Her mind screams— *Nothing! My friends. The entire wedding party: Who or what could have frozen us? God! We need your help.*

Human minds feel time passing. *How long?* Collectively repeats from the active minds. My awareness of the passage of time remains intact; I am aware that their gorgeous sun never set and the paralysis of all humanity, planet-wide has been going on for 81 minutes.

Beads of salty sweat percolate, slide, and stop, suspended before they ker...plunk.

Dafna's klutzy cousin's drink frozen in mid-fall. Her grandfather's affectionate squeeze of wife Miriam's tush... after 180 minutes not one digit unclamps from her substantial derriere.

That peculiar phenomenon is localized to the Earth and I-T-S solar system. No other solar systems are impacted. Paralyzed David isn't yet superhero me. Four hours now, fear attacks David's synapses. Time fluctuates between known and unknown variables.

I see every permutation of this unexpected new timeline. We're in the time after Ko'ach saved trillions upon trillions of righteous souls, by destroying their Realm.

18 miles from the wedding party's position, an immaculately fabricated embryo descends out of the blue-white righteous vortex. Swirling dust carried on sonic winds hits the human's unblinking, non-tearing, rough, rough eyeballs. *Ouch! If only I could blink and wash these particles away!* The gelatinous blue-white shell gently touches down, that holy DNA pulsates and gestates for 72 frozen hours.

Blinding hot glow emanates from blue-white thumb and index finger poking through membrane's 18 gelatinous layers. All 10 wiggling digits force righteous protoplasm to splatter and shoot up like a flesh searing geyser...god's genetic material seeds future anomalies.

God's second son, former leader within the Realm of the Watchers has rebirthed I-T-S self. That celestial baby has within I-T-S neural network a 27 trillion IQ. Shaking I-T-S holy placenta loose; that baby blinks one blue eye and one white eye and stares at my beloved Ima.

After crawling for 36 seconds, the baby's growth rapidly accelerates. Looking more and more like a human male, age 9 months. Baby tries to stand and falls multiple times. Baby's tumbling causes I-T to roll down an extremely dusty crusty hill. Growing stronger at 18-months I-T-S making good progress toward the wedding party; god-child picks himself up and starts running. Each pounding step causes god-child to age. Ancient-one reaches three human years in the blink of an encrusted pain needle pricking eye. Two more steps, and that fast-aging child becomes 13. The closer the ancient life force gets to 900-year-old Ima, the slower the lighting flares. I'm still referring to a time before the 18-million-year-old me-narrator was marooned for the first time.

Quicker than even I could react, god enters my beloved's eye with the speed of an unwanted searing poker. Scalding white-hot energy envelops Ima's brain, heart, limbs, and soul. On a scale of 1 to 10, her fear registers well over 18. Her super-nova radiance liquefies 360 seconds later. Her super-nova blast does not incinerate people, buildings, let alone the entire planet because all of that energy is contained within god's time bubble.

Oh, my God. Beloved! Where are you? I've told and retold these stories millions of times, and this never happened before! Please sweetie, try and reach out to me. Nothing! Please don't do this, god. Please, I'm begging you! I-I demand you return Ima to me this instant!

A demand! How dare you. I'm doing what I must. Ko'ach isn't what he appears to be. I've relied on others. Now, no longer. I have faith and truth in only myself.

You cannot.

Cannot!

Should not—over your father. Not even your judgment is as wise as your father's.

Agreed. I'm not that arrogant. Ko'ach certainly takes that prize. Father can't help me, nor help you. He's engaged with Malevolent Time and cannot for a millisecond become distracted. He must concentrate all his powers on that horrible beast. As much as I'd like to assist my father, I cannot break through Malevolent Time's lightning bursts. I've been unable to communicate with father for an uncomfortably long period of time, even for me.

Then, how do you know what your next step should be? How do you know you are not thwarting God's chance of defeating Malevolent Time?

We don't have time for this. The time for talk passed, within the context of disputed time fluctuations. The time for bold action is the only course left. The evil within Ko'ach must be annihilated!

I've never felt such anger from you before. You've never used the annihilation word before. Are you who you say you are? Could you be some variation of I-T?

Goodbye, David Sagacious. This is the night your story ends!

Ima Ancient-One combination hurtles through unknown dimensions faster than Ko'ach's best speed. That incredible gift is the reason Ima didn't break apart. I-T-S one of the reasons why that transformation worked.

Energy surge from god traverses time and space. Grand celestial smacks into Nephesh's heart. *Oh, my God. I was hoping not to be given...this curse. Now Ima more than a match for beloved. I don't want to do this. Do you hear me, god? I'd rather he destroys me than live with the memory of what I've done to him!*

Ko'ach gently touches down at the base of the Sierra Nevada. Stretching 150-foot Ko'ach yawns and cheerfully smiles after inhaling Earth's chilly thin air. He is eye to eye with dozens of smaller Sequoias. Ko'ach admires the Sierra Nevada's panoramic view. Crumbling boulders like pebbles beneath his wiggling toes. Ko'ach's footfalls boom boom boom!

Gargantuan Ko'ach's strides bring him closer to his enhanced beloved. Every 18 steps, Ko'ach shrinks.

Stomping naked Nephesh at 65 feet towers over diminutive 18-foot Ko'ach. She fumes.

"You!"

"Me? What's new, sweetie?"

"You mock me?"

"Never. I love you."

"How could I ever love...you! You who destroyed the only chance for our soul's everlasting..." Nephesh cries into her gigantic fingers. Tears leaking through. They land and gather together, forming a powerful flash flood. Ko'ach shrinks down to 9 feet.

"Run, puny insect!"

Ko'ach's tiny fingers tickle Nephesh's gigantic pinkie toe. She raises her leg. *Run!*

Bam! Nephesh's monstrous heel smashes boulders inches from Ko'ach's neck. Like a nuclear blast without radiation, her forceful stomp bends towering trees back beyond their flexibility limits. Ko'ach falls into her foot-created crater. Frustration builds within Nephesh; her building size fist pulverizes mountaintops. Permafrost breaks free. Melting snow gushes. Torrential run-off tickles her ankles. She grabs Ko'ach's legs and tosses his bloody chest toward squawking birds. Airborne, he playfully flaps his arms and joins in the squawking. His good-natured humor infuriates Nephesh beyond her breaking point.

Three rolling boulders knock Nephesh off her feet. She lands with a disheartened thud! Ko'ach zooms back to terra-firma. He's now only 3 feet and he trips over Nephesh's aromatic hair strands and falls hard into a deep sinkhole left by her voluptuous outline. Nephesh's finger pushes Ko'ach under the slushy mud. Suffocation enters his lungs. *Why does he not fight back? Too little, even for normal size human. Why does he not grow? Grow damn you! He's not even struggling against me. Oh my God. I must do what I must do. I don't want to murder you!*

Four bubbles rise to the surface. Each expelled gurgle shouts, "Release me!"

Nephesh hears Ko'ach's last gasping muddy cough and releases her finger pressure on her tiny beloved's crushed chest. Horrified, she shrieks, "Nooo!" She slaps her own face and cries, "I hate you!"

Nephesh's black mascara zigzags down her reddened cheeks. Bloodshot eyes rage. Looking heavenward. She searches for absolution and finds none.

Head down, Nephesh walks toward a jagged stone arrow the size of a 23-story skyscraper and stares at the killing stone. Bending her giraffe neck, she lines up her carotid. *Why the fucking hesitation? What the hell are you waiting for? Do I-T! God damn I-T! I said do I-T!*

Like a dead goldfish, Ko'ach's rigid body floats to the surface of the mud pit. Nephesh's loud cries mask Ko'ach's tiny footfalls. He's too weak to telepathically communicate.

"Don't," he shouts. Nephesh doesn't hear him. Glowing energy sparking and sputtering, he tries to fly. Three inches becomes three feet above Nephesh's indented footprints. His energy shorts out again and he lands face-first into her giant toe print.

Ko'ach waves his arms. "I'm here!" he shouts.

Nephesh backs away from the sharp edge. Fuchsia blood whooshes. Ko'ach's knuckles glow. Aiming beams with grand precision and loving care, he cauterizes the fleshy opening.

"You shouldn't have done that!" Nephesh tearfully screams.

"Dear sweetie Nephesh-ah-la. I didn't mean to cause you any pain." He sings, "All I Know."

"Too late!"

"Never too late for eternal love birds. We're Nephesh and Ko'ach. And we shall always be Nephesh and Ko'ach."

"Run! Save yourself from my wrath. I loathe my new orders. Why do you hold onto that tiny form? I must complete my mission. I must follow god's edicts to the letter. You taught me that a long time ago. I would prefer to die rather than be the source of your death. Nothing matters anymore. The end of our days should've come thousands of years from now...and when that finally happened, we should've been together for all eternity within the Realm of the Watchers. But we can't. We'll never be able to experience that joy...because you destroyed all our righteous futures!"

18 minutes pass. 65-foot Nephesh gently places her chin on the soft green grass and stares in silence at her 1.8-inch beloved. *Ko'ach, why can't I hear your thoughts?*

Reflexes faster than lightning, Nephesh scoops up Ko'ach. She squeezes his bones. Each crack and crunch causes Nephesh's giant-sized teardrops to pummel Ko'ach's face and body. *Do you hear me? Why won't you fight back? Why do you allow me to do these horrible things to you? How can you be so strong, at such an itty-bitty size? Ko'ach! Damn you! Answer me!*

Ko'ach's forearms push against Nephesh's huge digits; her finger's squeezing vise grip loosens up.

What are you doing? Is he making space so that he can break my hands? Why do you want to prolong our fight? Why won't you answer any of my questions?

Ko'ach caresses Nephesh's thumb and kisses her fingertips.

Beloved. My telepathy has returned. I can hear all your thoughts and communicate my love to you once more.

"Have a nice trip."

"What?"

Ko'ach tightly grips Nephesh's four fingers and flings her above the treetops.

No time to explain. Ima late for a wedding which must not be consummated.

Insect size Ko'ach smiles doing his rapid growing beanstalk routine. He flexes his elongated 70-foot body and flashes his golden smile. He slams his wrecking ball fist, freakish fissures form, making or creating mountainous landscape craters.

Confused, Nephesh bats her eyelashes. "No. Don't leave!"

Ko'ach's fuchsia energy glows. Teasing Nephesh his mind shouts, *Varoom. Varoom..*

Dust, boulder, and tree debris slam into Nephesh's knees. Her smiling face saddens, watching her beloved rocket into space.

Nephesh communicates with her righteous soul. *How many minutes are needed before I can re-engage my ability to fly?*

18...

Push the limits and finish the job in 9.

Nephesh shuts her eyes. Her concentration becomes impeccable. Partially repaired, she rockets into space and smashes into Ko'ach's dissipating time displacement wake. Black-fuchsia barrier prevents her from entering Ko'ach's time stream.

Nephesh's fists pummel her beloved's energy stream. Hours later she's neither dented the righteous structure nor caused the holy strands to help her. Without warning a singular self-aware energy strand enters Nephesh's body, and she grows to 900 feet. Her dagger fingernails the size of starships claw and crack open the first layer of Ko'ach's time barrier. Nephesh flings continent size time-barrier replete with disguised DNA fragments.

Time is a wondrous concept. In these confusing times, omniscient me is fully aware that Ko'ach and Nephesh's confrontation took place simultaneously centuries before and after their encounter with the frozen-in-time wedding party. That teenage me is unaware of 18-million-year-old me or any futuristic 900-year-old Ima, Dafna, or David.

Within the context of that altered timeline, Ancient-one—god-Ima symbiosis—walks up to 19-year-old Ima bride and David groom.

Out of place and time, naked Nephesh lands with the power of a furious 65-foot she-hulk.

Calm 9-foot Ko'ach smiles in Nephesh's direction. Her eyes nervously flutter. Ko'ach takes another satisfying lick of his sherbet. His smile widens, and his waving becomes more demonstrative.

"Over here, sweetie. MMM...great dessert after a wonderful human meal, burger, and fries with the works."

Ko'ach gobbles down the last cold sweetness and snaps his fingers. Everyone in the wedding party vanishes except Nephesh, Dafna, David, and Ima. Painful swirling black and fuchsia energy holds Nephesh in place.

Within the membranes of that peculiar matrix, her voice slows and deepens. "Ko'ach! I beg you, don't ki-l-l t-h-e-m!"

David, Ima, and Dafna's active minds shout, *God! Help us!* 18-inch triangle slices out from old Ima's chest cavity and merges with Dafna.

"Get back! Oh, my God! Noooooooooo!" teen Ima shouts at her glowing carbon copy.

Black energy wraps around Nephesh's ankles. She falls to her knees. Her powerful hands shred the shrieking eardrum shattering energy strands.

Ko'ach snaps his fingers and the encircling fuchsia vortex swirls faster and faster. This time, Nephesh is unable to break free. Fuchsia lightning tendrils reach out and engulf Dafna and young Ima. Poof! They are all gone, except for 19-year-old David.

"What's your preference? Jumping down the proverbial rabbit hole or sucking down the Matrix's red-blue pill?"

"Neither! What did you do to my bride? The wedding party, and my dear friend Dafna?"

"All of them live separate from you."

"What the hell does that mean?"

"None of your concern."

"The hell I-T-S not."

"Don't do that."

"Do what?" Fuchsia energy billows, gyrates and encircles David. Within the vortex, he can move. As hard as he tries, he's unable to push himself back out into our unaltered space-time-continuum.

Fissures open underneath David's feet, and he instantly liquifies. Two seconds later, Ko'ach liquifies. David's bubbling gurgling form coalesces into a one-inch version of himself.

Giant size 7-foot Ko'ach towers over frightened teen me. Ko'ach holds a giant-size fly swatter and transparent tube. Ko'ach flicks David; rubbing his bruised ribs, he rolls onto the black fly swatter. Screaming, David is batted into the seamy hot translucent tube. Noxious gas fills his tiny lungs. Choking David's mind shouts, "Why?"

David feels the sensation of falling down an 18-mile waterfall.

Ko'ach captures David's bio-magnetic DNA markers and forces fully whooshed and washed David fragments toward the lowest point on Earth. The Mariana Trench is located 36,729 feet below the surface. If you dropped the tallest mountain peak on Earth, Everest, into the trench, the distance between breathing air and the top of that peak would be over a mile of ocean. Ko'ach plans to use oceanic pressure as a tool to reshape what David must become.

The faster the glowing tsunami moves, the narrower I-T becomes. Water creates blue glowing bone and tissue. Two hearts beat, and three lungs expand parting female puffy lips. Her seductive slow opening and closing movements allow subatomic particles to replenish her sparkling salty blood-stream. Wise creature is reborn; she's both new and extremely ancient; she's keenly aware of the intricacies and conundrums of time travel. Gorgeous translucent blue-white woman sheds her fishy skin, revealing scalding thermal nuclear neural path-ways. She swims into Ko'ach's liquified soul. This merging bol-sters his power against all foes by a factor of 36 million.

Ethical microscopic strand breaks away from Ko'ach and swims to David. I-T pinches off pieces of specific genetic strands. He...that David is on his path...our path to becoming superhuman.

Ko'ach's luminescent eyes allow him to see everything within his pitch-black cave. Lifting one-inch glowing David from his cylindrical dungeon, he's plopped unceremoniously next to Ko'ach's dinner plate. David's illuminating footsteps are expunged by salty drips from a tiny crack in the ceiling.

Each drop hits with thunderous reverberations. David holds his hands over his ears.

Make me normal size again!

I've given you the power to do that, without my help. Concentrate on the sound of my voice. David's body vibrates. Doubling his height to 3 inches. His angry irritation temporarily fades. "Hey! I did I-T!"

"Don't!"

"What? I did what you asked." Grunting vibrates louder and sprouts up to 9 inches. "Wow! Wow! Look at me go! I-T-S crazy, right?" Grinning David stares up at giant size angry Ko'ach's face. "What did I do wrong?"

Ko'ach holds David down with his pinkie. "That hurts."

"Good!"

"Why good? I don't understand any of this. Turn me back."

"Push-ups!"

18-inch David rolls off the table. After 300 push-ups, exhausted dwarf stands 36 inches.

Ko'ach grabs David round the waist and tosses him toward the pull-up bar, and 200 pull-ups later, David drops down, standing 6-foot-3.

Ko'ach twists his torso and kicks out with his right foot against the cave wall. Hundreds of bright bulbs cast a warm eerie glow through the cave's cold grayness.

Pieces of Ko'ach's mind remain and try to clarify David's understandable confusion.

Time stream will protect. I give you, my word. Foreboding happiness changes. Rest you need: 45 hours should do the trick. Trust. Imperative loyalty. Forgiveness—yes. Thoughts become reality in this place. I feel your energy waning. You must start your regeneration. Have patience. Everything is as...should be. Your sleeping quarters are in the next room.

Walking like an 18-month kidlet, David's rubbery thighs can't keep him upright. *Splat!*

"Don't hit that!" Ko'ach laughs after the fact.

With the comical skill of Charlie Chaplin, David keeps hitting, getting back up, and hitting chairs, stools, books, and trash cans.

My nose and lips pushed against the cold cement floor. "Hungry," David's drool gurgles.

"You should want sleep. Okay, eat first. Then a good night of shluffy."

"Shluffy?"

"Human-Jewish-Yiddish word meaning to sleep."

Ko'ach gently helps wobbly David into his blue-white chair. Soft hum precedes a large plate filled with vegetables, baked potato and huge 21-ounce steak. Knife and fork feel heavy in David's grasp, aching teeth chew tiny pieces of meat.

Ko'ach slices off chunks big enough to gag a T-Rex.

"Your mutated metabolism will take three weeks. You know I can read your thoughts. That's not funny, David."

Weird kidnapper mentioned that thoughts become reality. Let's try that. Serrated knife materializes near David's toes. He coughs, bends low; two quick spinning pivots and he throws. Millimeters from Ko'ach's heart, knife liquefies. Pissed David sees a shimmering puddle. Ko'ach smiles, takes one step, and stretches 18 feet. Large hand wraps around David's waist. Ko'ach tosses him 36 feet toward the hundreds of feet tall cavern ceiling. He's suspended for 18 seconds before gravity brings shrinking David back down into his cylindrical prison.

Ko'ach's hot breath clouds the tubing. One-inch David leaps back, seeing Ko'ach's huge nose. "There will be time to act. Now you must sleep," Ko'ach's whispering voice booms.

"Fuck time!" enraged David gurgles.

"Yes, my boy, we're in perfect alignment. Fuck Time!"

Pounding tiny fists on the translucent tube, David says, "Mark my words! I'll escape! You can't keep me caged! What do you want from me? Come back, damn I-T! Asshole! Don't walk away from me!"

Feeling extreme exhaustion clouds his mind and weakens his body. David falls into a deep deep unnatural sleep.

Ko'ach sings, "We Are the Champions."

464

CHAPTER 32

Gravity Remains the 100-Foot Machine's Only Kryptonite; at the Bottom of the Mariana Trench, Ko'ach Trains David for the Ultimate Final Battle

Full circle, Ko'ach brings teen me to the place where I-T all began, a pocket of reality below the Mariana Trench. Ko'ach taps into the Earth's mantle to supply him with all the backup energy he'll ever need. Ko'ach's cave keeps a symbiotic imperative linkage to Ko'ach's unique time-engaging signature. I-T-S beyond I-T-S evil awareness.

Waves upon undaunting time and gravimetric gamma radiation waves pulsating around and through David and Ko'ach. Our cellular structure is uniquely designed to soak up that which would destroy all other mechanical and corporeal life forms. Only God, not god, and Malevolent Time would find that bombardment insignificant and trivial. God and Malevolent Time have always been beyond death's grip. Caging, exiling, sending them to realms beyond which the human or Fuchsia minds could ever comprehend; that's the only way to temporarily subdue each other, and only each other has the power to do that to one another.

Ko'ach clears his throat. I remain asleep. He shouts louder and the me, who is not me wakes out of his happy dream.

"Evil and Righteous time are in a constant state of flux. Nothing ever plays out the same way twice. I've cleaned up too many unforeseen variables."

"If unforeseen, how could you clean them up?"

"Hush! Ima dialoging here."

"And why are you doing that?"

Ko'ach's tight lip expression grows warm and inviting. His grin attempts to reassure frightened David. "I've trained hundreds of thousands of you throughout the Multiverse. But you're by far the most obstinate, with the greatest potential to become the strongest of the Davids.

"Who are you? Where am I?" woozy David asks.

"On God's orders, I've scattered the 18 trillion righteous souls within the Realm of the Watchers."

"You destroyed them? I thought you said you're one of the good guys. How can I believe anything you say or do?"

"I am a good guy. And so are you. And who said anything about destroying? I said scattered, and I did so to save them. Only the protective shell, which was the Realm, was destroyed. I sent those advanced righteous souls to the furthest corners of the Multiverse—a construct of God's making is the only place Malevolent Time can never go. I trust in God's strength. They will, in time, find host bodies, and the Multiverse will be all the better for that. The environment known as the Realm of the Watchers may have been inferred as heaven, but I-T isn't. Heaven does exist. That's where your mama and papa's human souls thrive.

"For them, thank you. I still don't understand why I'm here."

"Time."

"For what?"

"Training," Ko'ach whispers.

Ko'ach flicks David's elbow. He zooms and slams into a

comfortable blue-white chair.

Damn, he's strong. With the flick of his finger, he's broken my humerus.

"Why the hell did you do that?"

"I thought you heal rapidly."

"I do. But this is different."

"You must become more than you've ever thought possible. Your time with Greenie was child's play. You must find the grit inside to endure unprecedented agony. All that you've gone through hopefully prepared you for what must be."

Ko'ach's hand glows. Blue-white righteous energy repairs David's broken bone.

David massages his elbow and watches the bruising fade. "Thanks."

"Hit me."

David shakes his head. "I said hit me!"

"I don't want to."

Milliseconds later, he-me, changes our mind. We swing with all our might. Ko'ach blocks that powerful punch with his pinkie. To the vision of an ordinary human, my super-fast reflexes would be a blur; in comparison to Ko'ach I-T-S as if he's toying with a child.

Sweat trickles down my face. I pause to take a gasp of oxygen. Ko'ach's yawns are insufferable. Ko'ach pours himself a cup of milk, and quickly gulps I-T all. Smiling, he returns to block more of David's punches. "Come on, you're better than this. Okay. Okay. Sit."

Ko'ach digs his hand into a trough filled with large pieces of coal. Plink, plink, plink...he drops three onto his palm. Ko'ach extends his right blue-white glowing hand. The brightness grows more intense. David squints his eyes.

Ko'ach's distorted hairy arthritic gnarled skeletonized fingers slowly knit themselves back to healthy glowing tissue. For 36 minutes David watches time waves turn Ko'ach ancient and back to a super undetermined healthy age.

"Time and pressure. Time and pressure." Ko'ach opens his shaky fingers.

Shimmering in David's face are not three lumps of coal, but three huge diamonds.

"I don't care how long I-T takes. You'll gain your freedom from this place when you're fast enough to grab those diamonds from my grasp."

David wipes the sweat from his flushed cheeks.

"I might get the power to turn coal into diamonds. Fucking never! How the hell did you do that? I-T takes 2,500 degrees Fahrenheit at 825,000 pounds per square inch of pressure for billions of years. Did your hand pass through billions of years over these last 36 minutes?"

Ko'ach nods.

"Wow. Wow. Wow!"

"Catch!"

The medicine ball slams into David's chest. "Can't breathe."

Ko'ach easily lifts the 18-hundred-pound ball off David's chest. Blue-white beam descends, and David's lungs oxygenate once more. Ko'ach reshapes the cylindrical shape into a teardrop speed bag. Tractor beam holds the bag in place. Ko'ach's powerful fists rapidly pummel that bag.

"You want me to do that?"

"Eventually. You'll start with the light 36-pound bag. Oh, there's one catch. Everything you do over the next 3,000 years..."

"What? I get you have an incredible lifespan. But even advanced human lives won't go far beyond a single century."

"The moment you arrived here..."

"Arrived? Kidnapped, more like I-T."

Ko'ach admonishes with a long wagging finger.

"While here, your cellular degeneration will case."

"You're telling me, I'll no longer age. I'll be young, forever."

"While you're here, in this cave."

"And if I leave? If I join the people up top, will I rapidly age?"

"No, your aging process will remain much slower, but in time you too will be greeted with the ravages of full cellular decay."

"Why are you doing this?"

"You need thousands of years to become strong enough to complete your mission, save your beloved, save my beloved, save the Multiverse."

"When?"

"When you've achieved the impossible. When your basketball skill level is better than the most athletic NBA player. When your gymnastic, weightlifting, and swimming skills far surpass all Olympic gold medalists. Then and only then will you have a fighting chance. Slim though...maybe."

"Ready for what?"

"Mastery of gravity's nuanced peremptory proclivities will ensure you fulfill your destiny. You must harness the inner strength of a righteous celestial warrior, in order to wield the only weapon capable of bringing down our common enemy."

"God's Star of David. How did I know that? Don't walk away."

"Narrator David."

"Is that supposed to mean something?"

"Not something. Everything. The stories he tells repair not only your life, but the very fabric of our space. He is the future you."

"What! The...the hell I am!"

Ko'ach places his powerful hand on his captive's shoulder. "He, or rather you will in the distant future. His stories will always help to repair humanoid cell structures as well as the intricacies of every Multiverse. I also want you to practice your telepathy, telekinesis, and the most advanced martial arts techniques from Earth and my home world."

*

Three millenniums later, David's rippling muscles allow him to complete 18 thousand push-ups, pull-ups, and sit-ups against gravitational waves 18 hundred times Earth's gravity. Like his mentor, David's bones don't shatter when flying through a black hole. His skin doesn't burn to a crisp when encountering a supernova.

David practices the gymnastic Iron Cross. Forearms and shoulders are quiescent. Each bulging muscle, under David's control, refuses to twitch or shake.

Over the last millennium, David's reshaped body and muscle fibers are stronger than titanium. He holds the Iron Cross for 72 minutes.

Enormously proud Ko'ach watches David's superman routine. When the gravimetric beam is turned off, David can fly. Fuchsia steel is 18 hundred times denser compared to what's smelted on Earth. David has fun bending Fuchsia steel girders, and his thunderous punches pulverize Fuchsia fiberglass composites.

David is now ready to snatch a large piece of coal from Ko'ach's hand. Neither knows if he's yet developed the strength to squeeze that coal into a diamond.

Unprecedented time fluctuations splinter the cave's impenetrable ceiling and walls. Massive shards crumble and shatter at David's feet.

"What's going on out there?"

The answer is one Ko'ach has never given before. "I don't know." He waves his glowing blue-white hand over his instruments.

David and Ko'ach look upon a cracked viewscreen oozing sparkling time fragments. Ko'ach is shocked to see Nephesh, Ima and Dafna arrive fully awake in the year 2367. Earth's atmosphere is lit up like 18-trillion matchsticks.

Computerized feminine Nephesh's voice speaks before Ko'ach can ask a question. "In the year 2367, 6.66 million 100-foot malevolent minions consume all corporeal life."

"Oh my God, Ko'ach, am I reading this correctly—8.55 billion men and women were, are...boiled alive?"

The narrator's mind projects into Ko'ach's thoughts: *How can I still be alive? Is I-T because the younger version of myself is alive? Has God confided in you the reason why, for the first time in 18 million years, a new story plays out without my awareness beforehand?*

Sorry, old friend, I can't say. I'm calculating our best course of action. All of this is unprecedented.

Computer Nephesh explains that Ima, Nephesh, and Dafna, are safe from the carnage as long as they remain in their fuchsia time bubble. In that safe place, evil can't be made aware of their presence. Dafna, Ima, and Nephesh hover over Earth's magnetic north pole and watch 6.66 murdering machines depart incinerated Earth, like a swarm of malevolent locusts.

"Computer, extrapolate where they are going. Why are they leaving?" Ko'ach paces. He stumbles over a bucket filled to the brim. Diamonds slide left as the entire complex bank and hold that nauseating pose.

Faster and faster screeching machines orbit Earth's sun. Tornadoes blanket and suck every atom of heat. Human colonies on Mars, Jupiter, and Saturn's space stations are too slow to evacuate.

Microscopic metallic virus chews through Ko'ach's complex, similar to pinching the top of a balloon and letting out air. Millions of years of unprecedented time leak through microscopic opening in reality.

Ko'ach and David are nearly paralyzed, yet through their incredible strength, are able to move. In their minds, they run 18 times the speed of the fastest cheetah; in reality, they move slower than Flash, the sloth from the movie *Zootopia*.

Because teen David's training made him stronger than all other doppelgangers, my newfound strength surges, and I clench and unclench my fists. "What the hell am I supposed to do now, so far away from Earth, existing in timeless non-linear time?"

I could never find the talent to cut across so many millions of years.

"The only one who could do that is Ko'ach! Not the confused Ko'ach stuck in his time-altering cave. No, we need super demi-God Ko'ach caught in entropy's endless destabilizing conundrum."

On my angry world, artificially enhanced adrenal gland splinters dispassionate logic. Hulk-like rage surges. Gigantic fissures carve gigantic holes, *Punch! Punch! Punch!* I watch the bases of a dozen mountains crumble and collapse. Carried throughout this planet's violent hurricane breath are billions of tons of toxic debris. Shards slice through every one of my constructed dwellings. Choking, I rush underground and wait out this new storm.

I hear and feel an explosion of 18 dormant volcanoes spewing liquid rock for miles. *Oh my God, I-T-S pitting the ozone layer. Oxygen expelled into space. I-T-S hissing mocks my existence.*

God's righteous weapon calls to me. I walk through the valley of perpetual darkness. 18 seconds later every entrance and exit is blocked by 36-million tons of red hot debris. My blue, white inner light burns hotter than 36 simultaneous nova heat blasts. Fiery heat forms 18 rings around the entire planet. I feel God's righteous weapon's harmonics. Two doors before me. I punch. My blue, white heat blast shoots from my heart. Nary a scratch is left on those doors. They should have melted within 36-seconds. Releasing 18-million-years of pent-up anger. I calmly phase through the door on the right. God's blue, white glowing weapon speaks to me. The holy energy taunts my every step. I take three quick steps or 3600 steps. The weapon moves as I move. Always beyond my grasp. Remaining a single fingertip out of reach. Boulder rolls and knocks me into the holy God constructed weapon. *No matter how much I burn. This! Time! I! Will! Not! Let! Go!*

Dark energy barrier closes in on Nephesh, Dafna, and Ima. I-T mimics the bubble of the three hovering heroes in space. With the speed of time, disembodied dark lights wrap around withering righteous membrane.

Nephesh's mind reaches out to Dafna and Ima. *We must break free of this splintering time stream and neutralize evil's grip on that convoluted timeline.*

I won't let go! I won't let go! Blue-white flame ignites my body. My animalistic growling howls shake my body and the ground I stand on. Fissures open up and I fall through. *Do your worst, God! I will not release my grip! Oh, dear Lord, I'm melting! Ko'ach... not the one frozen in time watching the unthinkable take place...no, no, no! The Ko'ach who's out there, somewhere in the Multiverse. Save your beloved. Save my beloved. Save our Israeli friend. If I-T-S finally my fate to die, so be I-T. I promised not to let go and fail again, for I no longer have fingers. I'm gurgling a stream of goo. I live as a puddle with memories, longing for love with terrible regret. God, is this my fate to never die? To go on and on as a sputtering blue-white pond of agonizing goo?*

Malignant hand rips away Nephesh's golden-white-blue-fuchsia energy. Murderous fingertips flick, puncture and splatter Nephesh's oozing stomach.

Ima proud of your determination. Truth is, you three don't have the power to escape this place. No more time for delay. I must exit Ima's body.

In the deep recess of Ima and Dafna's mind, they hear Nephesh's brainwaves shout, *No! We're a team. We together can figure this out. You must not...*

Must? Be careful of your tone, Nephesh.

With all the respect in the Multiverse, this is a bad idea. You'll be stuck, locked in that never-ending time loop of I-T-S making. Fate worse than death. Agony beyond agony. Choked off, separated for all eternity from everyone you care about; evil's grip around your throat, not even God, your father will be able to breech that realm, for if he made the attempt the entire Multiverse would implode... And. And...

Yes? Say I-T.

What will become of the human-Ima leaving her body while she's under the influence?

I speak for the human, not the Ancient-One, when I declare to

Almighty God—don't worry about me. Follow your new destiny. Do what needs to be done.

"I'll stay with Ima," says nervous Dafna.

I appreciate the gesture. My way is the only way. Ima, we both will always share elemental particles of one another. Steady yourself for immediate extraction. Monumental seizures will slice flesh and soul... can't be prevented. I promise to mitigate 99 percent of delusion's disorienting dichotomies.

"Have you or any others from the Realm tried this before?" asks Dafna.

No, I have not. While the narrator lives, hope will remain eternal.

"The narrator?" perplexed Dafna inquires.

Indeed.

Why do you keep his identity from us? If he's as powerful as you say, why not make him aware of our predicament?

He's aware. And he's exceptionally powerful. But...um...the time isn't right, yet.

Dafna, Nephesh, and Ima's hearts beat as one, ba-da-bump, ba-da-bump. Surfing uncontrollably along Benevolent Time's ultimate undulating tsunami wave, all heartbeats in-sync.

Ear-shattering sirens blare throughout Ko'ach's complex. Hands over ears, his telepathy pushes beyond even their limits. Both men watch Dafna, Ima, and Nephesh vanish from the viewscreen. Ko'ach frantically manipulates the dials with his mind. Both men are shocked at the false historical events presented before them.

The following never happened in any previous scenario: Iran launches 27 ballistic missiles, each with nuclear warheads. Death flies toward anti-Semitic Europeans. The governments within those capitals lack Israel's missile and laser defensive systems.

Iran launches 12 nuclear missiles at Israel 36 minutes later. Five missiles malfunctioned. Heading off course, two explode into Iranian cities, two impact Iraqi cities, and the last one decimates Saudi Arabia's holy city, Mecca.

Two Iranian missiles get through Israeli defenses because I-T had infiltrated and transformed a squad of Israelis into 100-foot machines. Those machines are impervious to nuclear weapons. The helpless Jews, Druze, Christian, and Muslim populations living in Jerusalem, Tel Aviv, Haifa, and through the entire Negev are obliterated.

Biden's migrant sleeper cells make I-T possible for thousands of U.S. cities to become targeted with dirty radioactive bombs. Children in Jewish synagogues. Christian and Catholic churches, Sunni and Shiite mosques, and Buddhist and Hindu temples explode. More bombs detonate in pre-schools, kindergarten, elementary, middle, and high schools, emergency rooms, police, and fire stations.

In the chaos of death, Sunni and Shiite immigrants emerge from European cities slashing throats and raping Christian daughters, mothers, and grandmothers. Muslim boys and girls, ages 13 and 14, detonate conventional bombs coated in rat poison to ensure the slicing shrapnel impedes coagulation. Soft baby skulls, mother's eyes, grandmother's lungs, and grandfather's hearts are penetrated—all bled out.

David's empathy rages.

"Where the hell do you think you're going?" shouts Ko'ach.

"Let go!"

"Calm down."

"What the fuck! Calm down? How the fuck can you be so calm? Y-you told me part of my mission is to prevent all of... that!"

Catching Ko'ach off guard, David swings and connects—the first and last time his rage brings Ko'ach to his knees.

Grinning. Ko'ach rubs his aching jaw. "Nice one. Few beings are quick and strong enough to do that. In time, you'll save them by saving the narrator."

"Who?"

"Too complicated to explain."

"Time has no relevance in this place. Long ago, you promised if I diligently followed your directives and completed all your training, there would never be secrets between us. Who is this narrator you speak of?"

Electrical system explodes. Time's undulation manipulates every dial, lever, and flashing fuchsia button.

"David, I need your help!"

"Why isn't that working?"

"I don't know! This place is supposed to be impervious to all forms of malevolent manipulation," shouts Ko'ach.

Dafna's blue-white energy blast keeps the child-machine at bay. Her mother's thunderous metallic clap slams Dafna into falling debris. Machine mother's huge black boot crushes Dafna. Drooling tongue slurps Dafna's righteous essence.

"Reverse that shit!" David shouts.

"Beyond my abilities. No coming back from that specific type of death."

"Bullshit!"

"I wish to God I could save your friend."

"Send me to her before that happens. She's crunching something between her teeth. And licking her fucking fingers. Oh God! Why won't you turn the fucking view screen off?"

Nephesh takes on two larger machines, both with martial arts skills far above the one that killed Dafna. For 18 hours, Nephesh's fuchsia-blue-white energy sputters. Her two arms continue to block pulverizing metallic fists. From behind her, two large metallic males slam their fingers into Nephesh's back and crunch her heart. Metallic monsters lick squirting fuchsia blood off their lips. Creatures crack open her skull and scoop out her brains, making growling guttural throaty MMM sounds.

"You fucking asshole!" shouts Ko'ach.

Ko'ach's fingers swipe holographic images. Faster and faster, a blur, beyond David's ability to see that's Ko'ach's motion. I-T-S as if Ko'ach's fingers aren't moving at all.

Tears streaming down Ko'ach's face. He grabs David's shoulders. "I've scanned 18 trillion alternate timelines. And this fucking mess never happened before. You destroyed I-T. I've seen that history multiple times."

Righteous blue-white energy blasts from Ko'ach's right eye. Malevolent black energy blasts from his left eye. Energy streams entangle and fight each other.

"God! Instruct. How do I fix this mess? God? Excuse me, I must break out telepathy and link directly with God in a time and place you'll never know."

Ko'ach pushes his mind until fuchsia blood, with black flexes, pours out from his nose, ears, and eyes. Stampeding sequestering seizures reintroduce resonate redacted revelations. Icky idiosyncratic idioms instruct investigative cantankerous cockroaches; destructive displacement wave frequently fractures fentanyl flaming flamingoes. Pontificating parable paradoxically infiltrates a flock of starling murmuration. With each gobble, a kaleidoscope of butterflies aggressively attacks a swarm of succulent jellyfish.

David's internal force field protects his human shell. He tries to rescue his friend.

Proof Ancient-One sealed the opening. Ancient-One won't let evil escape, nor can the Ancient-One leave...that's the terrible trade off. That's the sacrifice which must be made.

"What of the human?" Ko'ach inaudibly utters.

"Human? Why did you say human? Which human?" frantic David gesticulates.

"I didn't say human. Let me be, David. I must reconnect without interruption."

He must never know about his enhanced beloved held captive by the Ancient-One.

This iteration is still not supposed to be. We must not deprive David of his Ima.

Follow the path.

God, please...the sacrifice is too great.

Follow the path! Trust me.

I see. Yes. Very well. Okay...I didn't know.

Ima battles four evil machines. With intense malice, Ima's limp body is thrown into a flesh-searing gigantic spider web. I-T-S metallic legs skewer her heart and lungs.

Noooo! David's mind shouts.

I-T-S jaws of death shred and masticate Ima's limbs and torso. Mocking song echoes in narrator's brain, "Always."

Ancient-One floats between Ima's neurons and multiple timelines.

I-T-S him! I-T-S him! I-T-S him!

"Caged righteous energy, the most exquisite dish of all," cackles I-T.

New history unfolds; trillions of righteous species and souls become tainted with malevolence: 50 percent are recruited, and 50 percent are consumed. That cycle of perversion continues for millions of years. If trainee David can escape Ko'ach's gravitational layer and enter normal space—millions of years will be equivalent to 100 Earth hours.

David and Ko'ach rise out of a pool of hybrid black, fuchsia, and red human blood. David's blue-white glowing forehead touches Ko'ach's insurmountable grief.

Ko'ach! You taught me time is flagrantly flexible. I-T-S fluidity is not forever set. We know the bastard's end game. We've never known when and where I-T would make I-T-S final stand. Now we know the exact century, decade, month, day, hour, second, millisecond. We can leverage those specific coordinates. Do you hear me! We can still fix all of I-T! Send me back before that apocalypse.

Everything you just said is true, but there's a catch.

What? You don't have the power to send me back to the exact moment we desire?

No, I can do that. Your memories cannot leave with you.

What! Why? What aren't you telling me?

How the hell can I help my beloved, your beloved, and our good friend Dafna without remembering what will happen? Without memories, I-T will happen all over again, and we won't have any backup plan.

When you break the envelope of this horrific timeline, I'm meant to be elsewhere.

And you can't divulge where and when?

Look, I give you my solemn oath, I'll never give up trying to find a way to save them all. I'll traverse infinite numbers of black holes. I'll do whatever I-T takes to keep this timeline from unfolding.

I-T will eventually sense what you're doing. You think that's what happened? You were elsewhere trying to find a weapon to decapitate that evil creature, and I-T sent you on wild goose chase after wild goose chase. Could I-T be the manipulator we fear?

No! That dishonor belongs to the one who created I-T.

Malevolent Time.

We'll be okay. I'm aware of God's struggles with her; he'll never let us down. This is part of his plan. We must have faith that God will prevent her devious transmission from reaching I-T.

"How do you know we haven't done this before in a twisted unending unyielding loop of timeless history?" asks David.

"This will work."

"You trying to convince me or yourself?"

"Yes..."

Both men fly toward blue-white energy portal and split off in opposite directions. Both sing the holiest Jewish prayer: Sh'ma Israel Adonai Eloheinu Adonai Ehad...

Time Kraken, the size of planets, bellows and undulates, crushing the rings of multiple solar systems. Creature's anteater nose sucks blue-white energy through the Multiverse. The lip of Ko'ach's portal fluctuates; his phased essence endures trillions of feelings, memories, and particulates duplicating and dissipating—forever.

He's gone. Be safe, dear friend. I wonder...will the dark side of Ko'ach's hybrid existence become the dominant force and work with I-T? Could I-T-S incursion into my world be imminent? Immortality's immutably inertness impales idealistic introspection. Mission derailed. Life force assailed, and infinities curtailed.

Gruesome fable, celestial actuary table. Hellish knife and fork. Friends becoming I-T-S pot pie pork. Fluctuations galore, iridescent sheath stabbing David's core. Heretofore, nothing is as I-T should've been before. Faustian winds huff and puff, regurgitation rough. Humanity bypassed. Memories trespassed...

Luminescent Ima hovers over steamy puddle of goo. Waving her glowing hand over my liquid essence, I'm yanked away from my hellish lava pit, sucked into God's swirling righteous blue-white tornado. I hear Ima's beautiful voice singing "Long Ago and Far Away."

My beloved shimmering essence phases through the blue-white energy vortex. Solidified nakedness, we hold and caress each other. My beloved sprinkles red rose petals over our bed.

Looking into Ima's sparkling emerald eyes, our lips taste millions of years of longing. Acoustic guitar materializes, and I sing "Time in a Bottle."

Licking her lips in anticipation, Ima sings in Spanish, "Eres Tu" (I-T-S You). David kisses her soft parted mouth and lingers on her last "Eres Tu."

His nose caresses Ima's nose. "Beloved Ima, I've never been happier."

"As am I. Make love to me, dearest David Sagacious..."

Lost in passionate lovemaking, the complexities of the Multiverse fade from our careening consciousness.

Decades later, my beautiful beloved sings, "Eternal Flame." I feel her warm touch become icy. Her shimmering sad face slowly dissipates. The planet's incinerating hot winds slap me into another alternate surreal evil reality. Rocking back and forth in a fetal position, my mind shouts, *No! Don't go! Please, I need you! Oh my God, no I don't want the return of those grotesque memories!*

I-T dropkicks Nephesh 16,000 meters. Limp rag-doll body bounces and crunches against I-T-S black force field. Enjoying I-T-S best day, I-T sings in a perfect recreation of John Denver's "Sunshine On My Shoulder."

Near death, young David painfully wheezes. Aspirating malignant darkness inflicts harm to his weakening, sputtering blue-white energy matrix. Black sparks crackle around his eyes, ears, and nose. Black metallic fingernail extends. A horrible crunching sound precedes black energy oozing from his cracked skull. His frozen expression exudes astonishment and loathing.

Defenseless, David's distended soul dives down decapitating decanter. Held hostage, his heinous hell, horrifically harvest...him!

I-T removes an emanating golden force field ring from I-T-S clawed pinkie finger. Trillions of righteous souls are trapped betwixt gamma-radiated shielding, their collective anxiety crescendos. All of that has never happened before. I don't have the means to reverse I-T...only God's righteous weapon could do that, and I-T alludes my every attempt to capture I-T without turning into another puddle of goo.

I feel I-T-S golden energy ring slam into David's heart. I-T recreates the slurping sound humans make when they reach the bottom of a big gulp slushy.

I-T rips and shreds David's righteous soul.

For the moment, Ima-Ancient-One is impervious to that agony. Secondary silver tube kerplunks from I-T-S earlobe. Black energy from I-T-S fingertips manipulates ends together, skewing all sources of light. I-T desires to keep Dafna Shaked alive so she can feel her organs rupture and sizzle from being skewered and rotated in I-T-S roasting pan. Bloody-black fingers slam, paralyzing Dafna onto I-T-S silver spike.

Red and white fluid flows up toward I-T-S metallic lips and multicolored blood-stained fangs. I-T continues to wrap I-T-S lips around that tube and suck righteous nectar. Black saliva drips over Dafna's face. Replicating George Takei's deep resonance, Oh my! Human Israeli meat is a wonderful delicacy."

I-T sings, "Come Rain or Come Shine."

Monstrous rage vibrates. I-T-S having a wonderfully joyous time murdering billions of souls and billions of timelines.

Ancient-One's light is unable to recharge. To discover, at the worst time, that which was never thought possible...there are limits to god's powers.

I-T creates an incandescent fuchsia wheel with black energy spikes. I-T takes immense pleasure pounding Ima's body and skull. I-T-S vocal cords resonate with Giuseppe Verdi's 1853 Opera II Trovatore, the Anvil Chorus blares with each metallic fist-denting, skull splattering, oozing brain matter.

I've learned to appreciate human songs. Let me see, how did that one start? Silly ditty. Round and round. Love singing in Perry Como's voice, and I believe Joe Shapiro and Lou Stallman wrote—not sure how I feel about singing something two Jews created. Damn fucking Jews have always been a tremendously innovative thorn in my side; too often, they fucked up my glorious plans. Planet-shattering cackles pulsate and thrum, splitting wide-open thousands of solar systems.

I-T continues to mock the narrator and capture righteous warriors by singing, "Young at Heart." I-T also recreates Roy Orbison's voice and sings, "I-T-S Over..."

Malevolent Time blasted God along the precipices of newly created time vortices. Could that be a contributing factor regarding why bad things continue to happen to good people? There are stretches of time when God fought to free himself. And he did, but that realm slammed God back. Malevolent Time erred; believing her dark thoughts could destroy God's holy weapon.

God's mighty justice pushes his emerging hand, the way a drowning victim ascends through a dark watery wasteland. Reaching speeds beyond time and space, God's holy weapon slices through the darkness. God's crescendo crushes his imprisonment. God's righteous arms extend upwards beyond that swirling galaxy's ingesting black vortex. God's base-baritone voice coordinates each letter, word, syllable. He powerfully repeats until his righteous weapon glows in his grasp.

ELOHIM ADON KADOSH MITS'VAH MISH'AHHAH.

God's energy weapon hurtles through dimensions neither Malevolent Time nor I-T could be aware of. God shatters Malevolent Time's essence. Pulverized into elements smaller than sub-sub-atomic, there's a slim chance Malevolent Time could grow I-T-Self once more. Ko'ach exists somewhere, directed by God. I'm not privy to the specifics of that holy mission.

God wields 18-trillion-mile long and wide blue-white glowing Star of David attached to an equally massive blue-white glowing staff. God's booming voice whispers... *He's ready. Merge into the one I sent 18 million years ago I-T-S time David's grasp on my righteous weapon no longer harms him. He's endured enough. Make sure you retain enough energy to destroy I-T and no longer harm the narrator.*

Commanded and directed by God. Righteous Star of David rockets faster than any warp driven starship. Holy justice pierces manipulative timelines and resonates singing: "Yerushalayim Shel Zahav" in Ofra Haza's voice. Trillions of murdered souls rise up and sing. Spiritual energy strengthens the barrier between Malevolent Time and God. Narrator David feels the love of beloved Ima waiting on the other side. *But first, I must do what God couldn't bring himself to do. Because I-T was long ago his, son.*

CHAPTER 33

After 18 Million Years, Narrator David Becomes Strong Enough to Wield God's Righteous Weapon

"DAVID!"

"Yes God."

"KO'ACH'S ETERNAL ESSENCE IS ENCASED AND FOSSILIZED WITHIN MALEVOLENT TIME'S HONEYCOMB: HIS MIND HAS BEEN FIGHTING THOSE DEMONS FOR THE LAST 18 MILLION YEARS. I CANNOT LEAVE MY POST. I MUST KEEP A WATCHFUL EYE ON MALEVOLENT TIME. YOU AND ONLY YOU CAN WIELD MY RIGHTEOUS STAR OF DAVID AND FREE YOUR MENTOR."

The star of David unleashes unprecedented righteous tornado. I absorb trillions of gigawatts of holy energy and grow to 36 feet. Sensing my approach, I-T absorbs dark energy from trillions of manipulated timelines. I-T-S dark heart and soul becomes enriched by the death of I-T-S unholy mechanical armada. David Sagacious, the narrator, is on a collision course with I-T; an 800-foot mechanical monster.

Hand over fist my righteous staff twirls. Supernova-engorged cell holds a microscope staff attached to a glowing blue-white Star of David. Each of those 36 trillion cells and Star of Davids split into an infinite number of boomeranging personas. With the support from all, I rocket through every point in time. 8000-foot monster bristles with indignant rage. Against I-T-S evil armor, my aim is precise and crackles 18-billion degrees hotter than any supernova.

Slice and puncture. We're too quick for I-T. From multiple ends of time and space, our righteous energy blasts. No matter how many out-of-sync David warriors I-T tries to consume, I-T can never find David prime.

Insect-like in comparison, 36,000 doppelganger David's jump on I-T-S back and put I-T in a sleeper hold. I-T flicks or squishes all of them.

Vomitus evil's breath expelled from I-T-S metallic lips. David prime becomes encased in I-T-S skin ripping dark vortex.

I began harnessing never-before-generated gravimetric waves within that caustic membrane.

For the first time in I-T-S existence...real fear takes hold, and I-T releases black tentacles; crushed, broken, and slammed against the hardest material ever created; my brain tissue leaks through my nose, ears, and eyes.

God!

God's 7,200-foot fist crushes I-T-S malevolent matrix.

Ima free! From an infinite number of angles, our Star of David burns blue-white hot energy. When one David exhausts his energy supply; 36 more take his place.

I allow myself to be caught by I-T-S monstrous hand. The harder I-T squeezes the louder my infuriating laughter becomes. I cut through I-T-S weakened armor. Slicing off pieces of thumb and finger. Twisted metal echoes in our minds.

From I-T-S black heart, dangerous energy spews and dissolves a million shrieking David Sagacious. I was wrong to think an infinite number of David Sagacious would be enough. *Has I-T tapped into an evil maelstrom not even God could have antici- pated? No! Not God's fault. I must do better. I must now finally murder I-T! I am all that's left of the Multiverse Sagacious.*

Expending all of I-T-S evil energy, I-T now stands a mere 88 feet. I became 99,000 supernovas. With my Star of David leading the way, we both melt through I-T-S metallic chest.

Over the next 72 seconds, I-T-S metallic shell recedes. I fly out and stare at Emet's righteous emerald eyes. For the first time in eons, pink, naked Emet is reborn.

God's righteous tears of joy and sorrow pity-pat, pity-pat, pity-pat.

Father?

Yes, my son.

Thank you.

For what?

My life. Long pause follows. *And death.*

I'm sorry I-T took so long.

Deep down, I knew you wouldn't abandon me. Is she destroyed?

No, not even I can do that. But her powers are dramatically reduced.

David.

Yes God.

Emet is ready. Do what must be done so that he can never be trans- formed again.

From her blue-white glowing cage, Malevolent Time blasts her most powerful black energy. So tiny and weak, her energy pulse can no longer endanger the narrator. That would change if she became larger. In time, which is a battle we might have to face and fight once more, but for right now, and for the first time ever, she no longer poses a threat to anyone, other than Emet. God hurdles through acidic Malevolent Time's Multiverse. Ko'ach slips into a by-design, temporary coma— and pink Emet screeches. He's once again metallic I-T.

Something black. Something smaller than sub-sub-atomic. Something of I-T-S own making floats out of God's blue-white containment field.

Reality goes haywire! I-T rips the time-space-continuum and stretches hundreds of feet. David's righteous blue-white energy matrix traverses in reverse. His knuckles become metallic.

"No! I-I won't!"

Righteous energy crackles and sputters, forming malevolent fissures along my blackening metallic fingers. Powerful pushback illuminates righteous reality. Flexing fleshy fingers, I push the purest righteous blue-white energy into I-T-S metallic core.

Causation, transformation restoration, supplication, veneration, salvation, elation, creation.

Goodbye, Papa.

Goodbye, my son.

Pink Emet's mind, body, and soul spread thinner and thinner—until not even a gaseous wisp remains. Malevolent Time will search for infinite time and space, but there is nothing left of Emet to manipulate. He's gone forever. God had the power to bring him back. I-T was his wish to cease to exist, to never again be transformed nor tormented by reliving his murderous sins.

Infinitesimal Malevolent Time's squeals echo through infinity's perdition. *Revenge shall be mine! I must get bigger. I will find the means to thwart God's magical physics, which, for now, prevents my enlargement!*

DAVID...

Yes, God.

YOU DID IT.

Where's Ko'ach?

SAFE. THE FUTURE IS NOT. THAT IS WHAT I MUST PROTECT. MALEVOLENT TIME'S DESTRUCTIVE POTENTIAL REMAINS. I MUST SEARCH FOR HER. THIS WILL BE OUR LAST COMMUNICATION. FEAR NOT, I'LL ALWAYS BE WITH YOU. I WILL NEVER ALLOW

MALEVOLENT TIME TO PERMANENTLY SEPARATE YOUR YOUNGER, LESS ADVANCED SELVES FROM THOSE WHO LOVE THE HUMAN YOU.

I thought I was all that survived.

THE EARTH YOU CAME FROM KEPT THAT SPIRITUAL FLAME ALIVE.

Ima.

YES.

And Dafna.

AND YOU TOO. YOU AND KO'ACH ARE NOW THE SAME, BOTH DESIGNATED AS PROTECTOR SUPREME. NO LONGER SHALL YOU BE MAROONED. YOU CAN VISIT ANYTIME. ANY PLACE. HOWEVER...

I must allow my human self to live his life with his Ima. That is the price...I must pay.

YOU CAN SHARE IN THE EXPERIENCES. SHARE THEIR JOY AND SORROW. ALL DONE FROM A DISTANCE, VICARIOUSLY. YOU'LL KEEP ALL THEIR MEMORIES—THOUGH YOU MUST REMAIN PHYSICALLY APART FROM THEM FOREVER. THE MULTIVERSE IS VAST. INFINITE TIME-TRAVEL IS, WELL...INFINITE. BE THE TRUTH BEARER. BE THE ONE TO HELP YOUR YOUNGER PRIMITIVE SPECIES TO FIGHT INJUSTICE. TIP THE BALANCE IN FAVOR OF GOODNESS. MALEVOLENT TIME IS NOT FINISHED. HER CHAOTIC SCHEMES WILL RESURFACE. AS TEMPTING AS THAT MIGHT FEEL, TO ACT AS GOD'S RIGHTEOUS INTERFERING GUARDIAN ANGEL; DO SO AS LITTLE AS POSSIBLE. ALLOW FOR FREE WILL. CHOICE OF ACTION MUST BE THE STALWART BY WHICH OTHER SPECIES LEARN FROM THEIR MISTAKES. YOU MUST ALLOW THEM TO FAIL, TO HURT, TO SUFFER, TO GROW, TO BE... I'VE ENCODED WITHIN YOUR RIGHTEOUS STAR OF DAVID, YOUR FIRST OF AN INFINITE NUMBER OF NEW MISSIONS. HAVE YOU INTERNALIZED THE COORDINATES?

*

Adventures through time is my forever calling. Before I joyfully disembark and vanish forever from human sight, I sing, "What a Wonderful World."

489

ABOUT ATMOSPHERE PRESS

Founded in 2015, Atmosphere Press was built on the principles of Honesty, Transparency, Professionalism, Kindness, and Making Your Book Awesome. As an ethical and author-friendly hybrid press, we stay true to that founding mission today.

If you're a reader, enter our giveaway for a free book here:

SCAN TO ENTER
BOOK GIVEAWAY

If you're a writer, submit your manuscript for consideration here:

SCAN TO SUBMIT
MANUSCRIPT

And always feel free to visit Atmosphere Press and our authors online at atmospherepress.com. See you there soon!

ABOUT THE AUTHOR

For three and a half decades within the Los Angeles Unified School District, **JOHN DAVID LIEBLING** taught government, geography, U.S. History, world history, and Middle East electives. John's career began when *Back To The Future* debuted on the big screen, and his retirement coincided with the MCU blockbuster *Endgame*.

In 2010, John started his Toastmaster adventure. He's won a number of trophies from his California and international Toastmasters clubs.

John is very much a dog person. His favorite was a shaggy, light brown Puli called Barney. He was a little guy who always believed he was bigger. Like John's fictionalized characters, real-life, demonstratively waggy Barney always exuded the heart of a champion.

John sees life through the lens of a historian. He's proud to be a Zionist. Verbally or by way of written commentary, he enjoys sparring with dishonest antisemitic bullies.

www.ingramcontent.com/pod-product-compliance
Lightning Source LLC
Chambersburg PA
CBHW021333150726
47989CB00005B/1962